THE OFFICER'S LOVER

Ten years ago Jordan Weiss suffered the devastating death of her boyfriend Jared, a gifted rower at Cambridge. Since then, work as an intelligence officer has taken her to the world's hot spots where she has faced terrible dangers. When a twist of fate sends Jordan back to London, she and rakish agent Sebastian Hodges are assigned to an investigation into mafia activities, which throws them into a whirlwind drama of lies, cover-ups and corruption. Who can Jordan trust? Secrets start to emerge that are strangely connected to her past and will ultimately shape the course of her future.

THE OFFICER'S LOVER

THE OFFICER'S LOVER

by

Pam Jenoff

Magna Large Print Books
Long Preston, North Yorkshire,
BD23 4ND, England.

British Library Cataloguing in Publication Data.

Jenoff, Pam
    The officer's lover

    A catalogue record of this book is
    available from the British Library

    ISBN   978-0-7505-3404-8

First published in Great Britain in 2010 by Sphere

Cover illustration © Mohamed Itani by arrangement with
Arcangel Images

The moral right of the author has been asserted

Published in Large Print 2011 by arrangement with
Little, Brown Book Group Limited

LP

Magna Large Print is an imprint of Library Magna Books Ltd.

Printed and bound in Great Britain by
T.J. (International) Ltd., Cornwall, PL28 8RW

To my family: past, present and future

If I should die, think only this of me:
    That there's some corner of a foreign field
That is for ever England.

–RUPERT BROOKE, 'THE SOLDIER'

the *MICHAELMAS TERM*

chapter ONE

I barrel through the double doors and across the lobby of the State Department, bypassing the metal detector and waving my plastic identification badge at the guard, who nods in recognition. My heels echo off the marble floor as I race down the corridor past the row of brightly colored flags, the tall glass windows revealing smokers huddled under umbrellas in the courtyard. A display of student artwork left over from Black History Month decorates the otherwise drab white walls.

I reach the elevators and press the up button. In an office across the hall, two jacketless, gray-haired men wearing identical brown ties lean over a cubicle divider discussing Cuba, their voices dispassionate and unhurried. A dying fluorescent lightbulb flickers angrily in the ceiling fixture above them. I turn back and press the button several more times, tapping my foot. The smell of scorched coffee, an empty pot left too long on the burner, hangs in the air. The door creaks open and I leap into the elevator, swiping my badge in front of the access scanner before pressing the button. Don't stop, I pray, leaning sideways against the faux wood paneling and watching the numbers light up as the elevator slowly rises.

A minute later, the door opens. I step out, then pause, momentarily forgetting my haste. August and imposing, the executive floor is worlds away from the bureaucratic lethargy below. Oil paintings of every secretary of state since Jefferson line the tastefully lit beige walls, staring down at me sternly, reminding me to stand straight. Large potted plants sit to either side of the elevator bank.

Steeling myself for the conversation I am about to have, I turn away from the closed double doors that lead to the Secretary's office, following the chronological progression of gold-framed portraits down the navy-carpeted hallway. At John Calhoun, I stop and adjust my collar before turning the knob of a familiar, broad oak door.

'Hello, Patty,' I say, entering the office and passing through the reception area before the stout, auburn-haired secretary can try to stop me. I knock twice on an unmarked door at the far end of the room, then open it without waiting.

'I want London,' I announce.

Behind the massive oak desk, Paul Van Antwerpen looks up from the cable he was reading and blinks once behind his glasses.

'Oh?' he replies, raising his eyebrows and running his hand through his thinning hair.

I hesitate. For the normally impassive Van Antwerpen, this is quite a reaction. He is surprised, I can tell, by the abruptness of my entrance as well as the nature of my request. The senior director of intelligence operations is a formal man; one schedules appointments to see him and does so sparingly.

'Yes,' I croak at last.

He gestures with his head to the two chairs opposite his desk. 'Sit down.'

16

I perch on the chair closest to the door. The office is immaculate as always, the desk bare except for a few tidy stacks of documents, the walls adorned only by the obligatory photographs of the President and Secretary of State. On the matching credenza behind his desk sits a telephone with direct lines to the Secretary and the National Security Advisor. Encrypted text, providing real-time updates on intelligence situations worldwide, scrolls down a computer screen.

I smooth my skirt. 'Sir, I know we had an agreement…'

'*Have* an agreement,' he corrects. 'One year.'

'Yes.' A year hadn't sounded that bad when the Director proposed it. Of course I was in the hospital at the time, two days out of Liberia, ten hours out of surgery, and so high on painkillers I scarcely remember his visit. Now, eight months later, a year seems like an eternity, indentured servitude. Not that working for the Director is exactly punishment; as his liaison to the National Security Council, I've spent my days shuttling between meetings at Foggy Bottom and the White House. I've gained a view of foreign policy at the highest levels of government, and I've seen things most people could not imagine in a lifetime. But I have to get out of here now.

And he's going to say no.

The Director, one of the only people who can still get away with smoking in the building, reaches for the humidor that sits on the far right corner of his desk. I fight the urge to grimace as he clips the end of a cigar and lights it.

'Don't get me wrong,' he says at last, puffing a

17

cloud of smoke away from me. 'I didn't really think I would be able to keep you here a full year. I've had five calls about you in the last month alone. Karachi, Jakarta, Montenegro, Lagos, Bogota, all of the garden spots.'

I smile inwardly. 'Garden spots' is a facetious term diplomats used to describe the real hardship posts. Those are the most interesting assignments and until now, I always sought them out, proud to say I had never been stationed in a place where one could actually drink the tap water.

'And now you're asking me,' he pauses, 'for London...?' He sets the cigar in an empty glass ashtray behind one of the stacks, then pulls a file with my name typed across the top from his desk drawer. My stomach twitches. I didn't know he kept a dossier on me. 'You've turned down London two, no, three times before. You don't even like changing planes there.' He sets the file down, eyes me levelly. 'So what gives?'

I avert my gaze, staring over Van Antwerpen's shoulder and out the window behind his desk. To the far left, I can just make out the Washington Monument in the distance, the pale stone obelisk muted against the gray sky. I swallow hard and shift in my seat. 'It's personal.'

I watch him hesitate, uncertain how to respond. Normally, such an explanation would be un-acceptable. As intelligence officers, we are trained to separate our work and personal lives, almost to the point of forgoing the latter. But I've earned my stripes, spent nearly the past ten years putting my life on the line. He'll feel that he owes me this much. He has to feel that way; I am

18

counting on it.

'If you'd prefer, I can take a leave of absence...' I begin, but the Director waves his hand.

'No, they'd kill me if I let you do that. You can have London. Martindale,' he pronounces the name as though it hurts his throat, 'will be glad to have you. She tried to steal you away from me months ago.'

I smile, picturing Maureen Martindale, the vivacious, red-haired deputy chief of mission in London and Van Antwerpen's longtime rival. I haven't seen Mo in three years, not since we worked together in San Salvador. My next move would have been to call her, if the Director refused my request. He closes the file. 'We're all set then. Just give me a few weeks to get the paperwork in order.'

I take a deep breath. 'I'm sorry, sir, that won't work. I need to get over there immediately. Tonight, if possible. Tomorrow at the latest.' I know that I am pushing the envelope, risking his wrath by asking too much. 'I'll buy my own plane ticket and use vacation time until the paperwork comes through. If it's a question of my projects here, I'll finish up remotely, help find my replacement...' The desperation in my voice grows.

Van Antwerpen is staring at me now, eyes skeptical. 'What's wrong, Weiss?'

I hesitate. It is a question I no longer know how to answer. 'Nothing, sir,' I lie at last.

'If you say so.' I can tell from his tone that he does not believe me, but I know he will not pry further. Paul Van Antwerpen is an extraordinarily distant man. In the years I have worked for him,

19

I've never learned where he is from or whether he even has a family, and he affords his officers the same kind of privacy. His standoffish nature bothered me in the early years when I mistook it for disapproval. Now I just accept it as part of who he is, like the Coke-bottle glasses and the cigars. He stands up, extending his hand. 'Good luck, Weiss. Whatever it is, I hope it works out.'

So do I. 'Thank you, sir.'

Two hours later, I climb into the back of a battered navy blue taxi. 'Arlington, please. Columbia Pike,' I request, pulling the door closed behind me. The taxi driver grunts and veers the car away from the curb onto the rain-soaked street. Garbled Indian music plays over the radio. I slump back against the torn vinyl seat, exhausted. The reality of what I've done crashes down on me like a wave.

England.

The cab lurches to a sudden stop as the traffic light at Virginia Avenue turns from yellow to red, sending the small cardboard box of personal belongings I was balancing on my knees to the floor. I bend to pick up the contents. Not much to it: a 'Solidarity' coffee mug given to me by Kasia, one of our Foreign Service nationals in Warsaw, as a going-away present; a few reports that I need to finish up in London that I cannot entrust to the diplomatic pouch; a wood-framed picture of my parents. I lift the photograph from the box, studying it. They are standing by the old maple tree in the backyard of our home in Vermont with identical burgundy wool sweaters tossed over their shoulders, looking like they stepped out of a J.

Crew catalog. I run my finger over the glass. My mother's hair, dark and curly like mine, is streaked with more gray than I remember. There won't be time to see them before I leave. I know, though, that they have come to accept my abrupt, un-announced departures, the weeks and sometimes months without communication that my work necessitates. They will understand, or pretend to anyway, I think, gratitude mixing with guilt. They deserve grandchildren, or at least a daughter who calls before moving out of the country.

As the taxi climbs the Roosevelt Bridge toward Arlington, I sit back and reach into my coat pocket for my cell phone. For a moment I consider following protocol for once and going through the State Department travel office for my plane ticket. Then, deciding against it, I dial zero. 'British Airways,' I request. The operator promptly transfers me to a prerecorded message of a woman's voice with an English accent asking me to hold for the next available representative, followed by a Muzak version of Chopin's Polonaise.

On hold, I lean sideways and press my forehead against the cool glass window, staring out at the white gravestones that line the wet, green hills of Arlington National Cemetery. I have been there twice for funerals, one several years ago and one last summer, both for diplomats whose patriotic valor earned them an exception to Arlington's military-only burial policy. I think of Eric and once again see him fall backward out of the helicopter as it rises from the Liberian ground, feel the Marine's arm clasped around my waist to stop me from jumping out after him. I swallow

21

hard, my once-broken collarbone aching from dampness and memory.

'How may I help you?' A British woman's voice, live this time, jars me from my thoughts. I quickly convey my request. 'London, tonight?' the woman repeats, sounding surprised. 'I'll check if we have anything available. If not, can you travel tomorrow?'

'No, it has to be tonight.' Panic rises. If I do not leave now, I might never go.

'One moment.' On the other end of the phone there is silence, then the sound of fingernails clicking against a keyboard. 'There are a few seats on the six o'clock flight, but we only have business class available.'

'Fine.' I am certain that Van Antwerpen will sign off on my reimbursement and that his signature carries enough weight to okay the upgrade, as well as the fact that I wasn't going through the travel office or flying an American carrier. I recite my credit card number, which I know by heart, then memorize the confirmation number the operator gives me. 'I'll pick up the ticket at check-in,' I say before closing the phone.

Five minutes later, the taxi pulls up in front of my apartment building, a nondescript high-rise that caters to transient government workers. Inside, I ride the elevator to the sixth floor and turn the key in the lock of my studio apartment. Opening the venetian blinds, I look around the nearly empty room, noticing for the first time how stark the bare, white walls look. Then I sink down to the futon bed, the only piece of furniture in the room. My mind reels back to the hospital eight months earlier, when I lamented finding a place in Washington to live. 'I don't want to sign a lease. I don't want to buy furniture,' I complained to my visiting mother.

'You can break the lease, you can sell the furniture,' she soothed, brushing my hair from my face as though I were five years old. 'It's not permanent.' Looking around the room now, I realize that she was right. The lease has a diplomatic transfer clause in it that will enable me to get out penalty-free. The rental store will pick up the bed the following day. In less than twenty-four hours, it will be as though I never lived here at all. Like everywhere else since England.

I reach into the large leather tote bag that serves as my briefcase and pull out the envelope that started everything. It was waiting for me at the reception desk of the apartment building this morning. At first I hesitated, surprised by the delivery; what little mail I received almost always went to my parents' house. Then, spotting Sarah's familiar return address, I tore open the envelope. I had not seen her in more than two years, not since I had changed planes in Johannesburg and she had driven six hours from her hometown of Durban to meet me. In a small airport café that smelled of coffee and rotten meat, Sarah told me the news: her mystery illness, the one that made her right hand go limp eighteen months earlier, had finally been diagnosed. 'It's amyotrophic lateral sclerosis,' she explained calmly. I stared at her blankly. 'ALS. What you Americans refer to as Lou Gehrig's disease.'

What Stephen Hawking has, I remembered. I

had seen the famous professor in his wheelchair once or twice on the streets at Cambridge. Picturing his wizened body, the way he slumped helplessly in his wheelchair, my stomach clenched. Would Sarah become like that?

'What will you do?' I asked, pushing the image from my mind.

'I'm going back to London,' Sarah replied. 'The doctors are better there.'

'Come stay with me?' I suggested.

But Sarah shook her head, laughing. 'Jordie, your home is a post office box.'

She was right, I realized; I didn't have an actual home to offer her. I took her hand. 'What can I do?'

'Nothing,' she answered firmly. 'I'll call you if I need you.' We hugged good-bye a few minutes later. Watching Sarah walk away, I was taken by her calm demeanor. She always had a hard time of it. Her mother died of Alzheimer's disease and her father disappeared into the bush when Sarah was ten.

When I reached my hotel room that night, I logged in on my laptop and researched ALS. It was a death sentence, I learned, my eyes filling with tears. Gradual, complete paralysis. No known cure. I pictured Sarah's freckled face as we parted, her blue eyes so unafraid. I never should have left her.

After that day, Sarah and I stayed in touch by letter and the occasional phone call. In the past year, though, her letters had grown less frequent until they had stopped entirely six months earlier. I tried repeatedly to reach her by telephone, without success. Then this letter arrived. A single typed page, signature barely legible at the bottom, it was mostly routine, an apology for not having written sooner, some small talk about the weather in London. And then there was the last sentence: 'I wish that I could see you again. If only you would come...' I sat motionless, reading and re-reading that one sentence. Sarah was there for my last days at Cambridge, knew how I felt about England and why. She never would have asked me to come unless she was desperate. It was, quite simply, the request of a dying woman.

I could say no, I realized, explain that I could not get away from work. Though Sarah would not believe my excuse, she would understand. But it was Sarah who was there for me at college, ready to listen over tea, no matter how small the problem or late the hour, who had put me on the plane home from England at the end when I was so overcome with grief that I could barely walk, and who had traveled the globe three times to visit me since. She was *that* friend, loyalty unmuted by distance or the passage of years. Now she needed me, and not in that three-day-visit-and-leave-again way, but really needed me. Now it was my turn.

I refold the letter and place it back in my bag, then reach across the futon and pick up a flannel shirt. Mike's shirt. I draw it to my nose and inhale deeply, seeing his brown hair and puppy dog eyes. We've dated casually these past few months – drinks after work at one of the L Street bars between his assignments on the Vice President's Secret Service detail, or, like last evening, a late visit when he returned from a trip. Physical comfort, warmth for the cold winter nights. Nothing serious, though I can tell from the way he looks at me that he hopes it will become so. I should call him, tell him that I am leaving. But I know that he will try to talk me out of going, and then, when he realizes he can't, he will insist on seeing me off at the airport. No, it's better this way. I fold the shirt and set it down. I'll mail it back with a note.

I stand up again and begin to pack my clothes and a few other belongings. Forty-five minutes later I am done. My whole life in two suitcases. There are other things, of course, dozens of boxes of books, pictures, and other mementos in government storage and my parents' attic, things I haven't seen in so many years that they feel like part of another lifetime. I think again of the photograph of my parents. Sometimes I wish I could live a normal life like them, full of backyards and dishes and plants. I wish I could be content.

'If wishes were horses,' I say softly, 'beggars would ride.' The expression of my mother's, one I haven't thought of in years, rushes back to me. Everything seems to be coming back today. I pick up my bags and head for the door, closing it without looking behind me. Twenty minutes later, I climb into another damp and musty cab bound for Dulles Airport. As the car pulls away from the apartment building, and the Washington skyline recedes behind me, my spirits begin to lift. I am on the road again, the only place that truly feels like home.

chapter TWO

'Easy oars,' I call to the crew, eyeing the tangled mass of boats that sits twenty feet ahead at the sharp corner underneath Chesterton footbridge. 'Hold it up.' As the rowers touch their blades to the water, slowing the boat, low thunder rumbles from the darkening clouds that have gathered over the flat grassy fenlands to the east. 'Damn,' I mutter under my breath.

'Steady there, Jordie,' Chris soothes, facing me from the stroke seat. 'Carnage?'

I nod, craning my neck to see around his head and the seven sets of broad shoulders behind him. 'Downing's jackknifed at the corner. Looks like they have a substitute cox.'

'Relax. There's nothing to be done about it.' Chris's voice is even, devoid of emotion. He is right, of course. Scarcely two boat widths' wide and only three miles long from lock to lock, the River Cam was never intended as the super-highway of rowing it has become.

I turn off the microphone. 'You want to call it a night?'

Chris shakes his head. 'Not with the way bow four were catching on that last piece. It'll clear in a few minutes.' I do not reply but wave at a swarm of gnats that has risen from the still water. Though the sun has dipped low to the horizon, the late spring air is warm and close. 'Uh, Jordie,' Chris jerks his head to the right. 'You might want to...'

I jump, noticing for the first time that the current is pulling us sideways toward the riverbank. 'Damn!' I swear again, as the bow of the shell angles into a docked houseboat with a thump.

A round window on the side of the houseboat flies open, and an unshaven, shirtless man sticks his head out. 'Fuck off and learn to steer your bloody boat!' he bellows, drawing laughter from the crews around us. I shift in my narrow seat, biting my lower lip and feeling my face go red. Then I turn the microphone back on. 'Stern pair, back it down one.' The two rowers closest to me slide forward in their seats, arms extended. As they catch the water in unison, they pull the shell slowly away from the houseboat. 'Easy oars,' I am forced to call again seconds later as we draw close to the crew behind us. I slump back in my seat. The current will surely pull us into the bank again, but there is nowhere else to go.

A minute later, the shells ahead of us begin to clear. 'All right, guys, let's take it on.' As I prepare to give the starting commands, I hear a loud and sudden hiss. I spin around in my seat, causing the boat to wobble precariously. Three feet behind me looms a large swan, raised up on its haunches, wings open. 'All eight, full pressure, go!' I shout, causing the microphone to screech. The shell lurches forward, but not quickly enough. The swan is inches behind me now, its breath hot and foul. I scream as the bird's sharp beak cuts into my neck. The enormous wings envelop me and everything goes black...

'...begun our descent into Heathrow,' the

28

pilot's voice, clipped and neat, crackles through the cabin. I open my eyes, my head jerking forward with a start. 'Please return your seat to the upright position...'

Blinking, I sit up and stretch, tuning out the rest of the pilot's familiar mantra. Had I really slept the entire flight? I look at the television screen on the seat in front of me. A white line arches across a world map, tracing a line between Washington, D.C., and London, showing the trajectory of our flight. The tiny airplane is nearing the end of the journey, marking our imminent arrival. My stomach clenches.

Easy, I think, pressing the power button on the armrest. The map disappears and the screen goes dark. I look around the cabin. My hastily booked seat is in the last row of business class, the space beside me mercifully unoccupied. From the other side of the flimsy blue curtain comes the clinking of flight attendants loading beverage carts in the galley, clearing the breakfast I missed. Across the aisle, a fiftyish man in a blue collared shirt reads the paper while his companion, a younger brown-haired woman (daughter? secretary? lover?) rifles through her purse, long red nails flashing into view every so often.

Turning away, I push up the window shade. The sky is ominous, shrouded in thick fog. Streams of condensation trickle along the outside of the glass. I imagine the airport below, controllers guiding the planes in with strong arm gestures, luggage carts and food service trucks scurrying among the aircraft like ants. The generic images should be comforting. We could be landing anywhere.

'Ma'am?' I turn to find a flight attendant standing in the aisle beside me, holding out a rolled hand towel with plastic tongs. I accept the warm, moist cloth and settle back in my seat. Ma'am. No one would have called me that the first time I'd taken this flight. Barely twenty-one years old, I had just graduated from American with an international studies degree that meant nothing in a recessed Washington economy. I was still looking for a job when the call came: the student who had beaten me for the fellowship to Cambridge was unable to go (pregnant, I would later learn). Did I want to take her place? For a moment, I hesitated; I had nearly forgotten about the scholarship, one of dozens I applied for the previous fall in a futile attempt to get over the boyfriend who had dumped me for my roommate at the start of senior year, taking all of our mutual friends with him. Still holding the telephone receiver, I looked around the cramped Adams Morgan apartment, which I shared with two girls I barely knew. There was nothing keeping me there. Three weeks later I was on my way to England.

England. I wipe my face lightly with the cloth. As a child, the very word sounded magical. England was the place of legends, the land of King Arthur and Dickens and Mary Poppins. I ran home from school in fourth grade to tell my mother that we had to go there now, because Nostradamus had predicted it would be washed into the sea. We did not go, of course; my parents seldom ventured farther than our cabin in the Berkshires or an occasional summer rental on Cape Cod. Ours were quiet vacations where my father could work on the journal articles that established him as a leading microeconomics scholar, my mother on the romance novels that had in fact long supported us. It wasn't until more than ten years later that I would board the plane for the land of my dreams, headed for Cambridge. I remember striding down the gate toward the door of the British Airways plane, my first passport crisp and new in my hand. My heart felt as though it might burst.

That was a different England. That was before.

I run my tongue over my teeth, fuzzy from sleep, pulling a half-empty water bottle out of the seat pocket, and take a large gulp. Then I reach for my bag, which sits on the seat beside me. A chocolate brown tote, it was a get-well present from my parents last year. 'Coach?' I protested when I opened it. I was never one for labels and couldn't imagine needing something so grand. But I quickly grew to love the soft leather, the versatility and size that let me put files in it one day, sneakers the next. I rummage through the side pocket, finding my compact mirror. My skin is dull and sallow, dark circles ringing my hazel eyes. I used to be able to travel for twenty hours on a cargo plane and step off ready for a meeting and now... I do not finish the thought as I work my dark curls into a ponytail low at the nape of my neck, using some of the bottled water to smooth the stray pieces.

The aircraft seems to hover parallel to the earth for several minutes, its wings wobbling and dipping from side to side, as though they might accidentally brush the ground. There is a small bump as the wheels touch down, followed by a second one, then a momentary gliding sensation. I place my hand on the seat in front of me to keep from being thrown forward as the brakes come on hard.

When we reach the gate, I remain seated as the other passengers fill the aisles and rush to pull their bags from the overhead compartments. I'll just stay here a moment more, I think as they shuffle past. The once-cramped cabin, strewn with magazines and airline blankets, seems safe, a familiar refuge. But it is nearly empty now and the flight attendant at the front of the plane is looking at me expectantly. It is time to go. I stand and hoist my small carry-on bag to my shoulder. Taking a deep breath, I head for the exit.

Inside the terminal, I follow the crowds toward immigration and customs. Bypassing the automated walkways, I stride down the corridor, savoring the opportunity to stretch my legs, stiff from the long flight. Familiar, brightly lit advertisements for West End musicals and duty-free shopping line the concourse. There are other signs, too, touting mobile phones and WiFi access, products that did not exist the last time I was here. As I advance through the terminal, weaving around the slower travelers, my gait grows long and purposeful. I smile inwardly, savoring the surge of energy that always comes from setting foot in a different country at the beginning of a new day.

At the entrance to the enormous immigration hall, I hesitate, studying the yellow signs that direct European Union and Commonwealth travelers into one line, everyone else to another. I am always reluctant to exercise my diplomatic privileges, but the hall is a swarming mass of people lugging children and suitcases through endless roped stanchions, shuffling with painstaking slowness toward the twenty or so immigration officers who sit in booths along the wide front of the room. Approaching a woman in a blue jacket who is directing arrivals, I hold up my black passport and try to ignore the angry stares of the travelers in line as I am led directly to a booth.

I hand my passport to the uniformed man behind the glass, who begins to leaf through it in a perfunctory manner. Then he stops and looks up at me. It is the stamps, I know, the pages and pages of markings from the countries I have visited, enough to give even a seasoned immigration official at one of the world's busiest airports pause. I usually have my passport 'scrubbed' before taking on a new assignment, removing most of my prior trips to avoid questions, but there wasn't time. I offer a smile to the immigration official, who flicks the passport cover with his thumb before handing it back and waving me through.

Proceeding to the baggage claim area, I collect my suitcases from the carousel and place them on a cart. I walk through the green 'Nothing to Declare' lane and out into the main terminal, scanning the awaiting crowd and the dark-suited drivers holding up placards. Not seeing my name, I exhale with relief. Maureen did not send anyone to meet me because either she knew I preferred to arrive alone or there had not been time to arrange a pickup. Either way is great.

I maneuver the cart through the crowded terminal, stopping at an ATM to withdraw a few hundred pounds, enough to last until I start work and have access to the embassy bank. The exchange rate will be better, I know, than going to one of the currency exchange kiosks. The smell of coffee wafts across the concourse, reminding me of the cup I missed earlier on the plane. I tuck away the bills that the cash machine dispenses, then follow the aroma to the Pret a Manger counter and order a small skim cappuccino. As the barista steams the milk, I eye the pastries behind the counter. But my stomach is still a rock, the prospect of eating unfathomable.

A few minutes later, I make my way across the concourse, the cardboard cup warm and reassuring in my hand. Licking the foam that has bubbled up through the lid, I take a sip of cappuccino, then step through the automatic doors of the airport. The fresh air hits me like a wall.

'Wow,' I say aloud, inhaling deeply. There was always something crisper about the air here, more alive. The sky is different too – it seems closer than at home, a cap pulled low and tight around the brow. In my memories, the weather here was eternally cloudy and gray. But the sky is a hypnotic field of intense, unbroken blue and the sun shines brightly now, mocking my fears.

I force my gaze downward, getting my bearings as I finish the remains of my cappuccino in two large gulps and throw the empty cup in a trash bin by the curb. Immediately in front of me, black taxicabs and airport hotel shuttles race past. LOOK RIGHT! a sign painted in bright yellow letters on the pavement cautions. On the opposite side of the road sits a bus terminal, dozens of coaches pulling in and out of its stations. My eyes travel instinctively to the far left, where a handful of young people, college students, I guess from their torn jeans and slouched stances, wait to board a blue and gray coach. The bus to Cambridge.

I step forward. What if I were to board that bus right now? I imagine stowing a rucksack beneath and climbing aboard, gazing out the window, my nose pressed to the glass as the bus makes its way up the M11 through the rolling fens of East Anglia, my eyes widening as the Cambridge spires break on the horizon. When I would arrive, I would walk the short distance from the Drummer Street bus station to my house on Lower Park Street to find Jared waiting for me there, joking with Sarah as he made me beans and toast for lunch.

Jared.

Stop, I think, but it is too late. The name rips through my lungs like a knife as his face appears in my mind.

'Jordan!' A booming voice jars me from my thoughts. Damn it, I swear inwardly. Maureen sent someone after all. 'Jordan Weiss!' The voice is female, I realize. Southern. I turn to see a large, familiar woman in a bright pink suit waving frantically at me from the other side of the road. Maureen did not send a car; she's come for me herself.

I feel the heads of the travelers around me swivel in Maureen's direction as she starts across the road, red curls bobbing wildly. Horns blare as she strides through traffic in her impossibly high heels, not bothering to use the crosswalk but stopping cars with an outstretched hand. My mind races. It is unheard of for the deputy chief of mission, second in charge of the entire embassy, to greet new arrivals. And Maureen didn't meet me when I arrived in the country for our two previous assignments together. What is she doing here?

But there is no time to wonder. Maureen, moving surprisingly quickly for a woman her size, is upon me in seconds. 'You!' she cries, oblivious to the stares. She throws her arms around me, enveloping me in a cloud of flowery scent. The strength of her embrace nearly lifts me from the ground. 'I've been waiting forever for this. Welcome to London!'

'Thanks, Mo,' I manage, breathless from being squeezed. 'But you didn't have to come all the way out here...'

'Don't be silly!' Maureen steps back, waving a hand dismissively. 'My driver is just pulling around.' I hold my breath, half expecting to see the pink Cadillac that attracted so much attention around Washington. But a black Mercedes appears at the corner. 'They wouldn't let me bring Bessie,' she adds, seeming to read my thoughts as the car pulls to a stop in front of us. 'Wrong side of the road and all that.'

I hand my bags to the driver and walk around the back of the sedan. I'd forgotten how strange it feels to climb into the right side of the car and find myself seated behind the driver. Sinking into the beige leather seat, I am surprised to see two cups of fresh, steaming tea nestled in the cup holders. I lift the one closer to me, smiling. Earl Grey, no milk or sugar. It's been years since I last saw Maureen, and the woman still knows how I take my tea, or did anyway, when I didn't need two cups of coffee to get out of bed in the morning.

Maureen climbs in the back beside me. We exit the airport, passing a large Beefeater Gin display, an enormous bottle still touting the company's sponsorship of the recent Oxford-Cambridge Boat Race. The Boat Race is the pinnacle of the rowing calendar in Britain, when the two varsity squads, the light Blues of Cambridge and the dark Blues of Oxford, face off in a twenty-minute race down the Thames. It is a grudge match with a hundred-and-fifty-year tradition, interrupted only by the two world wars. I look back over my shoulder at the retreating sign, wondering who won this year. My crew was a college boat, one of the feeder crews for the university squad. I never even considered trying out as a coxswain for the Blues, but some of the rowers could have made it. Jared, if he'd wanted to, and maybe ... well, Chris was good enough, too. He might have had a chance the following year, if things had worked out differently.

'So,' Maureen says, as we merge onto the M4 motorway. 'How'd I get so lucky?'

Typical Maureen, right to the point. I take a sip of tea, then set the cup back in its holder. 'Lucky?' I repeat, stalling for time.

She nods. 'To get you here. It was no accident. The Twerp would never give you up voluntarily. How is he, by the way?'

I bite my lip, fighting the urge to laugh aloud. The acrimony between Paul Van Antwerpen and

37

Maureen Martindale is legendary in the department, the cause a great source of speculation. Both are highly successful diplomats with more than twenty-five years of service. Some say that their feud stems from competition for a promotion or key assignment years ago. There is also a rumor they were once romantically involved, a passionate affair that ended badly. I like to believe that they are too professional to let either of these explanations, if true, affect their working relationship, preferring instead to think of it as a difference in style: Maureen is a brash Texan whirlwind, Van Antwerpen meticulous and precise.

'The Director's fine,' I manage at last. 'He sends his regards.'

Maureen snorts. 'I bet he does. Anyway, I know he wouldn't let you go if he could help it.' She takes a sip of tea then sets the cup down again, a half-moon of pink lipstick visible on the rim. 'So what gives?'

I hesitate. I've known Maureen for nearly a decade; she's the closest thing I've found to a friend in this business. Still, the first rule of intelligence is ingrained in my psyche: never admit to having a life outside work, much less talk about it. I clear my throat. 'It's personal,' I find myself saying for the second time in less than twenty-four hours.

But Maureen is not Van Antwerpen, and will not be dissuaded. 'Come on, what is it? I'd guess a guy, but I know you too well for that. Friend in need?'

'Excuse me?' I reply, startled. Maureen always could see right through me, but how could she

38

possibly know?

Maureen smiles. 'Just a lucky guess. I know you went to grad school over here and that you haven't returned since. Hard to think of what else could make you come back.'

'Yes.' I slump in my seat, relieved. Then I relay the story about Sarah and her illness. 'I don't know how long she has, but I'm here to do whatever I can for her.'

'I'm sorry to hear that,' Maureen says softly. 'I had a cousin with Lou Gehrig's. That disease is a bitch.' Had. I wince inwardly. Mo is not one to sugarcoat the truth, and I have not heard anything hopeful about ALS from anyone.

Maureen does not speak further but reaches in her purse and pulls out a BlackBerry, too new to be government-issued. I study her out of the corner of my eye. She has to be around fifty, I calculate. As ever, her strong features are flawlessly pulled together, a symphony of eyeliner, mascara, rouge. But her jawline has softened with time and her cheeks sit a bit less high. Do I seem changed to her, too? More seasoned, I hope, self-assured. I smooth the black wrinkle-free travel pants that had not quite lived up to their name, then wipe a smudge from the sleeve of my khaki jacket.

The motorway ends and we merge onto the A4, soon reaching a roundabout. A street sign, thick white writing on green, diagrams the spurs off the circle, eleven o'clock for Chiswick, one o'clock for Central London. The traffic light changes to yellow and red together before turning green. We continue through the roundabout, past Fuller's Brewery, pulling around a red Royal Mail truck as

39

we exit onto the Great West Road. A row of brown brick houses, identical except for a few odd-sized satellite dishes, sits close to the street. Tiny green buds dot the low hedge that runs along the sidewalk in front of the houses, and daffodils sprout from the narrow grass median. I gaze ahead at the tiny cars, the unfamiliar street signs. Everything looks so different here, picturesque, almost storybook. A warm feeling rises inside me, pushing up against the fear and dread, reminding me that there was a time when I loved it here more than any place on earth. I'd forgotten, I think, touching the glass with my fingertips.

'Forgotten what?'

I turn to find Maureen looking up from the BlackBerry, head tilted. I didn't realize I'd spoken aloud. 'Sorry, nothing. So, any idea what I'll be working on?' I ask, eager to change the subject.

Her expression turns serious. 'I can't say much here; it's classified. We're meeting tomorrow with the rest of the team. I'll brief you fully then.'

'Tomorrow?' I was hoping, as is department custom, I could take the day to unpack, get over my jet lag, see Sarah.

But Maureen nods, not noticing or choosing to ignore my surprise. 'Oh-eight-thirty in the Bubble.' The light changes and the car begins to move again, more slowly now in the traffic. 'I thought we would drop you off at your flat so you can get some rest,' she says a few minutes later, her tone light once more. 'See your friend if you'd like. You lucked out on housing, by the way. We had an unexpected departure.' She lifts her eyebrow as if to indicate a juicy story that she would share later out of the driver's presence. 'A unit in Hammersmith opened up.'

My breath catches. 'Hammersmith?'

She nods. 'It's gorgeous, and a great location. Normally you would have been up in Maida Vale or St. John's Wood.'

I do not answer but look out the window again. Hammersmith is right on the river. I see myself seated in the stern of the boat, facing Chris and the seven rowers behind him as they come forward in their seats, struggling to catch and bury the spoons of their oars in the choppy Thames wake. A faint wave of nausea rises in me.

Enough. I force the image from my mind as the car turns onto a wide thoroughfare, bustling with shoppers. The stores here are familiar chains: the drugstore Boots, a Tesco Metro grocery. Farther along, the wide windows of Marks & Spencer department store offers an end-of-season special on hooded jumpers while touting short skirts for spring. I am surprised – in my mind, I'd still seen the clothing here as loose-fitting and dark, the mid-nineties grunge I loved so much. But the outfits worn by the mannequins are snug and brightly colored, more Posh Spice than Pearl Jam.

We pass a bakery and a flower shop before turning onto a street lined with stately brown brick homes, compact cars packed tightly along both sides. At the end of the road, perpendicular to the main street, sits a row of ill-fitting modern town houses, a pub nestled in the corner. 'This is it,' Maureen says as we slow before the modular brick units. 'Yours is on the far right end.' Between the houses and the pub, there is a low hedge, a swath of unbroken blue sky behind. My flat is, quite literally, on the river.

She reaches for the door handle. 'Let's get you settled.'

'Mo, wait.' She turns back and looks at me. I hesitate. I do not want to appear rude, but if she comes in and stays to talk, it could be hours. 'You don't have to take me inside. If you want to give me the keys...'

Maureen raises her hand. 'I get it. You want to go see your friend, right?' Not waiting for an answer, she leans across the front seat and hands the keys to the driver. 'Harry, please put Ms. Weiss's bags in the flat for us.' She turns back to me. 'We can drop you at your friend's house.'

'That won't be necessary. It's all the way up in Notting Hill. I can take the Tube and...'

'Nonsense,' Mo interrupts. 'We'll swing round the park and drop you off.' I sink back in my seat, knowing that it is pointless to argue. 'What's the address?' Mo asks when Harry returns a minute later.

'Pembridge Crescent, number thirty-nine. Just off Bayswater, not far from the Tube station and Portobello Road.'

'Love the market there on Saturdays,' Maureen remarks as the car begins to move. 'We'll have to go sometime. Anyway, I need to give you a few things.' She hands me the keys that Harry gave back to her. She pulls a briefcase out from under the seat and opens it. 'Here.' She presses a cell phone into my palm. It is smaller than any I've ever seen and black, with no manufacturer's markings. 'It's the latest model. Satellite tech-

42

nology, you can make a call from anywhere, access e-mail, the Internet, texting, whatever. It has global positioning so you can find your way.' And so they can find me. I look at Maureen quizzically. 'You're going to be out in the field a lot on this assignment,' she explains. 'We need to be able to reach you at all times.'

My curiosity rises. I was expecting a desk job, maybe supervising some junior officers. But if Maureen notices my surprise, she gives no indication. 'This is yours also.' She pulls out a small case and hands it to me. Inside is my pistol, the Glock I left behind in the vault. 'The Director sent it in the overnight pouch.' I didn't think that I would be allowed to have my gun in England, a country where most of the police generally do not carry them. I lift the automatic from the case, check the chamber. It is unloaded, of course. The grip in my hand feels like home. There is a bond, I heard once, between a person and a gun fired to save one's own life.

Maureen passes me a folded piece of paper. 'This is your permit. You're authorized to carry that concealed everywhere. I don't want to tell you the strings I had to pull with the regional security officer to get that level of clearance.'

Why, I wonder, did she go to the trouble? She wouldn't have called in a favor with Diplomatic Security just to be nice. I push the questions from my mind as we reach Notting Hill, nostalgia tugging hard at my stomach as we pass Portobello Road. The street was legend in my mind as a child, immortalized by Angela Lansbury in one of my favorite childhood films, *Bedknobs and*

Broomsticks: 'Portobello Road, Portobello Road, streets where the riches of ages are stowed...' I came here often during my years at Cambridge, poring over old books and costume jewelry at the crowded stalls that lined both sides of the street on Saturdays. The market chaos is absent this weekday morning, only a few well-heeled shoppers walking unhurried among the chic cafés and antique shops.

As we turn off the main street onto Pembridge Crescent, I place the gun back in the case, then tuck it, along with the permit and phone, into my bag. The Victorian houses here are tall and wide, porches with pale stone columns behind low iron gates. 'Thanks, Mo,' I say as the car pulls to a stop. I reach for the door handle. 'I'll see you tomorrow.'

'Oh wait, I almost forgot.' I turn back. 'There's a reception at the Ambassador's residence tonight. It would be good if you could be there.'

Inwardly, I groan. I hate the niceties of diplomatic life overseas, the endless receptions and formal events, almost as much as the bureaucracy of Washington. I want to take a bath, unpack and sleep. But I can tell from Maureen's tone that this is not a request. 'Sure. No problem,' I reply, mentally scanning the clothes I packed to determine if I have something appropriate to wear.

'Great. Starts at seven. See you then.' Maureen smiles. 'And Jordan, it's good to have you here.'

I watch as the car pulls away, then look up at the row of stately houses that stand a few feet apart, their brick fronts painted various shades of faded white. Crossing the pavement to number thirty-nine, I hesitate at the base of the steps. The house is less well-tended than its neighbors, the gate handle hanging from its hinges, the window-trim rotting. I do not recall it being so dilapidated the last time I was here. The house, left to Sarah by her grandmother, had been in her family since before World War I, subdivided into flats in the fifties. The family kept the ground-floor apartment for its own use while renting out the others. Making my way up the cracked marble steps, I wonder if the rental income is no longer enough to pay for upkeep as well.

I study the row of buttons to the right of the front door and press the one farthest right, hearing a faint ringing inside. When there is no response, I turn the door knob and step into the musty foyer. The decor has not changed since my last visit. An aged chandelier casts the entrance-way in dim yellow light, revealing worn blue-flowered carpet and gray, peeling paint.

I walk past the wide staircase, pausing before the door to Sarah's flat, wondering about her condition, her reaction to my unannounced arrival. I knock once, then push the door open. 'Hello?' I call into the darkened room. 'Sarah?'

'Jordie... ?' Sarah's voice is filled with disbelief.

'It's me.' I step inside and adjust my eyes. The room is large, with a kitchenette in the left corner and a hallway leading off the far side. Sarah sits in a wheelchair by the back wall, the thick curtains behind her drawn. The floorboards creak as I cross the room.

Drawing closer to Sarah, my heart sinks. She was always thin, but she seems to have shrunk in half since the last time I saw her. All of her muscle tone is gone and as I bend to hug her, I can feel her shoulder bone protruding. Her skin is cool and clammy as I kiss her cheek. Her hair, a dull brown cap, shorter than I remember, smells of fresh soap. 'What on earth are you doing here?' Sarah demands, her Durban accent crisp.

'Oh, I happened to be in the neighborhood.' I step back, noticing how her right hand hangs limply by her side.

'I can't believe it's really you.' Sarah's voice cracks. This surprises me more than anything else. She was always stoic, unemotional. 'The Rock,' I used to call her. She was the strong one. How can this be happening to her?

I pull an old wooden chair from the kitchen table and bring it to her side, sneaking a glance around. The high ceilings and crown molding belie the house's elegant past, but the plaster is cracked now, the paint pocked with brown water stains. The furniture is sparse, a worn brown sofa and chair on a faded print carpet. The room is clean, though, dishes stacked neatly in a rack beside the sink, the air smelling faintly of rubbing alcohol and lemon polish. Someone is caring for her, I realize with relief.

Sitting down beside her, I draw back the curtains to reveal a small grassy patch separating her house from the row behind. 'You have night vision now?' I tease, gesturing to the book that lies in her lap.

Sarah looks down, dazed, as though she had forgotten the book was there. 'I must have dozed off a few hours ago, after the nurse left.'

'How are you feeling?'

She shrugs. 'Some days are better than others.' I make a mental note to ask the nurse about Sarah's condition. 'When did you arrive?'

'About an hour ago.'

'Where are your bags?'

She thinks I'm visiting. 'I had them dropped off.'

'Where? You didn't book a hotel, I hope.' Her voice grows brisk and commanding, the take-charge Sarah of old. 'I have plenty of room.'

I shift in my chair. 'No, at my flat, actually.'

'Your flat?' She blinks twice, eyes wide. 'How long are you staying?'

'Oh.' I clear my throat. 'About two years.'

'You mean ... you're moving here?' I nod. 'Why?'

'It's a good career opportunity,' I begin. Then, seeing Sarah's skeptical expression, I stop. I have never been any good at lying to her. 'Okay, the truth is, I have this sick friend...'

'Jordie...' Sarah's jaw drops. 'You came for me? But I'd never ask you to uproot your whole life.'

'I have no roots, you know that. Anyway, you didn't ask, I offered. It was a good excuse to get out of Washington.'

'But, how are you going to be able... I mean...' Sarah does not finish the sentence. She was there with me ten years ago. She knows exactly what I went through, what it has taken for me to come back again.

'I don't know.' My eyes fill with tears. Stop it, I think, mortified – I'm not the one with a reason to cry now. 'I'll manage,' I say when I can speak normally again, not meeting her gaze. 'Do you

47

need anything? I can go to the store for you or make you something to eat...'

'No,' she replies quickly, then clears her throat. 'Don't get me wrong, I'm delighted that you're here, that you'll be close by.' She raises her chin defiantly. 'But I won't have you treating me like a child, at least not now, while I can still manage on my own. The nurse leaves me what I need, and the rest I can do on my own. Just be my friend, the same as you ever have. I'll tell you if I want something more.'

I nod. She's setting the terms with her illness, I realize, as much as with me. 'I understand.'

'It's gotten so gray,' she remarks a moment later, gesturing with her head to the dark clouds that have gathered above the chimneys, blowing away the blue sky with mercurial ease.

'Sunday weather,' I add. She nods in agreement, a shared reference. Sundays at Cambridge always seemed gloomy and repentant, dark clouds gathered close and somber over the courtyards. It was the gods, we joked, frowning down upon us for the excesses of the previous night.

Neither of us speak further. A minute later, I look over at Sarah. Her eyes are half closed. 'Are you okay?' I ask, placing my hand on top of hers.

'Yes. There's a medicine I take for the symptoms. It makes me tired sometimes.' Sarah smiles weakly. 'I'm glad you're here, though.' Still holding her hand, I gaze out the window at two boys kicking a soccer ball farther down the grassy patch, open winter jackets flapping awkwardly as they run and play. When I turn back, Sarah's head is tilted sideways and her eyes are tightly shut. I can tell from her long, even breaths that she is asleep. Protectiveness rises in me. Maybe I should move in to help take care of her. But she's too proud for that. I'll just be close by instead. I pull out my new cell phone and scribble down the number on a small tablet on the coffee table. Then, I reach down and lift the cotton blanket that has fallen to her feet, pulling it up and tucking it around her.

As I stand to leave, a framed image above the fireplace catches my eye. I walk over and lift the picture from the mantel. It is a photograph of hundreds of college students, taken from above. The students, dressed in tuxedos and gowns, are looking up at the camera, their wineglasses raised. My breath catches. The May Ball. In the far right-hand corner, I can make out Jared's face between Chris's and my own. His dark eyes seem to leap from the paper, demanding to know what I am doing here, why I have come back. My finger trembles as I touch the image, the last picture of him ever taken. Hours later he was gone. I thrust the picture back on the mantel, as if it were hot to the touch. Then, tiptoeing carefully so as not to wake Sarah, I walk quickly from the apartment.

chapter THREE

I step out of the black taxicab onto the pavement in front of the Ambassador's Chelsea residence, following an older couple up the steps of the gated mansion. The fur-clad woman's dress is ankle length, I note, feeling underdressed in my above-the-knee black sheath and thin wool coat. I never quite get the outfits right for these formal occasions, just one of the reasons I hate them. Inside, guests crowd the high-ceilinged foyer, queuing for the receiving line that snakes beneath the crystal chandelier toward the entrance of the great room.

'Toilet?' I ask as I hand my coat to the butler, who points toward a hallway off the back of the foyer. Moving away from the din of voices, I pass a series of expensive-yet-hideous oil paintings depicting a hunting party, hounds chasing, then in the next catching, then finally devouring a fox. Inside the bathroom, I lock the door and pull a tube of lipstick from my clutch evening purse, studying my reflection in the mirror as I reapply the dusky rose, the darker of the two shades I own. My hair, which I painstakingly blew dry, falls smooth and full over my shoulders. But my skin is pasty from the Washington winter, faint under-eye circles of exhaustion visible through the powder.

Stepping out of the toilet, I walk farther down the hall, away from the receiving line, and reach the kitchen, a swarming hive of staff buzzing around large, stainless-steel appliances, stirring pots, arranging hors d'oeuvres on plates. 'Excuse me,' I say, swiping a glass of white wine from one of the trays before the puzzled waiter who is loading it can object. Continuing swiftly through the kitchen, I enter a small library just off the back of the larger room where most of the gathering has assembled.

I half face one of the high oak bookshelves lining the walls, pretending to examine the tomes while studying the guests. It would have been helpful if Maureen told me the occasion for the party. Some sort of military delegation, I surmise. The guests, clustered in small groups, are predominantly male, a significant number in dress uniforms from countries I cannot identify. Their hair is mostly dark, their complexions swarthy. Middle Eastern or South Asian. I recall reading an article in *The Economist* about an arms deal among the United States, Britain, and Saudi Arabia; perhaps the gathering has something to do with that. We'll do anything to get rid of that excess hardware from the Cold War, and someday it's going to come back to haunt us.

'Ornithologist?' a voice behind me asks.

Startled, I spin around to face the man who spoke. 'Excuse me?'

He gestures to the book I pulled from the shelf and I notice for the first time that it is an encyclopedia of birds. 'I was wondering if that was your profession or hobby.'

Scottish, I think, trying to place his accent. 'Neither actually.' I replace the book, studying the man. He is good-looking, I decide instantly. The thought is surprising; it usually takes a while for men to grow on me, and his tall, slim build bears no resemblance to the broad-shouldered athletic types I've preferred in recent years. His short brown hair, flecked with blond, flicks up stubbornly at the ends, as though it lost a good fight against a comb earlier. 'Just an excuse to avoid mingling.'

'Me too.' He shifts his glass and a small plate to

51

his left hand, then extends his right. 'Sebastian Hodges.'

'Jordan Weiss.' He is close to forty, I guess (though I can't tell on which side), measuring the crinkles at the corner of his deep green eyes as I shake his hand.

'Pig in a blanket?' Sebastian jiggles the plate slightly.

I look down and laugh. Only at an American diplomatic function would one find the miniature hot dogs, wrapped in puff pastry. 'Actually, I will, thanks,' I reply, taking one and popping it in my mouth. The taste instantly takes me back to childhood backyard barbecues, Fourth of July parades down Main Street. 'I flew in this morning and I haven't eaten since.'

'I'm the same way when I travel. It's the jet lag.' Sebastian takes a sip of white wine, then grimaces.

'Not good?' I raise my own glass, sniffing the wine in a way that I hope looks knowledgeable.

He shakes his head. 'To be fair though, pigs in blanket are a really difficult pairing.' I laugh again, feeling my shoulders relax for the first time since my arrival. I take a small sip. It tastes, well, like wine. I have never developed a discerning palate. My first real exposure to wine was at Cambridge, remainder bottles purchased at Oddbins for two or three pounds, taken to dinner at Formal Hall or student parties where the invitations invariably asked guests to P.B.A.B. ('Please Bring A Bottle'). There were Wine Society functions, too, complete with tasting note sheets that never quite got filled in, spittoons that nobody used. Ten glasses or so later, I never could remember what I drank. After the first, it didn't seem to matter much anyway. Since becoming a diplomat, I've had the chance to try many excellent wines, or so I've been told, but I can never tell the difference or remember the names.

'First trip to England?' Sebastian asks.

If only. I shake my head. 'Actually I was a postgrad at Cambridge. Read history. But I haven't been back in years.' I take another sip of wine, easing into the conversation.

'Cambridge? Well I won't hold it against you. I was a linguist at All Souls.' All Souls is one of the Oxford colleges. Oxford and Cambridge grads almost always identify themselves by the college attended within the university, even years after the fact. In the States and other countries, I had gotten used to saying I went to Cambridge, but with the Brits it was all Magdalene (pronounced 'Maudlin') or Trinity or Saint John's. The degrees might have come from the university, but the colleges were the lifeblood, the places where the students slept and ate and played. I had not known that at the start. I applied to Cambridge; Lords College was incidental because my fellowship was designated there. Within weeks, though, the college became my home. I simply could not imagine going anywhere else. 'Though I suspect I was there many years before you,' Sebastian adds.

'Oh, I don't know about that,' I protest playfully. 'I'm a good deal more mature than I look.' I finish my wine, then set the empty glass on the edge of the bookshelf.

'Indeed.' Sebastian's gaze sweeps from my eyes

53

downward, then back again, his expression deepening.

I feel a warm blush creeping upward from my neck. What am I doing? It is not like me to flirt with a complete stranger, especially not at a work function. Feeling the urge for another drink, I scan the room hopefully, but the bar is miles away, separated from me by a sea of guests. I turn back to Sebastian. 'So what do you...'

'There you are!' a voice roars, cutting me off. I turn to see Maureen careening into the library. She has abandoned her usual pink for a fitted, low-cut black dress that would look trashy on anyone else but somehow works perfectly on her ample figure. 'Trying to avoid me?' I shake my head, forcing a smile. Now that Maureen has found me, my time standing quietly in the library is over. 'Howdy, Sebastian.' Maureen nods in his direction, then turns quickly back to me. 'Come on, let me introduce you around.' Before I can respond, Maureen grabs my elbow and leads me away. I look back helplessly over my shoulder at Sebastian, who grins and winks.

'Maureen, who's...' I begin.

But she pulls me through the crowd, not listening. 'You skipped the receiving line,' she chides. 'Don't deny it. I saw you sneak in the back.'

I spot a waiter coming toward us, bearing a tray of white wine. 'I wanted to slip in so I could observe...'

Maureen shoots me a cynical look. 'Don't give me that, Weiss. You don't even have your assignment yet.' I consider arguing, then realize it is pointless. Instead, I manage to grab another glass of wine from the waiter as Maureen hurries me past.

As we make our way across the room, I scan the gathering once more. Scattered among the guests is a handful of diplomats, pale men in moderately priced American suits, feigning interest in their conversations while furtively canvassing the room to find more important people to corner.

'Ms. Martindale.' An olive-skinned older man in a uniform, speaking with a Middle Eastern accent too thick to identify, steps into our path and grabs Mo's arm.

'Excuse us, honey,' Maureen says, shaking him off, then flashing him her signature twenty-four-carat smile. 'Two secs, okay?' Had it been anyone else but Mo, the man would have felt snubbed, but he steps back, mollified.

A minute later, I find myself standing in front of the Ambassador, trying to ignore the stares of those waiting in line to speak with him. 'Mr. Ambassador, may I introduce Jordan Weiss?' Ambassador Raines is tall with an enormous stomach, and bald except for a ring of white hair surrounding his pear-shaped head. He is not, I know, a career diplomat. He made his money heading up a major defense company, donating handsomely in the last presidential election. Ambassadors at the major European posts are often wealthy political appointees, a fact that rankles the career Foreign Service officers to no end.

The Ambassador shakes my outstretched hand. 'A pleasure. I've heard a great deal about you.'

'Thank you, sir.' I study his face, trying to discern the meaning behind his words. I prefer to keep my own name out of the headlines, maneuver behind the scenes, but Public Affairs has written some releases involving my work that have been picked up by the media. Is he referring to those, or has Mo told him something more?

'And this is my wife.' The Ambassador turns to the much younger woman beside him. He does not, I notice, use her name. The Ambassador's wife is nearly as tall as he, but willowy, with flawless skin and perfect, shoulder-length blond hair. Her simple black silk dress, cut on the bias, screams couture. She wears no jewelry except for a diamond tennis bracelet that I am certain is worth more than my salary for a year. She is not, I decide, the Ambassador's first wife.

'Charmed,' Mrs. Raines (I presume she did not keep her own name) says in a voice that suggests anything but. She does not extend her hand but takes me in with a sweeping glance, making me feel instantly short and frumpy.

'So Maureen tells me...' the Ambassador begins. I steal a glance in the mirror on the wall. Behind my own reflection I see the growing line of guests in the foyer. Among a sea of dark-haired men, a shock of wheat blond catches my eye. The familiar color sends a jolt of electricity through me. There is only one man I have ever known with hair that particular shade. But it cannot possibly be.

'Ms. Weiss?' the Ambassador asks.

I force my eyes from the mirror. There had been a question, I realize, taking in the expectant looks around me, but I have no idea what it was. 'I-I'm sorry,' I manage.

'The Ambassador was asking...' Maureen

begins, prompting. My eyes dart back to the mirror. The blond man turns slightly, revealing his profile. At the sight of his wide jaw, I gasp.

'Excuse me.' I spin and start in the direction of the foyer, only faintly aware of the low murmurs behind me. I shoulder my way through the crowd, wine sloshing over the edge of my glass. 'Sorry!' I cry, feeling someone's foot beneath my own. Finally I reach the foyer and scan the crowd, but I do not see the blond man.

I look back into the great room, trying to ignore the quizzical expressions of the guests I trampled, then turn toward the hallway that leads to the kitchen, searching. Where is he? My head snaps in the direction of the front door, but my view is obscured by the reception line. Pushing my way through the waiting guests, I run out onto the porch, barreling down the stairs and through the gate. I reach the street, then look quickly in both directions. At the corner, a taxi turns and disappears.

The blond man is gone.

I stand motionless, my heart pounding. A coincidence, I think. A by-product of my jet-lagged imagination. But there is only one man I know who looks anything like that. It was Chris Bannister, I am sure of it. What is he doing here? Last I heard, he was reporting overseas for one of the papers, trying to outrun the same ghosts as me. There is no reason for him to be in London, much less at a diplomatic reception.

A hand touches my shoulder and I turn, expecting to find an angry Maureen. But it is Sebastian, his brow furrowed with concern. 'I saw you rush out. Are you okay?'

I look from Sebastian to the now-empty wine-glass in my hand, then back again, uncertain how to answer. Tears fill my eyes. I am most definitely not all right. But I will not break down, not in front of a man I barely know. Without speaking, I turn and run across the street, into a small park that sits opposite the Ambassador's residence.

'Hey!' Sebastian runs after me, catching me easily with his long strides. He takes me by the shoulders and turns me gently but firmly to face him. 'Wait a minute.' Breathing hard, he leads me to a bench by the side of the path and sits down. I eye the taxi stand at the corner and, for a second, consider running to it. 'I was a sprinter at school,' Sebastian says. 'But I'm completely knackered. Please don't make me chase you again.' Reluctantly, I drop to the bench beside him. 'Now what is it?' he asks, prying the wine-glass gently from my fingers and tossing it into the bushes behind us. 'What made you so upset?'

I do not answer. My stomach, nearly empty except for the wine, turns. I lean back, gazing up-ward at the trees. Through the sparse branches, the sky is clear and filled with stars, the moon a bright crescent. Then I turn to Sebastian, study-ing his face uncertainly. I just met him; I hardly know him at all. Yet there is something in his eyes that makes me want to trust him. 'I thought I saw someone I knew.'

'Must have been quite a someone,' he remarks.

'I have a lot of memories here,' I reply simply, then look away again. A sharp breeze blows through the park. I shiver, remembering the coat

58

I left inside. I cannot go back for it, not now.

I feel something on my shoulders and turn to find that Sebastian has taken off his suit jacket and slipped it around me. 'Thank you,' I manage, my voice barely a whisper. He does not reply but looks into my eyes. Something deep inside me stirs, breaks open. I lean forward, seized with the urge to tell him everything, why I have come back, why it hurts so much to be here again. 'It's just that...' I falter. His face is just inches from mine now, his breath warm on my forehead. Impulsively, I tilt my head upward and brush my lips against his. He hesitates for a second, surprised, then kisses me back, hard and fast. I reach up and clasp his shoulders, drawing him close, grateful to escape from thoughts and explanation. His hand finds the back of my neck, mouth parting.

A car horn blares from the street and I pull back. 'I'm sorry,' I say quickly, facing away.

'I'm not,' he replies and I can almost feel his smile.

I stare hard at the ground, willing myself to breathe normally. Then I remember the Ambassador's shocked expression, the murmur of the other guests as I ran away so abruptly. 'Oh God, I've really done it, haven't I? Ten hours in the country and I've managed to offend the Ambassador...'

'And the likely next secretary of defense.' I raise an eyebrow in surprise. 'He's considered to be the President's top choice since Robinson got caught in that spending scandal. You didn't know?' I shake my head. I keep up on the world affairs required for my job, but political speculation, the media all but making odds on cabinet appointees

59

like horses at the Preakness, was one of the things I liked least about Washington.

'Great, so I humiliated myself in front of a future cabinet member *and* the entire diplomatic community.'

Sebastian chuckles. 'I daresay you gave everyone something interesting to talk about, and for that they should be grateful. But I heard Maureen tell the Ambassador and his wife that you weren't feeling well, so all should be forgiven, if not forgotten.'

Except by Maureen, who forgives nothing and forgets less. Still my shoulders sag with relief. 'Well, at least I'm spared having to go back in there.'

'True. And you'll spare me the same if you let me take you home. My car is just around the corner.'

I hesitate, my insides aching. I desperately want to accept. The last thing I want is to be alone right now. But I know if I let him drive me home I won't be able to let him go. 'Thank you, but that's not necessary.' I stand, handing Sebastian's coat back to him. 'Good night.' Before he can answer, I turn and walk quickly toward the taxi stand at the corner, half hoping that he will chase after me again. But when I close the car, door and look back into the park, he is gone.

As the taxi starts forward, I sink back in the seat, trembling. What just happened? I replay the moment in the park in my mind, heat rising in me as I remember Sebastian's lips, full and warm on mine. I practically attacked him, I realize, mortified. It doesn't matter; I'll probably never see him again. A pang of regret shoots through me. The kiss left me wanting more.

As we drive through the darkened streets, my thoughts return to the blond man. Could it really have been Chris? He, too, fled after Jared's death, taking assignments as far away and fast as he could get them. He swore he was never coming back. But then again, so had I.

Ten minutes later, the taxi pulls up in front of my flat. As I pay the driver and climb out of the cab, my body sags with exhaustion. A good night's sleep, I think as I climb the steps wearily. Maybe a bath first, if I can stay awake that long.

I put the key in the lock. Then something on the ground catches my eye. I look down. Wedged in the crack underneath the door is a small cream-colored envelope.

I hesitate, uneasiness rising inside me. I kneel, lifting the envelope and turning it over as I straighten. Then I freeze. My name is handwritten on the front, the curved, familiar script reaching out like a long-forgotten dream. My heart races. Even without opening it, I know.

The envelope is from Chris Bannister.

chapter FOUR

I open my eyes and lift my head from the bare pillow, squinting against the pale sunlight that leaks through the yellow curtains. My head aches, a dull throb in my left temple. I raise my arm and

61

look at the watch I hadn't bothered to take off last night. Six forty. For a moment I wonder if I am still at the apartment in Washington, if the events of the previous day were all a dream. Then I roll onto my side. Seeing the cream-colored envelope on the pillow beside me, the note card sticking halfway out, I know that they were not.

I sit up in the bed, unmade except for the blanket and pillow I hastily pulled from the welcome kit. Across the room, my two suitcases lie on their sides next to a tall armoire, my black dress from the previous evening strewn across them. I swallow, my mouth sour with stale wine, and then everything comes rushing back: the party, my encounter with Sebastian, the note under the door. I carried the envelope inside the flat unopened, staring at it as I changed for bed. Finally, when I could avoid it no longer, I tore the flap and pulled out a thick card. A single sentence was written on it:

The honour of your presence is requested for dinner, Thursday, the twenty-fourth of April, at seven thirty o'clock in the evening at The Malta, Number Seventy-Nine Pilgrim Street.
Regards, Christopher Bannister

I lift the envelope from the pillow now and pull out the card once more. Chris Bannister. My stomach jumps. It is not that I am not glad to hear from him. He was one of the Eight and Jared's best friend. But why didn't he approach me at the reception? It was him; now I am sure of it. And how did he even know that I am here, much less where I live?

A horn blares on the street below. I blink, rereading the note once more. April 24. Today. My empty stomach flips, begins to burn.

Enough. Setting down the note, I swing my legs to the side of the bed and pad barefoot across the hardwood floor, pulling a bottle of Tums from one of my suitcases and popping three of the chalky tablets into my mouth. Still chewing, I walk into the living room. Sunlight streams through two wide skylights on the high, sloping ceiling. The flat is cozier than I anticipated from the exterior: built-in bookshelves, a wall of exposed brick. The blue overstuffed couch and chair are a welcome relief from the stuffy floral pieces that the government seems to buy in bulk for almost every other residence worldwide. I've been assigned to bigger houses, of course; the one in San Salvador had servants' quarters and a gardener's cottage in the yard. But for a major city such as London, where the property values are exorbitant and diplomatic housing notoriously small and drab, the flat is, as Mo promised, gorgeous.

I walk downstairs to the kitchen and pull a canister of coffee from the plastic bag of groceries that had been left on the counter, topped with a welcome card from the embassy sunshine club. Instant, I realize, replacing the canister and taking out a box of Earl Grey teabags instead. I fill the electric kettle, looking around as I wait for the water to boil. The appliances are white and smaller than in the States: a narrow stove and half-size refrigerator, compact washer and dryer stacked in the corner.

A few minutes later, I carry the cup of tea back up to the living room, then walk to the wide glass doors that cover the far wall and push the curtains aside. Yesterday, when I came back from Sarah's and first saw the panorama of the Thames, I gasped, amazed by the closeness of the water, overwhelmed by my memories. The river, then nearly at high tide, seemed ready to burst from its banks. Now the tide has waned, revealing a thin strip of muddy, debris-strewn bank on either side. Several dozen rowing shells dot the river, hugging the center, trying to find the deepest part of the current. I stare at one crew; transfixed, I appraise their strokes as they push for Hammersmith Bridge. Their blades aren't squaring early enough, and the rower in the four seat is catching too early.

Sipping my tea, I think of Chris once more. He found me, invited me to dinner. So what? He probably just wanted to welcome me back and catch up on old times. My stomach flips, unconvinced. His note gave no contact information, no means of reaching him to accept or decline. He simply assumed I would appear at the time and place given. Typical Chris. He had always, in his charismatic way, expected people to do what he wanted, and most of the time they did. Maybe I should not show up, just to prove a point, I think, toying with the idea. I wish that I could ask Sarah for advice. She would help me figure out what to do. Then I remember her wan, tired expression yesterday. I cannot burden her with this now.

I set my empty teacup down on the low coffee table then make my way into the bathroom, the white tile floor cold beneath the soles of my feet.

As I brush my teeth at the pedestal sink, I eye the large claw-foot bathtub that occupies the far wall. Baths are one of the things I remember most fondly about Britain. Our house at college did not have a shower, and I had grown to love the ritual of a long, hot soak in the mornings and often at night, too. The tub here is deep and inviting, with a new, single faucet, not the separate hot-and-cold taps that vexed me as a student. The best of both worlds. But there is no time; Mo called the meeting for eight-thirty. I turn on the shower and climb in without waiting for the water to warm. I still see Chris's face in my mind.

Nearly an hour later, I reach the edge of Grosvenor Square. Across the park, the embassy runs the entire length of one side, a massive gold eagle and American flag adorning the top. The hulking, bland building was designed in the bureaucratic style of the late 1950s, a Washington architectural eyesore plunked down in the middle of scenic London. It had not changed at all since I was last here more than ten years ago, lining up on a freezing Saturday morning in December along with dozens of other applicants to take the Foreign Service exam. I almost didn't come; there was a party at college the night before and I awoke nearly too hungover to stand. But Sarah dragged me from the warmth of Jared's bed, drove me to London, and waited as I hurriedly filled in the endless ovals with a number two pencil, answering questions on politics, economics, and current events. Green with nausea, I turned in the exam an hour early, certain that I would never hear from the State Department again.

A raindrop pelts my head, then another. 'Damn,' I swear, looking vainly toward the thin trees that line the park as it begins to shower in earnest. The light gray clouds I eyed when leaving the flat gave no hint of a downpour. I forgot how quickly the weather here can change, the constant need to have an umbrella close at hand. I run toward a red telephone booth half-way down the block, large raindrops splashing against the back of my white blouse. Pushing open the door of the booth, I duck inside, struggling to catch my breath from the unexpected sprint. I can feel the dampness soaking through my stockings, my hair turning from curly to frizzy. I'm going to look like a drowned rat at the meeting. If only Maureen would have let me start tomorrow. I imagine holing up in the cozy flat, drinking cups of tea and napping off my jet lag.

A clock in the distance begins to chime. I glance at my watch. Eight-fifteen. I dash across the rain-soaked street and up the steps of the embassy. Inside the lobby, I pause to catch my breath. 'Good morning, Ms. Weiss.' A white-haired woman in a prim gray suit seems to appear from nowhere. I take in her pressed jacket and flawless bun and feel like a wet poodle. 'I'm Amelia Hastings, Ms. Martindale's secretary. The DCM has been delayed at a meeting, but she's expecting you. She asked me to bring you to her office.' Her English accent is clipped, precise. She leads me to the security desk, manned by two Marines. 'New diplomat,' she says, gesturing toward me. 'Can she go around?'

One of the Marines shakes his head, all post-

9/11 seriousness. 'Not until she has her pass.' He points to the metal detector. 'Bag on the conveyor belt, please.' I empty my pockets into my purse, glad I decided to leave my gun at the flat. As the Marine scrutinizes the contents of my tote bag on the monitor, I study his baby face. When I started in the department, the Marines, who provide security at most of the major posts, seemed so attractive. In some countries, they were the only datable men. When, I wonder, as I set my bag down and step through the metal detector, did they get so young?

Amelia leads me across the lobby, past a large marble staircase. 'The consulate is through those doors,' she says, pointing to the right. Through the glass, I see a line of visa applicants waiting for the office to open. 'The Ambassador's office, as well as the DCM's, is located on the fifth floor,' she explains as we step into an elevator. I cringe as the car rises, praying I will not see the Ambassador. Facing Maureen after what happened at the reception is going to be hard enough. 'Economic is on four and political, where you'll be sitting, is on three. The library is on two and the commissary is in the basement. I can give you a tour later if there's time.'

The doors open and I follow Amelia down a wide corridor, lined with portraits of white-haired men, former ambassadors. We reach a large oak door bearing Maureen's name. 'You're soaked,' Amelia says as she ushers me through the reception area and into Maureen's office. Her tone is observant, noncritical. 'I'll bring you tea.'

I consider asking for coffee instead, then decide

67

against it. 'Thank you.' After Amelia disappears, I stand in the middle of the office, not wanting to sit on the chairs while wet. No wonder Maureen and Van Antwerpen hate each other, I think, looking around. The two are like night and day. Van Antwerpen's office had been bare and austere. Maureen's, on the other hand, is a mess. Her enormous mahogany desk looks as though a paper truck has capsized on it. The walls are covered with presidential commendations and photos of Katie and Kyle, the now college-age twins she adopted from Vietnam as infants, as well as her aging Doberman, Teeny. Even the furniture is explosive: overstuffed rose colored cushions and matching drapes, as brash as Maureen herself.

A few minutes later, the doorknob turns and Amelia reappears, carrying a steaming cup. 'Do you want–' she begins, but she is interrupted by a clattering noise at the far end of the room.

'No time for tea!' Maureen cries, barreling through a second, private entrance to the office. 'Meeting in five. We'll grab coffee afterward. Thanks, Amelia.' The secretary retreats from the room, still holding the cup. 'What the hell happened to you last night?' Maureen demands as soon as the door closes. I cringe, bracing myself for the inevitable tirade. She walks to her desk, pulls something off the chair. My coat, I recognize, as she throws it at me. 'Are you okay?'

I fold the coat over my arm, shifting uncomfortably. 'Fine, sorry. I just...' I falter, looking for a good excuse for my abrupt exit and finding none. 'I didn't feel well and I had to get some air,' I finish lamely.

68

Maureen frowns, biting her lip as though there is more she wants to say. 'Let's go.' I follow her through the door at the back of the office into a narrow hallway to an elevator that seems to pre-date both world wars. We descend in silence. At the bottom, the doors open, revealing a cavern-ous basement. The Bubble, a large, trailer-like structure, stands in the middle.

I follow Maureen to the door of the Bubble, then stand aside while she punches several num-bers into a keypad by the door. The lock snaps open. She leads me into the room and the vacuum-sealed door closes behind us with a sucking sound. Outside, I can hear the low hum-ming noise of fans, designed to ensure our conversation cannot be overheard or recorded.

A young woman with a blond bob is already seated at the conference table that runs the length of the room. 'Good morning,' she chirps, rising to her feet.

'Good morning, Sophie,' Maureen replies. 'I'd like you to meet Jordan Weiss, Senior Intelligence Officer. Jordan, this is Sophie Dawson.' I shake Sophie's outstretched hand reluctantly. She has a tiny upturned nose that seems to pull her mouth into a bow, a tailored suit, and well-coiffed hair that gives no indication of the rain outside. It is as though she has stepped out of the recruiting brochure for the Georgetown School of Foreign Service. She hardly looks old enough to drink.

'I must say, Ms. Wei– I mean Jordan, it's a great honor to meet you,' Sophie babbles, sounding nervous.

Over Sophie's head, Maureen winks. 'We need

to get started,' she says, walking to the head of the table. 'Any sign of–' She is interrupted by a clicking sound at the door to the Bubble, fingers punching in numbers on the keypad. I turn toward the door and as it opens, a rock slams into my chest.

There, standing at the entrance to the Bubble, is Sebastian.

'There was a service interruption on the Central Line,' he says, his Scottish accent more pronounced than I remember from the reception the previous evening. His hair gives no pretense of behaving today, but flares wildly in all directions, as though he has just gotten out of bed. What is *he* doing here? 'Sorry I'm late.' Dimples I didn't notice the previous night appear in both cheeks as he smiles at Mo.

Maureen shoots him a withering look. 'Par for the course with you.' But there is no anger in her voice. 'You already know Sophie. And I believe you met Jordan last night.'

'Indeed.' A look of amusement, almost imperceptible, flickers across his face. He is not, I realize angrily, surprised to see me in the least. He knew exactly who I was at the reception last night, but said nothing. Did he seek me out purposely?

'Sebastian is from SOCA, the Serious Organised Crime Agency, and he's detailed to us for this investigation,' Mo adds. 'Let's get started.' I pull out the chair across from Sophie's, not looking at Sebastian as he sits down next to me. As I lay my coat over the arm of the chair, I feel his gaze, making me conscious of my still-damp blouse clinging too snugly across my chest. 'Jordan, I haven't had a chance to debrief you, but the short version is that we've recently been assigned to tackle an issue related to Albanian organized crime.'

I blink, surprised. It is not what I expected to work on in London. Then I try to recall what I know about Albania. Not much – I've never been there. It's in southeastern Europe, on the Adriatic, I think, and it's struggled like the other post-communist nations toward democracy and a free market.

Mo continues speaking to me: 'We put this team together a few weeks ago, and when your transfer came up, you seemed like a natural fit. Sebastian, why don't you outline the problem for us?'

'Thanks, Maureen.' Sebastian places his rumpled navy suit jacket on the back of the chair. As he walks past me to the front of the room, a hint of aftershave tickles my nose. I see his face in the moonlight, feel his lips on mine once more. If only I had known. 'Over the past few years, the Albanian mob has grown to be a major player in underground criminal activity throughout Europe. In Britain, they're edging out other groups, including the Turks and the Russians. They now dominate all areas of the black market: drugs, weapons, prostitution.

'Until recently, infighting among the major families that control Albanian organized crime made it difficult for us to pinpoint targets. But in the past year the Radaj family has emerged as the dominant clan with respect to the British market. Two weeks ago, police in Leeds were able to intercede at a major drug operation and arrest Bakim

71

Vasti, a highly placed member of that syndicate.'

'Have they been able to learn anything from him?' Sophie pipes up, trying to sound knowledgeable. Why is Sophie on the team? I wonder. She cannot be more than a first or second tour officer. Is she CIA? It is, I know, a question that people often ask about me. CIA operatives are often placed under Foreign Service cover, their true identities only revealed on a need-to-know basis. 'Spot the spook' – guessing who is really a spy – is a popular, if officially frowned-upon, diplomatic pastime. It hardly seems possible that the vacuous blonde has passed the Foreign Service exam, though, much less that she is a spy.

Sebastian shakes his head. 'Vasti killed himself in prison two days after his arrest.'

Now it is my turn to interject. 'How did he manage that?'

'Cyanide. He must have hid it on his person, somewhere that the guards missed during the body search.' Unless someone gave it to him, I think. It is not inconceivable that one or more of the underpaid prison guards is on the mob's payroll. But the question is moot. Vasti is dead, and even if he was not, the Eastern European gangs are notoriously tight-lipped. He would not likely have broken, told us what we wanted to know, even under the most extreme questioning.

Sebastian drops into the chair beside me before continuing. 'When the police searched Vasti's car they found documents confirming what some of us have long suspected: that the mob has someone, corporate or maybe even institutional, laundering money for it in Britain. We need to identify the source in order to stop them.'

'And that is where you all come in,' Maureen adds. She pauses, noticing the expression on my face. 'What is it?'

I hesitate. 'Why us? I mean, shouldn't the British government be handling it?'

'They are. It's their investigation, in fact. SOCA has a team working on this as well and the Brits will take the lead in acting on any information we acquire,' Mo replies. 'Sebastian is here to co-ordinate our efforts. He's got full U.S. clearances and reciprocity, by the way, so the usual foreign national restrictions don't apply. But they've asked for our assistance, and this is our business too; the Albanians have major criminal enterprises in the U.S. and many of their exports to us pass through Britain en route.'

'And some of the targets we will be investigating are actually subsidiaries of American corporations,' Sebastian adds.

'Our task is to find the person or persons who are funding and laundering for the Albanians,' Mo adds. 'Fast.' She walks to the front of the room and presses a button on the wall. A large screen descends from the ceiling. Then she opens a laptop that sits on a podium at the front of the room and a typed list of a half dozen names appears on the screen. CLASSIFIED-NOFORN ('No Foreign Nationals') is typed across the top in bright red. 'This is a list of possible contacts that have been preliminary identified by SOCA, individuals who might shed light on the suspect companies or organizations. They aren't current intelligence assets, but potential sources of information.'

I scan the list. About halfway down the page, I stop. 'Duncan Lauder,' I read aloud, a shiver of recognition running through me.

'Yes, he's finance director at a company called Infodyne. It's the British subsidiary of a large American company. And it has a significant portfolio of interests on the Balkan peninsula, which raised a red flag.'

I nod, seeing him in my mind. Duncan was a lanky rower at Downing, one of Lords's rival rowing colleges. His relationship with Vance Ellis, a talented actor, was one of the worst-kept secrets in Cambridge. 'I know Duncan from college. Do you think he's involved in all this?'

'Not necessarily. He was just identified as a potential informant,' Maureen replies. 'How well do you know him?'

'Well enough to reach out to him.'

'Okay, you can cover Duncan.' I look at the paper again, my skin prickles. Duncan Lauder. How odd. This is England, I remind myself. So much smaller than America. Sarah used to say, only half joking, that two British people meeting on the street of Bangkok could invariably trace mutual friends back to the same sixth-form college in Surrey.

There is a click at the entrance to the Bubble and Ambassador Raines appears in the doorway. As he surveys the room, I fight the urge to sink lower in my seat. 'Ambassador,' Maureen says, clearly caught off guard by the interruption. 'I was just briefing the team on the Albanian investigation.'

He does not answer. His eyes flick coldly in my direction and I brace myself, waiting to be rebuked for my behavior at the reception. But he looks away dismissively and turns toward Mo. 'I need to see you as soon as you're done here.'

'Right away, sir,' Mo replies nervously. She has spent her career dealing with senior officials. What is it about Raines, I wonder, that makes her so ill at ease?

After the Ambassador leaves, closing the door behind him, Mo clears her throat. 'All right, let's wrap this up.' Ten minutes later we have covered the rest of the people of interest, Sophie and Sebastian dividing the names among them. 'Now I want you to listen to me,' Maureen says, her voice turning grave. 'You need to be careful on this assignment.' She pushes a button on the laptop and the list disappears from the screen, replaced by a gritty black-and-white photograph. I squint, trying to make out the image. Across the table I hear Sophie gasp. It is a naked woman, lying on the ground, dark, gaping holes where her eyes, breasts, and genitals once were. 'This was taken in Tirana two weeks ago. One of our local assets.' Maureen pauses, letting the image sink in. 'Don't be fooled by the fact that we are in England. This assignment is every bit as dangerous as Bogota or the Sudan. The Albanian mobsters are ruthless and they will kill anyone who gets in their way. The people who we are going after aren't playing games, and they have everything to lose. I want you to be careful ... and get the job done.'

I stare at her, surprised. We're in London; it's hard to believe things could get that dangerous here. But Mo is not one to be overly dramatic. I understand now why she made sure I had my gun. She presses another button and the screen goes dark. 'Okay, we'll meet back here same time next week.' She closes the computer and the screen retracts back into the ceiling. 'Unless something comes up that one of you needs to discuss before then. If so, you can call my private line.' She hands us each a small card containing her number, as well as the cell phone numbers for Sebastian, Sophie, and me. 'Don't go through Amelia. She's a nice woman, but she's not cleared for this. Jordan, political is on three. If you check in there at some point, Bob Maxwell will show you to your desk.'

I nod. The desk is a formality; Mo knows that I almost always work from the field. 'Thanks,' I reply as she starts for the door. For a minute, I consider following her, taking her up on her earlier offer of coffee. There is much that I want to ask her about the assignment out of the earshot of the rest of the team: 'What is it, exactly, I am meant to be learning from Duncan? How probable is the Infodyne connection relative to the other companies that are being investigated? Our meeting was brief, the information unusually thin. But she is already through the door of the Bubble. Sophie follows close on her heels, leaving Sebastian and me alone. I stand and pick up my bag and coat, not looking up at him.

'Nice seeing you again,' Sebastian says, coming to my side.

I look up, eyeing him coldly. 'You knew last night, didn't you? That we would be working

76

together, I mean.' He does not answer. 'Why didn't you say anything?'

He hesitates. 'I was going to at first. But then you ran out of the reception. And afterward in the park, you were so upset that, well, the timing just didn't seem right.'

But it was right enough to kiss me, I want to say. Or at least not to stop me from kissing you. I am staring at his lips, I realize. I look away, feeling the heat creep up from my collar. 'I don't like to be played, Sebastian.' He opens his mouth but I raise my hand, silencing him. 'This is bad. Mission teams are built on trust.'

'I'm sorry.' His eyes are wide, like a little boy reproached. 'Let me buy you a drink after work to make it up to you.'

I hesitate, unprepared. Is he seriously asking me out? 'I have plans,' I reply, remembering Chris's note.

'Tomorrow then.' It is more a challenge than a question. My anger rises, eclipsing attraction. Is he so arrogant as to think his charm can erase the fact that he duped me?

'Sebastian, we're colleagues. Let's just leave it at that.' I turn and walk quickly from the Bubble, hoping that he didn't see me blush.

chapter FIVE

It is nearly dark as I make my way past the closing shops of Fleet Street, buttoning the top of my coat against the chilled air. The pavement, still damp from the earlier rain, is sour with rush hour exhaust fumes. A group of barristers, gowns folded over their arms, walks ahead of me, discussing a case in self-important tones as they turn into a narrow cobblestone passageway.

I gaze up at office buildings that rise several stories on either side of the street. A yellow light burns behind a third-floor window. I imagine a reporter, clacking away at an old typewriter, working on a big story for tomorrow's press. Most of the newspapers are no longer located on the famed thoroughfare, having relocated to Wapping and other more spacious and economic locations. But I cannot help but wonder if Chris's office is nearby. Chris. I stop, seized by the urge to turn back toward the Tube station. Running is pointless, though. He will find me, whether I appear for dinner tonight or not.

Steeling myself, I continue walking. As I round the bend at Fetter Lane, Saint Paul's comes into view, its massive dome bathed in light. Excitement rises in me. The cathedral was one of my most beloved childhood images of London as a child. When I climbed its steps for the first time, I half expected to see the old woman from

Mary Poppins selling bags of birdseed for a tup-pence. Chris once teased me about my senti-mentality over what he called 'a silly children's film.' Still, perhaps he purposely chose our meeting place so close to the cathedral, since he knows how much I loved it.

Still staring at Saint Paul's, I press forward and turn onto Pilgrim Street, stopping in front of the address on the invitation. The Malta is a wine bar, crowds of well-heeled young bankers filling the front window. My shoulders slacken slightly with relief; maybe Chris just intended a casual meeting after all. The people look so different than in America, I think, as I make my way through the clusters of patrons that spill out onto the sidewalk. The complexions are paler, the teeth more askew. People here always seemed less focused on physical appearance, more at ease with themselves. It is, I suspect, part of the reason that I used to feel so at home.

Inside the dimly lit bar, jazz music plays from an unseen piano. I scan the room, searching unsuccessfully for Chris's blond head above the crowd. 'Excuse me,' I say, squeezing past two young women, trying to reach the hostess stand that is wedged into a corner by the window.

A hand grabs my elbow. I jump and spin around. Chris towers above me in a gray sport coat. My breath catches. I had planned a witty greeting: 'Oh Captain, my Captain.' It was an old joke between us, a reference to our shared love of Walt Whitman, and Chris's leadership of the boat club. But standing here, I am struck dumb. The memorial service, I think, remembering the last time I saw him. From my hiding place in the back of the college chapel, I watched him and the six other boys seated in the front row, heads bowed. There was an empty place beside him intended for me. But I fled before the service began, unable to bear hearing the hymns and platitudes that were so inadequate for my grief.

'Chris!' I gasp finally, more air than voice.

He stares down at me, as though making sure I am really there, then bends and kisses my cheek stiffly, his scent a mixture of damp wool and Burberry. 'Come on then,' he says, his posh accent thicker than I remembered. Still holding my arm, he guides me expertly through the bar, his broad shoulders seeming to part the dense crowds by will alone. At the rear of the room, he opens a door and gestures for me to go up the narrow marble staircase on the other side. Uneasiness rises in me as I climb, the noise of the crowd below fading. At the top of the stairs there is another bar, empty except for a handful of men puffing cigars around a snooker table.

I steal a hurried glance in the mirror above the bar. There was not time to go home and change after work, but I hoped to at least be able to freshen up before seeing Chris. I turn to ask him if he knows where the ladies' room is but before I can speak, a hostess appears. 'Mr. Bannister, your usual table is ready if you would like to be seated.' She turns to me. 'Take your coat?'

I hesitate, not ready to give up this layer of armor. 'I'm still a bit chilly, thanks.'

A private club, I realize, as the hostess leads us across the bar to an elegant dining room. I remember hearing of such places when we were at college, though I have never been in one. They were the province of the students from wealthier families, the ones who spent winter breaks in Nevis, Easter holidays in Gstaadt. I imagined such places to be formal and stuffy. But the furniture here is sleek, the decor modern. A Coldplay song I cannot name plays in the background.

The hostess leads us to a secluded corner table by the window. Chris pulls out my chair and I sit down awkwardly, conscious of his presence, the way he hovers a second too long behind me as though afraid I will flee. Forcing myself to breathe normally, I look out across the restaurant, concentrating on the other patrons. They are almost all young and impeccably dressed. As we sit, I recall reading not long ago in *The Economist* about the new generation of rich twenty-something Londoners who made their fortunes in investment banking and private equity. I feel out of place, a civil servant who does not belong here. I look across the table at Chris. Surely journalism does not pay this well. His family, I recall vaguely. Chris always liked to play the rebel, but his father was chairman of some large company. The stories of his family home in Kent, with its horse stables and indoor pool, were legend.

A waiter appears, filling our water glasses with Pellegrino. 'What are you drinking, red or white?' Chris asks.

I shrug, taking off my coat and putting it on the back of my chair. 'I don't mind.'

'Why not one of each?' I wince inwardly. I can no longer drink as we did in college; even the small amount of wine at the reception the previous night left me rough around the edges. Chris orders two bottles by name without looking at the wine list, an Australian sauvignon blanc and a Chilean pinot noir. I study him out of the corner of my eye, taking in his strong jawline, the fullness of his lips. He was always striking; more handsome, many would say, than Jared, at least in a conventional sense. He does not, I think now, look English at all. His blond hair and bronzed skin are more Los Angeles than London, his broad, muscular build better suited to American football.

He turns back to me and I shift my eyes quickly, gazing just over his shoulder. 'You'll love the food. Ever since the new chef arrived, it's been top-notch.' The words tumble out on top of one another. He's nervous, too, I realize with surprise. I try to remember seeing him anxious before but cannot. My insides soften. Chris was always a great guy, the loyal friend I could call in the middle of the night if I was locked out of the flat or the computer crashed. Almost a male version of Sarah, at least in that respect. It is silly to be afraid of him now.

He is staring at me. 'You look lovely, Jordie.' I hesitate, caught off guard by his abruptness. My mind races. Is that what this is all about? Has Chris contacted me simply for a date? That would be a little direct, even for him. There was always a kind of base physical attraction between us, but he could not possibly imagine, after all that happened... 'I didn't mean,' he continues. 'That is...' He clears his throat.

'It's fine,' I say quickly, looking away.

The waiter returns with the wine bottles, holding them out for Chris's inspection. He pours a small amount of the red into Chris's glass and the white into mine. I sample the wine and nod. 'Excellent,' I say, pretending.

'I've ordered the chef's tasting menu,' Chris says as the waiter finishes pouring. His voice is normal, as though the previous moment had not transpired. 'You have to request it when you book because all of the ingredients are flown in fresh. It's bloody fabulous, the best meal in town.'

And the priciest, I am certain. 'Sounds great,' I reply, my hopes of a quick getaway fading. I notice then how the azure blue of his shirt matches his eyes perfectly.

'So...' Chris says, when the waiter has left us alone once more.

I stare at the tablecloth, fighting the urge to play with the silverware. 'So.'

'What brings you back to London after all these years? Work, is it?'

I look back up at him. 'I thought you would know.' I can hear the bite in my voice. 'I mean, you knew I was back, practically before I got here. You knew where I was living.'

'I have my sources,' he jokes. Then his expression turns serious. 'I'll admit, it was all a bit cloak-and-dagger.'

'Especially the part where you appeared at the Ambassador's reception,' I reply tersely. 'Then vanished again.'

'You saw me,' he says, a note of surprise in his voice. I nod. He looks away, not speaking for several seconds. 'I'm sorry about that,' he says at last. 'I wanted to talk to you, but I lost my nerve. I didn't know how you would, that is, if you would...' Now it is his turn to look away. 'I'm glad you're back, though.' The waiter returns with a basket of warm bread and sets down two starter plates in front of us. 'Cheers,' he says to the waiter, then turns to me. 'Toro tartare.'

I look down at the molded pink lump of tuna, ringed with seaweed salad. I'm wary from past experience of eating raw fish in foreign countries. But Chris is watching me expectantly so I fork a small amount, dip it in the wasabi sauce. It is surprisingly fresh, with a faint ginger flavor. English food has come a long way in ten years. 'So, how's life been treating you?' I ask, eager to change the subject.

Chris shrugs. 'As well as can be expected. I'm still with *The Times*. They forced me to come home to a bureau position a few years back. It's a desk job, but at least they allow me to do the stories I want.'

I nod, understanding his restlessness, the need to keep moving to stay two steps ahead of the ghosts. Then I hesitate. 'And Caren?' I picture the tall, brown-haired girl who tried so hard to win Chris's affections, to be there for him after everything that happened. 'I mean, now that you're settled back here, I thought maybe...'

Chris shakes his head. 'All over long ago. Re-married to an insurance broker. Has a little girl.' He delivers the news in short staccato bursts. 'I ran into them once in the West End. Seems like a nice enough bloke. I'm happy for her. Caren is great. It was me who couldn't adapt.'

She didn't have a chance, I think. I notice the faint lines in his brow, the puffiness beneath his eyes. An aged movie star. 'Maybe you'll meet someone else.'

His laugh has an edge of bitterness, his expression a cynical one I've never seen him wear. 'Not likely. As a friend of mine once said I think marriage is a great institution; everyone should try it once.' His eyes dart to my left hand. 'And you?'

'Never married. I'm still pushing papers at State.'

'Hardly!' Chris exclaims, his tone light once more as he attacks his plate. 'I've caught glimpses of your exploits on the wire. You were in Liberia, weren't you?' I nod. 'I saw a photo that one of our guys took there and recognized you in the background,' he adds, sounding as though he needs to explain. 'He confirmed it was you.'

'I was there.' I choose my words carefully. Chris is still a foreign national, and a journalist at that. 'When all hell broke loose, it turned into a rescue mission.' My collarbone begins to throb, as it always does when Liberia comes up.

Chris whistles. 'That couldn't have been easy.'

'It wasn't. I lost a friend.' In my mind I see Eric's unmoving back on the ground, growing smaller as the helicopter rose. We did not receive official word for almost two days, but in that moment I knew he was gone. First Jared, then Eric. Are all of the men I get close to doomed to die young?

'I didn't know. I'm sorry.' Me too, I think. For Eric, and all of the people there we weren't able to help.

We finish our appetizers in silence. Chris pours

more white wine into my glass before I can protest. A server clears the plates and a minute later the waiter returns with two covered dishes. He removes the lids simultaneously to reveal the main course, shrimp in a light batter, surrounded by a thin, raw-looking meat. 'Rock shrimp tempura with Kobe beef carpaccio,' he announces.

'The new surf and turf,' Chris jokes after the waiter walks away. 'Absolutely brilliant.'

I smile, then reach for a piece of bread to quiet my stomach, still gurgling in protest from the tartare. 'So who do you still keep in touch with from college?' I ask, suddenly hungry for news.

'No one, really. I've run into Andy a few times in the pub and Roger once on the Tube. Mark lives out in the country in Oxfordshire. Wife and two kids.' I smile, trying to picture the skinny, freckle-face rower with a family of his own. 'You?' he asks.

I shake my head. 'No one.' I take a bite of the beef, swallow. 'This is delicious. I mean no one except Sarah Sunderson. My grad friend from South Africa.'

'Oh yes, I remember her,' Chris says, but I can tell he is trying hard to picture Sarah's face. To me, Sarah was everything, but she was quiet, and tended to fade into the scenery for others.

'She's the reason I came back. She's alone and very sick. I wanted to be here for her.'

'That's too bad,' he says. He does not, I realize, look surprised. Of course not. He already knows about Sarah. He knows everything.

'Why?' I blurt.

'Why what?'

I take a deep breath, meet his eyes levelly. 'Why did you track me down?'

'I heard you were coming back,' he replies, trying unsuccessfully to make his voice light. 'I wanted to say hello.'

I shake my head. 'No good, Chris. No one just "hears" about my travels, not in my line of work.'

He manages a weak smile. 'Found out through a mutual friend?'

'Not even Sarah knew I was coming.'

He leans back and clasps his hands behind his head, exhaling sharply. 'Okay, Jordie, you've got me. I tracked you down, called in a few favors at the Foreign Office to learn your whereabouts.' I guessed as much. 'I expected to find you in Africa or Asia something,' he continues before I can ask why. 'I was surprised you were on your way back here. Just dumb luck on the timing. But I would have tracked you down wherever you were.' He swings forward, grasping the table with both hands. 'I had to find you, Jordan. I need your help.'

'Help?' Wariness rises in me. I have been approached by friends for help before – generally it involves information or access, something related to my job that I'm not able to give. 'I don't understand.'

'It's about Jared, Jordie.' At the sound of his name, I freeze. The piece of beef I have just swallowed seems to stick in my throat, making it difficult to breathe.

'What do you mean?' I manage several seconds later.

'I want to find out what happened to him.'

'We know what happened. He died.' I remember then the sharp rapping sound, and how, through a fog of sleep and alcohol, I threw on my robe, stumbled downstairs, and opened the door. There stood Chris and Mark, wordless, their hollow eyes illuminated by the flashing light of the police car behind them. In that moment, even before they spoke, I knew.

'The police said that Jared drowned,' Chris says.

'He did,' I reply quickly. Found by a fisherman – a strange voice behind the boys in the darkness of the doorway explained, when their words failed them – down by the lock.

Chris shakes his head. 'In the River Cam, eight feet deep and twenty feet wide? Impossible. Jared was one of the strongest swimmers I knew. I saw him go five times that distance when our pair capsized at Henley, and he wasn't even out of breath. There's no way he wouldn't have made it to shore.'

Suddenly it is as if an enormous hand is squeezing my chest. I look away, forcing myself to swallow, breathe. 'So what are you saying?'

Then I turn back. Chris is staring at me, eyes wide.

'Jordie, Jared's death wasn't an accident.'

It is difficult to hear over the buzzing in my ears. 'They said alcohol ... the May Ball.'

'We were all drinking, but none of us enough to walk into the river and drown. Especially not Jared.'

'He didn't...' I start emphatically, but I cannot bring myself to finish the sentence. After Jared's death, there was speculation. Suicide, some said. People knew that he had been withdrawn. A wave of guilt washes over me. We fought that night and he stormed off in anger...

'He didn't kill himself,' Chris finishes for me decisively. 'Jared had everything. He was happy.'

Or should have been. Jared was about to complete his doctoral program and had secured a prestigious teaching fellowship at Oxford for the following year. But he was moody in the weeks before his death, distant. I attributed it to the end of the school year, to my departure, which hung between us, looming and unspoken. 'So what then?'

'I don't know, Jordie. There's so much we never learned. Like what was he doing down by the river in the middle of the night, alone? He wasn't with you or me or any of the others. And it's not like there was another woman.'

'No,' I said quickly. Jared was faithful. Of that I am certain. 'Why now?' I ask.

Chris pauses. 'I've had my doubts over the years. Something about his death, the way it was explained, just never made sense. My gut always told me that–'

'Your gut?' I interrupt. 'You're a journalist, Chris. I'm in intelligence. We deal in facts.'

'I know, but I keep thinking back ... the whole thing was such a circus, and the college wanted it over and done with as soon as possible. We only had access to what they wanted us to know. We were young, numb ... we didn't know to ask questions. And then I received this.' He reaches in his back pocket and pulls out a folded sheet of paper. 'It came in the post a few weeks ago.' At the sight of the familiar article, my stomach churns. It is the front page of the *Cambridge Evening News* from the day after Jared's body was found. STUDENT DROWNED, the headline reads. Underneath it is Jared's college photograph and a picture of the river.

'Someone sent you a newspaper article, Chris. Probably some nut who doesn't like something you wrote or the way you covered a story.'

He shakes his head. 'It's more than that. The article doesn't mention me. This came from someone who knew us, our connection to what happened. No, I don't know who or why, but getting this, ten years after the accident ... it's like someone is trying to tell us something. I think we owe it to Jared to figure out what it is. And to ourselves.'

'What do you want from me?'

He reaches across the table and takes my hands. 'I want you to come with me.'

'Where?' I ask softly, already knowing the answer.

'Cambridge. Help me figure this out. I need you. No one knew Jared like you did.'

I look away, swallowing hard. Now I am the one who is drowning, cold water running thick into my nose and mouth, filling my lungs.

'Jordie, what is it? Are you okay?' I turn back to Chris, his face a mask of concern.

Nausea rises up in me. 'No,' I gasp, pulling from his grasp. I stand up, grabbing my bag and coat. 'I have to go.'

'Please wait.' I hear him calling after me as I dash across the restaurant, feeling the stares of the other diners.

I barrel down the stairs and make my way through the crowded bar as quickly as I can. Outside, I speed to a run, expecting to hear Chris's footsteps chasing after me. I careen blindly down the street, barely seeing Saint Paul's as I skirt the edge of the cathedral grounds. He has not followed me, I realize, several minutes later, looking over my shoulder. I slow to a brisk walk. The nausea subsides, soothed by the cool air, but my breathing is ragged, as though I have just finished a race. This is the second time I have fled in two days, and it isn't like me. At least this time I remembered my coat.

Outside it is dark now, the traffic thinner, sidewalks nearly deserted. I am close to the river, I recognize instinctively. I make my way down the winding street toward the water, still seeing Chris's wide eyes as he leaned across the table, feeling his hand warm and heavy on mine, taking me places I did not want to go. Pain rips through my chest like a knife. The past, neatly buried for so long, has been released from its moorings. It seems to loom before me now with all of its questions and recrimination, ominous and unyielding. This is why I didn't want to come back, why I avoided it all of these years.

I reach the concrete embankment at the river's edge, then stop, taking in the panorama of the Thames, the boats nestled along the near shore for the night. The Millennium Bridge, an arched pedestrian walkway not here a decade ago, spans the river, connecting the City to the South Bank, ending at the Tate Modern. To the far right, I can make out the top of the London Eye, also new since my last visit, framing a tall office building in an enormous circle of red and blue lights.

I inhale deeply, brackish air filling my lungs, before continuing east along the concrete promenade. Streetlights cast yellow pools on the pavement, illuminating a couple kissing on a park bench, the tree branches lashing the sky above. Chris's words play over and over in my mind: Jared's death was not an accident. He does not believe that Jared drowned, or that he committed suicide. That means... I halt. My breath catches. Though he hadn't said it, Chris was suggesting that Jared was murdered. Another wave of nausea overcomes me and I double over, vomiting what I had eaten of dinner into a sewer grate.

A moment later, when the heaving subsides, I straighten, willing my stomach to calm with slow, shallow breaths. Stop overreacting, I tell myself as I wipe my mouth and start walking again. Just because Chris is suspicious because he received an article in the mail doesn't mean that Jared was murdered. Chris is wrong. He has to be.

But as I continue walking, the nagging sensation in my stomach grows. There is something about Jared's drowning that does not make sense. Always has been, at least in those fleeting middle-of-the-night moments when I permitted myself to think about it. I attributed my uneasiness to the grief. In my darkest places, I never allowed my mind to go there, to make the leap that Chris just had, that someone could have deliberately caused Jared's death. And even after the paradise I knew as Cambridge had been shattered, it still seemed impossible that something so evil could have happened there.

What if Chris isn't wrong? I turn the idea over in my mind, considering. For ten years, I managed to live with the fact that Jared, the only man I ever loved, somehow drowned in the river. But what if that isn't true? What if, as Chris said, there was more to Jared's death than we thought? I shake my head. The idea is unbearable.

And now Chris wants me to go to Cambridge, to open up the door to all that had happened. Even in making the deal with myself to come back to England and be here for Sarah, I never imagined actually going *there* again, walking those paths that I locked away so many years ago.

Then in my mind's eye, I see myself and the seven rowers who remained the morning after the memorial service. As if by silent agreement, we arrived at the boathouse before dawn and climbed in the boat and rowed down the river, the June air thick and stale, gnats hovering over still water. We rowed more slowly, of course, with six than we would have with eight, Ewan holding his oar still, not rowing to compensate for the empty seat behind him where Jared would have been. When we approached the middle of Plough Reach, we pulled the boat into the right bank and climbed out, forming a circle around the freshly covered grave. We stood there not speaking, heads bowed. A flock of geese, flying low over the railway bridge, called out low and guttural, breaking the silence. In that moment, as the sun rose over the fens, it had seemed that a silent pact was made: the remaining members of the Eight would be there for one another forever.

Owe it to Jared, Chris said. And to ourselves. I see his haunted eyes across the restaurant table as he had spoken. We won't find anything. But maybe opening these old wounds is what it will take to put it behind us for good.

I turn and begin climbing the road that leads away from the river. About halfway up the block, I step into a red telephone booth and dial directory assistance. 'Bannister, Christopher,' I request, hoping that there will only be one listing. The operator gives me the number, then connects the call. The phone rings five or six times, and it occurs to me that I might have a wrong number or that he might not be home.

'Hello?' Chris's voice sounds thick with sleep. How long was I walking?

'It's me,' I say, clutching the receiver.

'Oh, hello.' His voice is alert, filled with anticipation.

'I hope I didn't wake you. I didn't know it was late.'

'It's not. I'm just knackered. I didn't sleep well last night.' Chris was always a sound sleeper, able to nod off anywhere. He must have been nervous about our meeting. 'Dozed off a little while ago. Too much wine.' I wonder if he finished off the second bottle after I left. 'Jordie, I'm so sorry if I upset...'

'It's okay,' I reply, cutting him off. I bite my lip. 'I should apologize for running off like that. It was terribly rude of me.'

'I understand,' he says, and I can tell he really does.

'The thing is ...' I pause, taking a deep breath.

'Yes. I mean, I'll go up with you.'

There is silence on the other end of the line. I wonder if he is mad. Maybe he has changed his mind about going altogether. 'Really?' he asks a moment later.

'Yes. When do you want to go?'

'As soon as possible.'

I am reminded of the other obligations in my life. I have a terminally ill friend to care for, mobsters to thwart. I don't have time for this. Then I remember once more the rowers at Jared's grave the morning after the funeral, and know I have no choice. The sooner I put this behind me, the better. 'Tomorrow,' I reply at last. There are questions I want to ask him. How does he propose to get information about Jared's death? What will we do in Cambridge? A wave of exhaustion sweeps over me. There will be time for questions later. 'Meet me at two-fifteen at the Chimney,' I say quickly, before he can suggest we travel to Cambridge together. I need time, and I need to go there alone. 'Oh, and thank you for dinner.'

'No, thank you,' he replies. 'You won't be sorry, Jordan.' I do not answer, but set the phone back in the cradle with a click. I'm already sorry, I think, stepping out of the phone booth and into the night air, which has suddenly grown thick with fog.

September 1997
The predawn air is brisk and still as I close the door behind me and step into the darkness of Lower Park Street. Cool moonlight illuminates the row of gray

brick houses set close to the winding road, servants' quarters turned student housing. At the top of the street, a deliveryman moves between the doorways, putting down glass bottles of milk.

I make my way to the edge of Jesus Green. The nylon sleeves of my splash top rubbing against my sides, breaking the silence as I follow the path across the flat parkland. Though the trees are still full with leaves, the air is cold enough that I can see my breath if I look closely and a faint early frost covers the grass. In the narrow canal that hugs the right side of the park, a family of ducks nestles close to bank, heads tucked in sleep. The fetid smell of still water mixes with the smoky remnants of a bonfire the previous evening.

I first made this pilgrimage almost a year ago on a morning much like this. Then, as I crossed the deserted park, my skin prickled. What was I doing? I had been persuaded by an attractive blond-haired boy at the Freshers' Week activities fair two evenings prior: everyone at Lords joined the boat club, he said, and since perhaps I was a bit too short to row, wouldn't I like to cox? In the rush of alcohol and excitement, I'd accepted, and then forgot until the next day when I received a notice in my pigeonhole informing me that rowing started at six the following morning. I'd considered canceling, but there was no contact information on the note. So I made my way across the park, questioning my safety and my sanity, cursing my inability to say no. Perhaps it was a mistake, I thought as I reached the road that separated the green expanses of Jesus Green and Midsummer Common, taking in the sleeping boathouses across the river. Maybe there will be no outing. But as I started to turn back, a moving speck of light appeared at the far end of the

96

park. A bike light, I realized, as a second, then a third appeared, dancing like fireflies, forming a beacon to the river.

This morning I do not see bike lights. It is late September, nearly a week before term time, and only a handful of crews from the bigger rowing colleges are back early to get a head start on the season. The novices will come the following week after being recruited as I had been, first learning to row in metal tubs and later clogging the river with slow wooden boats. The boy at the Freshers' Fair (Chris, I would later learn) had not lied – everyone, it seemed, rowed at some point in their college careers. It is as egalitarian as it is popular, one of those rare sports that you didn't have to start as a child, that you could learn at eighteen and advance as far as your talent and physical form would allow.

And then there is me. Normally a second-year would not be coxing the first boat at a top rowing college like Lords – there would have been some snotty little guy who coxed at Eton, or at least a seasoned third-year. But owing to various transfers and situations, there is something of a coxing vacuum and so, Chris explained at me at the end of the May term before we went down for the summer, I am it.

I cross the deserted roadway without waiting for the light. Halfway across Midsummer Common, I pause, taking in the pub Fort Saint George and the footbridge beside it, which leads across a thin, winding strip of river to the boathouses. The anticipation that has been building inside me through the long summer months rises, breaks wide open. I am home.

On the far side of the footbridge, I make my way along the hard, sloping pavement that runs between

97

the boathouses and the water's edge. Lights come on in one of the boathouses to my left, and I hear voices joking, the clacking of oars being pulled from the racks.

Ahead, fifth on the left, sits Lords boathouse, dark wood and square. The three wide metal garage doors, painted black with red stripes, are still closed. I am early, as usual; it is a family curse, a dominant trait inherited from both of my parents. But here I do not mind – I've always welcomed the few minutes of quiet, the chance to collect my thoughts, to assess the current and the wind and how they will affect our outing.

As I reach the boathouse, I gaze back across the water at the skyline, unchanged in the months I have been gone. Beyond the park, Lords sits closest to the river, its chapel and chimneys rising above the still-sleeping courtyards. To the right, over the city center, the spires of Trinity, Saint John's, and King's are dark against the pinkening sky.

Turning away, I walk to the boathouse and open the wooden door, inhaling the familiar mixture of sweat and dampness as I climb the stairs. At the second-floor landing, I stop short. A tall, dark-haired boy I do not recognize stands on the balcony, his back to me.

I wait for him to turn and acknowledge that I am there, but he continues studying the horizon, shielding his eyes with his hand as though it is sunny, gazing left down the river to where it bends out of sight. 'There's an east wind today,' he says abruptly, as though we have been having a conversation. 'You won't feel it until you hit the long reach but you'll want to hug close to the bank.'

I hesitate, caught off guard. 'I'm Jordan Weiss,' I say, suddenly aware of my American accent.

He turns, revealing strong, chiseled features, high

98

cheekbones, a slight cleft in his chin. His brow is thick, predatory. 'I know. Second-year coxswain. You were elevated when Fergus went down unexpectedly.' It is clear from his scowl that he does not think I deserve the promotion. 'Eight stone, though that could stand to come down a bit.' His eyes are an icy emerald green.

Anger rises in me. Who is this stranger to criticize my weight? I open my mouth but my reply is cut off by loud, lumbering footsteps on the stairs behind me. 'Good to see you, mate!' Chris, tan from the summer holiday, leaps onto the balcony, brushing past me to pump the stranger's hand like a politician on speed. He is shorter and broader than the other boy, with wide-set features, a handsome bulldog. Then he turns back and, before I can protest, lifts me from the ground in a bear hug, spinning me around. His hair smells freshly of soap. 'Jordie!' he cries, kissing me on both cheeks before setting me down again. 'Good summer in the States?' I step back, trying to catch my breath. He does not wait for an answer. 'You know Jared, of course.'

Jared Short. My stomach twists. I know of him. Jared Short is a legendary rower. He rowed for Oxford three times as an undergraduate, trialed for the British national team. There was talk that he could have made the Olympics were it not for a recurring shoulder injury. So he had come to Cambridge two years earlier to pursue his doctorate. Then the news came at the end of the May term last year before the summer holiday: Chris, a friend of Jared's since school, persuaded Jared to transfer from Caius College to Lords for his final year of studies, to row for the college and help us reclaim the Head of the River.

'W-welcome,' I manage, glad I didn't get the chance to tell him off.

Jared does not answer but turns to Chris. 'I was looking at the boats,' he begins and I know I am dismissed. I retrieve the cox's headset from the women's locker room, then start back down the stairs, hearing Jared and Chris discussing the new Aylings shell that the boat club trust purchased over the summer. Jared's words are spare, his tone terse.

Downstairs, the others have assembled, a half-dozen fresh-faced boys in Lycra shorts and long-sleeved t-shirts. My boys. 'Jordie!' Mark cries, spotting me and bounding over for a hug. Ginger-haired with freckles, he is the youngest of the crew, a second-year who made the boat because of his experience at school.

'How was your summer?' I ask.

He gestures with his head toward the cluster of boys. 'Went inter-railing with this lot.' Mark and two of the third-years, Andy and Nick, have been an inseparable trio since the previous winter. Beside them, Roger, a sweet but nerdy boy with thick glasses, listens eagerly, wishing to be part of the banter.

'Wait 'til you hear what our Markie got up to in Munich,' Andy winks, then rolls his spaniel eyes. 'We were at the Hofbrauhaus when…'

'All right,' a voice behind me interrupts. Jared has come downstairs, Chris close behind. The boys look at him, unfamiliar with his businesslike tone. They talked about Jared coming to Lords with great anticipation, excited about what it might mean for our chances in the May Bumps. But I knew it was a bad idea. The crew, almost entirely intact from the previous year, was cohesive, bonded. An ego like Jared's would surely only hurt us. 'Enough messing around,' he snaps, confirming my impressions. I look at Chris, wondering if as boat club captain, he will intervene. But he only

100

watches Jared, his expression rapt.

'Why don't you boys warm up with a two-bridge run?' I suggest.

Jared turns to me. 'There's no time for that. We're late. A six o'clock start means warmed up, in the boat, ready to push off at six. Not standing here, joking around.'

'But if they don't warm up…'

He cuts me off. 'Land warm-ups are a waste. A good cox,' he adds, making clear from his tone that I am not, 'can warm up the crew entirely in the boat.'

Feeling the eyes of the other boys on me, I bite my tongue, fighting the urge to retort. Dissent will only hurt us now. 'All eight, hands on,' I say instead. Keeping my eyes low, I follow the boys through one of the now-open garage doors to the racks of long rowing shells. I struggle to keep my voice even as I give the commands to lift the boat and carry it to the river's edge. 'The blades should be here and ready,' Jared growls when we have set the boat to the water, sending the boys scrambling to retrieve the oars. Holding the boat in place from the stern so it will not drift away, I stare at him angrily. Who does he think he is?

The boys lock their blades into the metal riggers that jut triangularly from the boat, four on each side. The bow-side rowers climb in first, extending their blades across the water for balance before they are joined by the four on stroke side. As they tie their socked feet into the shoes that are affixed to the boat, I study the crew, which sits backward facing me: Mark farthest from me at the bow of the boat, Roger in front of him at two, then Andy and Nick at three and four. Simon and Ewan, seated at five and six, spent last year rowing for the Blues squad; I do not know them as well as I do the

101

others. Chris is at stroke, of course, seated closest to me, Jared in the seven seat behind him.

'What are you waiting for?' Jared snaps.

I hesitate, caught off guard by his nastiness, then reach across the boat, supporting my weight on my hands as I climb into the narrow seat at the back. As I plug in the cox box, I feel my cheeks burn. 'Number off when you're ready,' I instruct into the mouthpiece, fighting to keep my voice from cracking.

'Bow,' Mark calls, and each of the boys shouts his position in succession, signaling that he is ready.

'Stroke,' Chris says when the count reaches him, winking as if to say, Don't mind Jared. But the rock in my stomach grows. All summer I looked forward to this moment, to pushing back from the bank and feeling the water beneath me once more. But now, looking down the boat at Jared's stony face, I know that rowing as I loved it is gone.

chapter SIX

'Tickets,' the conductor calls as he walks through the train car. I refold the copy of the *International Herald Tribune* that I had been trying unsuccessfully to read and hand him the day return I purchased at King's Cross an hour earlier. When he has punched the ticket and returned it to me, I sit back, gazing out the window. The last time I looked up, more than thirty minutes earlier, we'd still been winding through North London, past industrial buildings and gritty block flats, a gold-

102

domed mosque set against the gray sky. Now green fields, dotted with sheep, slope gently on either side of the train. We're somewhere north of Royston, I estimate as the fields give way to a cluster of brown brick houses, then a small shopping center. Not more than fifteen minutes out of Cambridge.

Cambridge. I shiver involuntarily. What am I doing here? I asked myself the same question last night as I brushed my teeth. Then I climbed in bed and lay awake, staring in the semidarkness at the wide-beamed ceiling. When I made the decision to come to England, when I summoned the courage to ask Van Antwerpen and get on the plane, I never considered this. I knew, of course, that Cambridge was just an hour north of London – quicker than a trip around Washington Beltway at rush hour. I suppose if I'd had time to think about it, I would have planned on ignoring Cambridge while I am here, simply pretending that it did not exist. I certainly never dreamed of going there, just a few days after my arrival, to ask questions about Jared.

I lift the cappuccino from the seat beside me, dipping my head downward toward the opening, inhaling the rich aroma. The cardboard is still faintly warm against my palms, the familiar bitter taste comforting. I gaze over the lid across the train car. It is nearly empty, a few students with luggage returning late from the Easter break, a couple of gray-haired tourists with cameras and fanny packs consulting a Lonely Planet guide, plotting their route through the colleges.

My parents, I think. Guilt rises in me. It's been

four days since I left Washington and they have no idea where I am. I pull the cell phone from my bag. Earlier, I called Mo's number and, relieved not to have reached her directly, left a message that I would be working from the field today. Now I dial the code for the United States, then the number. The phone rings twice. 'Hello?' My father's voice, sleepy and confused, comes over the line, as clear as if he were next to me.

I smile, remembering the crackling static, the line delays of our calls a decade ago. 'Dad, it's me…'

'Jordan.' There is instant panic in his voice. 'What's wrong?'

'Everything's fine,' I reply quickly. 'I'm sorry for waking you.' It's after eleven, I note, glancing at my watch; after six at home. My parents' early rise time seemed to have muted in recent years, a silent concession to semiretirement, if not age.

'It's fine. I was just getting up. But the connection sounds funny … and the phone number … Jordan, where are you?'

'I'm in England, Dad. I'm sorry I couldn't call before leaving; it was all very sudden.'

'Oh…' I can almost hear him sitting up, turning on the light, and reaching for his glasses as he processes the information. 'But I thought you said you would never…?'

'I did.' I hesitate. 'I had to come. Sarah's sick.'

'Oh.' His voice deepens with concern. My parents met Sarah once when she visited Vermont with me several years earlier, and they were quickly taken with her simple, unassuming demeanor. 'How bad is it?'

'Pretty bad. Lou Gehrig's. I don't even want to talk about it now.'

'I understand. I'm sorry. How long are you staying?'

'It's a permanent assignment. Two years, maybe more.' There is silence. 'Don't worry, I'll come home to visit before too long. And maybe you and Mom can come here.'

'Maybe.' But I can tell from his voice it won't happen. My parents have never been out of the country. Their passports, which I insisted they get in case of an emergency, lie untouched in a kitchen drawer. 'At least you're somewhere safe this time,' he adds.

Safe. England would never feel that way to me. Right now, just minutes out of Cambridge, I'd almost rather be dodging sniper fire in Monrovia again. 'How are things there?' I ask, changing the subject.

'Fine. Lot of planting.' I smile, picturing the garden, my parents' collaborative pride and joy. My mother cultivates fruit trees and vegetable plants while my father grows prize-winning flowers and ivy that climbs the nineteenth-century stone wall in vines. 'Do you want me to wake your mother? She'll be sorry to have missed you.'

'No, let her sleep. I'll call again soon.' I give him my new cell phone number, knowing that they will never use it, but will wait for me to call.

'Love, you, Jord.'

'You too.' I close the phone, picturing my parents nestled together under their down wedding quilt against the brisk New England morning, Buster, their border collie, curled up stubbornly at the bottom of the bed.

Outside the gently rolling hills have flattened into the fenlands of East Anglia. We are almost there. Eager for distraction, I look down at the newspaper once more. The bottom half of the front page carries a story about Kosovo's recent declaration of independence from Serbia, the concern that it may be bring war back to the already battered region. There has always been a tension, the article says, between the Serb state and Kosovo province, which is comprised largely of ethnic Albanians.

The mention of Albanians reminds me of the mob, the fact that I have a job to do. Setting down the newspaper, I reach in my bag and pull out a thin folder of papers, research on Infodyne I printed from the web. The company's website was generically corporate, all pledges of environmental awareness and global citizenship. It took several more clicks before I was able to find a list of the conglomerate's various businesses, ranging from shipping and containers to security staffing. I flip now to the contact page, the company's name in boldface type, an address, phone number, and website listed beneath, then I open the phone once more and dial the number listed. An automated recording answers and I follow the prompts, punching in Duncan's last name until the computer recognizes it and transfers me to his extension.

I hold my breath as the phone rings several times. Usually it takes weeks to make contact on a new assignment: identify the target, learn his or her routine, plan an incidental encounter. This

time it is simply a matter of calling up an old classmate. But the same adrenaline I always feel surges
through my veins, making my heart quicken.

'Duncan Lauder' a gentle male voice answers,
its familiarity through the years startling. I pause;
I expected a receptionist, another few seconds to
figure out what to say. 'Hallo?'

I take a deep breath. 'Duncan? This is Jordan
Weiss. I don't know if you remember me from
Cambridge? I coxed for Lords College.'

'Of course I do.' He does not sound as surprised
as I might have imagined. 'How are you, Jordan?'

'Um, fine, thanks,' I reply, caught off guard by
the routine nature of his question. 'Back in the
U.K. for work. I was wondering if you might have
some time to get together for coffee.'

There is silence on the other end of the telephone. I can almost see Duncan, an older version
of the wiry boy I knew, pursing his thin lips,
trying to figure out what I wanted. 'Certainly,' he
replies at last. 'When?'

I hesitate, surprised; I half expected him to say
no. But of course he is too polite to refuse my
invitation. 'You're in Luton, aren't you?'

'Yes.'

'I'm going to be in Cambridge today, actually.' I
fight to keep my voice neutral, to avoid sounding
too eager. 'Are you free sometime later this afternoon?' I promised this time to Chris, I remind
myself. Then I push down my guilt. A meeting
would provide an emergency escape hatch if the
day in Cambridge got to be too much.

'Umm...' Duncan clears his throat. 'Today isn't
good for me, lots of meetings and such. I'll be in

London on Monday, though. Why don't we say Trafalgar Square, by the Waterstone's, at ten?'

I wonder if he is telling the truth, or if he doesn't want me coming to Infodyne. But I don't know him well enough to push. 'Perfect. Why don't you give me your cell–' I stop, correcting myself. 'I mean your mobile number, in case anything comes up.'

There is a slight hesitation and for a split second I wonder if he will refuse, but then he rattles off the numbers and I scribble them down on the top sheet of paper in the folder before giving him mine. 'Cheers.' There is a click.

I pull the phone from my ear, studying it uncertainly. I should call Sarah. See how she's doing, let her know where I am. But I'm not ready to tell her about Chris, what he has asked me to do. And I cannot bear to tell her that I am going to Cambridge, or to answer the many questions the news would surely bring.

The train rounds a gentle curve and slows slightly as buildings begin to appear on the horizon. I straighten, placing the papers and phone back in my bag, then inhale deeply. I close my eyes, counting to ten slowly as I let the air out, willing my stomach to unclench as the train wheels screech to a halt. The buzzing in my ears grows until I can barely hear the conductor's voice over the loudspeaker announcing that we have reached Cambridge.

Steeling myself, I follow the other passengers from the compartment. There is another train on the opposite track, waiting to make the return journey to London. Fighting the urge to jump on it, I walk down the platform, and for a moment it seems as though I might have been returning to college from a day trip to London, instead of coming back for the first time in a decade.

I exit the station, drawing my coat closer around me against the colder-than-expected air as I pass the racks of chained bicycles. I eye the taxi stand, the small buses unloading passengers. I could ride to the city center and be at the college in minutes. But I need to do this slowly. I begin walking straight down Station Road, past the large brown brick buildings, once grand houses now turned into language schools for foreign exchange students.

As I turn right on Hills Road, my shoulders slacken slightly. The outskirts of Cambridge are like any other English town, the streets lined with pubs and shops. A few minutes later I cross the busy intersection at Lensfield Road, which marks the edge of the city center, and make my way up traffic-clogged Regent Street past the University Arms hotel. The narrow sidewalk is crowded, shoppers from the villages jostling with students on their way to lectures. In my mind, Cambridge was grand and imposing. But now the buildings lean in, hovering over the pavement, giving everything a too-close feel. Farther along to my right sits the entrance to Emmanuel College, an ornate archway, high brick walls on either side. The thirty or so colleges are scattered throughout Cambridge, some in the city center, others like my own on the periphery. Feeling my stomach tug, I turn away from the college, walking instead toward the arcade of shops that line the narrow passageway of Petty Cury.

Soon the street gives way to an open-air market-place, rows of awning-covered stalls. The air is thick with the smell of fresh fish and flowers and soap. I blink. What am I doing here? This is out of my way; I do not need to come here to meet Chris, to fulfill the bare minimum of my promise. It is more, I know, than just stalling for time. I continue through the marketplace, past the used book sellers and secondhand clothing merchants, as if pulled by a will not my own, until I have reached the far side and am standing on the cobblestones of King's Parade. In front of me sits King's, the grandest of the colleges, its hypnotic chapel steeples climbing toward the sky like giant sentinels. The clouds above seem to part and a single beam of sunlight breaks through, casting light on the chapel roof, illuminating the stained-glass windows. I gaze upward at the sight that I have forced so long from my conscious mind. Now the spires seem to stare down at me, de-manding a reckoning. Where have you been? a voice asks in the breeze. What have you done to be worthy of this? And why have you come again?

A bell rings, jarring me from my thoughts. I jump as a bike speeds by, its rider swerving to avoid hitting me by just inches. I stare at the back of the rider as he passes. There is something about the boy, about the way his hair flares in the wind, that reminds me of Jared. I force myself to look away. I am still standing in the middle of the street. All around me, students pass in every direction, racing to the library or lectures, laugh-ing and talking with friends. I am, I realize, the

110

only one who is standing still.

I turn away, making my way down Trinity Street, not looking at the other colleges or shops, aiming for the one place I actually need to go. At the top of Jesus Lane, I stop again. I am almost there. The rock in my stomach grows. But it is too late to turn back now. I force myself to keep walking. The road curves slightly and the high wall breaks, revealing a simple iron gate, the entrance to Lords College. My breath catches. A whiff of honeysuckle, carried on the wind from a garden unseen, wafts underneath my nose, hurling me back through the years. On the other side of the gate runs the Chimney, a walled passageway several hundred feet long, dozens of bicycles propped in the gravel on either side of the path. It ends at a brick tower, three stories high, crowned with a crest of red and black bearing three roosters.

'Oh,' I cry aloud, bringing my hand to my mouth. My eyes fill, begin to burn. I wasn't prepared for the sameness of it all.

Beneath the archway, a figure crouches, tying a shoelace. Jared, I think for a second. But then the figure straightens and I see that it is Chris. Wiping my eyes, I start toward him. A flicker of surprise crosses his face as I near, as though he did not really expect me to show. Then, as I step through the archway, his eyes flood with relief and the haggard expression that lines his face breaks. 'Jordie,' he says, bending to kiss my cheek. I do not answer but stare over his shoulder into First Court, transfixed by the familiar brick buildings that line three sides of the square, the horse sculpture on the manicured lawn in the center. 'As if we never left, eh? How are you holding up?'

'Fine,' I manage, forcing my gaze away from the courtyard.

'Good.' His eyes travel from my face to my khaki jacket and jeans, lingering a split second too long on my fitted white t-shirt. 'Wait here for a moment, okay?' Before I can answer, Chris turns and enters the rounded doorway on the left side of the arch that leads to the Porter's Lodge, the office from which most of the administrative details of the college are handled. I watch through a narrow-paned window as Chris confers at the counter with a gray-haired porter I do not recognize. Behind them, a rugby game crackles on a black-and-white television.

I turn away. Opposite the Porter's Lodge, a low chalkboard runs the length of the arch, crammed with scrawled announcements of rowing schedules and rugby practices, the starting time for mass in the chapel. It is the beginning of the May term, I realize, resetting my brain to the long-forgotten academic calendar. The school year is organized around eight-week terms: Michaelmas in the autumn, the Lent or Easter term running January through March, and finally the May term, which actually ends in June. I remember each as a sprint, a flurry of athletic and social activity, building to a fever pitch, then four weeks' holiday to recover before the next one began.

A group of students, unfathomably young, passes by me into First Court, their laughter ringing out, echoing off the brick buildings as they walk the path that lines the grass, red-and-black

112

striped college scarves flapping self-importantly behind them. One of the students is talking animatedly on a mobile phone, discussing plans for the evening. We did not have those when I was here. Most students did not have phones at all, using instead the pay phones underneath the bar stairs. Among ourselves, we communicated by paper, notes scrawled hastily on scraps and put in pigeonholes, the narrow slots in the mailroom outside the Porter's Lodge. The notes, confirming plans, proposing dinners and parties, formed a tapestry of daily college life, and in the beginning I saved every scrap of paper, planning to intersperse them with the many photographs I'd taken of dinners and parties and such in an album someday. Then the sirens came in the night. I left with one suitcase, the notes and photographs and all of my other belongings still in my room, as though I had only gone for a visit to the States. As if I was coming back. What became of those things? I picture my room on Lower Park Street, frozen in time. Did the bedders throw everything out? No, Sarah would have taken care of it. She would not have allowed a stranger to go through my belongings. I imagine her left behind to deal with it all, sorting through my clothes, taking them to the charity shop. And what of Jared's things? Someone must have packed them up, sent them home. I make a mental note to ask Chris.

I stare after the students as they disappear through the archway at three o'clock, which leads to Cloister Court, one of the half-dozen courtyards that make up the interior of the college. Do they know about Jared, about what happened

113

here? Most, I assume, do not. The rowers might – there is a plaque down by the boathouse, Sarah told me once, purchased with donations made in his memory. I remember thinking that there should have been more, a section of the college named after him, or at least a scholarship fund. But Jared was not rich like Chris; his family could not have championed such a cause. I left and so did the others; within a few years, anyone who knew Jared was gone.

No, it is as if he vanished, his memory disappeared like smoke. It is largely, I know, because of the circumstances of his death. If Jared had died after a brave struggle with illness, the story would have been touted. But an inexplicable drowning was unseemly. The college would have tried to minimize the tragedy, fearful of the effect on alumni donations and admissions. There were surely whispers among the students in the years immediately following our departure, urban legends about what transpired. Now it was reduced to a footnote, a piece of college lore.

A moment later, Chris reemerges. 'Let's go.' He walks back out of the archway into the Chimney, kneeling in front of one of the bikes that leans against the wall.

'I don't understand,' I say, as he unlocks the bike and steers it in my direction.

'I thought this would be the easiest way to go.'

'Go where?' I demand, taking the handlebars. I had not previously thought to question Chris about his plan. But, I realize now, I have no idea what we are doing.

'We have an appointment at the medical

114

examiner's office at three-thirty. The police were no help at all, claimed their file was sent away years ago. But my cousin knows someone at the hospital who got the medical examiner to agree to talk to us.' He gestures to the bikes. 'I arranged to borrow these to get us to Addenbrooke's.'

'Oh.' I do not know why I am surprised. Cambridge students go everywhere by bicycle and Addenbrooke's Hospital is on the outskirts of town. I was never the strongest rider, though, and I haven't ridden in years. I study the bike. Old and rusty, it looks as though it could have been leaning against the wall since the last time I was here. I am annoyed. If Chris had told me where we were going, I could have just taken a cab from the station to Addenbrooke's and avoided all of this.

I follow Chris and wheel the bike down the Chimney and through the gate. 'Ready?' he asks when we reach the street. I nod, putting my bag in the basket and climbing on the bike, trying not to wobble as we pedal east along Jesus Lane, away from the city center.

As we reach the roundabout at Maids Causeway, I catch a flash of green out of the corner of my eye. To the left sits Midsummer Common, the river and boathouses just behind it. My eyes travel instinctively to the Lords boathouse. The bike begins to wobble beneath me, swerving into traffic. A car horn blares. Chris brakes hurriedly, rolling back to me and pulling me onto the sidewalk. 'You all right?'

'I–I think so,' I manage. 'It's just that...'

He follows my gaze toward the river. 'Did you go?' I know he is asking whether I went to the

115

river earlier that day, down the towpath to Jared's grave. I shake my head. 'Me either.' He clears his throat, his hand heavy and warm on my shoulder. 'Let's just get to the coroner, shall we?' I do not answer but start pedaling again, forcing myself to look straight ahead.

Addenbrooke's Hospital sits on the southern edge of the city, a chunky collection of adjoining 1970s-style block buildings set among the more modern structures of the biomedical campus that have gone up around it. I was never here as a student; I only glimpsed it from the motorway, heard references from Andy and the other medical students who came here for rounds. Now I follow Chris to an overflowing bike rack, then dismount so he can chain the two bikes together.

We do not speak as we enter the hospital. The corridors are a drab white, lined with gurneys and medical equipment, and permeated by a metallic smell that reminds me of my own hospital stay a year earlier. Chris leads me down one corridor and then another to an elevator without hesitation, as if he has been here before. As we descend to the basement, I imagine the coroner's office, half-dissected bodies lying on tables. But we reach a door to an office and as Chris knocks I am relieved to see through the glass window that it is just a desk and chairs, no corpses in sight. 'Come in.' Inside, a petite Asian woman, her hair short and gray-flecked, sits behind an old metal desk piled high with papers. 'You must be Mr. Bannister.' The woman rises slightly and extends her hand.

'Chris,' he says, shaking her hand. 'And this is Jordan.'

'Nice to meet you. I'm Rachel Peng, the deputy coroner.' The woman gestures to the chairs. 'Have a seat.'

'We really appreciate your seeing us,' Chris says.

'Anything for your cousin,' she replies. 'I understand that you wanted to have a look at the file for a man named Jared Short.'

'Yes.'

Dr. Peng lowers her bifocals to stare at us. 'May I ask why?'

Chris clears his throat. 'Jared was a friend of ours in college,' he begins and I can hear him choosing his words carefully. 'He drowned.'

'I'm sorry,' Dr. Peng replies.

'And at the time, we were too young and upset to really understand what happened. Now,' he pauses, 'we're just trying to get some closure.'

'Typically, you would need a release from the family or a police authorization,' Dr. Peng says. Hope rises in me. Perhaps we will have to leave without seeing the report. She continues, 'But your cousin has been a good friend and I owe him more than one favor, so...' She reaches across her desk and picks up a file. 'Here it is. I pulled the file this morning but I haven't had the chance to review it. If you'll just give me a second...' She opens the cover. 'The report indicates that the body, I'm sorry, I mean Mr. Short, was found in the river and that he had been there about three hours judging by the decomposition of the, I mean, his condition.' She looks up. 'I hope you'll forgive my crudeness. I don't often deal with the families and, well, tucked away in the lab all day, one can get a bit clinical.' She

117

returns to studying the report. 'There was some alcohol in his blood…'

'How much?' I interrupt.

'About .10.' I nod. Chris was right; Jared was drinking at the ball, enough that he shouldn't have been driving a car, but not enough to make him fall in the river and drown. 'There was no evidence of trauma to the body,' Dr. Peng continues. Her forehead crinkles. 'Hmm, this is odd.'

Chris leans forward. 'What?'

'The autopsy photographs are missing.' My stomach flips. Somewhere in my rational mind I knew that there was an autopsy, that the nature of his death would have required it. That is the very reason we are here. But hearing it now, the notion that such things were done to Jared, that there are pictures, is almost more than I can handle.

'They would typically be in the file?' Chris asks.

'Yes. I'm not sure why they're missing.' She holds up the file to show the empty page where only two pieces of tape remain. 'I'm sure there is a duplicate set in the file in London. Would you like me to request it?'

'Please,' Chris replies. 'That'd be great. If you could send the file to Jordan at the American embassy in London, that would probably be easiest.'

I cringe; I do not want to look at the pictures. 'May we see the file?'

Dr. Peng nods and passes it across the table. I pick it up. Inside, there is a three-page report, the handwriting slanted and faded with age. I run my finger over the paper. Whoever wrote this touched Jared.

Chris leans close, reading over my shoulder. 'Dr.

Antony,' he reads, then looks up. 'Who's that?'

'My predecessor. He's the one who performed the autopsy.'

'Does he still work here?'

Dr. Peng shakes her head. 'Unfortunately, he died of a heart attack about eight years ago.'

I skim the handwriting. A twenty-two-year-old male, it reads. Six-foot two, one hundred ninety pounds. There are several paragraphs of medical terminology that I cannot comprehend. 'I'm sorry,' I say, handing the folder back to Dr. Peng. 'But I don't understand this.'

She scans the first page. 'It says here that your friend was found approximately three hours after he died, and that the body was largely intact, consistent with someone who had been in the water for that period of time. That the toxicology report found he had a blood alcohol level of .10 and no drugs in his system. He...' Dr. Peng pauses as she flips to the second page of the report.

'What is it?' Chris asks. Dr. Peng does not respond but raises her hand, then turns to the third page. A moment later she moves back to the second. Her forehead crinkles again, deeper this time. 'Is something wrong?' Chris demands. I can hear the impatience in his voice. I put my foot on his, pressing down, warning him not to push too hard.

'Can you tell us what the rest of the report says?' I ask gently.

'It's nothing,' Dr. Peng replies quickly. But her expression has changed, her eyes now guarded. 'It must be a mistake.'

I lean forward. 'Dr. Peng, please.'

Her hands tremble as she closes the file. 'I

shouldn't have done this, let you see the file without authorization. I could lose my job.'

'We're not going to get you into trouble, we promise,' I reply. 'We won't tell anyone we've been here. We just want to know what it says.'

She hesitates, then clears her throat. 'Look, if anyone asks me, I'm going to deny that we ever met. Dr. Antony was my mentor and he was a great pathologist. But something isn't right with this report.'

'How so?' Chris demands. I press harder on his foot.

'Well, here.' Dr. Peng leans across the desk, holding up the folder and pointing to the front page. 'The cause of death given is drowning, like you said.' She flips to the second page. 'But here, it says that there was no water in the subject's lungs at the time of the autopsy.'

A chill runs up my spine. 'What does that mean?' But even as I ask, some part of me already knows the answer.

'It means that your friend Jared didn't drown. He was dead by the time he hit the water.'

chapter SEVEN

Jared didn't drown.

Dr. Peng's words echo in my ears as I lean against the side of the hospital building, not moving. A few minutes earlier, when it was clear that the visibly shaken coroner was not going to

120

say anything further, we hurriedly thanked her and left her office.

'She said that Jared didn't drown,' Chris says, echoing my unspoken thoughts. His voice does not register surprise.

'But she also said it was probably a mistake,' I point out.

'Either there was water in Jared's lungs or there wasn't. Seems like a pretty simple call, especially for an experienced pathologist like Dr. Antony.' He gestures with his head toward the bike rack. 'Come on.'

I follow him, staring out across the motorway at the fields as he unlocks the bikes. The clouds have thinned now, sunlight shining through, belatedly warming the day. As we walk to the edge of the road, Dr. Peng's words play over and over again in my mind. It is impossible to believe. For so long, the manner of Jared's death was a fact, part of the tapestry that made up my life: I studied at Cambridge and had a boyfriend there who drowned. Now someone had ripped that piece out, leaving jagged threads, a blank space where it had been.

I straddle the bike, then turn to Chris behind me. 'Even if the coroner's report is right, even if Jared didn't drown, then how...?' I ask, my throat dry and scratchy. 'How did he die?'

Chris shakes his head. 'You're asking the wrong question. The question is not, how did he die? The question is, who killed him?'

Killed him. The words slam into my stomach like a rock. 'Just because he didn't drown in the river doesn't mean he was...' I cannot finish the sentence.

'Killed? You're joking, right?' he asks, voice rising. His eyes burn. 'He didn't drown, Jordan. We know that. So what do you think happened, Jared died and then happened to fall into the river on his own?'

'I–I don't know,' I stammer. 'I just think we're jumping to conclusions.'

'If Jared did not drown in the river, then he must have been killed. What other conclusion could there possibly be?' he demands. I do not answer. My mind races, searching for other plausible explanations and finding none. I remember Chris's voice in the restaurant last night, strong with conviction. He believed Jared was killed then and he is convinced of it now. I begin pedaling furiously, desperate to get away from the hospital.

'Jordan, wait!' Chris's bike creaks as he pulls up beside me. Then he grabs my handlebars and slows gently until I am forced to a halt. 'I'm sorry for yelling.' He stares into my eyes, searching. 'But now do you believe me about Jared?'

'I don't know.' I look away. But the facts seem unavoidable. Dr. Peng said that Jared was dead before he reached the water. At a minimum, someone else had to be involved. 'Yes,' I whisper, swallowing hard.

'Thank you,' he replies and there is a calmness to his voice that makes me think, for a second, that being right is enough for him, that this will end here. But then his face hardens once more. 'Now let's figure this out together. For Jared.'

Forty minutes later, we enter the Maypole, a pub that sits close to college, below Jesus Lane where Park Street meets Lower Park Street.

'What are you drinking?' Chris asks.

I hesitate. The Maypole had always been known for its cocktails, creamy and brightly colored concoctions with fancy names, served in big glasses with umbrellas and fruit. But such drinks seem ridiculous now. 'Coffee,' I say, still feeling the chill that has been with me since Addenbrooke's.

As Chris walks to the bar, I look at my watch. It is nearly six o'clock, I note, surprised at how quickly the afternoon has passed. The pub is growing full with a happy-hour crowd. I make my way to an open table and drop into one of the chairs, listening to a group of students at the next table discuss how their rehearsal had gone today. Situated steps from the Amateur Dramatic Club theater, the Maypole has always been popular with the thespian crowd. The walls are lined with posters from various productions, framed clippings of newspaper reviews. Above the table hangs a blue and green poster touting a production of *As You Like It* that I recall seeing as a student. I lean closer, studying the list of the leading actors, printed below the title in smaller letters. Vance Ellis. I see him in my mind, tall and raven-haired with pale porcelain skin. Vance was Duncan Lauder's lover and companion. The two could not have been more different, Duncan soft-spoken and athletic, Vance temperamental, prone to wild binges of drinking and drugs. Yet they were inseparable, one of the most enduring relationships I had known at Cambridge. Were they still together now after so many years?

A few minutes later, Chris returns with two steaming glass mugs, setting them on the table as he sits, choosing the chair closest to me. 'Thanks.' I take a sip, surprised at the strong taste of alcohol that mixes with the coffee.

'Baileys and Jameson,' Chris explains in response to my raised eyebrow. 'You always liked it, and I figured we could both use something stronger.' I nod, cupping my hand around the cup, grateful for the warmth.

'So who killed Jared?' he asks matter-of-factly, as if discussing the weather.

'I just can't believe it.' I stare hard at the table. 'I'm still trying to get my head around the idea that it wasn't an accident, that the coroner's report isn't wrong.' I take another sip of coffee, forcing myself to push the emotion down, to think as I would for a work investigation. 'I think the first question is, why was he killed? I mean, who would want to hurt him? He was such a nice...' I stop midsentence, seeing Chris's skeptical expression. 'Okay, maybe *nice* isn't the right word.'

'Jared was a lot of great things, Jordie. Brilliant scholar, talented rower, a great friend. But I wouldn't call him nice. He could be a bastard.'

I nod, picturing Jared storming away from the boathouse when the crew hadn't rowed well. He was intense and exacting, with little patience for anyone who did not rise to that standard. But there was another Jared, too, that only I knew, the one who would curl around me like a child and bury his head in my neck to escape his problems, who would awaken in the middle of the night, sweat-soaked and terrified, clinging to me from the nightmares that he would not talk about and could not escape. 'He was intense,' I agree. 'But

124

that didn't give anyone a reason to hurt him. We're assuming, of course, that it wasn't random.'

'Not in this town,' Chris replies quickly.

He's right, of course. Cambridge is the epitome of small-town Britain; with the exception of an occasional alcohol-fueled fist-fight between local youths and students, violent crime was almost nonexistent. 'So where does that leave us? Jared didn't have any enemies.'

'That we know of.'

I tilt my head. 'What are you saying?'

Chris finishes his coffee and sets down the cup. 'Jared had everything. Someone could have been jealous.'

'Of what?'

'I don't know.' Chris looks directly at me. 'You?'

I shake my head, feeling a blush creep up my neck. 'That's crazy!'

'Maybe. I'm just exploring all of the possible theories.'

'No,' I insist. 'There was no one else.'

'Not for you. But maybe there was someone with a crush...?'

Only you, I think, the air thick with the unspoken. 'That can't be it.'

'Then what else?'

'The Eight...?' I am surprised to hear the words come out of my mouth. A look of realization passes over Chris's face. Rowing at the major colleges like Lords was a competitive business, especially in the May term as the top crews vied feverishly for the Head of the River. There were rowers who were angry when they didn't make the first boat, who thought they deserved a spot.

And competition between the colleges was even more intense. I heard rumors of crews over the years sabotaging one another's shells or blades to ensure victory; an urban legend of one crew tainting another's prerace dinner so they couldn't row due to food poisoning. But the notion that someone might actually kill to get into a boat or to win is unfathomable.

'I wish we were able to get a copy of the coroner's report from Dr. Peng,' I say, changing the subject.

'You mean like this?' Chris reaches into his coat and pulls out a few folded sheets of paper.

I look from the papers to his face, then back again, amazed. 'How did you?'

'There was an extra copy at the back of the file that I was able to slip out. She'll never miss it; she didn't even know it was there.' He hands the papers to me. 'You hang on to these for safekeeping.' I put them into my bag quickly, not wanting to see the writing that confirms the truth about Jared's death. 'So what's our next move?' he continues. 'I mean, this can't be the end, not after all that we've learned. You'll keep helping me, won't you?' His eyes hold mine, pleading.

I hesitate. A big part of me wishes that I never agreed to this day in the first place, that I still believed, even falsely, that Jared died accidentally in the river. But we opened the door and now we have to follow the path, wherever it leads us. I cannot turn away. 'Yes,' I say at last.

'Good.' Chris stands up. 'Because we've got a lot of work to do. Let's go.'

I hesitate, looking at the clock above the bar,

which reads five to seven. 'What now? I'm not sure there's much else we can accomplish today.' Despite my promise to help, I am eager to board the next train out of Cambridge.

He shifts uneasily. 'Um actually, there's one other thing. This morning when I was waiting for you by the P'lodge, I ran into Lady Anne.' Lady Anne is the wife of Lord Colbert, the Master of the College. 'She invited us to dinner at Formal Hall.'

My heart sinks. 'And you accepted?'

He nods. 'I figured it wouldn't hurt to ask some questions, see what they remember.' I look at Chris, annoyed. He knew this all day. He also knew, though, that I wasn't ready to hear it earlier. Chris was always good at giving people the information they needed, no more than he thought they could handle.

For a second I consider confronting him about the subterfuge. Then I stop; it's who he is, and I learned a long time ago not to waste breath or energy trying to change people. And he's right – the Master and his wife are good potential sources of information. But inwardly I groan. It is my third night in the country and I still haven't had an evening in the flat to relax and unwind.

Still I hesitate. 'I don't know. I'm still fairly exhausted from the jet lag.' I look down at the bottom of my jeans, muddy from the bike ride. 'And I'm hardly dressed for hall.'

'We'll be wearing gowns, so one will notice,' he says dismissively. 'Now let's go or we'll be late.'

Outside, it is growing dark and the streetlights have begun to come on. We do not speak as we

127

walk the bikes the short distance back down Jesus Lane to the front of college, leaning them against the wall of the Chimney. Chris stops outside the Porter's Lodge. 'Wait here,' he instructs before walking inside.

I stare into First Court once more, across the open western side where a low wall separates the hockey pitch, the field leading to the Lower Park Street houses. The setting sun flickers on the horizon. In my mind I see a girl walking across the field. It is me in my younger years, twenty, or twenty-one maybe, backpack full of library books, flannel shirt untucked. I am speaking to someone I cannot see and my face lifts, breaks open with laughter. And then I know it is not just the pain I have been running from all these years. It is the joy. The memory of a paradise ripped from its roots in an instant, of a joy so breathtaking and so real that is gone, never to be touched again.

'Here.' Chris emerges through the doorway and hands me one of the sleeveless black gowns he carries. As alumni of the college ('Old Members,' they call us), we are required like the current students to wear the black cloth gowns over our street clothes for Formal Hall. I slide my arms through the holes, leaving the gown open in front.

The bells in the college chapel chime seven fifteen as we cut across the edge of First Court, passing through another arched doorway and up a set of stone steps inside. At the top, I pause. The cavernous dining hall looks exactly as it did ten years ago, the dark wood walls and oil paintings of past Masters unchanged by time. I follow Chris down the length of the room, weaving in and out of the students who scramble among the benches to find seats together at the wood tables that run the length of the room. Though Formal Hall is held almost every night, most students attend only once or twice a week, eating the rest of their dinners at the less expensive, cafeteria-style meal served earlier. This is a special occasion for most students, a chance to enjoy slightly better food, to sit down with friends over a bottle of wine.

At the front of the Hall on an elevated dais sits High Table, reserved for the Master and fellows and their guests. Several professors I do not recognize are already seated at one end of the table, engrossed in conversation. Lord Colbert and Lady Anne rise as we approach.

'Welcome,' Lord Colbert says in a deep baritone, shaking Chris's hand, then kissing me on the cheek. He must be about seventy-five now, though his bald head and regal features seem unchanged in that timeless manner of the already old.

But Lady Anne, never a small woman, is considerably rounder than I recall, her puff of hair more white than gray now. 'What good fortune to have you back!' she exclaims. A bell sounds and, still standing, we take our places: Lord Colbert at the head of the table, Lady Anne to his right, Chris to his left, then me beside. The room grows quiet as a student comes to the front and reads the traditional grace in Latin. There is much shuffling, the scraping of benches against the floor, as the students are seated.

'My wife tells me you're up reliving memories,' Lord Colbert says as the first course, breaded mushrooms, is served. 'It's always wonderful to see our Old Members.'

'Thank you, sir,' Chris replies.

'It's been what, about ten years, since you left?' Lord Colbert asks. I nod. 'Christopher, you're with *The Times*, aren't you? I've read some of your pieces,' he adds, not waiting for an answer. Then he turns to me. 'And what have you been doing, that is professionally, since you left us?'

'I'm a Foreign Service officer. A diplomat with the State Department. I've been stationed in a number of countries and spent the last year in Washington.'

'And you're posted to London now?'

'Only just. I arrived a few days ago.' I consider mentioning Sarah, then decide against it.

'I've met your Ambassador Raines on a number of occasions,' Lord Colbert says. 'He seems like an admirable chap. I'm told he has a promising future in Washington.'

'Well, how lucky for us that you've returned,' Lady Anne interjects before I can respond. 'Do either of you have families?'

Chris and I exchange uneasy glances. We must seem like such anomalies among our classmates, most of whom have gone on to marry and have children. 'No ma'am,' he replies at last.

'You know, the college has an alumni dinner scheduled for June to coincide with the college's quincentenary,' the Master says, changing the subject. I had almost forgotten that the college would be five hundred years old this year. 'We'll be unveiling the new Mortensen Library.'

I take another bite of mushroom, stifle a hiccup

130

I suspect would be loud, and reach for my water glass. Half listening as the Master continues talking about developments in the college, I look out across the sea of gowns that fills the Hall, the student conversations growing more animated with wine. I was young like them once, I know, with nothing more to worry about than being able to cox after a night of revelry, preparing for a supervision on Monday. But I cannot remember how it felt to be so carefree. My eyes travel upward to the balcony at the rear of the hall. Through the high-paned window I can make out the edge of the adjacent chapel roof, a nearly imperceptible corner perch where the two buildings meet. My heart quickens, remembering.

'We've received the notices about the reunion,' Chris is saying. I turn toward him, forcing myself to focus on the conversation as the waiter clears the starter plates. 'And we'll certainly make every effort to attend.' I nod, though I cannot imagine coming back again, much less for a reunion. 'But when I saw Lady Anne earlier today, I didn't have a chance to explain the full purpose for our visit.' Panic rises in me. Chris is going to tell the Master what we learned about Jared. It is too soon, too direct. I grab his arm under the table but he shakes me off, continuing, 'You see, we're gathering some information about an old classmate of ours. It's an unexpected stroke of luck that we have the chance to speak with you. Perhaps you can help provide some of your recollections.'

'I'll certainly try.' Lord Colbert sits back, lifting his wineglass. 'Who is it?'

'Jared Short.'

'Oh?' the Master replies.

Lady Anne interjects, 'The lovely boy who drowned so tragically?'

I hold my breath, waiting for Chris to correct her, to tell her what we learned from Dr. Peng. 'Yes, ma'am,' he replies, his eyes wide, face sincere. I relax slightly. Maybe he isn't as unsubtle as I thought.

'What is it that you want to know?' Lord Colbert asks.

'Anything you can tell us,' I answer.

Lord Colbert clears his throat. 'I'm not sure I can be of much use. I didn't know him well. He was a great rower and a brilliant student. He had a lot of friends. But you already knew all of that.'

'Yes.' Chris picks up his own wineglass and swirls it, feigning nonchalance. 'We knew Jared well as a student. I was wondering if you could tell us what you know about his death.'

'Nothing,' Lord Colbert replies, a second too quickly. 'I mean, I was out of town at a conference the night that he passed away. I only know what the police told us and what was reported in the papers.'

'And what was that?' I press, studying the Master's face.

'You know the story as well as I do.' There is an undertone of impatience in his voice. 'It was the night of the May Ball. He went missing and was found drowned in the river.' He pauses. 'Why are you asking these questions now?'

'It's such an unpleasant subject for dinner,' Lady Anne chimes in.

But Chris is not dissuaded. 'It just seems that

the details around Jared's death are a little vague. One day he's the college's star rower, and then the next day he drowns and it's like he was never here.' I press Chris's leg under the table, urging him to remain calm. 'No funeral, no mention of it in the annual alumni bulletin.'

'His parents wanted it that way.' Lord Colbert says, his voice matter-of-fact. 'There was a memorial service.'

'We understand,' I interject, forcing empathy into my voice. 'Still, I'm sure that you can appreciate that his closest friends might be a little curious to learn additional details.'

'Ms. Weiss,' Lord Colbert replies evenly. 'There are no other details.'

Chris jumps back in. 'None that you know of.'

'None whatsoever.'

Chris opens his mouth to reply, but I kick him under the table, warning him not to share what we learned. We eat the main course, venison in puff pastry, silently for several moments. I pick at mine with disinterest. I was never a fan of the gamey foods that they always seemed to serve for formal dinners here. I eat around it, trying to satisfy my nearly empty stomach with the potatoes and peas.

Finally the waiters come to clear the plates. 'You won't object, will you, if we have a look around the college to see if we can learn anything further?' I ask Lord Colbert as dessert is served, testing him.

Lord Colbert sets down his fork. 'About what, pray tell?'

'The circumstances surrounding Jared's death,'

Chris replies.

The Master, unused to being pressed, exhales sharply. 'Haven't we just been through all of this?'

'Are you suggesting there may have been more to Jared's death than met the eye?' Lady Anne asks. Lord Colbert's head snaps in her direction. His expression does not change but I can see his eyes working furiously, communicating with her in the secret language of long-married couples, cautioning her to be quiet. Is he simply warning her not to encourage our questions or is there something he does not want her to say?

'We don't know,' I answer quickly, before Chris can mention the coroner's report. 'That's what we want to find out.'

The Master shakes his head dismissively. 'You're wasting your time. We know what happened. He drowned.'

I can feel Chris biting his tongue, struggling not to respond. 'Maybe. But we'd like to look around and see if anyone else might remember anything,' I reply.

'I'm sorry, but there's simply no point. I'm afraid that I'm going to have to ask you to refrain. I can't have you bothering the staff, digging up painful memories. If this got out, the publicity for the college wouldn't be good. Now, I apologize, but I am rather tired and have an early tutorial tomorrow morning, so I am going to skip dessert. Lovely seeing you. Hope to see you at the reunion.' He stands up and is gone, Lady Anne following close behind.

'Well that was interesting,' Chris remarks ten

134

minutes later as we make our way down the stairs, the laughter of lingering students fading behind us. Outside, the cool night air is a welcome relief from the stuffiness of the hall.

At the end of the Chimney, the taxi Chris phoned on his mobile idles in front of the gate. 'The train station,' he says to the driver as he climbs in behind me. He moves closer than is necessary, his leg warm against mine.

'I don't think we should have told them why we were here,' I reply as the taxi starts down Jesus Lane.

'No, that was perfect. I knew he wasn't going to tell us anything but his reaction was exactly what I wanted to see.'

Hearing the deliberateness in his voice, I turn to him. 'So you wanted to be invited to Formal Hall with the Master?' He nods. 'And you ran into Lady Anne on purpose?'

'Absolutely.' Chris's voice is plain and unrepentant. 'I remembered that Lady Anne took her constitutional about that time every afternoon. And I'm glad I did. Did you see the look on Colbert's face when we mentioned Jared? He knows more than he's letting on.'

'I don't know...' I hesitate, looking out the window as we drive along the edge of Parker's Piece. The flat, grassy park, bustling with cricket games and picnics by day, is deserted now, except for a couple huddled on a bench beneath one of the streetlights. 'Maybe he was just nervous about poking around. Or he might just think we're being foolish.'

'I don't think so,' Chris replies. 'And I'm going

135

to find out.' Neither of us speak further. I study his face out of the corner of my eye. He stares intently into the space in front of him, a man driven by a quest.

The taxi pulls up in front of the train station and Chris pays the driver. 'There's a train leaving at nine forty-five,' he says, checking the board as we enter the station.

Seven minutes. 'You don't have to wait. I can manage,' I reply as we walk toward the platform.

He looks down at me protectively. 'I don't mind. Do you want something to eat for the ride? Or read?' He gestures toward the newsstand, which is about to close for the evening.

I shake my head, lowering my hand to my bag. 'I've got some work to do. And I'm still full from dinner,' I add, feeling a twinge of guilt as I tell the fib. I barely touched my meal. But I do not want to miss the train, and I am eager to get away from my memories and all that we learned.

'I understand. I'm sorry I can't drive you back to London,' he says as we walk down the platform. 'But I want to stay up here and do some more digging tomorrow.'

We reach the door of the train. 'What are you going to do?'

'Ask some questions around college. Some of the staff have been there for decades. They have to remember something.'

'But Lord Colbert said...'

'We're not in college anymore, Jordan. The Master can't control our lives. I can talk to whom I want. I just hope he hasn't gotten to them already.'

136

'Keep me posted.' I look up at the clock. Two minutes. 'I'd better go.'

'All right.' He leans forward, enveloping me in his thick arms. I find myself folding into the warmth of his chest, drawn close by the comforting smell of his aftershave. I linger, a second or two longer than usual. We have shared the weight of our discovery all day. I do not, I realize, look forward to being alone with it. 'Be careful.' Pulling away, I turn and board the train, not meeting his eyes.

Inside, the rear car is empty except for a man in a suit at the far end reading a newspaper. I take a seat toward the middle, setting my bag beside me and turning to look behind me as the train begins to pull from the station. Through the window, I see Chris retreating down the platform, shoulders hunched, head down. Finding out that he'd been right about Jared's death was no great thing for him.

Facing forward, I reach in my bag for the stack of papers regarding Infodyne that I didn't get through on the train this morning. As I do, my fingers brush against other papers, folded in half. The coroner's report. I pull my hand back quickly and zip the bag shut. But it is too late – the thought rises up like a wave, dark and menacing. Jared did not drown. I lean my head back against the seat, closing my eyes. Someone killed him. I had always imagined, naively perhaps, that his drowning was painless, as though he simply went to sleep in the water. But now a thousand dark images flood my mind. Did he suffer? Had he known that he was going to die? I bite my

137

knuckles, fighting the urge to scream aloud. I am not a stranger to death, or even murder. In my line of work, I have seen too often the horrors that people can invoke upon one another. But this is different. This is mine.

Exhaustion overtakes me then, and I release the images from my mind, soothed by the gentle rocking of the train. Some time later, I awake with a start. I open my eyes. I had fallen asleep, for how long I do not know. I blink, looking out the window, trying to figure out how far we have gone. But the terrain is nondescript, shrouded in darkness.

As I turn back, something catches my eye. It is my bag, lying on the floor of the train. Uneasiness rises in me as I lean forward to pick it up. It was on the seat beside me when I dozed off. Did it fall? But it sits perfectly upright, the contents not jostled or spilled. No, someone moved it.

I spin around to look behind me but the car is empty, except for the businessman dozing beneath his fallen newspaper. The seats in front of me remain deserted as well. For a moment I wonder if the conductor had come through, but he surely would have woken me to ask for my ticket. Hurriedly I pick up the bag, noticing for the first time that the zipper is half open.

'Dammit!' I swear as I reach into the bag, berating myself for falling asleep where I should not. Have I been robbed? My wallet is still there, as are my cell phone and keys. Calmer now, I rummage through my bag, taking inventory. Maybe it really did just fall. Perhaps I forgot to close it. But as I reach past the Infodyne papers and my hand closes around emptiness I know that the movement of my bag was no accident.

The coroner's report is missing.

November 1997

The early evening air is frigid against my stock-inged legs as I cut across the field that separates the Lower Park Street houses from the back of college. I stick to the stone path so my high heels do not sink into the muddy earth. As I reach the edge of North Court, my shoulders sag. Usually before a boat club dinner, I have a ritual: a long nap and a hot bath, lots of water, and a snack to line my stomach for the night of drinking ahead. But today I spent nearly six hours at the University Library, looking for an obscure article to support a point regarding the Paris Peace Conference I want to make in my thesis. My eyes grew dry from scanning faded microfiche, my nails jagged from searching among the dusty stacks. I lost track of time and returned late, with barely enough time to iron my little black dress and throw on some makeup before heading toward Hall.

Normally, I would look forward to the boat club dinner, the post-race highlight of each term. But this morning's race, the Fairbairn Cup, left little cause for celebration. It was a simple timed race down the river, designed more for the novices than for the senior divisions. We rowed poorly, though, becoming dis-jointed when the adrenaline of a race kicked in for the first time and finished eighth out of eleven boats in our division. Today's fiasco made it impossible to ignore the truth: something is not working with this crew.

It is not for lack of effort. We train six days a week,

staying on the water more than two hours each outing, doing exercises designed to enhance the crew's speed, strength, the precision of the strokes. I've heard the boys speaking in low tones through the doorway of the locker room or over breakfast in Caff, speculating on the source of the problem. Some think Mark is too inexperienced to be in the boat, or that he and Nick are not strong enough to be bow pair. Others say it is a problem with the new shell. But I know it is not any one of these things. I know that the problem is Jared.

Jared's presence at the boat club has proved to be worse than even my initial fears. He is perpetually angry, and his nastiness affects the entire crew – I can see from the cox's seat how the boys tense up, waiting for him to explode at one of them for catching the water too early, not holding on long enough at the stroke's finish. And he seems to save most of his bile for me. Rowers tend not to appreciate coxes. They see us as deadweight at the back of the boat that adds no speed or power. They never see the work that goes into steering the boat, straining to see over eight sets of massive shoulders, aiming for the most direct route, figuring out how to make the sharp turn at Ditton between the two stalled boats and the swans without crashing into the bank. And then there are the commands – it is my job to watch the movement of the blades as their spoons come in and out of the water, to gauge the length and spacing of the water displaced by each stroke, and to try to figure out what is wrong and what to say to fix it. No, the crew never sees any of that, but for the most part the others regard me as a necessary evil, and because they like me, they don't give me too hard of a time when I occasionally set us off balance by pulling too hard on the rudder or cause

140

us to lock oars with another crew.

But Jared is different. He acts as if I am the root of all problems in the boat, screams at me constantly. Underqualified for the job, I am an easy target – a second-year cox, even a good one, does not always have the technical knowledge to know what is wrong or the confidence and poise to make split-second calls. This morning, after the race, I leapt from the boat, trying to stop it as I was supposed to do. But in my haste I forgot to take off my headphone and the wires tore from the cox box. 'Idiot!' he berated as the rest of the crew looked on, sympathetic but powerless to help. I left the boathouse shaken and demoralized. The tension has begun to affect me outside of rowing as well. I sleep restlessly, have nightmares, and wake with a sense of dread in the morning, knowing I have to return again to the boathouse.

I make my way across First Court and up the stairs, hanging my coat on the rack before entering the Hall. The room is already crowded with a hundred or so rowers in tuxedos and little black dresses like my own, finding seats, balancing the predinner drinks that I missed. Chairs replace the benches that normally flank the long wood tables and the chandelier has been dimmed low to give the room an elegant feel. I make my way through the crowd to the table at the front left of the room reserved for the first men's eight. The rest of the crew is already seated. I take the last empty seat beside Roger and across from Nick. Jared, I note with relief, is at the far end. The table is set formally with cloth napkins and china bearing the college crest; folded menus announce the courses.

The room grows warm and voices rise to be heard above the din. Waiters circulate pouring white wine. I

141

take a sip, grimacing. Boat club dinners, like any other college event, are about the quantity of alcohol, not quality. A hand touches my shoulder. 'Boat race,' Roger says. Inwardly I groan. A boat race is a drinking contest, a relay down both sides of the table. He gestures with his head toward Jared and Chris at the far end. I am surprised – I would have expected Jared to look down upon such revelry but he faces Chris, glass raised. The race begins, Chris empties his glass in a single gulp on our side, then Simon. Across the table, the progression is a split second slower, Mark hesitating for a second as Jared finishes. Poised with my own glass, I watch as Roger drinks beside me. I cannot be the cause of our defeat. When it is my turn, I tilt my head back and swallow the wine in two mouthfuls, then set down the glass to indicate we have finished.

'Winners!' Roger and Ewan cry as jubilantly as if it were a real race. Across the table, Nick demands a rematch. As the glasses are refilled, this time with red, my eyes catch Jared's. A look of amusement crosses his face, as if to say, 'Now isn't this silly?' dimples crushing his usually smooth cheeks. I look away quickly, feeling my neck grow warm. It is, I realize, the first time I have seen him smile.

This time the race begins at our end of the table. I drink my wine as quickly as I can, but I am no match for the avenging Nick, who downs his in a single gulp, sending his side on to victory. 'Tiebreaker!' Chris insists as the first course, baked brie, is served. My empty stomach burns in protest. I cannot bumper another glass of wine so soon.

'Excuse me,' I say to no one in particular, standing up unsteadily and making my way to the door. The same games and banter are playing out at tables

142

across the Hall, mini-tableaus of college life. As I reach the door, nausea rises in me. I pause, grasping the door frame for support.

There is a hand on my elbow. I look up confused. Jared hovers above me, wearing a serious expression. I wonder what he is doing here, whether he is going to yell at me about something. 'You all right?' he asks, sounding concerned.

'I'm fine,' I manage. 'Just going to the loo.'

'You looked a little green when you stood up. I'll walk with you.' I consider protesting, then decide against it, allowing him to lead me up a short flight of stairs to the ladies' room on the mezzanine.

'Thanks,' I say, pulling my arm from his grasp. Inside, I stare down at the toilet, which seems to be moving in small circles. A cold sweat forms on my brow. What is wrong with me? Two glasses of wine should not affect me this way. I remember the questionable-looking tuna sandwich I ate late this morning at the library tea room. My stomach rolls. Should I make myself throw up? A tactical chunder, the boys call it. It is a deliberate way to rid the body of some of the alcohol either to avoid being drunk or, in many cases, to be able to continue on drinking. But it's not likely to help with a sandwich eaten so many hours ago. I decide against it and wash my hands.

Outside, I am surprised to find Jared still standing by the door. 'You didn't have to wait.'

'No problem. I was just going to get some air myself.' He presses a glass into my hand. I start to protest. The last thing I need is another drink. 'It's water,' he adds.

I wrap my hands around the cool glass and take a sip. 'Thanks. I couldn't handle another boat race.'

'Come on.' He starts up the stairs. I hesitate, sur-

143

prised. He is not heading back to dinner, or outside, either.

'Where are we going?' I ask as we climb the steps, passing the darkened doorway of Upper Hall. The dining rooms are stacked like tiers on a wedding cake, each smaller than the one beneath it.

Jared raises a finger to his lips as we pass a half-open pantry door where two waiters are discussing a bottle of wine that has been spilled. 'Bloody idiot,' one says and I cannot tell if he is referring to the waiter or one of the students.

We reach the Prioress's Room, the third and smallest of the dining rooms. It is dark, with tables and chairs stacked in the corner. 'Where are we going?' I repeat as we cross the room.

Jared does not answer, but opens a window. 'Let me go first.'

'Go where?' I look over his shoulder into the darkness beyond.

'Shhh.' He slips through the window, then holds his hands back through to me. I hesitate. Climbing out on the roof is surely forbidden and doing it at night after drinking is madness. I start to protest but Jared has already disappeared into the gaping darkness on the other side.

Taking a breath, I reach out and put my hand in his. As he pulls me through the window onto the ledge, I am greeted by an icy blast of air against my bare arms and neck. I think longingly of my coat hanging idly two stories below. 'Slide this way. Careful, it's a bit sooty.' He guides me into a corner where the side of the building abuts the chapel, forming a small nook. We move onto the chapel roof; the edge is slightly wider here. But the space is only eighteen inches deep, and beyond the precipice is a four-story drop down.

I draw my knees to my chest and wrap my arms around them, trying to make myself as small as possible. 'You wouldn't be trying to kill me, would you?' I ask, teeth chattering.

Jared laughs, his breath forming a tiny puff of smoke in the moonlight. 'Nah, what would I do for a cox?' A bad cox, I want to say, is better than no cox at all. I decide not to antagonize him while we are perched at this height. He reaches around me, holding me in place as he closes the window. 'So the porters won't notice.' Then he takes off his dinner jacket and drapes it around my shoulders. The scent of a lemony shampoo wafts from the collar. I smelled it once before, I recall, a quick whiff mixed with sweat as he leaned over my seat to fix the cox box, cursing my technical ineptitude. I stop as the oddness of the situation strikes me. This is Jared who screams. Jared who gives me nightmares. We hate each other. Why is he being friendly now?

He sits back but his arm remains locked firmly around my shoulder, holding me in place. I relax my grip on the edge of the building, noticing for the first time the gargoyles that guard the rooftop corners like sentries. 'Look.' He gestures outward with his free hand. Across the horizon, the towers and steeples of Trinity, King's, and Saint John's are silhouetted cool and pale in the moonlight, the clear sky a blanket of stars behind them.

'And as for the more earthly pursuits.' I follow his gaze downward. Through a tall arched window, we have a bird's-eye view of the dinner in the Hall below. At our table, the boys have folded their cloth napkins into makeshift hats. Faint singing wafts upward. 'And did those feet, in ancient time...' An off-key

145

chorus of tenors and faux basses croon 'Jerusalem,' the hymn based on the Blake poem extolling England's green fields. Soon the singing will turn sillier, I know, ending with the inevitable roasting of the boatman, 'Tony Johnson is a Horse's Ass.'

Out of the corner of my eye, I peek at Jared. He watches the gathering below with a faint smile, a parent watching his children play. So he really is fond of the crew after all.

'I never knew you could get up here,' I remark.

'I found it accidentally about a month ago. I like to get away sometimes. I'm from the countryside and, well, Cambridge is just so crowded sometimes, you know?'

I open my mouth to disagree. Coming from Washington, I find Cambridge peaceful, quaint. But on some level I know what he means. We live, study, and play with the same few hundred people in the same space day in and day out. 'It can get a little claustrophobic,' I agree.

'And this is a good spot for thinking about things,' he adds. I cock my head. I had not imagined him as pensive. 'Just things. About my dissertation.

'What's it about?' I ask. It is the first conversation I've ever had with Jared that is not about rowing and I find myself curious to learn more.

He hesitates, as if surprised by my interest. 'I'm working on some issues related to the war – war criminals and such...'

'I didn't know you read history,' I interrupt. I pictured him doing something drier and more clinical, like natural sciences or computers, perhaps. 'I've never seen you at the faculty building.'

'I don't really spend time there. My supervisor is

146

down in London and I research mostly out of the Public Records Office at Kew. It's not so much history, though that's where my degree is based, as international affairs and politics. I'm looking at where some of the lesser-known war criminals escaped to, the ones who got away. I'd like to publish it after I'm finished to maybe shed some light on the topic.'

'Oh.' I consider mentioning my own thesis, but economic development after the First World War seems esoteric and irrelevant by comparison.

'Anyway, there are still some holes in my research and I've got to get that wrapped up. And then there's the boat to consider – what's wrong, how we are going to fix it in time for the Mays.'

I nod, unsurprised by his abrupt change of topic. The crew is never far from my mind, either. Though the May Bumps are more than six months away, he is right to be concerned – the guts, the foundation of the boat, need to be built now. Bumps, held few places in the world other than Cambridge and Oxford, are races where seventeen boats are lined up a length and a half apart. The objective over the course is to bump, or contact the boat in front, before getting hit by the boat behind. If a crew is successful in bumping, then it will switch places with the crew it bumped for the start of the race the next day. The race goes on for four days and the goal is to advance as many places as possible or – if you are us and are already second from the top – to hit the one crew in front of you and then stay on top, thereby claiming the Head of the River. The Lords women's first boat did it last year to great fanfare, including a bonfire after the boat club dinner where a wood boat was burned in celebration. Our men have been second for the past three years, trying

147

in vain to overtake Trinity Hall and reclaim the Headship that has eluded us for decades. But even as we chase, the crews behind us are hungry, too, nipping at our heels. There is an unspoken urgency this year – if we do not claim the Headship now, we will begin to slide down in the rankings.

And Jared was brought to Lords to help us reclaim the Headship. He feels as though our success or failure is on his shoulders. Suddenly I understand his intensity. It is not that he is mean. He is driven. It's like he is chasing something and that keeps him from being able to stop and play like the rest of us.

'What do you think? About the boat, I mean.' I look up at Jared, surprised. He has never asked my opinion about the crew. 'I know you can feel things from the cox's seat, see things that I can't.'

I hesitate. Do I dare to tell him the truth? The alcohol warms me, making me bold. 'I think that you scare the crew.' He opens his mouth but I raise my hand before he can speak. 'I know that you need to be tough with them to instill discipline. But they're tense. They're so afraid of angering you that they aren't able to loosen up. They need to relax, to laugh, bond a little.'

Jared does not answer but looks down and for a minute I worry that I have angered him. 'Look.' He gestures to the Hall below, where dessert has been served. A contest called a no-hands bumper is under way, the goal to clean one's plate by eating without hands or silverware. I follow Jared's gaze to the far right corner of the room, where Chris is talking to Michelle, a female rower from the second year. He shakes his head. 'That boy always leaves with someone.'

He's right, I realize. Chris has hooked up with a lot

148

of women, even by college standards. It sometimes seems as if he is on a mission, driven to prove something. But it is more than that: Chris is always the one hosting late-night parties in his room, inviting people back for drinks after events. 'It's like he can't stand going home alone.'

'Sooner or later, we all go home alone.' He exhales heavily, an almost-sigh. 'Anyway, that boy needs a good woman.'

'Just waiting for the right girl to walk into the wrong bar,' I quip, borrowing a line I heard as an undergraduate.

'I think he thinks you're that girl,' Jared says bluntly.

I turn to look at him, startled. What is he talking about? 'We never, that is, I never...' But now there seem to be a thousand signs: Chris's protectiveness of me, the way he seems to always be close by. I took it as a stroke looking out for his cox. Could Jared be right? 'That's impossible,' I say finally. But my head swims.

'Maybe,' he replies indifferently.

What about you, I want to ask? I have never seen Jared with a girl. A thousand questions flood my brain. What is he doing here with me? Why does he normally hate me so? I turn, expecting to find him watching the party, but instead he is staring out across the rooftops, a faraway look in his eyes.

'This is kind of strange,' I say abruptly. He turns to me. 'Us, I mean, hanging out tonight, talking like normal people. Like we don't hate each other.'

His expression crumples slightly. 'I don't hate you.'

'You think I'm a shitty cox.'

'Not even. I think you could be a good cox.' Now it is his turn to be candid. 'You've got the technical skills. *But you feel too much. A cox needs to be calculating, precise. You should be driving the crew like highly trained racehorses, not coddling them like babies. The boys trust you and that's a good thing. But in the boat, you can't be their friend.'*

I look away, stung by the truth in what he's said, hoping he cannot see my cheeks burn in the darkness. In the distance a bell begins to chime. 'We should go,' he says abruptly. 'The porters lock the upper floor just past nine and I don't think we want to spend the night.'

Downstairs we stop by the door to the Hall, listening to the roar of singing on the other side of the door, a train that has gone on without us. I take my coat from the rack and, as if by silent agreement, we continue down the stairs and out the door. Jared stops and turns to me. 'I've got to get the train to Kew early tomorrow,' he says, an apology perhaps for not carrying on to the bar or inviting me around for coffee. I am relieved and yet strangely disappointed.

He reaches out with his hand and I freeze. Does he mean to hug me good night? But he brings his hand to my face. 'You've got a bit of a smudge...' Nice, I think, as he brushes his thumb against the corner of my lip. Classy. 'There, that's better. Have a nice Christmas break, if I don't see you.'

He turns away. I fight the urge to call after him, to ask him to wait. I don't hate you, either, I want to say, remembering his hurt expression earlier. But he is already halfway across the courtyard, shoulders hunched, head tucked low against the wind.

the *LENT TERM*

chapter EIGHT

Trafalgar Square on a Monday morning is a swarming mass of activity. Cars and buses move along the roadway in fits and starts, jamming up at the traffic lights, filling the air with thick exhaust. Swarms of commuters, invisible beneath a sea of black umbrellas, jostle as they make their way from the buses to the city, from Charing Cross Tube station to Whitehall. Across the road, the square itself is packed thick with tourists who, undaunted by the fine misting rain, feed the pigeons that cluster by the lion statues beneath Nelson's Column and snap photos from the steps of the National Gallery.

I press back against the glass window of Waterstone's, looking for shelter from the chaos as much as the weather, then close my umbrella. This time I came prepared, determined not to turn up soaked at another important meeting. I look at my watch. Nine-fifty. I pull my cell phone from my pocket. The message button blinks once. Someone must have called while I was on the Tube. I open the phone and punch in the key code hurriedly. I tried to call Chris twice, once from the train station and again when I got home to tell him that the documents had been stolen, but he didn't answer, nor had he returned my calls over the weekend.

When I woke up on the train and realized the

coroner's report was gone, I searched my bag a half dozen times, looked under my seat and the one across from it, and checked between the cushions. Then I walked the length of the train, scanning the handful of other passengers who dozed or read as we neared London until the conductor asked me if everything was all right. I did not know how to answer. The notion that someone had stolen papers of seemingly little or no worth from my bag while leaving my wallet and other valuables intact sounded illogical, paranoid. The papers could simply be lost, I reminded myself, sitting back down. They could have fallen from my bag at dinner or in the taxi, though I thought my bag was closed the entire time. In any event, the report was gone. So I dialed Chris to tell him as the train pulled into King's Cross.

But the voice that fills the receiver now is not his. It is Sarah, politely asking if I've settled in okay, do I need anything? Guilt slams into me. It's been two days since I've spoken with her. I stopped by to see her on Saturday morning, hoping to persuade her to come with me to the shops to buy some items for my new flat. She hesitated, looking longingly out the window, then down at her wheelchair, and I could see her worrying about getting down the stairs and navigating through the crowds that thronged Portobello Road on the weekends. 'I'm a bit tired,' she said finally, and though I pressed her a few more times, I knew it was futile. No amount of cajoling could move Sarah when she made up her mind. I left soon after and spent the rest of the weekend settling into the flat, napping off my jet lag, reading some background on Infodyne. I meant to call, but ... it doesn't matter, I cut off my own mental excuses. You came here for her. Quickly I hit the call return button. The phone rings twice before her soft voice answers. 'Hello?'

'It's me. I just got your message.'

'Jordie, I just wanted to make sure you were all right.' There is concern, but no hint of reproach in her voice.

'Yes, I'm sorry for having been out of touch. I think I slept half the weekend...' I had not told her about my trip to Cambridge when I stopped by on Saturday. It just seemed too soon, the information about Jared too raw to share. Now I am seized with the urge to tell her everything, to have her help me make sense of it all. But I can't, not here. 'I'm just on my way to a meeting but I'd love to catch up. Dinner tonight?'

'I'll have to check my calendar,' she replies drolly, 'but I think I'm free.' Of course she is.

'Great. I should be there by seven. I'll pick something up on my way.' I close the phone then brush a piece of lint from the front of my white sweater beneath my coat. I fretted over the outfit choice, changing several times before settling on the simple twin set and camel-colored light wool skirt, trying to achieve a serious yet not intimidating look.

'Jordan,' a voice calls behind me. I spin around to see Duncan Lauder striding toward me, closing a large black umbrella.

'Duncan!' I exclaim as he bends to kiss me lightly on both cheeks. He is taller than I

155

remembered, and paler, the healthy color and form that came from hours on the river replaced by a gray office pallor, a slight paunch. His always wispy brown hair has thinned, revealing patches of scalp.

'I hope you weren't waiting long. The trains were running a few minutes late.' His teeth seem to lean against each other, overlapping in a way I hadn't remembered.

'Not at all. You're right on time. Thanks for meeting me.' He reopens his umbrella, holding it over me as we navigate through the crowds. Uneasiness nags at me: Duncan said that he would be nearby for meetings. So why was it necessary to take the train? Why not pick somewhere more convenient? I remember his hesitancy on the phone the previous day when I suggested coming to Infodyne. Perhaps he does not want to be seen with me.

Enough, I think, silencing my questions. Paranoia has never served me well. Most likely I am his first meeting of the day and he's just taken the train in from wherever he lives. I turn to him. 'Where shall we go?' I ask brightly as we reach the northern edge of the square.

'There's a coffee shop a few blocks up,' he replies, leading me around Saint Martin-in-the-Fields church. But as we turn the corner, he looks furtively over his shoulder in both directions. No, my first instinct was correct: Duncan is definitely nervous about our meeting, and I haven't even told him why I want to see him yet.

We continue along a narrow street that seems to parallel Charing Cross Road. It is a no-man's-land between the darkened theaters of the West End and the lively stalls of Covent Garden, lined with local shops that are of little interest to the tourists who crowd the larger thoroughfare. Rainwater mixes with garbage waiting to be picked up at the curb, giving the air a sour smell.

'How's Vance?' I ask as Duncan opens the door to a small coffee shop and sets his umbrella by the front door. It is a calculated risk, assuming that they are still together, hoping that the question will break the ice if they are.

'Brilliant, thanks.' Duncan's face brightens at the mention of his partner. 'He's in a show right now in the West End, a reprisal of Sondheim's *Company*. Fabulous reviews. You really should see it. And we bought a lovely flat in Bethnal Green last year.'

'That's East London, right?'

He nods. 'It's really coming around. Not as dodgy as it used to be and you can get good value for money on property.'

'That's a bit far for your commute to Luton, isn't it?' I ask after we have ordered our cappuccinos.

I reach for my wallet but he waves me away. 'I've got it. It is. But well worth it. I can't imagine us living outside of London.'

'Are you still rowing at all?' I ask.

'I am, actually. Nothing serious, but there's a group of us that manages to go out once or twice a week. In an eight, if we have the bodies, if not in a four. You should join us. We're always in need of a cox.

I manage a laugh. 'Not sure the early mornings are for me anymore. But I'll think about it.' Inwardly, I shudder. I haven't been in a boat in a decade, not since our row to the site of Jared's grave the morning after the funeral. I cannot imagine ever doing it again.

Duncan picks up cappuccinos and leads me to a table in the back of the shop. As far from the windows as possible, I notice. 'So what brings you to England?' he asks after we are seated. He stirs brown sugar into his cup.

I hesitate. In other countries, I would have had some degree of cover, a fake job or purpose to use when getting close to a target, so as not to arouse suspicion. England is different, though. Too many people know me here to keep my work a secret. 'A friend of mine from college, Sarah Sunderson, is terribly ill with ALS. I wanted to be close by, so I took an assignment here.' I speak slowly, choosing my words with care.

Duncan's brow furrows, his lips pulling downward. 'I didn't know her, but I'm so sorry to hear that.' His sadness is genuine. Duncan was always such a nice guy. I wish I didn't have to approach him under these circumstances, to involve him in my work. 'Is this the first time you've been back since...?' He does not finish the sentence.

'Yes.'

'Well, I'm sorry about that, too. I never had the chance to see you, afterwards I mean, to speak with you at the memorial service.' Because I ran out before it started, I think, slipped out the side door of the chapel, unable to bear the very kind of condolences he wanted to offer. 'I wanted to tell you how sorry I was. How much I liked Jared.' His words come out in a tumble now, the regret as fresh as if Jared died yesterday. 'I knew him from the boathouses, of course, and a conference we both attended once in Madrid. I wanted to send a note but I couldn't ... anyway, it was a terrible loss.'

Even more than you know, I think, remembering all that Chris and I learned yesterday. For a minute, I consider telling Duncan about our trip to Cambridge, to get his thoughts. But I am here for work; I cannot jeopardize my assignment for personal reasons. 'Thank you,' I say at last. I take a sip of cappuccino, fighting the tears that seem to form in my eyes whenever Jared is mentioned these days. I blink them back, cursing inwardly. This isn't me. Coming back has made me soft, and I hate it.

'And I wish I could be of more help,' Duncan adds, 'but I really don't know anything more about the night he died than you do.'

I swallow, too fast, nearly choking on the hot liquid, then set down my mug with a thump. 'Excuse me?'

'I mean that I don't have any information about the night Jared died. I assumed that's why you wanted to see me. Like I told Chris...'

'Chris Bannister?' I cannot keep the surprise out of my voice. 'You spoke with him?'

'Oh, I thought you knew.' Duncan's eyes widen. 'He called me about a week ago. Said he thought there was something off about Jared's death and asked me what I remembered. He said that you and he were trying to get some answers.' My

159

mind races. Chris didn't mention that he contacted Duncan. And he spoke with Duncan a week ago, before he even saw me, before I agreed to help.

I take a deep breath. Concentrate. Get the information you came for and deal with Chris later. 'Actually, I didn't come here to talk about Jared. I need to ask you about something else.'

He frowns. 'I don't understand.'

'Duncan, I'm not sure if you're aware of this or not, but I work for the State Department. I'm part of an investigation team...'

'Investigation?'

I pause, careful not to say too much. 'It has to do with organized crime syndicates and the contraband they traffic into the U.K. and the States.'

His eyes widen once more. 'I can't imagine what I might know about anything like that.'

'You're finance director at Infodyne, aren't you?'

'Acting finance director,' he corrects, his voice rising slightly. 'But we're the eleventh-largest company in Britain. We're hardly a – what did you say? An organized crime syndicate?'

'I know, I didn't mean to imply...' I take a breath, regrouping. 'We're concerned that a British company could be somehow involved, laundering money maybe. Not necessarily Infodyne, but the company does have significant Albanian interests.' I pause, studying Duncan's face. His expression remains impassive, except for a slight twitch in the corner of his left eye. 'It wouldn't likely be the whole company,' I continue, 'but it could be some part, a few players. Small, repeated transactions that can't otherwise be accounted for to unfamiliar entities. With a company so large, it would be possible someone could be doing things without your knowledge.'

'I'm familiar with how laundering works,' he replies, a second too quickly. 'And I can assure you there's nothing improper going on at Info-dyne. I'm sorry. It just seems so preposterous.'

He's lying. I take a deep breath. 'Duncan, do you know something about the Albanians? Because it's critical that you tell me if you do. We have reason to believe–'

'I don't know what you're talking about.' His voice is calm, but beneath his freckles his face has paled a shade further. 'I'm sorry I can't help you with what you're looking for. Now if you'll excuse me, I have an eleven o'clock meeting with one of our brokerage houses in the city.' He pushes back from the table and stands up.

'Duncan, wait.' I leap to my feet, placing my hand atop his. 'Maybe you could do some checking, let me know if you find anything.'

'I'm afraid that's impossible.' He pulls away, shaking off my hand.

'Duncan, please … if it's a question of security, I'm cleared. I can get you my credentials. If Info-dyne is somehow involved...'

He cuts me off. 'Such wild accusations do nobody any good. None of us.'

He's afraid, I realize, a chill passing through me. I wonder who the 'us' is he's referring to. 'Duncan, if it's a question of security, we can help, offer protection...' But even as I speak I know that it won't make a difference.

'I have to go.' He starts from the table, then

turns back. 'Take care of yourself, Jordan.' And before I can speak further, he walks quickly out of the café.

chapter NINE

'Duncan, wait!' I cry, taking a step forward. Then I stop. I cannot match his pace without running and I do not want to make a scene. He's not going to say more anyway.

That went well. I sink back down in my chair, staring at Duncan's nearly untouched cappuccino, then reach for my own drink, replaying the conversation in my mind. Duncan knows something about the Albanians, that much is certain. He looked like he'd seen a ghost when I mentioned them. If only I'd gone about things differently, asked the right questions, maybe he would have confided in me. But what are those questions?

I pull my cell phone from my bag, as well as the card Mo gave me with the team's phone numbers. I hesitate, considering the names. I need information. Sophie is useless, Mo too busy. I hate to ask Sebastian for anything, but he seems to be the only choice. I dial his mobile.

'Hallo,' a sleepy-sounding voice on the other end says a moment later.

An image of Sebastian, shirtless in bed, pops unbidden into my mind. 'It's Jordan Weiss,' I say, feeling silly for using my last name. 'I hope I didn't wake you.'

'I'm not much of a morning person.' He does not sound surprised to hear from me.

'It's almost eleven,' I point out, pushing down my annoyance. 'Late-night assignment?'

He yawns, then stretches audibly. 'Something like that. What can I do for you?'

'I need some background for the investigation. I was wondering if you can help.'

'Certainly. There's a file an inch thick in the vault. Just ask Amelia...'

I shake my head. I don't have two days to spend reading up on the subject. 'I thought maybe you could give me the short version over coffee. I'm buying.'

'Then make it breakfast. Where are you now?'

'Near Trafalgar Square.'

'I'll meet you at the benches in front of Westminster Abbey in half an hour.'

Twenty-five minutes later, I make my way across Parliament Square, juggling two hot dogs and cans of soda I purchased from a street vendor, as well as my umbrella and the one Duncan abandoned at the front of the café. The rain has stopped, though, and bits of sunshine peek through the clouds behind Big Ben to my left.

I am surprised to see Sebastian waiting for me on a park bench by the grassy strip that runs along the side of Westminster Abbey, set back a few feet from the crowds of tourists that fill the pavement. His hair is still damp, his jeans and white t-shirt rumpled. A worn tan leather briefcase sits by his feet. He is completely unprofessional and, I decide instantly, even better looking

163

than I remembered.

'What's this?' he asks as I near. His eyes flick from my twin set to my legs, then back again.

I hand him one of the hot dogs, trying not to notice the warmth as his hand brushes against mine. 'Breakfast.'

He grimaces, taking a can of soda from me. 'Not exactly what I had in mind. I was hoping for fried eggs, some toast.' He shakes his head. 'You Americans and your hot dogs.'

'It was the best I could do on short notice. You seemed to like them well enough at the Ambassador's reception.'

'I was trying to impress you.'

'Whatever.' I wipe the still-damp bench with a napkin, then sit down, ignoring his obvious attempt to flirt. 'So I just met with Duncan Lauder.'

Sebastian cracks open his soda, reaches into his pocket, and pulls out two aspirin, blowing on them to remove the lint, then downing them with a mouthful of soda. 'And?'

'He didn't exactly give me the keys to the kingdom,' I continue, unwrapping the foil around one end of the hot dog and taking a bite. 'But my questions provoked quite a reaction. He seemed terrified at the mention of the Albanians.' I pause. 'Sebastian, I need more information.'

He does not respond, but looks across the grass at two squirrels playing by the base of a tree. As I study him out of the corner of my eye, a shiver runs through me. Enough, I think, but it is too late. My mind reels back to another bench, the night of the Ambassador's reception, Sebastian's lips on mine.

164

He turns to me abruptly and I look away, staring hard at the pavement. 'And you're asking me for background, not Maureen.'

I hesitate, trying to answer the question buried in his statement. 'Maureen is one of my closest friends.' It strikes me then that other than Maureen and Sarah, I do not really have any friends at all. 'And I trust her implicitly. But she's deputy chief of mission now.'

'A lot of politics and red tape at that level,' he observes.

'Right. She's not an operative like you and me anymore...' I pause, caught off guard by a sudden sneeze.

'Bless you,' Sebastian says, producing a somewhat clean-looking tissue from inside his coat.

I sniffle and wipe my nose. 'It's the dampness. I always get a bit of a cold the first few days here.' Then I look up at him once more. 'So tell me about the investigation, Sebastian. Tell me what I really need to know.'

He looks up and holds out his palm. 'It's going to rain again any second now.' He tilts his head toward Westminster Abbey. 'Want to go in?' Not waiting for an answer, he stands and picks up his briefcase, then starts for the door. I follow, finishing off my hot dog and throwing the foil and soda can in a bin before slipping a piece of gum from my pocket and popping it in my mouth. Walking a few feet behind Sebastian, I notice the slight lilt to his gait, the flash of lower back that is revealed as his t-shirt pulls away from his jeans with each step.

Inside, I stop, gazing upward in awe as

165

Sebastian pays our admission. I have only been in the massive church once during a sightseeing trip to London during my first weeks at Cambridge. I forgot the scale of the flying buttresses, the opulent stained-glass windows. The smell of damp stone seeps heavily from the floor.

Sebastian leads me away from the tourists who pack the main sanctuary and over to one of the side crypts, illuminated only by a dozen or so small candles flickering at the front of the nave. I watch as he lights a candle and then crosses himself. 'Are you religious?' he asks when he has finished.

I am surprised by his question. I was raised with the typical upbringing of an East Coast reformed Jew: enough Hebrew school to get through a bar mitzvah, then services twice a year on the High Holidays. During my first assignment in Warsaw, I sought out the synagogue and the surviving Jewish community most Friday nights, in part because I was lonely and in part because observing as a Jew there seemed an act of defiance against the Nazis, a sign that they failed to wipe us out. But after I left, I reverted to my secular ways and I haven't been inside a synagogue in years. 'Not really.'

'It's amazing what people have done to each other over their religious beliefs. The Crusades, the Inquisition, the Holocaust.'

'True,' I say, struggling to keep the impatience out of my voice. It was something Jared loved to discuss, too, putting his research of war criminals into a larger historical context. But I was never good at theoretical debates. And I need to know

166

about the Albanian mob, not the history of world religious intolerance.

'How much do you know about the Balkan conflict?' Sebastian asks, looking up at the stained glass above the candles.

I hesitate. The topic seems closer to the Albanians, at least geographically, but I am still not sure where he is going. 'I know about it,' I reply curtly, not wanting to send him into a long-winded discourse on the subject. In truth, not as much as I should. I know that Yugoslavia was created by the Allies after the war, forcing various ethnic groups with centuries of animosity to coexist as one country. That after the fall of communism, some republics, like Croatia and Slovenia, successfully pulled away. But in other places, most notably Bosnia, ethnic conflict escalated to civil war. But the timelines are hazy to me, the events and players a jumble I can never keep straight.

'I was there, in Sarajevo, as a peacekeeper, so-called,' Sebastian says, a somber note creeping into his voice. 'In fact, there was very little we could do except stand by while the various groups killed each other. Imagine it, Jordan.' He turns and looks levelly at me. 'Sarajevo had been an international city of arts and culture, the site of the 1984 Winter Olympics. Less than ten years later, it was reduced to rubble. There were bodies in the street and the people were killing their neighbors, putting each other in camps. It was like Berlin or Munich in the late thirties. But this was the 1990s. We had CNN, television.'

Thirteen years ago in Bosnia, I think, thirteen minutes ago in Darfur. I saw the footage of what happened in Rwanda, glimpsed the violence myself in Liberia. Time hasn't changed the visceral hatred among people, the groups into which we choose to divide ourselves. And despite the awareness brought on by technology, we seem no more willing or able to stop the violence.

Sebastian continues, 'So after the Dayton Accords, the fighting for the most part eventually stopped in Bosnia. But there was another problem: Kosovo.'

'Kosovo just declared independence,' I offer, recalling what I learned from the newspaper on the train.

He nods. 'Kosovo has always been a key piece in the Balkan chess game. It's a province within Serbia, which was one of the Yugoslav republics. But the population is mostly ethnic Albanian with a strong Serb minority.'

Albanians, finally. Now we're getting somewhere. 'During the communist years, Tito suppressed the Serbs because he thought a weaker Serbia meant a stronger Yugoslavia and that empowered the Kosovar Albanians,' he adds. 'But then in the late eighties, Milosevic stirred up the Kosovar Serbs as part of his campaign for power.'

'Interesting,' I say, not entirely meaning it. I sink to the bench in front of the candles, the stone cool beneath my palms. 'But I'm not sure how this ties into our investigation.'

'Have you heard of the Kosovo Liberation Army?'

I shake my head. 'Vaguely.'

'The KLA was a guerrilla movement in Kosovo, ethnic Albanian insurgents who fought against

Serbian control. Originally, it was just a bunch of disorganized rebels scattered throughout the country. But with the chaos in Bosnia and the fall of the communist regime in Albania, they were able to consolidate their operations and amass a fairly staggering cache of weapons.' I follow his movements as he paces in front of me, willing him to get to the point. Reading the file in the vault, I realize, might have been quicker. 'Then in the mid-nineties they made their move, launching an attack on the Serb minority, trying to seize power and gain autonomy for Kosovo. It was another brutal war, thousands of civilians killed.'

'Kind of a second Bosnia,' I observe.

'Exactly.' He stops, turning to me. 'Don't get me wrong: the Serbs fought back and they slaughtered many innocent people, too. No one's hands were clean. But the KLA benefited from NATO air strikes against Serbia, and a considerable amount of support from Washington.'

'I don't understand? Why would we...?'

'Forge a relationship with ruthless killers?' he finishes for me. 'Come on, Jordan, don't be naive.' He's right, I realize. We have a history of supporting questionable insurgent groups when it suits our aims. 'I'm not another Brit beating up on American foreign policy,' he adds, sitting down beside me. 'That would be cliché.' And easy, I think, especially these days. Iraq has made being an American diplomatic representative abroad tougher than ever. 'But sometimes our governments choose the least bad ally and after Bosnia, the West wasn't eager to empower the Serbs, so we forged relationships with the KLA.'

'So then what happened?' I ask, trying to move the story forward.

'After the U.N. came in and settled things down, the KLA effectively ceased its military operations. But many of its members found places in the police forces and provisional administration.' His voice is a low growl now and there is an angry burning in his eyes that makes him even more attractive. 'And the organization itself still had other business enterprises. During the nineties, the KLA had become deeply involved in the black market as a means of raising money for arms: narcotics, human trafficking. Profits from heroin alone financed most of their arms supply. With the war over, they were able to devote all of their resources to these activities.'

Suddenly the connection is clear. 'So the Albanian mob grew out of the KLA?'

He nods. 'Effectively the Vastis of the world are just rebel fighters who graduated to running crime syndicates. The same feudal clans that raised insurgent armies are now sparring over drug turf in Manchester.'

'How did they get to England?' I ask.

He pauses as there is a shuffling sound behind us. A group of older women, their white sneakers and fanny packs screamingly American, fill the entrance to the crypt. A minute later, when they have moved on, he continues, 'They started by achieving dominance over the black market in the Balkans, then spread up through Europe. They largely edged La Cosa Nostra out of the heroin trade in Italy, which is pretty remarkable. Even the Russians are afraid to go up against

170

them for the most part.'

'Why?'

'Because they're ruthless. The Albanian mobsters live by the *kanon*, or code of loyalty, that comes from feudal times. They won't hesitate to kill anyone – mobster, police officer, prosecutor...'

'Government informant,' I add, remembering the photo Mo showed us in the Bubble.

'Even their own family members, if they betray the code. Anyone who gets in their way. So now they control almost all of the illegal transit in Europe and the U.K. Pretty much anything bad that comes into Europe comes through the Albanians. And it goes much further than drugs – weapons, humans–'

'Human trafficking? Here?' I interrupt. I know about slave labor of course. But in my mind that is a problem in the less developed world, workers from impoverished Asian nations taken advantage of as they seek a better life.

He nods. 'With the expansion of the European Union, it's become easier than ever to transit sex workers and other forced labor. They've got operations in Brussels, Amsterdam, London, New York...'

'Why haven't we done more to stop them?' I interrupt, fearing another lecture.

'In the nineties, everyone was focused on getting the cease-fires in place, bringing the Bosnian war criminals to justice. And then since 9/11...' He shrugs, not needing to finish the sentence. Since 9/11, it has been all about Iraq and Afghanistan. 'There's always been a suspected connection between the Albanian mob and some Muslim terrorist groups, money sent back to the Balkans to help various causes. But in recent months, we've picked up chatter that indicates that money from the Albanians is going directly to support al-Qaeda and other major terrorist organizations. Finally, our governments woke up and realized that something had to be done and that is how this task force got funded.'

'But...' My mind races. How could a company like Infodyne possibly be connected to the Albanian mob? And what made Duncan so terrified?

I open my mouth to finish the thought, but before I can speak my cell phone begins to vibrate against my leg. As I reach for it, Sebastian's phone begins to ring, too.

'Shhh!' a docent scolds in a hushed whisper from the entrance to the nave. 'No cell phones!'

Sebastian takes the phone from his belt, silencing it. 'It's Maureen,' he says as he flips it. Mine stops vibrating. 'Hodges. Hi, Mo. Yes, she's here with me now.' He smiles. Then, as he listens, his expression grows serious. 'I see. I'll tell her. Thanks.' He closes the phone. 'We have to get to the embassy right away. Maureen's called an emergency team meeting and she wants to see us immediately.'

chapter TEN

Maureen is already in the Bubble when we arrive, pacing the front of the room. Sophie sits immediately to the left of the head of the table, hands folded. I cross the room to Mo. 'What's going on?'

'Sit down.' I drop into a chair opposite Sophie. 'There's been a slight change to the directives,' Mo says as Sebastian sits beside me. 'We've been ordered to terminate our investigation of Infodyne immediately.'

'What?' I explode, unable to control myself. Beneath the table, Sebastian nudges me with his knee, urging me to stay calm. I swallow, regroup. 'I just met with Duncan Lauder this morning. He seemed nervous. I'm certain he knows something.'

'Jordan, I'm sorry. The order was delivered by Ambassador Raines personally: Infodyne is off-limits. He assured me they've looked into it: the company's clean.'

'Right.' I can hear the sarcasm in my own voice. 'So we stop investigating one of our best leads, just like that?'

Maureen leans across the table, eyeing me levelly. 'Just like that. You'll receive a list shortly detailing the redirected targets.' She picks up her briefcase from the floor. 'That's all for now. Except for you, Weiss,' she adds. 'Come with me.'

I stare after her, dumbfounded. The meeting lasted less than a minute, which was quick, even for Maureen. Why not tell us over the phone? Something doesn't smell right.

I start after Mo, who is already out the door. Sebastian grabs my sleeve as I pass. 'Call me,' he mouths silently. I nod, then race out of the Bubble, struggling to match Mo's long, brisk stride.

I hop into the elevator car as the door is about to close. Expecting to go to her office, I am surprised when she presses the button for the ground level. Her mouth works silently as though chewing on a piece of gum. She has something on her mind, I can tell. Something she did not want to discuss in front of the others.

'Let's take a walk,' she says at last as the doors open. I follow her through the lobby and down to the street. 'Are you hungry?' she asks as we cross the square, not looking at me.

Not really, I think, remembering the hot dog I ate with Sebastian an hour earlier. 'Sure.'

'I thought we'd go for tea.'

'Okay,' I reply, surprised again. Mo seldom breaks for meals when she is working. But I can tell this is not going to be just a social occasion.

She does not speak as she leads me through the well-appointed streets of Mayfair, past several of the smaller embassies, an art gallery that resembles a museum; she dodges the puddles that remain from the earlier rainstorm with surprising agility. A few minutes later, we stop in front of a five-story brick hotel, its grand entrance draped in flags. Claridge's is one of the grandest hotels in

London. Mo means to have Tea, not tea. 'It's the closest place,' she says by way of explanation as we walk up the steps and cross the black-and-white checkered lobby. The atmosphere, heavy with the hush of self-importance, seems too pretentious to be one of Mo's usual haunts. 'And I haven't eaten yet today.'

The waiter ushers us into the Reading Room, an elegant salon with crème walls and dark wood columns. The furniture is done art deco style of the 1930s, chairs covered in a green and beige geometric pattern, square silver lamps on each linen-covered table. When we are seated by the fireplace, the waiter starts to hand us menus with a selection of teas longer than most wine lists, but Mo waves him away. 'English breakfast is fine. I'm sorry about Infodyne,' she says when he has gone.

I hesitate, considering her words. Mo seldom apologizes for anything and I wonder for a moment if she is simply reiterating her order to stop investigating the company. But her voice sounds genuinely regretful. 'Whose call was it?' I ask. 'Ambassador Raines?'

'No,' she says a bit too forcefully, as though trying to convince herself. 'I mean, he's a good foot soldier for the administration, but the directive came from higher up, I'm sure.'

'Do you believe them?' I unfold my napkin. 'That the company's clean?'

'It doesn't matter what I believe. You know how the game is played. We step on the wrong toes, we might get ordered to terminate the whole investigation. Or one of you could get PNG'd.' I raise an eyebrow. *Persona non grata* is the term used to describe a diplomat who has been ordered to leave the country by the host government under threat of having his or her diplomatic immunity revoked and being arrested. It usually arises when someone in the intelligence world is caught spying. People were PNG'd regularly during the Cold War in the Soviet Union and other Eastern Bloc countries. It is no laughing matter, but the notion of it happening today in England is hard to imagine. Something isn't right about any of this.

Maureen continues, 'Kosovo is just such a sensitive topic right now since the province declared independence last month.' I nod, familiar with how the game is played. Balkan experts in Washington and capital cities across the globe scrambling to explain why peace efforts failed, trying to find a justification for why the millions of dollars in aid pumped into the region these past ten years were not in vain. 'Sometimes you have to make choices, Jordan. Punt the ball now so maybe you have time to get it back again and score.' I smile inwardly. For some women, sports analogies are just a way to sound tough and fit in with the guys. But anyone who has ever served with Mo knows she's a diehard Dallas Cowboys fan, talking stats with anyone who will listen. Her annual Super Bowl party is a favorite at every post, as much for the buffalo wings and submarine sandwiches as for the game.

'Anyway, it's out of my hands. Infodyne is off the list.' Maureen stops speaking as the waiter returns, depositing a tiered plate heaped with scones and other pastries. He prepares the tea,

176

pouring hot water over a tiny strainer holding tea leaves, steeping it directly into each cup. I look around for a paper napkin to get rid of my gum. Then, finding none, I dig an old receipt out of my pocket and deposit the gum in it while Mo watches the waiter.

'I hope this all isn't a result of my conversation with Duncan Lauder,' I say after the waiter has gone.

'How did that go?'

'Not well. I mean it was clear that my questions were making him nervous about something. But he clammed up and left before I could learn anything.' I reach for a scone, break it in half, and spread the inside with clotted cream. 'I tried to handle him delicately but I think I may have botched it.'

'I'm sure you did fine,' Mo reassures. 'Actually, Lauder was not the problem.'

'Then what was?'

'Your conversation with Lord Colbert.'

My hand freezes in midair. 'I–I don't understand.'

'You went to Cambridge yesterday, correct?'

Remembering the GPS in my cell phone, I know I cannot lie. 'Yes. If this is about my being out of the office...'

'And you had a conversation with Colbert.' She is not asking a question.

My mind reels. How does she know? And more important, why does she care? I set down the scone and, willing my hand not to shake, pick up my teacup. I take a sip, stalling for time as I try to figure out what is going on, how to best position my answer. 'Yes. Lord Colbert is the head of the college I attended at Cambridge. I saw him at a dinner I attended there.'

'What did you discuss?'

'Just old times,' I reply carefully.

Maureen slams her hand down on the table, sending the dishes rattling. A few of the other patrons glance in our direction, then look away politely once more. The waiter starts to approach. 'Is everything...?'

'We're fine.' Mo raises a hand and he retreats once more. 'Jordan, let's cut the bullshit. Why did you talk about the investigation with Colbert?'

I start to protest, but she interrupts me, her voice low and terse. 'Lord Colbert is a very powerful man. One call from him to the Foreign Office and our investigation gets tanked.'

'Maureen, I'm sorry, but I don't understand. I never mentioned the investigation to Colbert. What does he have to do with any of this?'

'He's on the board of directors of Infodyne.'

'What?' The news slams into my stomach like a rock. 'That's impossible!' But even as I say this, I know that it is not. To the students at college, Lord Colbert was a wizened academic, plodding through the courtyards, attending conferences on linguistics. But beyond that he comes from a wealthy family and holds a seat in the upper house of Parliament. It is entirely possible that he sits on the boards of any number of corporations, including Infodyne, which, as Duncan pointed out earlier this morning, is one of Britain's largest.

'Does that mean you weren't pressing him as

part of the investigation?'

I lean forward, rubbing my hands against my temples, which have begun to throb. 'Like I said, I never even mentioned Infodyne.'

'Then why were you talking to him? And what spooked him?' I open my mouth but before I can speak Maureen raises her hand. 'And don't tell me it was just a social call, or I'll take you off this investigation and bust you down to the visa line for a month.' I look away, uncertain where to begin, how much to tell her. She reaches over and puts her hand on my forearm. 'Jordan, we're friends. We've always trusted each other, sometimes when lives were on the line. I know you and I know something is going on. And I want to help, but I can't do that if you won't level with me.' Looking into her eyes, I feel my insides begin to crumble.

I take a deep breath. 'My conversation with Lord Colbert really had nothing to do with the Infodyne investigation. You know I went to grad school at Cambridge, right?'

Maureen nods, cutting a scone and taking a bite, settling in for a story. 'Ten years ago. That's where you met your friend Sarah, the one who's sick.'

'Yes. And I had a boyfriend there.' The word sounds so inadequate to describe what Jared was to me. 'His name was Jared Short. He died two weeks before graduation.'

She presses her napkin to her lips, leaving a pink stain. 'I'm so sorry. How?'

'Drowned, or so we thought.' There is no point in holding back now. Quickly I tell Maureen about Chris contacting me the night of the Ambassador's reception, our visit to Dr. Peng. 'Jared was dead before he hit the water. Somebody put him there.' It is the first time I have spoken the words to anyone other than Chris – in fact the first time I fully believe them myself – and as they tumble out, I am almost relieved.

'That must have come as quite a shock. And now you want to know who did it.'

'Yes. And why.'

Mo exhales sharply. 'Well, that's quite something. Jordan, this must be incredibly painful for you. It's hard not knowing. But you're trying to solve a murder that happened ten years ago. We're diplomats, not detectives.' I fight the urge to remind her that the lines have never been that clear. 'And you're working on a dangerous, urgent investigation for us. I need your full attention here.'

'I've handled multiple cases before, Maureen. I promise this won't interfere with my work.'

'It already has. Your bothering Lord Colbert drew attention to us, just when we can least afford it.'

But how had Lord Colbert even made the connection between me and Infodyne? I think back to our conversation. I told him that I was a diplomat, nothing more, nothing that should have aroused suspicion. Unless ... could Duncan have somehow spoken to Lord Colbert, warned him about my questions? It seems impossible that there is a connection between the two men, other than their mutual affiliation with Infodyne, or

180

that Colbert could have gotten the investigation stopped so soon after my conversation with Duncan. But it is the only explanation I can come up with.

I turn to Mo, who is watching me expectantly. 'I'm sorry, Mo. We never planned to see Lord Colbert, but when his wife invited us to dine at the Hall, I guess it just seemed like a good opportunity to ask some questions about Jared.' I look down at my teacup. 'But like I said, I never mentioned the company. I don't know how he made the connection.'

'Everything's connected, Jordan, in ways we cannot possibly imagine.' There is a strange undertone to her voice. 'You know I could order you to stop looking into Jared's death.' She raises her hand again before I can speak. 'And I'd be tempted, if I thought it would do any good. But I know you: you're going to do what you want, what you think is right, no matter what.' She smiles. 'Reminds me of me when I was younger. And I would want answers, too, if I were in your shoes.' Her expression turns serious again. 'But I am going to insist that you keep me informed of what you find out. And that you be careful.'

'I will,' I promise. 'Thanks, Maureen.'

'I guess that's it for now.'

I take a last sip of my tea. 'Are you heading back?'

She shakes her head. 'I'm going to have another cup of tea and catch up on some paperwork. I've got a meeting at Whitehall in an hour.' She pulls a file from her briefcase and sets it on the table.

I can tell from her tone that I have been dismissed. Pushing back from the table, I hesitate. 'Mo, I have a question.'

She looks up from her papers. 'Yes?'

'What's the deal with Sophie?'

Maureen's brow wrinkles. 'The deal?'

I shift uncomfortably. 'I mean, why do we have a rookie agent on such an important case?'

'Sophie's smarter than she looks, Jordan. She has a double Ph.D. in international studies and finance and she is fluent in Arabic.'

Impressive, I think, if not particularly relevant here. 'And her father was Albert Morrell,' Mo adds.

'Oh.' Albert Morrell was one of the most distinguished Arabists in the history of the department. He served as ambassador to several Middle Eastern countries, then resigned a few years ago after marrying his second wife, a descendant of the Saudi royal family. 'I didn't make the connection.'

'There was no way you could have. Sophie uses her mother's maiden name.' I understand then Sophie's competitiveness, her overeager demeanor. She's trying to show that she's not just her father's daughter, that she can make it on her own. Perhaps I should try to be nicer to her. Maureen continues, 'You can see where her finance background might be useful when we get deeper into the money laundering piece of this investigation.'

'Sure,' I reply, picturing the girlish blonde. Looks certainly could be deceiving.

Outside the hotel, I retrace the route to the embassy, my mind racing. Colbert is connected to Infodyne. But how did he make the connection between *me* and the company? He knows that I am a diplomat. Nervous from our questions at dinner, he could have called a contact at the Foreign Office for information. But our investigation is classified; it would not have been easy to learn about my assignment, even for a man of his stature. No, something more has to be going on here.

A few minutes later, I step off the elevator onto the third floor of the embassy. The political section is a sea of cubicles, junior officers and secretaries typing away in front of monitors, phones cradled between shoulder and ear. A row of offices, occupied by more senior diplomats, lines the far wall. Mine is a narrow office to the far right, a concession to the privacy my work requires, but small enough not to raise eyebrows among the other officers. The furniture, an old metal desk and cracked vinyl chair, are vintage government issue. A yellow Post-it note is stuck to the bulky computer monitor that predates flat screens. 'In Sophie's office. Come see me when you get back. – S.H.'

I thumb through my office directory and discover that Sophie's office is in the economic section one floor above. When I knock on Sophie's half-open door, Sebastian is sitting alone at her desk, facing away, feet propped on the window ledge. 'You rang?'

'No,' he deadpans. 'I wrote.' He motions with his head for me to close the door. I drop into one of two chairs that sit in front of the desk, looking around. The tiny office is neat, the desktop nearly as bare as my own. But there are the little touches I never remember to bother with: a vase of daisies on the corner of the desk, a framed Matisse print on the wall. 'How was tea?'

I shrug. 'Okay. Another warning to leave Infodyne alone. Not much else. So what's up?'

He holds up a piece of paper and passes it to me. 'We've received the revised list of targets.'

'And...'

'And it's nonsense. There's nothing new that's been added, just the removal of Infodyne. I was able to download some financial data on the company the other day, wire transaction records for the past year.' I cock my head. 'Called in a favor with an old classmate of mine who's in banking and owed me a big favor. Sophie has been running an analysis of the data, looking for patterns.'

'But Maureen just said...'

'Maureen said we had to terminate the official investigation. She didn't say anything about looking around on our own.'

'That's not a valid distinction and you know it.'

'I know that Maureen Martindale is a pit bull. And that, regardless of politics, she wants us to find the company that is laundering for the mob.'

'All right, show me,' I relent, my curiosity winning out.

He stands and gestures for me to come around the desk where a laptop is open. 'Something doesn't add up.'

I take the still warm seat, studying the spreadsheet displayed on the monitor. Sebastian leans over my shoulder, closer than is necessary, the inside of his bicep pressing against my shoulder. 'Infodyne, as you know, is a huge conglomerate. We have to look at the various businesses, try to identify any suspicious patterns to see where there might be layering, or placing of cash that doesn't belong.'

I shake my head, studying the endless columns of figures. It might as well be Latin. 'I don't understand,' I say, turning toward him. Our faces are just inches apart now, his breath warm on my cheek.

He smiles. 'You really were a liberal arts major, weren't you?'

Before I can answer, the door to the office flies inward and Sophie's blond head pops around the corner. 'Sebastian, I...' Then, seeing me, she hesitates. 'Oh, hello.' She clearly expected to find him alone.

Sebastian straightens. 'I was just showing Jordan the financials on Infodyne.' As he pulls away, I exhale. I've really got to get a grip on this. 'It's a little hard to scroll through, though.'

'Maybe this will help,' Sophie replies, passing a sheet of paper across the table. It is easier to comprehend than the data on the computer screen, neat columns of dated transactions, like a bank statement. 'I ran the report through the anti-money-laundering program developed by Treasury, applying a number of different criteria, link analysis, time sequence matching.' I look up at her impressed. I'm not familiar with the technical aspects of money laundering, but I know from departmental cables I've read that the types of programs she's describing are cutting-

185

edge, among the most sophisticated tools our government has at its disposal for this kind of thing. She continues, 'Most of the businesses check out. But there is a subsidiary based in Glasgow, which is supposedly an import-export company. On the surface, the books look legit. There are cash inflows and outflows, payments and accounts receivable.' She pauses to point across the desk to a row of numbers with manicured pink nails. 'But when you run the analysis, there's a series of irregular wire transfers, made from two banks, one in Geneva and one in Dubai, every other week for months.'

'What does that tell us?' I ask.

'On its own, not much.' Sebastian runs his hand through his hair. 'It's possible that those are legitimate transactions.'

'Possible but unlikely,' Sophie adds. 'We need to verify the transactions, find out who the money is coming from, whether actual services were provided for the money paid or if it's all fictitious.'

'How do we do that?'

'Infodyne is publicly traded and there's lots of filings and shareholder information still to dig through,' Sebastian replies. 'And I can circle back with some of my banking contacts too to see if they have anything else. Of course the quickest way would be to get a source on the inside at Infodyne. But I'm not sure that we can do that anymore without triggering attention.'

'And it would help to know the real reason the Infodyne investigation was terminated,' Sophie adds.

'Unfortunately, that's an easy one,' I reply. Quickly I tell them about Jared and my trip to Cambridge. It is the second time in an hour I have recounted the story and the words roll off my tongue more easily now, though my voice still catches whenever I say his name. As I reach the part about his death not being an accident, Sophie's eyes grow large. 'It's all my fault,' I finish. 'I had no idea that Lord Colbert was linked to Infodyne. I don't even know how he knew I was investigating the company.'

'It's spilled milk, Jordan,' Sophie says.

'Nothing to be done about it now,' Sebastian agrees. 'If anything, your conversation with Lord Colbert may have helped us.'

'Helped? I don't understand.'

'The fact that Infodyne was such a hot button with Lord Colbert likely means we're on to something.'

'Infodyne is our most promising possibility. So we...' Sophie hesitates, looking up at Sebastian. 'We think that we should all concentrate on Infodyne.'

We, I think, watching Sophie's cheeks grow pink. Does she have a crush on Sebastian? 'So you intend to go after Infodyne? I mean, the financial analysis is one thing, but you're planning a full investigation, despite a direct order to the contrary from Maureen not an hour ago?'

'Despite that,' Sebastian answers firmly. 'Or maybe because of it. You know Maureen; she would be going after Infodyne herself if she wasn't caught up in the high-level politics. And asking her to give us the go-ahead would only

187

implicate her if anyone found out.'

Sophie leans forward. 'What do you think?'

I look from Sophie to Sebastian, then back again. 'I think it's a bad idea. Crazy even. We'd be violating a direct order.'

'I'm wondering what it is you're afraid of.' Sebastian's words, a challenge, stop me cold. Am I becoming one of those spineless bureaucrats I have always despised, more concerned with procedure and protocol than the mission, too afraid to take risks? If so, it is time to hang it up. Fear is what gets you killed in this business.

'All right, I'm in,' I declare. 'Let's go after Infodyne.'

'I thought you might say that.' Smiling, Sebastian reaches into his desk drawer and pulls out a file. 'I've run profiles on the board and senior officers and other key players at Infodyne. There's nothing obvious on the surface, of course. But Sophie and I will split the list, find out where they came from, run the vulnerability profiles.'

I nod. Vulnerabilities are anything that could make a person an easy target for blackmail or manipulation, such as a drug problem, financial troubles, or secrets he or she did not want revealed. 'And of course we'll keep running down the other companies on the list, to be sure we aren't missing anything,' he adds.

'What do you want me to do?' I ask.

'Get back in touch with Duncan Lauder. Ask him about the wire transfers, see if you can get anything more based on the new information we've obtained.'

188

I agree, though as I picture Duncan's pale, pinched face, I am certain I will get no further. I need to figure out a way, too, that I can reestablish contact without the news getting back to either Maureen or Lord Colbert. But I do not want Sebastian to accuse me once more of being afraid. 'I'll try.'

'We can do this, you guys,' Sophie says. 'I know we can.'

She sounds like a high school coach in a sports movie. But for a second, part of me almost believes her. I stand up. Then, reaching the door, I stop again, turning back. 'Just be careful,' I caution. 'We're going out on a limb here, without departmental knowledge or approval. There's no safety net if anything goes wrong.'

chapter ELEVEN

I shift the grocery bag to one hip and twist the doorknob to Sarah's apartment with my free hand. 'Hello?' Receiving no response, I slip inside and close the door behind me. 'Wait 'til you see what I've...' I pause. The room is empty and nearly dark, except for the computer monitor left on at the desk in the far corner. The smell of unwashed breakfast dishes hangs heavy in the air. 'Sarah, where are you?'

'Here,' comes a muffled voice from the hallway beyond the living room. Alarm rising in me, I drop the bag and race toward the sound. Sarah is

189

lying facedown on the bathroom floor, her legs sprawled out into the hallway.

'Sarah!' My heart stops. Somewhere in the deepest recesses of my mind I know that Sarah's illness is terminal. And I am no stranger to death – I lost Jared, a few colleagues at State. But seeing Sarah like this now, realizing that someday I could find her like this, only gone for good, brings her condition home in a way I am not ready to comprehend.

'What happened?' I ask, moving around the wheelchair that blocks my path. I kneel down and gently grasp her by the shoulders, turning her over. Closer now, there is a sour smell, as though she has soiled herself. 'Are you okay?'

She exhales, brushing her bangs aside with her good hand and gesturing with her head toward the shelf above the sink. 'The nurse forgot to leave my medicine where I could reach it. And silly me, I thought I could manage.'

The nurse only came in the mornings. It is almost seven now. How long has she been lying here? The nagging guilt I've felt for not spending more time with her since arriving breaks wide open. I am, I decide, the worst friend in the world. I pull the wheelchair closer. 'Are you hurt?'

'Just my pride.' She's light as air, I realize, as I lift her back into her chair. I pull the medicine bottle from the shelf above the sink and hand it to her. She gestures toward the toilet with her head. 'If you can give me a minute … and maybe some fresh clothes.'

I walk farther down the hall to where it ends at a small bedroom, just big enough for the twin bed

190

and white dresser. I open the top drawer and pull out fresh underwear, then move down, finding a fresh t-shirt and blue sweatpants in the lower drawers. As I straighten, I notice a small framed photograph amid the clutter of pill bottles and crumpled tissues. Sarah and me in long, flowery dresses. A garden party, I realize, picking it up; one of the rare social occasions when Sarah joined us. We traipsed through town from one college fete to another, drinking Pimm's with lemonade and champagne, basking in the sunlight. I study our bronzed, smiling faces. Could those smiling, healthy girls possibly be us?

Setting the photograph down, I carry the clothes back to the bathroom and hand them to her. 'Can you manage?' She nods and I notice for the first time the thick metal bars fitted at waist height along the walls. She must not have been able to reach them from the floor to pull herself up. For a minute I consider staying with her while she changes but I do not want to insult her pride. 'I'll be just outside.'

'Wait in the living room,' she instructs firmly. I close the door behind me and reluctantly walk away, listening as I retrieve the grocery bag in case she needs help.

'So what did you bring?' Sarah asks brightly, wheeling herself back into the living room a few minutes later. Her face is freshly washed, hair brushed. As if she had not spent the day on the bathroom floor, I think, my heart breaking once more. I walk to the grocery bag, which I'd set on the kitchen counter. 'Well, we can go old school.' Forcing myself to sound cheerful, I hold up a

DVD of *The Princess Bride*. 'Or really old school.' I pull out *Casablanca*. 'We have not one but two bottles of wine. And' – I shake the box or pasta– 'I'm cooking!'

'Pesto?' I nod. 'Ugh!' Sarah groans, then laughs. Pasta with stirred-in pesto was my staple meal at college, and my culinary skills have not improved since. 'Then I definitely need some of that wine before we eat.'

Thirty minutes later I carry two steaming plates of green-colored penne to the living room, the smell of basil and pine nuts tickling my nose. 'So how's the job?' Sarah asks as I set a plate before her, arranging the condiments on the low table so they are within her reach. I refill our wine glasses, then put *Casablanca* in the DVD player and press play. The movie will be nothing more than a backdrop for our conversation, I know. We've both seen it so many times that neither of us will mind.

'Job's fine.' I take a sip of wine, debating how much to say. My instinct has always been to tell Sarah everything, but my assignment is classified and she is still a foreign national. 'Mo's great as ever, though she seems to have a lot on her mind these days. But my team...' Sarah cocks her head as I pause to take a bite of pasta. 'I'm working with a junior officer who looks and acts exactly like Lucy McFadden.' The comparison is probably an unfair one, given what Mo told me earlier about Sophie's credentials, but I know that my reference to the posh, vacuous student whose father sat in Parliament will give Sarah an immediate image. 'Except that it turns out she's annoyingly smart. And a Scottish liaison who thinks he is God's gift. He walks into a room...'

'Looking as though he already shagged everyone in it?' she finishes, taking a bite of pasta.

'Exactly!' It is an old joke between us. My shoulders slacken as I take another sip of wine. It feels good to laugh with Sarah like we did years ago, as if nothing is wrong. But everything is different now. I know then that I have to tell her. 'There's something else.'

Noticing the change in my tone, Sarah's face blanches. It is the look of a woman who has gotten used to bad news, who is bracing herself for the worst. 'What is it?' Her fork hovers midway between her mouth and the plate, trembling.

'Everything's okay,' I reply quickly. 'It's just that I learned some new information about Jared.'

Sarah's brow furrows. 'I don't understand.'

'How he died.' I begin telling her what has happened, more slowly and in greater detail than I had with Mo or the others at work, starting with Chris's note. At the mention of the reporter's name, her mouth puckers slightly. Sarah never liked Chris. She found his brash, energetic style overwhelming – putting them in the same room was like letting a Great Dane puppy run amok in a china shop. 'So I met him for dinner and he told me that he didn't think Jared's death was an accident.'

'What an awful thing to say to you,' she replies quickly, and I can hear the protectiveness in her voice.

'But the thing is.' I pause, setting down my fork. 'I think he could be right.'

193

'Jordie...' Sarah is using her gentle, patient tone, the one she saves for when she thinks I am being foolish.

'No, really. We went to see the coroner at Addenbrooke's and she told us–'

'You went to Cambridge?' she interrupts. 'When?'

'Friday. I meant to tell you when I was here at the weekend.' I stare hard at my plate, feeling strangely defensive. 'Why?'

'No reason.' But her answer comes too quickly, her words pinched. Is she angry? She's jealous, I realize. She never thought I'd go there, but if I did she wanted to be there with me, by my side like she used to be.

'Anyway, the coroner told us...' I swallow, still having trouble saying the words. 'She told us that Jared didn't drown.'

'Didn't drown,' Sarah repeats slowly. 'How is that possible?'

'He was already dead when he hit the water. Chris is convinced that Jared was murdered.'

She takes a small sip of wine. 'And you?'

I hesitate. 'There doesn't seem to be any other explanation. I want there to be, but nothing seems plausible. I'm having a hard time accepting it, though. I mean, I'm not naive, I've seen plenty of death in my line of work. But Jared? Who would want to kill him? That something evil could have happened there, of all places. It's just unbelievable.'

'It wouldn't surprise me,' she replies. I cock my head. 'I'm not talking about Jared, of course,' she adds quickly. 'But at college generally.'

'Really? Foul play at Cambridge?'

'Makes perfect sense. Look, the place has been turning out world leaders, captains of science and industry, for five hundred years. With all that money and power, there's bound to be a few dark secrets.'

'Oh, come on! Maybe some duke put arsenic in some prince's port a million years ago, but murder? In our time?'

'All I'm saying is that I wouldn't be shocked,' she insists.

I take another bit of pasta. 'The Master, it seems, would disagree.'

'Lord Colbert? Is that old bufty still kicking around?'

I nod. 'We went to Formal Hall with him and Lady Anne.'

'Formal Hall? Good God, Jordie, next you're going to tell me you took a spin down the river and played table footie in the bar just for old times sake. You really have jumped back in with both feet, haven't you?'

'No...' I start to protest, then stop, considering. For years I avoided even the slightest thought or mention of Cambridge. Now, back only a few days, I am completely immersed. 'Anyway the Master went apoplectic when we started asking questions about Jared's death.'

'I'm sure he doesn't want you stirring all of that up, tarnishing the college image again. Plus he's probably afraid of what else you might find.'

I open my mouth to tell Sarah the real reason that Lord Colbert was jumpy, then close it again quickly. Infodyne is part of my investigation, off-limits. 'I think my two coworkers have the hots for each other,' I offer instead, changing the subject abruptly.

'The princess and God's gift?'

I nod. 'She was making eyes at him the whole time during our meeting this afternoon. And he didn't seem to mind.'

'Did you?' Sarah asks. 'Mind, I mean?'

'Not at all!' I reply quickly. 'I mean as long as it doesn't interfere with our work...' She shoots me a knowing look. 'No, I'm not jealous of Sophie. Sebastian's attractive and he did kind of hit on me the other night, before I knew we were working together. But he's arrogant and we're on assignment and...' Hearing myself babbling, I stop. 'She can have him. Really. It's just that, I don't know... For the past ten years, being on my own has been normal. Now, being back here...'

'Reminds you of how alone you are?' I do not answer. She continues, 'It's understandable. You deserve someone wonderful.' So do you, I want to add. Sarah has been on her own for as long as I've known her. Once, years ago, she wrote to me about a brief affair with a man in Paris who I suspected was married. But other than that she has always been alone. And now with her illness, her chances of ever having a relationship seem nonexistent. 'What about Chris?' she asks.

'What about him?'

'As a potential someone, I mean. He always adored you.'

'Oh!' The question catches me off guard. 'There's nothing...' I start to protest. Then I stop again. I've seen it in Chris's eyes, the way he

196

watches me when he thinks I am not looking. 'There's always been an attraction between us, I guess. But too much has happened, too many years.' There is an awkward pause. I clear my throat. 'Is the pasta all right?' I ask, gesturing toward Sarah's plate. She has not raised her fork for some time and the penne are practically untouched.

'Very good. But I think I'm finished.'

'You've hardly eaten.'

'I ate,' Sarah protests with a laugh. 'You piled it on. Nobody but you could eat that much.' I smile, looking at my own empty plate. I've always had an enormous appetite for carbs. With my running and constant activity, I can still get away with it for now, but it's going to catch up with me someday.

I look at Sarah again, wondering if the effort of feeding herself is becoming too much. 'Would you like me to help you eat some more?'

'Absolutely not,' she replies firmly. 'I'm full. But it was delicious, really.'

I carry the plates to the kitchen, then fill and turn on the electric kettle, washing the dishes while the water boils. A few minutes later, I return to the living room with two cups of tea and a plate of chocolate-covered HobNob biscuits. I hand Sarah her cup, putting the plate on the low table between us close to where she can reach. Then I sit back down on the sofa, leaning back against the cushion. Onscreen, *Casablanca* has flashed back to Paris on the eve of war, Rick waiting at the train station for an Ilsa who would never show. Star-crossed lovers who met at the wrong

197

time, destined to be pulled apart. At least Ilsa got to see Rick again, even if it was too late for them. I close my eyes, imagining what it would be like to walk into a café and find Jared.

'Hey!' A pillow smacks me in the face. I snap my eyes open and sit up, blinking. 'Wake up, you're snoring!'

'Mmph.' Rubbing my eyes, I lift my head from the sofa cushion. Though it feels as though only a few minutes have passed, the film's ending credits are rolling.

'You never could stay awake through a movie,' Sarah chides. 'Jeez, I'm the one who's supposed to be medicated.'

'It's the wine.' I point to the second, half-empty bottle on the coffee table. 'My tolerance isn't what it used to be.' I stand up unsteadily. 'I'll be right back.' I make my way to the bathroom. At the entrance, I stop, remembering the sight of Sarah lying sprawled on the floor. 'Um, Sar,' I say when I have finished, returning to the living room. I hesitate, taking a deep breath. I am treading on dangerous ground here. 'Do you think maybe it's getting too hard for you to be on your own?'

Her cheeks color. 'I can manage,' she insists. 'I mean, full-time nursing is too expensive. National Health would make me go to a home before they would pay for that, and I don't want some bloody stranger around all of the time anyway.'

'Maybe I could...'

'What, move in here?' She cuts me off, her eyes flashing. 'Play nursemaid to me? Forget it.'

I raise my hand. 'Sarah, please. I didn't mean—'

'Well I do mean it, Jordan. Like I told you

before, I adore you and I'm very glad that you've come to be close to me. But if you're thinking of putting your life on hold to watch me die, you can just hop on the next plane home!'

I stand watching helplessly as she navigates around the furniture and wheels herself down the hall to her bedroom, slamming the door behind her. For a minute I consider going after her and apologizing. But that would just make things worse. She needs a few minutes to cool off. I walk to the back door and step out into the cool night air. The chirping of crickets echoes in the darkness.

There is a gentle buzzing against my leg. My cell phone. I pull it from my pocket. 'Hello?'

'It's me, Chris.'

'Chris! I've been trying to call you. Where have you been?'

'It's a long story but I'm on my way back to London. I need to speak with you.'

'Me too,' I reply, remembering the stolen papers. 'I have to tell you that–'

'Not here,' he says, cutting me off. 'We should talk in person. But I'm still a few hours away.'

Where on earth, I wonder, has he been? 'How about tomorrow after work?'

'There's a pub on the Marylebone High Street, just below Weymouth, called the Spade & Bucket. Can you meet me there at seven tomorrow?'

'See you then.' Closing the phone, I walk back inside. Sarah sits by the desk in the corner. Her face is freshly washed, but there is a tiny streak by her eye where a tear has fallen. 'I'm sorry. I never meant...'

She shakes her head. 'It's not your fault. You were trying to help. I should apologize for snapping. I just get so frustrated sometimes,' she adds, her voice cracking.

I want to tell her that I understand. But how can I possibly know what she is feeling? It was the same when Jared died. She was by my side every moment, but she couldn't go through it for me. I squeeze her shoulder gently. 'Let's just forget about it, okay?'

She nods. 'Who was that on the phone?'

'Chris. He found something but he wants to discuss it in person. I'm going to meet him tomorrow to talk about it.'

As I carry the last of the dishes to the sink and rinse them, Sarah turns on her computer, a laptop plugged into a docking station with a flat screen monitor. 'That's nice,' I remark, drying my hands and walking to the desk.

'I just got it last month. It's my one luxury. This computer is my link to the outside world so I pulled out all the stops. High-speed Internet. Video.'

I think about all of the time I spent trying to reach Sarah by post. She was just a click away the whole time, at least recently. If only I had known. 'Nice.'

'I didn't have this the last time we spoke,' she explains, seeming to read my thoughts. 'And I didn't know your e-mail address.' I start to ask her why she hadn't put her e-mail address in the letter she'd just sent me, but before I can speak, she continues, 'There's a whole international community out there of people who have ALS or

200

other things that limit their mobility,' she adds, a note of pride in her voice. 'Sometimes we chat about research into cures or medicines that help with the symptoms. But we talk about all kinds of other stuff. I'm a bit slow typing. There are voice-activated programs too.' I know she is thinking about the future, when she will no longer have use of her left hand.

'Well I'll leave you to it. Enjoy.' I bend down to kiss her cheek. 'And try to get some rest. I'll call you tomorrow.' I start for the door.

'Jordie?' I turn back. 'Thanks.'

Forty-five minutes later, I climb the steps to my flat and unlock the door. Inside, I walk upstairs into the bathroom and turn the hot water tap of the tub on full blast. Undressing as the tub fills, I think about the investigation once more. We've been pulled off Infodyne, at least officially of course, because of my conversation with Lord Colbert. My mind reels back to the dinner at Formal Hall once more, trying to remember if I said anything that might have made him uneasy. But Chris did most of the talking. Chris. I wonder where he's been, what he's found out about Jared's death. A few days ago, I thought his suspicions about Jared's death were paranoid. Now I want answers, too.

A few minutes later, I step gingerly into the tub, savoring the heat that envelops me. As I lean back, a dark flash on my lower torso catches my eye. I hesitate, fingering the spot above my right hip. I seldom notice the black swan tattoo, no bigger than a silver dollar. Now I press the spot softly, remembering.

201

March 1998

'Damn,' *Chris swears as he bends down and lifts me from the cox's seat. I wrap my arms around his neck, holding tight, shielding myself from the sharp wind that blows off the river. Normally I do not like to be picked up, but the sloping bank of the Thames makes it impossible to pull all the way in as we do on the Cam, so the boys carry me to and from the boat to avoid my having to join them wading calf-deep into the cold, dirty water. He sets me down on land as the others collect the boat. 'That was bloody awful.'*

Teeth chattering, I nod in agreement. The Tideway race proved to be a comedy of errors. The day was bitter and blustery, with gusts of wind that drove the boat nearly sideways, making the twenty-minute course seem twice as long. To make matters worse, Mark insisted on rowing despite a stomach virus and vomited midway through the race. 'Gross!' Nick cried as the sick-tainted water splashed upward. Then, about twenty meters from the finish line, Andy broke the rigger that held his oar in place, making it nearly impossible for him to continue rowing, and we limped through the remainder of the race.

When the boat is put away on the trailer that will carry it back to Cambridge the next morning, we shower and change at the boathouse we've been using during our weeklong stay. Then we migrate to a nearby pub to await the results of the race. 'Fifth!' Chris cries when they are posted, sending up a collective whoop from the boys. Fifth place in the division would normally have been abysmal, but under the circumstances we are just relieved not to

202

have come in last. Fifth means we had real speed, a good deal of precision before the catastrophes set in.

Later, someone suggests food and we make our way to an Indian restaurant we passed earlier on Putney High Street. The wind has settled now, the March air cold and damp after the rain. Seated inside the restaurant, the boys tear into the meal with ravenous, post-race gusto: heaping plates of warm naan bread and papadums, curries of every variety served over steaming jasmine rice, washed down with pints of lager.

Rubbing my nose, still red from the cold, I look down the long table at the boys as they eat, heads down, their seemingly never-ending banter momentarily quieted. At the far end, Jared lifts his head and his eyes catch mine, then dart away once more. My heart quickens. It has been more than three months since the Fairbairn dinner and our conversation on the roof. I did not see him again until I returned in January from the winter break and went to the boathouse for the first time. Part of me expected him to be warmer but in fact he was more aloof than ever. He seems changed in other ways, too, though, not all bad. He yells less at the crew this term, even me. He is still demanding, but I can see him restraining himself as he corrects a point that he thinks should have been obvious, struggling to keep his voice calm. It is as if he took to heart my advice about not scaring the boys.

Forks scrape against plates as the boys finish the last of their meals and the chatter resumes. 'If we did this well on the Thames with a busted rigger, just imagine what we can do in the Bumps,' Nick says.

'If Mark doesn't chunder,' Ewan adds, chiding.

Embarrassed, Mark raises his pint. 'To the Head-

ship!' he proposes loudly. The others hesitate, reluctant to jinx our chances by toasting the ultimate prize.

I clear my throat, wanting to break the awkward silence. Then I raise my mug. 'To the Eight,' I propose instead, saluting the crew rather than the goal. The others lift their glasses, heartily echoing my toast.

'This crew,' Chris says, after the plates have been cleared and another round of lager poured, 'is a crew like no other.'

'We should get a tattoo to commemorate it,' Mark suggests jokingly. A few of the boys laugh.

'He's right.' The group turns in surprise to Jared, who has been silent for most of the evening. 'A tattoo would bind us forever.' No one speaks for several seconds.

'Right now?' Roger asks, blinking through his glasses.

Jared shrugs. 'Why not?'

'All right then.' Chris drains his beer. 'What are we waiting for?'

We make our way outside onto the darkened street, the boys still debating the logistics of getting tattoos. 'I've heard of a place in Fulham,' Nick offers.

As we walk to the bus stop, I hang back, noting how the boys seem to move as a unit, Chris leading at the front, Jared bringing up the rear. A cohesiveness has developed among the crew these past few months. Partly it comes from the hours and hours of training together, the quiet confidence as our speed and strength continue to grow. But it is more than that: freed from Jared's harsh demeanor, the boys have been able to relax and laugh together. One unusually warm day a few weeks ago, we turned up at the boathouse expecting to row as usual. But Jared was

204

waiting on the grassy patch beside the boathouse, holding a rugby ball.

'Agility exercise,' he said, shooting me a knowing look as impromptu teams formed. The boys laughed and joked as they tossed the ball to one another, running and catching, their faces bathed in sunlight. Then Chris bumped into Jared and they fell to the ground, taking two or three other players with them. And though the change had in fact occurred gradually over the term, it seemed as if in that one moment, Jared became one of the crew and the Eight was born.

The bond goes beyond just rowing. They are often seen together at meals, in the bar. It is exactly what needs to happen for us to take the rowing to the next level, to have a shot at winning the Mays. I only hope that it is enough.

We board a night bus for Fulham, sprawling out across the empty seats. As the bus climbs Putney Bridge, my thoughts return to the tattoo. Do they mean for me to get one as well? My parents would be horrified. I toyed with the idea of getting one with my freshman roommate at college, but backed out at the last minute. This is different, though. I have to do it, to cross the divide between coxswain and crew and truly be one of them.

A half hour later, we enter the tattoo parlor on an unmarked side street, a tiny, dark shop run by a man who doesn't have any visible tattoos of his own, but is all too willing to brand nine inebriated people. 'The Boys Are Back in Town' blares from an unseen radio.

'What should we get?' Roger asks as the crew scans the illustrations of dragons and demons that line the shop wall.

'There!' Chris exclaims, pointing to a drawing of a swan. The other boys murmur in agreement.

Inwardly, I recoil. The swans on the river are nasty and terrifying; I don't want one permanently etched on my body. Still, I can understand Chris's choice. Swans represent power, grace. And the drawing is impressive in its detail, the bird poised on its haunches, wings spread.

'I'll go first,' Chris says, unbuttoning his shirt as he steps behind the curtain.

'There's a pub next door.' Simon starts for the door. 'We'll wait for you there.'

'I'm going, too,' says Andy. 'Come get me when it's my turn.' Roger and the others follow him, leaving only Jared and me behind.

I look up at him uneasily. 'You're not going with them?'

He shakes his head. 'Nah, might as well get it over with.'

An awkward silence passes between us. For a minute I consider going to the pub, rather than being alone here with Jared. But the other boys are already gone, their laughter fading down the street. Jared drops into one of the plastic chairs, picking up a copy of the Financial Times that has been left on a low table. I study his face, and want to say something to break the tension between us, to get back to the place we were on the roof that night, but I cannot. Instead, I turn and study the drawings of tattoos on the walls.

A short while later, Chris emerges. 'It wasn't bad. I've already paid for everyone,' he adds as he exits the shop. 'My treat.'

'Okay, who's next?' the man behind the curtain calls.

Jared and I look at one another. 'I'll go,' he offers.

'Want me to hold your hand?' I whisper jokingly. But Jared nods, his face solemn. He's nervous, I realize, surprised. I follow him behind the curtain. As Jared pulls his shirt over his head, I cannot help but notice his muscular torso, the way it tapers before disappearing into his jeans. I've seen him this way at the boathouse, of course, walking around as all the boys do between the erg machines and the showers in various states of half-dress. But close now, an unfamiliar twinge of longing pulls at my stomach.

Jared climbs onto the table and lies facedown. 'Here?' the man asks, touching the spot on the back of Jared's right shoulder that Chris chose. He nods and the man transfers the swan design from a piece of paper onto Jared's skin. I position myself on the low stool that sits at the head of the table. Jared takes my hand, his large, calloused fingers interlaced with my own. His grip tightens as the man brings the tattoo gun to his skin. His face remains expressionless, his eyes locked on mine. Out of the corner of my eye, I see a thread of blood running down his shoulder to the table.

'Not bad,' he remarks, rising stiffly from the table when it is done. But his complexion is pale. 'You don't have to do this, Jo.'

Jo, I think, feeling my cheeks grow warm. It is the first time anyone has called me that. 'I know.' I sit down. The table is still warm where he laid. 'I would like it to be very small,' I say to the man, holding my fingers about an inch apart. 'Here.' I pat the space just inside my right hip.

'Do you want me to leave?' Jared asks as I unbutton my jeans. I shake my head, lying back and pulling

207

my pants down just below my pelvis on one side, exposing a fine strip of pink lace underwear. Jared's breath catches slightly behind me. As the tattoo gun presses down on my skin, I close my eyes and reach behind my head, gripping Jared's forearm hard.

Thirty minutes later, we step out from behind the curtain. Roger, who has come back from the pub, sits in the waiting room. 'The others are locked in,' he reports. Some pubs lock the doors at the legally required closing time, letting patrons already inside remain and continue drinking. 'But we ran into some guys from Downing and they invited us to a party at the Tideway Scullers. We'll probably head there when we're all finished.'

'Good luck, pal,' Jared adds, clapping Roger on the back before we leave the shop.

Outside, the air has grown colder, the March night still belonging to winter, not spring. Zipping my coat, I look both ways down the street, which is deserted except for two men emerging from a kebab shop on the opposite corner. 'It's late.'

'I'm not sure I feel like going to the party,' Jared replies. 'But it's not as though we have a choice.'

I nod. We cannot get into the pub and neither of us has the key to the flat where the crew is staying.

We hail a taxi at the corner and I slide across the backseat. Jared climbs in behind me, giving the driver the address for the party. As I sit back, something brushes against my shoulder. I look up. It is Jared's arm, draped above me I expect him to pull back but he stares out the window, not seeming to notice.

The party is in full swing when we arrive, music blaring from the second story of the boathouse. The large common room is crowded with male and female

208

rowers, talking and drinking from plastic cups of beer. We pass the makeshift dance floor to the corner where people cluster around a keg. Jared emerges from the crowd a minute later, holding two plastic cups above his head to keep from being jostled. 'Come on.'

We step through an open doorway onto the balcony. It is deserted, owing to a sharp breeze that gusts off the river. I pull my jacket closer around me. 'Do you want to go back inside?' he asks.

I shake my head. 'It feels good.' We move toward a corner of the balcony away from the doors. 'Not as quiet as the chapel roof,' I add. 'But considerably less scary.'

He looks away, not answering. He's embarrassed about that night, I realize. I understand then why he has been so aloof. It is as though he regrets letting his guard down, as if the intimacy of our conversation somehow showed weakness.

'Are you upset about the race?' I ask finally, changing the subject.

'Not at all. A bad race can be just as useful as a good one, maybe more so. You know what I mean?'

I do. Learning how to handle disasters in a race, how to keep going no matter what, is as important a skill as any for the Eight to develop. 'We're still a long way from there, though,' he adds, before I can reply. 'I mean, this was only a head race. But in the Bumps...' He does not need to finish the sentence. Today was simply a timed head race, just us against the clock. It did not have the distractions of a boat beside us, as would be the case in a side-by-side regatta, or worse yet, the panic of being chased by another crew in the Bumps.

I nod. 'They've really come on, though, haven't they?'

'We're as cohesive as any crew I've seen,' he agrees. 'You were right, you know, about what you told me that night on the roof. I needed to relax a little to let them bond.' His eyes meet mine now, locking in. 'You're much better, too, in case I haven't told you, Jo. The way you handle them has really made a difference.'

Jo again. A lump forms in my throat, making it difficult to speak. 'Th–thanks,' I manage at last. 'I guess we each learned something from the other.'

He does not answer, but leans toward me. He is going to kiss me, I realize, and a split second later, before I have time to finish the thought, to decide whether or not I want him to, his lips are on mine, full and warm. I am paralyzed. Warmth surges through me and then I am kissing him back hard. His mouth opens, drawing me deeper. A second later we break apart. What just happened?

Jared looks away, breathing hard, not meeting my eyes. He stands and starts for the door and for a moment I think he means to leave me. 'Come on,' he says abruptly, his voice gruff. Not turning around, he reaches back for my hand and leads me inside, through the crowds toward the exit.

Outside we stop, hesitating, unsure where to go. I hear laughter coming from the darkened road. I look desperately over my shoulder. I do not want to see anyone else, not now. 'Here,' I whisper, pulling Jared around the side of the boathouse, opening the door to the bays where the shells are kept. Inside the air is damp, the scent of wood and turpentine familiar.

Jared reaches for me, his lips finding mine again in the darkness, feverish and more demanding as he guides me backward past the boat racks. He presses *me up against the concrete wall, running his hands hungrily down my body, never breaking from our kiss. I wrap my arms around him, drawing him close, heedless of the dull ache at the site of my tattoo and the pain I might be causing as I grasp his shoulders. This is different, I think. Normally sex moves slowly at college, with making out the norm, intercourse the eventual exception. But I know from the way he lifts my shirt that there will be no courting in stages with us. It will be everything, here and now. I unbutton his pants, push them down.*

'Are you sure?' he asks breathlessly between kisses. 'It's so cold here, so dirty.'

'I don't care,' I reply, drawing his mouth to mine once more. His questions silenced, he lifts me up and I wrap my legs around his waist, not caring who hears as I cry out in the darkness.

chapter TWELVE

I walk into my office, looking at my watch as I flip the switch to the laptop I was issued earlier today. It is after five o'clock and I still have not had the chance to call Duncan. I planned to reach out to him first thing this morning but I arrived this morning to find a junior officer from political named Bryce waiting to shepherd me through all of the embassy in-processing I'd managed to avoid until then. Not bothering to hide his lack of enthusiasm for the task, he led me from one bureaucratic office to another, where I was given

211

forms to complete, enabling me to get my permanent identification badge, my laptop. Then I'd spent the rest of the day making the required courtesy calls on the heads of various sections of the embassy, a series of ten-minute meetings scheduled by Amelia that consisted of little more than where-have-you-served-oh-really-do-you-know-so-and-so. The political counselor, Bill Wright, an ambitious and prematurely bald man in his forties, was particularly icy, resentful of the fact that I'd been seated in his section for appearance's sake when in fact I work directly for Mo.

I pick up the phone now and dial Duncan's office number. But the phone rings three times, goes into his voice mail. He must be gone for the day. I could call his cell, I remember. But I don't want to risk alarming him. Better to wait and try again tomorrow. I turn to the laptop that sits in the docking station. The scratched cover makes clear that it has been used before, but I can tell from the initial scans that are running down the screen that it has been updated to meet agency encryption security requirements. I log in, and when desktop comes up, click on the e-mail icon. I scroll through the junk mail, a welcome message from the commissary, a reminder from the regional security officer about keeping laptops secure. Halfway down the in-box, I spot a message from Sebastian. Easy, I think, as a jolt of excitement runs through me. He is just a colleague; you've made that clear. I click on the message. 'Found this after we spoke. S.' it reads.

I open the attachment, a report from a United

Nations human rights committee on the trafficking of women. I skim through the pro forma language about commitment to human rights, the statistics about trafficking. At the back there are several addenda, handwritten sheets in a language I do not recognize. Behind is a typed translation. 'Statement of Anna B. from Pristina,' the heading reads. There is a photograph of a young woman, but her face has been blurred so it is not recognizable. The translation reads:

It was a morning in August 1996, I don't remember the date. We were just preparing to leave for school when the men broke through our door. I was in the toilet and they did not see me but I could hear most of what they were saying. I thought they were soldiers at first but I did not recognize their uniforms. Five, maybe six men. They accused father of being a spy for the government and they did not believe him when he said he was only a librarian. They shot him in the kitchen and my brother too as he tried to flee. My mother ran to my brother screaming and I was certain they would shoot her too, but they pushed her down on the bloody floor between them and they each raped her. Then they cut her throat with a knife. They set our house on fire, but I was able to escape after they had gone...

I pause, bile rising in my throat. I had some idea of what happened in the Balkans, of course, even before Sebastian explained the details today. But the war coverage had focused on the politics of ethnic separation, the bombings that destroyed ancient bridges and buildings. It was not until

213

years later that we would hear about the geno-
cide, the rapes, and by then I was halfway around
the world, working for the government, fighting
injustice in other places. But now, sitting here
again, I cannot avoid the truth – the slaughter
had taken place while I played at Cambridge, a
few hours' plane ride away. What was I doing
when Anna's family was destroyed?

Guilt rises up in me. Growing up Jewish, the
lessons of the Holocaust were deeply imbedded in
my consciousness. 'Never again' was a familiar
refrain. My parents, though not religious, saw this
as their personal mandate. They had marched
with the civil rights movement in the South in
their younger years, protested on behalf of the
Soviet Jews not permitted to emigrate during
communism. Social justice, my father told me
once at Passover, was our obligation as Jews, to
free all people from the bonds of oppression as we
had once been freed. But we are still failing.

I look at the screen again, scrolling to the second page and forcing myself to continue reading.
Anna recounts how she was taken by the soldiers
to a camp, locked up in a shed with a half-dozen
other girls, and raped several times a day. She
was luckier, she said, than some. The girls who
became diseased were taken outside and shot.

*After the war, when the soldiers had fled, men from
the Liberation Army freed us from the camp. They told
us that once the U.N. came we would be forced to go
back to our villages. But we had nothing to go back
to; our families were dead, our homes destroyed. The
people who were left would be no help, the men said.*

They would blame us for sleeping with the enemy, collaborating willingly. They would let us starve in the street, if they did not kill us themselves. We had nowhere to go. The men said they would help us leave, get to the west. They got us passports and visas, arranged passage in a lorry. They said the trip cost five hundred dollars and that we could pay it back when we got there by working.

I thought they meant working in a restaurant or cleaning houses. But we were forced to go on dates with men, to have sex with them for money. I was one of the lucky ones – I was allowed to meet the men in a bar and sometimes they would buy me a drink or meal before taking me to a room or car to be alone. Others, like my friend Olga, had to work on the street corner all night, no matter how cold or rainy the weather. There were a lot of men, sometimes five or six each night. Some hurt us as much as the soldiers in the camp. We were only allowed a few hours' rest before we had to work again, even if we were sick.

Anna's statement ends abruptly. The report goes on to describe how, once they arrived, the women's passports were taken and they were charged exorbitant fees for shelter and food so that their debts grew and they could not leave. When the police broke up the prostitution ring, they found Anna in a room in Manchester with a dozen other girls, sleeping on the floor, two and three to a mattress. The door was padlocked from the outside. Two of the five girls Anna traveled to England with were dead, Olga from illness and malnutrition, another girl strangled by a 'client.'

I scroll back to the front page. The data at the

top indicates that Anna was born June 8, 1981. She would be almost twenty-seven now. Where is she? How did she manage to go on? I want to imagine that, liberated from prostitution, she was able to start a new life, find a job or maybe even go to school. But the government has limited resources for supporting the women they rescue, and Anna, on her own with little or no money or skills, with no resources, would likely be forced to return to the streets.

I close the screen, not wanting to read the reports of other girls that surely follow. Would Anna and the others have been better off staying in their homeland? The problem is larger than Bosnia, I know – it is the human desire to escape suffering, to strive for a better life, which creates the very conditions that the mob needs to exploit people. These are the people we are trying to stop. This is not the busy work I anticipated when I asked for London to be near Sarah. This is real. Then again, I hadn't expected to be confronted by the cold reality of my college boyfriend's murder, either. Overwhelmed, I turn off the computer and walk out of the office.

I take the elevator to the ground floor. As I start across the lobby, I see Maureen in the far right corner, engrossed in conversation with a man I do not recognize. She is holding an open file, pointing to something. I take a step toward her, trying to catch her eye, but she does not look up or notice me. I hang back, several feet, so as not to appear to be eavesdropping. A few minutes later, she shakes hands with the man, who starts for the front door.

'Hi, Mo,' I say, walking toward her.

She blinks, as though surprised to see me, then closes the file and tucks it under her arm. Is there something, I wonder, that she doesn't want me to see? 'Jordan, how's it going?'

'Fine.' I hesitate, wanting to update her on my investigation into Jared's death, all that Chris and I have learned, to show her that it isn't a waste of time. But this is not the place. 'Just heading out.'

'You've started on the redirected targets?'

'Yes,' I say, feeling instantly guilty at the lie.

'Good.' She smiles, but her expression is strained. Is it our investigation or something else that is stressing her? 'Let's catch up tomorrow.' Before I can speak further, she turns and heads for the elevators.

Outside, I make my way across Grosvenor Square. The air is warmer than it has been since I arrived, the setting sun peeking determinedly through a layer of clouds. A few minutes later I reach Oxford Street, weaving my way through the sidewalks packed thick with the tourists and shoppers who spill out of the department stores.

I cross the busy intersection and pass Selfridges, turn onto a smaller street that continues north. The crowds begin to thin, the commercial stores giving way to trendy boutiques and sidewalk cafés, high-end restaurants and wine bars. The atmosphere, almost festive, is a jarring contrast to the dire report of Anna B. I've just read. This is a London she and the other girls have likely never known.

Soon I reach Marylebone High Street, spot the Spade & Bucket not far up on the left. It is more restaurant than pub, the walls painted a pleasant shade of cream, large potted plants in subtly lit corners of the room. Chalkboards over the bar boast an extensive wine list and a menu of fresh, healthy dishes. Gastro pubs, I read in the airplane magazine, are very much the fashion, replacing many of the old fish-and-chips establishments in the upscale neighborhoods. Here the trend seems a popular one; patrons overflow the bar, cluster around standing tables. Through a window at the back of the pub, I can make out a small garden, equally as crowded.

A moment later, Chris bursts through the double doors of the pub. 'There you are!' he exclaims, sounding as if I, and not he, had just arrived. He would not, I decide, make a good undercover operative. He hugs me hard, as though it has been years, not days, since our last meeting. Then he turns abruptly, crossing the room in two strides and claiming a table as its occupants stand to leave. 'Come on.' He waves me over.

As we sit, I notice him taking in my black V-necked sweater and slim khaki pants. I study his face, my conversation with Sarah fresh in my mind. Am I attracted to Chris? He's certainly handsome in that broad-shouldered, athletic/military way that I've been drawn to in recent years, perhaps because it is the furthest thing from Jared's dark, brooding style...

A waitress approaches, jarring me from my thoughts. 'Wine?' Chris asks.

'Sure,' I blurt, hoping he has not noticed me looking at him.

'I've got a lot to tell you,' Chris begins after the

waitress has brought our drinks, a pint of Guinness for him and a glass of pinot noir for me.

'Me too. I've been trying to reach you.' His brow furrows as I tell him about the coroner's report being stolen. 'I know you gave it to me for safekeeping. I'm sorry.'

He cocks his head. 'That's strange. At least it was just a copy. Dr. Peng said she would get the original from the archives, anyway. The one that has the photos. I'm just sorry I put you in danger.'

'Danger? What do you mean?'

'Someone came after you to steal the report. I worry what might have happened if you'd woken up.'

'That's a little dramatic, don't you think?'

'Did they take anything else?' I hesitate. He is right, of course. A thief would have taken my wallet, my gun. 'Someone didn't want us to have proof that Jared's death wasn't an accident,' he adds.

I shake my head. 'Nothing we can do about it now. So what did you find out?'

Chris swallows a large mouthful of beer. 'I went back to the Porter's Lodge and spoke with Peter Mason.'

I smile, remembering the elderly head porter who seemed to have been there as long as the college. 'I'm surprised he would talk to you. I would have thought the Master would have warned him not to.'

'Peter's an old mate of mine. I used to bring him whiskey and we would watch telly together sometimes when he was on the late shift.' I look at him, surprised. I had not imagined Chris, posh and self-important, spending time with the college staff. Then again, he was always very social and would have done anything to delay going home alone at the end of the night. He continues, 'Anyway, I got to him after our dinner at the Hall, before the Master had a chance to speak with him.'

'So what did he say?'

'I asked him if he remembered anything unusual about the time around when Jared died. He had to think about it for a while. I guess ten years is a long time, even for something like that. The only thing he recalled was that a package was delivered to the Porter's Lodge for Jared shortly before he died.'

'So? That could have been a lot of things, even a care package from his mother.'

Chris shakes his head. 'A week before the end of term? Not likely. Anyway, Peter remembered this package in particular because it didn't come in the post. It was hand-delivered by a man in a suit.'

'Oh!' I feel as though I'd been pricked by a pin. I remember seeing such a man from a distance, talking to Jared in the car park. He was older, ill-fitting among the flannel-and-jean clad students, too formally dressed to be one of the academic fellows. Later, when I asked Jared, he was evasive. Something to do with the teaching position he'd been offered for the following year, he said. It seemed strange at the time, but I didn't push. There were so many little things that I swept under the rug, wanting to enjoy our days together

220

before my departure without incident.

'What is it?' Chris asks.

'It's just that...'

Suddenly there is a hand on my shoulder. I look up. Standing there, balancing two pints, is Sebastian. 'Good evening.'

'Oh hello,' I say, surprised. My stomach flutters involuntarily. 'Funny meeting you here.'

'I'm just meeting a friend for a drink.' He gestures with his head across the bar. 'Saw you and thought I'd say hi.'

I scan the room, wondering if he is with Sophie or another woman. But my view is obscured by the crowd. 'Sebastian, this is my friend Chris Bannister. We went to college together. Chris, Sebastian Hodges is a colleague of mine.'

Chris nods. They do not shake hands, but eye each other coldly. Ironic, I think. The two men Sarah suggested I might like, just an hour earlier. They are completely different, yet both attractive in their own ways. 'Well,' Sebastian says, after an awkward pause. 'I'd best be getting back. Enjoy your evening. See you in the office, Jordan.'

'That wasn't very friendly of you,' I say to Chris when Sebastian is out of earshot. 'What's wrong?'

Chris shrugs, turning back to his drink. 'Nothing. I just don't like the look of the chap is all.'

There is more to it than that, I decide, studying his face. It is not like Chris to be so rude. Perhaps he is jealous. 'So Peter told you that Jared received a package,' I say, changing the subject.

He looks over his shoulder once more, then clears his throat. 'You know, maybe we shouldn't be discussing this here.' I look at him, puzzled. No one is going to hear us in the crowded, noisy room. 'I mean, after what happened to you on the train ... well, you just never know who's around. My flat is just a few blocks away. Why don't we continue our conversation there?'

I hesitate uncertainly. I was alone with Chris dozens of times at college, of course, drinking and watching movies or playing cards in one of our rooms late into the night. But things are different now. It's been years, and Sarah's question an hour earlier about his possible interest burns fresh in my mind. 'Oh, come on,' he persists. 'I won't bite. And there's something I want to show you.'

He's right. I'm being silly. 'Okay, let's go.'

Outside, it is dark now, the air a few degrees cooler than it was earlier but still pleasantly mild. I follow Chris as he continues north along the High Street until we reach Marylebone Road. Traffic whizzes endlessly in both directions along the wide thoroughfare until a minute later, the light changes and the cars and buses stop to let us through. At the corner, a homeless woman sits on the ground, begging for change. I study her, newly aware. How did she come to be here? Was Anna B. on a corner like this somewhere? I reach in my pocket, pull out a five-pound note, and hand it to the woman.

Chris leads me down a smaller street and the traffic and commotion fade behind us. 'So after I left Cambridge, I drove to Wales and visited with Jared's mum,' he continues in a low voice as we walk. 'His dad passed away several years ago.'

'Oh.' I hadn't known. I always imagined Jared's parents as they were years ago, the one time I met them at college. His father was a tall, quiet man, a retired laborer with thick, calloused hands. His mother, a tiny, wizened woman, was born in the same seaside cottage where she raised her only son, not leaving the hamlet more than a handful of times in her life. I remember how they eyed the college buildings fearfully, as though they might be asked to leave at any moment, painfully aware they did not belong.

'I hope you don't mind that I didn't ask you to come with me. I know it's hard for you to get away from work,' he adds.

'Sure,' I reply. But Chris is being polite. He knew Jared's mother would speak more freely with him alone. She eyed me suspiciously when we met: I was an outsider, the woman who threatened to take her boy away. I was relieved when his parents didn't come down to college for the memorial service and I was not forced to face her. No, I am glad not to have joined Chris on his trip. But part of me wishes I could have gone to see Jared's childhood home, touched the earth that was so much a part of who he was.

He stops in front of a row house and opens the door. Inside is a well-kept foyer, print rug on hardwood floor, a low table with a vase of daffodils. 'After you,' he says, gesturing for me to go first up the stairs. 'I've got the top floor, I'm afraid.'

I start forward. Three steps up, I stop again. 'Okay, but first I need to ask you something. I ran into Duncan Lauder.' It seems ironic, lying to

Chris about the circumstances of my meeting with Duncan, even as I am asking him for the truth. But I cannot tell him about my work, any more than I could Sarah. 'He mentioned that you asked him about Jared. Why didn't you tell me you met with him?'

Chris hesitates, considering the question. 'I don't know,' he replies, his voice sincere. 'It didn't seem important.'

'How so?'

'Well, I tried to do some background checking before we met. I wanted to make sure I had as much information about Jared's death as possible to convince you that I wasn't totally crazy in what I was trying to do. Jared mentioned Duncan a few times at college; they consulted on a project or something. So I spoke with Duncan, but he didn't really have anything of value to offer. I didn't mention it because it seemed inconsequential.'

'Oh.' I study his face. My work has made me an expert in when people are lying, but Chris doesn't sound the slightest bit defensive and his explanation makes sense. I am suddenly embarrassed at how suspicious I must have sounded. 'Okay. Just wanted to know.' I continue up the flight of stairs, then another. At the top, I step aside to let Chris unlock the door.

'Welcome to Chez Christopher,' he says, flicking a light switch then gesturing grandly with his arm.

'Very nice.' The loft-style flat occupies the entire length of the building, unbroken except for the slight indentation where a wall had been torn down between two previously separate rooms or apartments. The decor is modern and sleek. Dark hardwood floors have been buffed to a glossy finish and recessed lighting gives the room a soft glow. A wall of exposed brick, freshly restored, runs the length of the flat.

Chris gestures to a sitting area at the center of the room, low, futon-style couches around a metal and glass coffee table. 'Have a seat. I'll get drinks,' he says as he walks to a kitchen with stainless-steel appliances and dark granite countertops at the front end of the flat. I drop to one of the cushionless orange sofas, still taking in the apartment. The walls are adorned with black-and-white photographs, done by a well-known artist whose name I cannot remember, a framed poster marking an exhibition at the Tate Modern. The apartment is well put together, a decorator's showcase. But something is missing: there is nothing personal here, nothing of Chris. I remember then the photographs from college I'd seen during my visits to Sarah's. How is it that Chris, so obsessed with the past, has no mementos of it?

'What do you think?' he asks as he crosses the flat and sets down a bottle of red wine and two glasses on the coffee table. His expression is hopeful, a little boy eager to please.

'It's beautiful.'

His face breaks into a wide smile. 'My sister's a decorator so she did it up for me. Lots of my own things are still in storage, though, from when I was overseas.'

So that explains the lack of photos, I think,

chiding myself for again being suspicious. 'I hear you on that. My whole life is in my parents' attic.'

He sits down beside me, then gestures with his head toward the rear of the flat. 'Sorry about the mess. The housekeeper doesn't come until Friday.' I notice then for the first time a wide, unmade futon bed, clothes strewn across it. The disarray is somehow comforting, proof that he didn't plan to have me back here.

He pours the wine and hands me a glass. 'Cheers.'

I clink my glass to his, then take a sip. 'Mmm,' I sigh, savoring the rich, full flavor. Even my unrefined palate can tell the difference between this and the glass I just had at the pub. 'You always could pick them.'

Chris laughs. 'Wine, at least. Seriously, I'm glad you like it. It's the last of a limited vintage I brought back from Jo'burg last autumn.'

'Oh.' The mention of South Africa reminds me of Sarah. I picture her lying on the floor, her expression of wounded pride.

'What is it?'

'Nothing. So tell me.' I cross my legs. 'What did Jared's mother have to say?'

'She was surprised to see me, of course, but glad.' I nod, imagining her initial suspicion melting to Chris's charm. 'She wanted to know why I was there, asking questions about Jared.'

'What did you tell her?'

'The truth, more or less. I didn't go into the whole business with Dr. Peng. There's no reason to hurt her with that, at least not until we know more. But I told her that I had questions about

Jared's death, that I thought there were some things that were never fully explained.'

'How did she take it?'

'That was the strange part. I thought she would be surprised, and maybe upset. But she wasn't; she seemed almost relieved. She said she had questions, too. She hadn't brought them up all these years because she didn't know how or to whom, and who would listen to a grieving old lady anyway? But she was glad someone was asking.'

'Questions?' I ask, draining my wineglass.

'Well for one thing, she wanted to know why they wouldn't let the family bring Jared home to be buried.'

'What?' I set the glass down on the coffee table, harder than I intended, missing the coaster. 'The Master said that Jared's parents wanted him to be buried at college.'

'Apparently not,' Chris replies, refilling my glass. 'According to Mrs. Short, the college told her it was some sort of tradition for students who died at college to be buried there.'

A tradition of one, I think as I take another sip of wine, picturing Jared's lone grave by the river. Maybe she misunderstood. 'That's bizarre.'

'And it gets stranger. Mrs. Short said that it was Lord Colbert who told her about the burial spot when he called to break the news that Jared died.'

My hand, still clutching the wineglass, freezes in midair. 'But he told us–'

'That he was out of town the night of Jared's death.' I rub my temples. 'None of this makes any sense.'

'It does if Lord Colbert has something to hide.'

If he didn't want us to think he was around that night. A Cambridge interment would have meant Jared could be buried quickly, without being examined by a coroner in Wales. I exhale slowly, trying to calm the thoughts that are spinning through my brain. 'I think we're getting ahead of ourselves here. 'What else did she have to say?'

'Nothing else about his burial. But there was one other thing. She said that Jared called her a few days before he died.'

'So?'

'Normally they spoke only on Sundays.' I nod. Jared and I would sometimes go to the pay phone beneath the bar after Sunday lunch, each of us waiting while the other called home. 'But according to his mum, he called the house that Tuesday, asking to speak with his father, who was out fishing. So he asked her instead.'

'Asked for what?'

'Money. He wanted her to wire him money.'

'Oh.' This surprises me more than anything else. Jared never seemed short on cash. He was on scholarship and received a stipend. It wasn't a lot, but enough to cover our meager expenses, the occasional pizza, a bottle of wine for Formal Hall. 'How much did he ask for?'

'She didn't say exactly, but it sounded like a lot. Whatever she could send. Or in her words, enough 'to clean out her whole biscuit tin.'

My stomach twists. Jared's parents were not rich people. He told me once how his mother took in odd laundry and sewing jobs when he was a boy to supplement his father's income. I always sensed a certain guilt he felt at his living among so much Cambridge grandeur while his parents worked hard to stay afloat. He was determined to make it through university on his own and to start helping them as soon as he was earning an income. He never would have asked for their help, unless it was an emergency. 'He didn't say why he needed it?'

'No.'

'That doesn't sound like Jared.'

'I know,' Chris replies. 'But she didn't seem to know any more, so I didn't press. Anyway, after Jared's death, the college sent home a trunk of his papers and belongings. She showed them to me.'

'Did you go through them?'

Chris shakes his head. 'Better. I convinced her to let me borrow them.' He reaches around the back of the sofa and lugs a medium-sized steamer trunk into view.

'Chris, how did you...?' I stand up and walk around the coffee table, approaching the trunk from the opposite end. Kneeling in front of it, I run my hand along the dusty oak lid, remembering. Jared's trunk, the one he tucked away in his closet at college. 'I'm surprised she let you take it.'

'Promised her I would bring them back personally next week and stay for a visit. The poor dear is starved for company, I think.' A wave of guilt washes over me when I think of Jared's mother, alone in her tiny cottage with only her memories. I could have written, sent a Christmas card. But part of me feared her, thought that she blamed me somehow for her son's death.

Slowly, ceremoniously, Chris opens the lid. Inside sit two piles of neatly stacked papers, a nest of folded clothing beneath. It is meticulous, as if Jared had arranged the trunk himself. 'Have you gone through them yet?' I ask as he lifts the stacks of papers from the trunk.

He shakes his head. 'I just got back an hour ago and I called you right away.'

I lean over, reaching into the trunk and pulling out a jacket. It is a red and black splash top, one of the nylon and fleece pullovers worn by rowers everywhere. But it is too small for Jared. Mine, I realize, sinking from the sofa to the floor. I bring the jacket to my face, inhaling the mixture of sweat and dirty river water, preserved ten years in this crypt. 'I must have left this in his room.' I lost the jacket, or thought I did, sometime in the middle of the May term. Now I wonder if Jared kept it purposely, wanting to have a part of me near him after I was gone.

I set down the top beside me on the floor, then reach inside the trunk once more and pull out a large blue shirt. It is the one Jared wore the night of the Tideway, I remember instantly. The night of our first kiss. I shake it out. A small bloodstain still marks the shoulder where he got the tattoo. I lift it to my nose, inhaling. The room blurs and for a minute I am in the galley of the boathouse on the Thames, the concrete damp and hard beneath me, my head buried in Jared's neck.

Chris clears his throat. My vision clears. He has looked up from the papers and is watching me. An expression I cannot decipher crosses his face. 'Mrs. Short wouldn't mind if you keep that, I'm sure,' he says gently. I do not answer. He lifts some of the papers from his lap and holds them out. 'Here, let's divide these up.'

Reluctantly, I set down the shirt and take the stack from him. Jared kept everything, it seems: college bills, invitations to parties, notes people left for him in his pigeonhole. A paper narrative of his life at college. I rifle through each one, scanning it quickly as I would an investigation file at work, parsing through the needless bits, looking for kernels of information. But it is mostly routine, notes sent to him about rowing practice, plans for the weekend. I thumb farther down the stack. A piece of paper, folded, heavier cream-colored stock, catches my eye. I open it. 'Memorandum of Understanding' the heading reads. It is a letter agreement; Jared's signature and another I do not recognize at the bottom. 'Chris, what do you make of this?'

He takes the paper from me, his eyes darting from side to side as he reads. 'This has to do with Jared's scholarship. It was privately underwritten by the MacLeod Foundation out of New York. Apparently, they paid for his tuition and provided a stipend.'

'I don't understand.' I take the paper back from him, processing. I knew Jared had a scholarship, of course; but I always assumed it was just from the university. Why would an American foundation fund his studies? Suddenly he is a stranger to me. We were together such a short time. Despite our instant closeness, there is much about him I do not know. I pick up Jared's shirt again, clutching it as though it might contain answers.

'Look,' Chris says a moment later. I set the shirt and paper aside and turn to find him holding a racing number from the Nottingham Regatta, a race that I had long forgotten. 'It's funny, isn't it? Jared was so terse and practical. You wouldn't have thought him nostalgic. But he kept everything. These papers are like a documentary of our time at college.'

'Yes.' I reply, wishing that I kept something. I planned to keep it all of course, the invitations, the notes, every little scrap of paper. But that was before.

I look down at the papers in my lap once more. Another thick crème piece of paper catches my eye. I pull it out quickly, wondering if it will shed more light on Jared's scholarship. But it is a piece of stationery. 'Vincci Via Hotel,' it reads across the top. Beneath is a street address in Madrid. Perhaps Jared was there on holiday before he knew me. The thought sends a small stab through my stomach. Like most people, I think little of life beyond the immediate place where I am. I picture Jared's life as the single year that I knew him. It hurts to remember that I missed most of the years that he was alive, to acknowledge that there were vacations and lovers and laughter that came before me.

I scan the paper. Written in Jared's chaotic scrawl are some unintelligible notes, a phone number. He'd scribbled at the bottom, 'M.J.A., Trin.H. #3' and beneath it the numbers '3284'. There is a date in the upper right-hand corner: May 10, 1998. A chill shoots up my spine. We'd been together then. Perhaps the stationery was old, a piece of paper he brought back from vacation and later grabbed from a drawer to write something in haste. He left Cambridge for a conference one weekend that spring, through I don't recall, or hadn't known, where. London, I assumed. But it could have been abroad.

I hold up the paper. 'Hey, what do you make of this?'

His brow furrows. 'Don't know. Might be nothing, scrap of paper from an old holiday.'

'Maybe.' I start to return the paper to the stack. But my hand lingers on it, not wanting to let go of something that was written by Jared, touched by him. 'Mind if I keep it?'

'No worries. I don't think Jared's mum will notice.'

I turn back to the stack once more. Farther down there is a clump of papers, stapled together. I pull them out. They are photocopies of a document of some kind written in Arabic. 'Check this out.' I pass them to him.

Scanning them, he shrugs. 'Looks like research of some kind.'

'But Jared was studying war criminals in Europe,' I press. 'And he certainly didn't speak Arabic.'

'No clue.'

'Can I take these, too? I can have them translated by someone at the department.'

He nods. I take the documents back and tuck them in my bag, then turn back to the stack of papers. My vision blurs slightly and I blink, realizing how dry and heavy my eyes have become. I glance at the clock on the wall. It is after eleven.

'It's late,' I say. 'I had no idea.'

He looks up reluctantly. 'We can keep going tomorrow if you want.' He starts to set the papers back in the trunk. 'What's this?' I lean over. Wedged in the base of the trunk, nearly obscured by a pair of faded jeans, is an envelope bearing a red-and-blue pattern. He tugs, pulling it out. Closer now, I recognize the design as British Airways.

'Probably some ticket stubs from an old vacation,' I reply, wondering if it is Jared's ticket to Madrid.

Chris, who has opened the envelope, hands it to me. 'I don't think so.' Inside is an unused plane ticket, the detachable kind the airlines issued before e-tickets. I unfold the itinerary that is stapled to the top of ticket. A nonstop flight, Gatwick to Rio de Janeiro. The departure date is July 1, 1998, just a few weeks after Jared died. 'Maybe he had vacation plans for the summer...' But even as I say it, I know that this is not the answer. Jared would not have gone away like that, not without telling me.

Chris shakes his head, then points to the top of the page. Number of travelers: two. 'Jared wasn't traveling alone.'

I thumb quickly down to the second page of the tickets. 'Oh my God,' I gasp, seeing my own name.

'He was planning on taking you with him.' Chris's voice is grim. 'And Jordie ... these tickets are one-way. 'Wherever he was taking you, the two of you weren't coming back.'

chapter THIRTEEN

I stare silently at the tickets for several seconds. 'I don't understand,' I say at last.

'He never mentioned anything to you? Did you two have vacation plans after term ended?' I shake my head. 'Maybe it was a surprise,' Chris persists.

'Impossible. I was scheduled to move back to America that week and Jared knew it.' I rifle through the envelope the tickets came in and pull out a small receipt. 'He paid cash for these.'

'Maybe he didn't want anyone to know where you were going.'

'But if that was the case, why would he have used our real names?' Chris shrugs, not answering. 'I guess that's why he asked his mother for money,' I add.

'Not likely,' he replies, leaning over my shoulder. 'Look here.' He points to the purchase date, May 18. 'He bought the tickets almost a month before he called home for the cash.'

But only a few days after he returned from Madrid, I think, remembering the hotel stationery. My mind reels back to the last semester at Cambridge. There was a sense of desperation in our final month together. 'Come away with me,' Jared often said, closing his eyes and pointing to a faraway corner of a map that hung over his desk. I assumed it was just his way of saying that he didn't want our time together to end, that running away was a metaphor for escaping our inevitable separation, for not letting circumstance tear us apart. I didn't realize that he actually might have meant it.

Chris takes the tickets from me and sets them aside. 'Well, let's keep looking tomorrow. Maybe we'll find something else that will explain the trip.'

Reluctantly, I pick up the stack of papers I'd been searching and start to put them back into the trunk, still thinking about the tickets to Rio. My hand catches on something thick in the middle of the stack. 'Oh,' I say, pulling out a photograph. It is a picture I took of the Eight playing rugby on the grassy patch beside the boathouse that March day when Jared turned up with the ball. I always had my camera with me in those days, never wanting to miss capturing a moment. When was the last time I'd taken a picture, I wonder now? I run my finger over their smiling, carefree faces. A month later, Jared would be dead and the Eight would be broken forever. In that moment, though, we were eternally young and happy.

Chris leans over to examine the picture, his breath warm on my cheek. 'I'd almost forgotten that day.'

'Me too.' Tears well up in my eyes too quickly to blink them back.

'Don't,' he says, leaping up. 'Let me get you a tissue.' He never could handle sadness, I think as he disappears into the bathroom. A moment later he returns, looking sheepish. 'No tissues. I think I have a towel somewhere...'

I shake my head. 'It's all right. I'm sorry,' I say, wiping my eyes with my sleeve as he drops to the floor beside me. 'It's just that...'

'I know.' He reaches out and wraps his arm around my shoulders. Gratefully, I close my eyes and let him draw me in close. His warm, musky scent reminds me of college and the boathouse, of the last time I felt happy and safe, and for a moment it is as if Jared is holding me, stroking my hair. But Jared is dead and none of these things – not his clothes nor his papers, nor the embrace of his best friend – can change that. They just make the loss more real. Suddenly I am falling into a bottomless well of grief, the pain is as raw and fresh as if he died yesterday. This is what I dreaded most about coming back again, what I spent a decade trying to outrun. I cry harder now into the front of Chris's shirt, not caring whether he minds.

A few minutes later my sobs subside. 'I'm sorry,' I say, struggling to catch my breath.

Chris does not answer. I look up. He is staring at me intensely, his face just inches above mine. Then he reaches down, cupping my face, brushing the wetness from my cheeks with his thumbs. A strange expression, one that I have not seen in years, crosses his face. 'Jordie...'

'Chris,' I say, but before I can speak further, he brings his lips down hard on mine. I freeze, caught off guard. I never meant for this. But the warmth feels good, his touch a welcome respite from all of the worry and hurt. I am kissing him back now, reaching for anything to push away the pain.

My mind reels back to the May Ball and a kiss that never should have happened, one that sealed all of our fates. *Don't*, I think, forcing the image from my mind. This is not that kiss. We are not those children. Heat rises in me, eclipsing memory, as Chris presses me back against the floor, cushioning me with one arm, unbuttoning my blouse with the other. My gun, I think, as his hands run down my torso, before I remember I'm not carrying it today. I look up at him, a thousand conflicting feelings running through my mind. We should stop, and talk about what is happening between us. But Chris's eyes are closed and as his hands travel beneath my hips, I close my eyes, yielding to his touch. I reach up, clasping his shoulders, running my hands down the rippled muscles of his back. Then I climb on top of him, tearing at his jeans, choosing to ride, rather than fight, the waves of desire that crash down upon me.

Afterward, I roll to one side, closing my eyes. 'Did I hurt you?' Chris asks, still cradling the back of my neck, holding me close. I shake my head. He kisses my eyelids, my cheeks. There is a reverence to his touch that tells me all I ever wondered about his feelings for me, his un-requited love.

I shift and feel something beneath me. Jared's shirt. A cold tide of regret washes over me. I should have stopped things before they went this far. Ten years ago I would have stopped things, knowing that it was wrong. Ten years ago I *did* stop things. But now it is too late. Chris is mov-ing lower, his kisses tracing a path from my neck, down my still half-buttoned shirt to my stomach. For him, this is just beginning.

My stomach twists. I pull away, sitting up. 'I should go.'

His face falls. 'You're leaving? After what just happened, I thought...'

Then I understand. To me this was an impulse, a way to dull the pain. But this is something he's always wanted, a dream come true. I turn to face him. 'Chris, we can't do this.'

He smiles. 'I think we just did.'

'Seriously.' I pull up my pants. 'You know what I mean.'

His cheeks flush. 'Why not?' he demands, un-accustomed to not getting his own way.

For about a thousand reasons, I think. Exhaustion overwhelms me. I should set this straight, but I know how stubborn Chris can be and I cannot handle a long debate right now. 'Look, I'm sorry. I'm just tired and I have a super-early morning for work. Let's talk about this later, okay?'

'No worries,' he replies quickly, mistaking post-ponement for acquiescence. 'Maybe when you come back to finish going through the trunk tomorrow...'

'Okay,' I agree, standing up, eager to leave. I look down at the splash top and blue shirt that still lie beside the trunk. I hesitate. Is it weird to ask the man I've just slept with for a memento of my dead ex-boyfriend? 'Is it still okay if I take those?'

But Chris nods quickly, giving no indication that he finds my request strange. 'We found some great stuff in this trunk and we're making real progress,' he says eagerly, following me to the door. He looks as happy and relaxed as I have seen him, the Chris of college days. He thinks we are going to be together now. 'If we walk to the corner, there's a taxi stand...'

'I can manage, thanks.' He leans down and, before I can react, kisses me long and full on the lips. I break away gently. 'I'll talk to you tomorrow.'

On the street, I pause to catch my breath, then walk to the corner and climb in the first of two awaiting taxicabs. What just happened, I wonder? As the car winds through the darkened streets, I think back to the moment before our kiss. Did I do something to invite it? And why didn't I stop him? On some level, it felt right – I was always attracted to Chris – never with the passion I'd felt for Jared but the kind of base-level attraction women feel watching David Beckham or George Clooney. It was, I decide, a physical need, intensified by the emotions brought on by Jared's belongings.

But for Chris it was more than that. I see his face the moment before we kissed, the burning intensity in his eyes. It was a look I recognized from years ago, something I had not wanted to acknowledge since coming back. His feelings are not in the past. And now I've stirred those emotions, toyed with them. He looked so hurt when I left abruptly.

My thoughts shift to Jared and the plane tickets. Why didn't he tell me of his plans for us? And why Rio? Our talks of fantasy vacations centered around Africa or Greece and the Mediterranean. We never discussed South America. Rio was a huge, teeming city, not at all the outdoorsy kind of trip we would have planned. The millions of people would have made it easy to get lost in the crowd.

I reach in my bag and pull out the plane tickets. Jared purchased them just days after the Madrid conference. Something happened there, something that made him want to flee and take me with him.

Duncan said something about Madrid, I remember. Maybe he knows something about what happened to make Jared want to run. I promised Sebastian and Sophie that I'd contact Duncan again anyway to ask about the financial documents. I've already jeopardized our investigation once by asking the wrong questions about Jared. Do I dare risk it again? But as I clutch the plane tickets in my hands, my resolve grows. My gut tells me that whatever happened at Madrid is linked to Jared's death. It is worth taking the chance.

Twenty minutes later, I unlock the door to my flat and walk upstairs. I am exhausted but cannot bring myself to climb into bed like this, so I go to the bathroom and turn on the shower full blast. I stand under the hot spray for several minutes, not thinking, numb, then scrub myself everywhere, as if trying to wash away what just happened. Then I collapse in bed, still damp and naked but for a towel. I fall asleep quickly, clutching Jared's shirt in my arms.

Some time later, I awake. The bedroom is still

dark, but I can tell from the rumble of a garbage truck on the street below that it is almost dawn. My head is thick from too much wine and my muscles are strangely sore, an ache like after a workout but in all the wrong places. Chris, I think, feeling the hardness of the wood floor beneath me, his weight above. Jesus. What have I done?

Unable to lie still with my thoughts any longer, I roll over and sit up. Five forty the clock on the nightstand reads. I am dying to call Duncan to ask about Madrid, but it is too early. I walk to the bathroom and brush my teeth. My own reflection stares back recriminating, eyes puffy, cheeks red and scratched from Chris's stubble. I eye the shower. A run first, I decide, splashing water on my face instead. I need to sweat this out. Five minutes later, after changing into navy sweatpants and a long-sleeved white t-shirt, I lock the apartment door behind me and jog down the stairs onto the street.

The morning air is brisk and cool, the pavement still damp as though it has rained overnight. Forcing my eyes from the river, I turn and start running toward Hammersmith Bridge, past a row of narrow houses that back up to the river. The uneven dirt surface is reassuringly solid under my feet. Chris's face appears in my mind and I push it away. No thinking during the first five minutes of a run; that is the rule. The houses on my right begin to thin, giving way to unkempt parkland.

I reach the base of Hammersmith Bridge and begin to climb, passing a few other runners,

242

some early morning pedestrians walking dogs. My blood pumps more quickly. I can feel my legs begin to lose their stiffness, my head begin to clear. Through the fog that hangs low above the water, I make out an eight, chopping their way through a warm-up exercise.

The bridge begins to slope downward and a few minutes later I reach the far bank. I hesitate. Going to the left will take me toward Putney Bridge, enabling me to run home in one continuous loop. But it will take me past the boathouses and I cannot face that, not today. Instead I turn right toward Barnes. Here the bank is less developed, the deserted path lined with sparse trees and brush. The fog is thicker now, obscuring the road ahead. A bird chirping mingles with the pounding of my footsteps, our chorus breaking the early morning silence.

I run harder now, a thin layer of sweat beginning to form beneath my sports bra. Chris's face reappears in my mind. Five minutes are up; I have no excuse for avoiding the thought any longer. For me, last night was a physical need, born out of the grief of digging into the past. And it was over for me the minute it happened. My curiosity satisfied, any questions about an ongoing relationship seem ridiculous, moot.

But this was not some casual encounter for Chris; to him it really meant something. And he thinks it is going to continue. He did not want a one-night stand. He wants me. I have to talk to him, today. To set him straight that we cannot – will not – be more than friends. It will not be an easy conversation. I adore Chris and the thought of hurting him is more than I can bear.

Apprehension wells up in me. I hate conversations like this. I had them with Mike several times during my months in Washington. He didn't understand why I did not want to meet his parents, was so hurt when I refused to discuss the future. With Jared it was different – our commitment just was, like our breathing, present without conversation since the day we first kissed.

Suddenly there is a sharp scuffling sound behind me. I stop running, spin around. The fog has closed in, shrouding the path, making it impossible to see more than a few feet in the distance. Uneasiness rises in me. I snap my head from side to side, trying vainly to see the riverbank, the hidden trees.

'Hello?' I call aloud, my voice fading into the mist. There is no response. My skin prickles. Another runner perhaps, but I have not seen one since crossing the river. I remember the train ride back from Cambridge, how the papers disappeared from my bag. Have I been followed?

My hand rises instinctively to my waist but closes around air. Damn, I've left my gun at the flat. Despite Maureen's warning, I didn't think I'd need it, not here. Hearing another crackling sound, I jump. The noise comes from ahead of me now, but it is more muted, farther away. Probably just a squirrel. I shake my shoulders, trying to cast off the chill. There's no one here. I am not reassured. The instinct of knowing when I am being watched is one that I have honed well in this line of work, and I am seldom mistaken. Casting a final glance into the thick fog in front of me, I turn and run swiftly toward home.

April 1998

As we pedal along the road that leads out of Cambridge, the colleges recede behind us and the town noises fade. The road narrows to a single lane in each direction. The fens, their spring grasses still ascending to lush, stretch endlessly on either side, broken only by the occasional house or farmer's shed. A few wisps of feathery cloud mar the bright azure sky.

Ahead, Jared cycles with long, sure strokes. My own movements are short and jerky, my balance uncertain. The muscles above each of my knees, unaccustomed to this form of work, burn in protest. The faint perspiration beneath my shirt begins to pool, trickling down my sides.

Jared. I watch his shoulders beneath his t-shirt as they flex and work, warmth growing inside me. It has been more than a month since the night of the Tideway. Afterward, as we lay breathless and intertwined on the cold concrete boathouse floor, I wondered what just happened. Nothing, I told myself quickly. Cambridge, perhaps even more so than American universities, was a place for hooking up, lots of young people with too much alcohol and time on their hands living in close quarters. So people did – a lot – though most of it was just snogging, groping after a drunken night. It seldom went as far as we had. And afterward, the parties almost invariably went their separate ways.

The dampness of the boathouse reached me then and I shivered. 'You okay?' Jared asked, drawing me closer and pulling his coat around my naked shoulders.

245

I noticed for the first time his hand buried in my hair. 'My tattoo is a little sore, but—'

'I mean okay with this.' He cut me off and there was an urgency to his voice.

'Sure,' I shrugged. 'Just surprised, I guess.'

'Really?' he asked. 'I'm not. I think it's been building since the night of the boat club dinner. Maybe before. Not that I planned this,' he added defensively.

I laughed. 'I thought the cold damp boathouse floor was an unusual seduction technique.'

But he did not rise to my teasing. 'I tried to avoid it in fact. For the sake of the Eight.'

So that was why he was so aloof these past few months. 'You're cold,' he said, his tone growing concerned. 'We should go.' But instead we drew our bodies closer, neither rising. The movement stirred desire in me again, deeper than I had ever felt. I ran my hand down his hip and, finding him ready, rolled on top of him, moaning as we moved in perfect rhythm once more.

Afterward we lay in the darkness, fingers laced, listening to voices outside as the last of the partygoers made their way down the steps and past the door, finding their way home. I do not remember who spoke first, but soon we were talking in low whispers. Jared told me about his family in Wales and I discovered that we were both only children. I told him a few things about my parents and our home in Vermont, but mostly I listened as he talked about his years at school, trialing for the national rowing squad. His words came out in a tumble, any hint of his usual terseness gone. It was as if he'd had no one to speak with in years.

At some point I noticed faint light peeking beneath

the boathouse door. 'Morning?' I asked with disbelief, pulling away and standing up.

'Only just.' He sat up, pulling his shirt over his head. 'And don't forget we didn't get to the party until late. But we should get back if...' He did not finish the thought. I knew he meant if we wanted to sneak back into the flat without being seen and facing the questions our absence all night would bring from the other boys.

Later that morning I left for spring break, slipping from the flat before anyone else awoke, and caught a cab to Heathrow. The next two weeks were agony – I milled around my parents' house in Vermont, trying to act as though I was glad to be there. But in my head, I played the night in the boathouse over and over, wondering how things would be with Jared when I returned to college. Would things return to normal, as though our night had never happened? And, more important, what did I want? My mind whirled, trying to reconcile the man I disliked for so long with the one who clung to me as we talked in the darkness, who brought me to places physically I hadn't known existed. It was hard to picture being with him but impossible to imagine coming back from where we had been.

When I returned to England after break, I did not go back to college, but instead took the train west for another rowing camp. The name was a misnomer – the crew went away, not to the woods, but to the home of one of the boys, someone whose parents lived by a river and didn't mind having nine students sleep on their floors, throw wet rowing clothes over their heaters, and cook fantastically large meals in their kitchen. This time it was Andy's house, a spacious

247

home on the sprawling hills of Herefordshire. We rowed three times a day on the River Wye, narrow and calm like the Cam. The less crowded water gave us the chance to row for long stretches without interruption, though I had to navigate around the rocks and shallow bits. In between, we returned to the house, where the boys ate, napped, and nursed their blistered hands as they watched football on television.

I arrived at camp to find the boys unloading the boat from a trailer. Through the others' greetings, my eyes found Jared, who worked on assembling a rigger on the boat several feet away. He did not look up. So that's it, I thought, my heart sinking. He did not speak to me that first day as we rowed, nor over dinner at a local pub. I begged off early, claiming jet lag, and retired to the narrow single bed, surrounded by the boys' sleeping bags. Alone, I could not contain my disappointment: Jared was acting as though nothing happened between us.

In the middle of the night, I woke and felt something slip into my hand. Fingers, I realized, opening my eyes. Jared's fingers. He was sleeping on the floor beside my bed, his hand clasping mine. The next morning he was gone and I wondered if I had imagined it. But that night, his hand found mine again in sleep.

A week later camp ended and we made our way back across the Midlands to college. As I unpacked, my mind reeled back to Jared. What was happening between us? Other than his holding my hand at night, there was no acknowledgment of anything between us; in fact, we had barely spoken. I fought the urge to go to his room, to knock on his door and demand answers, to throw myself in his arms. My insides ached with longing. Then, taking a look at my disheveled appearance, I thought better of it and fell into bed.

Sometime later, I was awakened by a strange noise. It's just the wind, I thought. Branches scraping against the side of the house. But beneath the scratching came another sound, a rapping noise once, then again. I walked to the window as another pebble bounced against the glass. Below, Jared's face looked up hopefully in the moonlight. I did not bother to open the window but raced downstairs and flung open the door. Jared wrapped his arms around me as he stepped into the house. Wordlessly, he swept me up and carried me up the narrow staircase into my room, closing the door with his foot and in that moment all of my questions about what would happen between us were answered.

The days since then have been the happiest I have known. I turned in my thesis just before spring break and so there is little for me to do but wait. I fill my days with novels I always wanted to read, sunning myself on the edge of the cricket pitch, with visits to friends for tea and a game of Scrabble or gin rummy. Of course with the Bumps just two months away, the crew is more intense than ever. We row in the evenings now, meeting at six, then making our way quickly down to the lock. There, instead of turning back, we pull into the bank. The boys remove their blades from the gates and set them down in the grass, then lift the boat from the river and carry it in their stocking feet around to the other side of the lock, navigating the steeper bank. The extra work is well worth it. There the water is calm and still, the silence broken only by the occasional geese or a fisherman on the shore and the rhythmic catch of the blades as they slice into the water, accelerate and break free.

Jared sits in the five seat now, farther back in the boat. He said it was to give bow four a better rhythm to follow. In truth I know it is for his benefit and mine, to keep him farther away from me now that we are lovers. Even with the additional distance, his presence makes it hard for me to concentrate. Occasionally his eyes flicker in my direction. There is no smile, no change of expression, but in the deepness of his eyes I can see everything – his assessment of how well the outing is going, his preoccupation to get back to the library and finish up the section of his dissertation he has been working on. His desire for me. Then his eyes flick away, so quickly I wonder if I might have imagined it all.

I watch his back now as he turns from the main road, then slows down, coasting to a stop as we near the American cemetery at Madingley. We set our bikes down in the grass, then walk toward the platform beneath the American flag. TO YOU FROM FAILING HANDS WE THROW THE TORCH – BE YOURS TO HOLD IT HIGH, reads the inscription at the base of the flag pole, taken from the poem 'In Flanders Fields.' Behind it, thousands of small white crosses fan out in arched rows, the spokes of a wheel.

We walk toward the Memorial Wall, which lines one side of the cemetery. I look up at Jared. His Adam's apple bobs slightly as he studies the names etched in stone. The trip was my idea – the cemetery was one of the places I wanted to see before… Before. My imminent departure is always hanging out there unspoken between us. The great irony is that we found each other just months before I will graduate and return to

America for good.

I step up beside Jared and slip my hand in his. I was surprised when he agreed to my suggestion to take the bike ride. I'd hesitated in suggesting it, knowing that it would mean time away from his work. He has been at it nonstop, finishing research even as he writes up his dissertation. Each night after Boatie Hall, the late dinner for the crews that row in the evening, Jared returns to the library above First Court instead of joining the rest of us in the bar. When the bar closes, I go home alone, knowing that he will slip in beside me late, his body cool from the night air. He rouses me from sleep with cajoling hands, stirring my desire. But in the mornings I awaken in the mornings to find him gone, returned to his research, the rumpled bed beside me the only evidence that he was not a dream.

He turns and gestures now across the fields to the clouds that have gathered above the trees. 'We should go.'

We wheel the bikes to the entrance of the cemetery before climbing on. At the junction with the main road, he does not turn back toward Cambridge but continues south. He is heading to Grantchester, I surmise in the easy unspoken way that has developed between us in the short time we have been together. The small village, immortalized by the poet Rupert Brooke, is another place I mentioned wanting to see.

It does not matter where we are going, I think. I am content to follow and enjoy the timelessness of this Sunday afternoon, the rare opportunity to be alone together. Not that our relationship has been a problem for the crew. After we returned from camp, Jared and I kept things secret for several days, leaving the bar separately at night and then meeting in one of our

251

rooms shortly thereafter, sneaking out before dawn. It was as if we wanted to nurture our newfound relationship, savor it privately, before exposing it to the scrutiny of others. Then, one night, as if by unspoken agreement that we could hold back no longer, we walked into the bar hand in hand. I held my breath, worried about what the Eight might think, the effect that it might have on the cohesiveness of the crew. But they have been silently accepting, even if surprised at the couple they could have least predicted. Except for Chris. He has been distant, sitting as far from me as he can at Boatie Hall, not laughing or joking in the boat. He is angry with me, I think. Chris adored Jared, idolized him, and I committed the ultimate betrayal by taking his friend away.

My thoughts are interrupted as thick rain begins to fall, drops pelting hard through my cotton shirt. 'There's shelter just ahead,' Jared calls over his shoulder, going faster, and I stand against my pedals, breathing hard, struggling to keep up. Around the next curve we reach a crumbling pile of stone. It is the ruins of a chapel, I realize as we drop our bikes and run toward it. Though the roof is nearly gone, thick trees bow overhead, forming a canopy of leaves. The air is heavy with the smell of wet earth and stone.

Jared spreads his jacket out on the ground and I sit down, accepting the water bottle he offers. He drops beside me and pulls from his backpack snacks I hadn't known he'd brought; nuts and cheese, apples and grapes. Neither of us speaks as we eat.

The rain falls heavier now, parting the leaves above, sending a spray of drops down on us. 'Sorry about this,' he says, as though personally responsible for the storm. 'We could have made a dash for Grantchester.

But I was worried about the road getting slippery. I didn't want one of us to fall.' He of course means me, the weaker rider.

I notice him staring at me. 'What?' I ask, aware of the water as it seeps through my t-shirt, mats my hair to my head.

He does not answer but leans in and kisses me with wet lips, long and deep. His hands are icy on my damp skin, the air cold as he lifts my shirt from my head. I wrap my arms around him for warmth. He draws me closer, lifting me into his lap, and I pull his pants down, straddling him and drawing him inside me, burying my nose in his dark, wet curls.

Afterward, as the waves of desire ebb, I shiver, wrapped in Jared's coat and arms. The rain has stopped, I notice for the first time, except for the drops that pour down upon us when the breeze blows, shaking the trees.

A minute later he clears his throat. 'We should get back. Get out of these wet clothes.'

I gesture to my jeans, still bunched around one of my ankles. 'I think we just did. Get out of them, I mean.'

He smiles patiently at my joke. 'I mean before we catch a chill. Neither of us can afford to get sick now. We'll come to Grantchester another day.' But some deep part of me knows that we never will, that I have traveled as far down this road as I ever will and that we will not come this way again. It is the same sense I have had every day as my time at college winds down, watching a movie of myself doing things for the last time. Even our fledgling relationship is heavy with the irony that each day together is another day closer to when we will part.

'I love you,' I say then, not caring that I am saying

253

it first, or whether it is wrong or right or too soon. There is no such thing as too soon when time is running out. My words echo unanswered through the stillness of the churchyard. 'I love you,' I repeat. He draws me close once more, and as he buries his head in my neck, I feel a hot wetness against my skin and realize that he is crying.

chapter FOURTEEN

The earlier fog has lifted as I cross Grosvenor Square, the morning sun burning off the last of the dampness. Birds call to each other from the trees that line the path as if proclaiming the chance for a real spring day. My sweater, short-sleeved and pink, overlaps the matching floral skirt, concealing the gun I've secured neatly beneath.

As a clock in the distance chimes eight, I pull my phone from my bag, then hesitate. I want to call Duncan as soon as possible, but using a cell that Maureen can trace is just bad business. Instead I hurry to the red phone booth at the corner and fish some coins from my pocket, then pull the folder with the Infodyne papers from my bag. I decide to try his mobile first; he may be more comfortable if he, too, is not speaking from his work phone. I dial the number I scribbled down on the train, waiting for the ring. But instead there is a click and the phone goes right to voice mail.

Quickly I scan the paper and dial the main number for Infodyne, following the automated instructions that lead to an alphabetical voice directory. I punch in the letters of Duncan's last name. 'There is no name recognized,' a recording announces brightly. 'Please try again.' I carefully respell Duncan's name into the keypad. 'No name recognized. Please hold for assistance.' Damn these systems, I think as I am transferred. They never work as they should. A moment later, a live woman's voice comes on the line. 'Infodyne, how can I help you?'

'Duncan Lauder, please.' There is a pause, fingers clicking on a keyboard.

'I'm sorry, there's no one listed by that name.'

'L-A-U-D-E-R,' I spell impatiently. 'He works in finance.'

Another pause. 'We do not have an employee by that name.'

'There must be some mistake,' I insist. 'I spoke with him a few days ago at this number.'

'Let me check the paper directory in case there's a problem with the computer,' the woman offers. There is a thump, followed by low, muffled voices. 'I'm sorry, nothing.'

'When was your paper directory last updated?'

'Three months ago.'

I grip the phone harder. 'Would you please transfer me to someone in the Finance Department?'

The operator puts me on hold and background music begins to play. 'Maria Jones,' a different woman's voice, lower this time, answers a few seconds later.

I take a deep breath. 'Hello, I'm hoping you can help me. I'm trying to find the direct extension for Duncan Lauder.' There is silence on the other end. 'Hello?'

'There's no one here by that name,' the woman replies flatly.

'But there has to be!' I splutter. 'I don't understand. I spoke with him just a few days ago. I called his voice mail yesterday!'

'There's no one here by that name,' the woman repeats. 'You must be mistaken.'

'Did he quit?' I demand, my voice rising. 'Go on a leave? Do you have a forwarding phone number?' There is a moment of silence, then a click as the line goes dead.

I set down the receiver. Duncan is gone. I push open the door to the phone booth and run across the street, taking the steps of the embassy two at a time, ignoring the puzzled stares of the other diplomats and staff as I fly past. Inside I flash my badge at the guard and bypass the metal detector, then race to the elevator.

In my office, I plug my laptop into the docking station and flick the switch, not bothering to sit down. Hurry, I pray, tapping my foot as the machine boots up. Leaning over, I click on the Internet Explorer icon. The screen defaults to the embassy home page, a smiling, official photograph of Ambassador Raines, thinner and with more hair than he has now. I pull down my browsing history. Infodyne is still there from the other day. I scroll down to it, then hesitate. There will be a record of my going to the site, today, after Maureen forbade the investigation. But I am too rushed to care.

I click on the address and a second later, when the Infodyne website pops up, I select the link to personnel then type 'Lauder' in the search box. A message appears: 'No such listing.' I select the browsable personnel list instead, scrolling to the *L* names. Lane, then Lewis. No Lauder.

My mind reels. Where is Duncan? Did he quit, or take a leave in the few days since we spoke? But the operator said he did not exist in a directory that is three months old. And his own department was unable or unwilling to acknowledge his existence. Something is not right. I pick up the receiver of the phone on my desk and dial directory assistance. 'Lauder, Duncan.' I say when the operator comes on the line. 'East London,' I add, remembering what he said about the flat he and Vance purchased.

There is a pause. 'No such listing.'

I hesitate. 'How about Ellis, Vance Ellis?' It seems unlikely that Duncan's telephone would be listed under the name of his partner, a semi-well-known actor, but it is worth a shot.

'I have that listing.' Relief washes over me as I jot down the number the operator recites. 'Would you like me to connect you?'

'Please.' There is a moment of silence before the phone begins to ring. Come on, I pray, drumming my fingers on the desk as it rings unanswered a second, then a third time. Be there.

'Hello?' a groggy voice, not Duncan's, answers.

'May I speak with Duncan, please?'

'He's not here.' The voice is awake now, instantly sharp. 'Who's calling?'

257

'Is this Vance?'

'Who's calling?' he demands again.

'Vance, I don't know if you remember me, but my name is Jordan Weiss. I went to Lords College when you were at Downing. I knew Duncan through rowing. I think we met once at a party. I–'

'I know who you are,' he interrupts coldly. 'What do you want?'

I twist the telephone cord in my hand. 'I'd like to speak with Duncan, please. It's important.'

'I told you, he's not here.'

'Do you know when he'll be back?' I persist.

There is silence on the other end of the line. 'He won't be,' Vance replies at last, his voice hollow and terse. 'He's gone.'

I gasp involuntarily. 'Gone? Where did he go?'

'Leave him alone. You've done enough already.' Vance slams down the phone. I stare at the receiver, stunned. Duncan is gone. It could have been a lover's fight; maybe Duncan and Vance split up. But something in Vance's voice, angry and protective of his partner, tells me that Duncan's disappearance has nothing to do with their relationship. No, Duncan did not leave only his home, but Infodyne as well, and I am certain that his disappearance has everything to do with my questions.

I pick up the phone again, then hesitate. My first reaction is to call Maureen, but that of course is impossible, since she ordered not to pursue Infodyne any further. Instead I dial Sebastian's work number, but his voice mail picks up after three rings. Figures, I think, looking at the clock, which reads ten to nine. I hang up, then dial his cell. Pick up, dammit, I think, as the phone rings over and over. I know you're there. There is a click on the other end of the line. 'Hello?' a voice, not Sebastian's, says. Female, I register slowly. American.

I hesitate, unprepared. 'Hello?' the voice repeats.

'Sophie, is that you? It's Jordan.' There is no response. On the other end of the line I hear movement and muffled voices.

A male voice speaks now. 'Sebastian here.'

I fight the urge to say something about Sophie. 'It's Jordan.'

'Oh, hi.' His voice sounds casual and sleepy, as though there is nothing unusual about Sophie answering his phone first thing in the morning. 'I was just on my way into the office. What's going on?'

I bite my lip, uncertain how to respond. Sebastian and Sophie are sleeping together. A dozen emotions collide in my brain. How long has this been going on? Did it predate my arrival, or did he become involved with her after I rejected him? 'I need to talk to you,' I say at last. Then I falter. There's no way I can discuss the investigation over the phone. 'Can you meet me?'

'Sure.' Hearing Sebastian leap to his feet, I imagine Sophie's face. 'Did you want to meet at the office?'

'Not for this, no.'

'How about Covent Garden Tube station in half an hour?'

'Perfect. See you there.'

Twenty-five minutes later, I make my way

across the sun-soaked piazza at Covent Garden, weaving through the tourists who mill to and from the arched market stalls. A mime, clad in a white flowing robe and face paint, juggles oranges while balancing on a milk crate, surrounded by a large circle of onlookers.

Sebastian emerges from the Tube station as I approach, holding two cardboard cups with one arm, tucking in his shirt with the other. He has, I realize, what the boys at college used to refer to as an RSL, a 'recently shagged look.'

Seeing me he stops, his eyes momentarily darting to my skirt, then back again. 'I brought coffee,' he offers brightly, holding one of the cups out to me as he approaches, a peace offering. I take it from him, not answering. Seeing my expression, his face falls. 'Jordan, it's not what–'

I hold up my hand. 'It's not my problem. No need to explain.' I begin to walk away from the Tube station toward the shops that line the far side of the street.

'Fine. I wasn't going to anyway,' he replies evenly, following me.

Finally, unable to hold back any longer, I turn to him. 'Sebastian, she's on the mission team.'

'Sophie's not my subordinate. We don't even work for the same person. Technically, I haven't violated any protocols.'

'Technically. What is she, anyway, twenty-three?'

'What are you, jealous?' he retorts.

'No,' I reply quickly, starting to walk again. But the question sticks between my ribs. I am a little jealous, I realize with surprise. Not that I should

260

be. Sebastian hit on me and I rejected him. I stop in front of an art gallery at the corner, staring hard at a large painting in the window. It is modern, with great indiscernible swaths of red and orange. 'I just don't think it's a good idea, getting involved with a member of the investigation team.'

'So you've said.' I remember then our conversation in the Bubble the day after the cocktail party. He is still stung, I can tell, by the fact that I rejected his advances. He shrugs. 'It could have been us, you know. If you weren't already involved.'

My mind reels back to the pub the previous evening, the icy stares exchanged between Chris and Sebastian. 'Chris and I are just friends.' It is not exactly a lie, if you exclude the past twenty-four hours. An image of Chris, above me on the floor the previous evening, flashes through my mind. Sebastian is not, I realize, the only one guilty of complicating things with sex. I swallow, forcing the image from my mind.

Sebastian shakes his head. 'I'm not talking about Chris, though you two did seem rather cozy in the pub last night. I mean your boyfriend from college, the one who died. Whether or not you want to admit it, you're still in love with him. You can tell yourself whatever you want, but we both know that's why you've kept me at arm's length, not the mission.'

I look down, feeling as though I'd been slapped. 'That's not fair.' I cannot have this conversation, not now. 'Anyway, I didn't get you out of bed to discuss my love life. Or yours.'

261

Sebastian eyes me skeptically. 'So why did you call?'

I take a deep breath. 'Duncan Lauder is gone.' Quickly I tell him about my calls and website search, my conversation with Vance. 'I obviously spooked him with my questions.' I study his face, wondering if he will tell me I am being illogical, making a leap not supported by the facts.

But he does not. 'Damn. If we hadn't been ordered to cease the Infodyne investigation...'

'I know. We could have had an official detail watching Duncan to make sure he didn't flee. But that's moot at this point. The question is: What are we going to do now?'

'We need to find him,' he says, bringing his right hand to his forehead. 'Sophie and I are still working the other angles, but Lauder is still our main contact at Infodyne, and the only one who can shed light on those transfers. If we lose him, we really are back to the start. I'm going to put out a search for him. Unofficially of course.'

'But if he's really gone, he's surely left the country.'

'I have friends,' he replies cryptically.

'Okay, and I'll follow up on him, too.'

'How?' I hesitate. I don't want to tell Sebastian my plan in case it doesn't work. 'Come on, Weiss. You know the rules: no one goes in without back-up.'

He is right. 'I'm going to try to get in touch with Vance.'

'But he already refused to talk to you.'

'That was on the phone. If I go to the theater, approach him in person, I'm hoping it will be harder for him to say no. At least then I'll be able to read his face and know if he's lying to me.'

'It's worth a shot. But be careful. Duncan Lauder is probably desperate right now.'

And Vance will do anything to protect him. 'I know. I will.' I remember then the research notes I'd taken from Jared's trunk at Chris's last night. 'I want to ask you another favor. Unrelated.' He tilts his head, listening. 'I need to have something translated from Arabic.' I hesitate. Sebastian's comment about my feelings for Jared still stings and I do not want to admit that I am even now caught up in finding out what happened to him. But I have no other choice. I pull the papers from my bag. 'Chris and I found this and we think it might be related to Jared's work.'

'And you want me to ask Sophie to translate it.'

I shrug. 'She's a bigger fan of you than me. I just need the gist. I don't know anyone here well enough to ask yet. If not, I can find a translation service—'

He waves his hand, cutting me off. 'It's fine.' He takes the papers from me, then looks at his watch. 'Let me see if I can catch her before she leaves for the office. You heading back?' I nod. 'I'll see you later.'

As I watch Sebastian disappear into the crowd, longing tugs at my stomach. I could like him I realize, really like him. 'Which is exactly what makes this so dangerous. But he is with Sophie now. And he thinks I am still in love with Jared. There is more truth in his words than I would like to admit.

A vibrating sensation against my side shakes me

263

from my thoughts. I reach in my coat and pull out my cell phone. Chris. I can't handle a conversation with him, not now. But he could have new information about Jared.

The phone beeps and the message light comes on. Reluctantly, I dial my voice mail. 'Jordan, it's me, Chris.' His voice sounds nervous. 'Um, I don't know if you're there and not picking up, but I'm sorry about last night. We can talk about it if you want, or just pretend it never happened. Finding out what happened is too important to let this get in the way. Call me, okay? I want to...' I do not finish listening to the message, but delete it and tuck the phone away in my bag.

chapter FIFTEEN

It is well after nine o'clock when I emerge at Piccadilly Circus, moving slowly in the crush of passengers who climb the stairs from the Tube station to the neon-lit street. When I reach the pavement, I swim to one side of the crowd and pull up alongside a building. I turn to a store display window behind me, studying my reflection in the glass: black pants and a turtleneck, covered by my dark wool coat, intended as much to keep my appearance nondescript as to ward off the faint evening chill.

As I make my way down Shaftesbury Avenue, the sidewalk is thick with tourists and theater-goers and young people setting out for the evening, all making their way in different directions. At first I try to weave my way through the throngs, eager to move more quickly than the shuffling mass will allow. But then I give up, finding a stream of traffic that seems to be going in the direction I want and join it, allowing myself to be carried by the momentum of the crowd.

Soon the theaters begin to appear, signaling the edge of the West End. Patrons cluster under one of the marquees smoking and for a second I wonder if the shows have let out, if I am too late. But a moment later a bell rings, signaling the end of a late intermission, and the smokers extinguish their cigarettes and disappear back inside.

My cell phone vibrates in my bag. I reach down, distracted by the interruption. 'Hello?'

'Jordan, it's me.' Chris's voice comes over the phone, husky and pleading. 'Please don't hang up. About last night...'

'I can't talk right now,' I reply hastily. 'I mean, I'm in the middle of something for work.'

'I understand.' But I can tell from his tone that he does not. 'Are you coming over tonight?'

I wince, remembering my promise to finish going through Jared's papers. 'I can't,' I blurt out. 'The work thing I mentioned came up unexpectedly and I can't get out of it. I'm so sorry.'

'Okay,' he replies slowly, trying unsuccessfully to mask the hurt. 'I guess I'll just keep looking through the papers myself.'

I hesitate. Despite any awkwardness I may feel about what happened between us, Chris is my friend, and we are trying to find out what happened to Jared together. I need to talk to him, to clear the air and make sure he is comfortable with things. Soon. 'I'll call you if I get done earlier than expected, okay? And if not, then tomorrow night for sure.'

'Sure.' His voice brightens. 'I'll be home all night if your plans change.'

As I close the phone, a clock begins to chime ten in the distance. The shows should let out any time now. I turn right on Charing Cross Road, making my way past the closed secondhand bookstores, the chain steakhouses catering to tourists. Closer to Leicester Square, the shops that line the street tout cheap pizza and T-shirts, souvenir replicas of Big Ben.

Remembering the directions I got on Map-Quest before leaving my flat, I turn left down a smaller street. About fifty yards down on the right sits the Marlbery Theatre, its marquee advertising the *Company* revival Duncan mentioned so proudly. I approach the theater, studying the actor's black-and-white headshots mounted behind glass next to a large poster for the production. Vance's photo is second from the top, his dark hair and thick mustache giving him a more dramatic appearance than he had at college, now reminiscent of Freddie Mercury.

Through the cracked door of the theater, music builds to a crescendo. The show will be over soon. Looking in both directions to make sure I am not being watched, I duck into the alleyway that runs along the right side the theater, stepping over a puddle that reflects the bright marquee lights. Halfway down the alley there is a closed stage door. I imagine Vance coming out

266

there, wonder whether he will be alone or with colleagues, how he will react. Will he talk to me?

From inside the theater come triumphant strains of music, followed by thunderous applause. The curtain call, I think, as the clapping grows louder, falls off slightly, then swells again. Moments later, the front doors of the theater open with a bang and the din of the crowd spills out onto the street. 'Try to get an autograph,' an American woman says. Footsteps grow louder now, approaching. Quickly, I scurry to the back of the alley and hide behind some cardboard boxes stacked beside a garbage bin. I duck further into the shadows as three heavyset women in leggings, fanny packs, and white sneakers enter the alleyway, clutching programs, and position themselves in front of the stage door to get better access to the cast when they emerge.

Several minutes later the stage door opens and a handful of actors walk out. The women cluster around them for autographs, chattering in high-pitched voices. The door opens again and the women snatch their programs back and race to the door once more. From my vantage point in the shadows I recognize Vance at once. Towering over his fans in a calf-length orange leather coat, he is even more dramatic looking than his photograph, his angular features unchanged in the decade since I saw him last.

I hover uncertainly. What now? I cannot very well pop out from behind the boxes. I remain hidden while Vance signs obligatory autographs and receives compliments on his performance in a perfunctory manner that suggests he repeats this routine nightly. 'Excuse me,' he says a moment later after he signs the last autograph, handing the pen back to one of the women and making his way from the alley.

When the women have turned their attention to another actor, I slip from behind the boxes. At the edge of the alley I pause, scanning the street in both directions. I do not see Vance. But a second later I spot him, fifty feet ahead to the right, walking briskly, skirting the edge of the crowd. I follow, not taking my eyes off him, as he turns one corner, then another. Faint perspiration forms under my shirt as I struggle to match his long-legged stride.

When I am about ten feet behind, I slow down so that he does not notice me, maintaining my distance as he crosses the busy intersection at the Strand. He's headed for Embankment, I realize, as he turns down Villiers Street, heading toward the Tube station. As he descends the stairs, I hesitate. What now? I could return to the theater the next night and try to approach him at the stage door again. But there will surely be fans then, too, and I have to find Duncan as soon as possible. No, I need to follow him and confront him now.

Careful not to get close, I follow Vance down the escalator and through the turnstile, grateful for the travel card I purchased earlier, then through the station's labyrinthine tunnel onto the platform for the District Line headed east. Where is he going, I wonder, studying the route map? Duncan mentioned a flat in the East End. I hang back on the platform several feet away from where he stands and hide behind a group of jostling teenage boys.

When the train pulls into the station, I board the car behind his, picking up a copy of the *Daily Mail* that someone left on the seat. Pretending to read, I peer around the edge of the paper. My breath catches. Vance is sitting in the last seat of the subway car, facing me on the other side of the glass. Does he recognize me? But his head is tilted back, eyes closed. Even from this distance I can see the worry and fatigue. Guilt washes over me and for a second I consider turning around and going home. I have caused him enough pain, intruding on his world with my questions, causing his lover to flee. I have to find Duncan, though. Quickly, I hide behind the newspaper once more.

'Liverpool Street,' a woman's recorded voice announces. Vance stands and heads for the door. I leap to my feet and follow him from the train and up the escalator. He makes his way up into the main station, from which the regional trains depart. My pulse quickens. Is he going out of the city somewhere to see Duncan? But he continues through the station, taking the underground passage that leads to the far side of the street.

Outside we pass a handful of large office buildings, the last frontier of the city, lobbies dim and vacant at this time of night except for the security guards. Vance turns off the main thoroughfare onto a winding passageway, no more than a few feet wide, lined with tiny boutiques and pubs. Then, without warning, he stops. I freeze, ducking into a doorway of a closed sandwich shop. My heart pounds.

Has he noticed me? He bends to tie his shoe-lace. Straightening, he lights a cigarette, its tip forming a beacon as he continues walking. More cautious now, I hang back farther, trying not to let the soles of my low-heeled pumps scrape too loudly against the cobblestones.

We cross a wide thoroughfare, then start down another narrow street. A minute later Vance turns right at another broad roadway and I follow, relieved by the anonymity that the noisy traffic and pedestrians provide. 'Brick Lane,' a sign at the corner reads. Spicy smells from a series of curry restaurants on the far side of the street tickle my nose and I stifle back a sneeze. Two blocks up, Vance stops and enters an unmarked building, letting the door slam shut behind him.

Carefully, I step out of the doorway, studying the building. It is a brick low-rise, indistinguishable from the buildings on either side, an empty shop on the ground floor, three stories of flats above. Is this where Vance and Duncan live? My heart sinks as I study the half-dozen buzzers beside the front door. I would not know which one to ring even if I dared. And I cannot wait all night on this dark, deserted street for him to emerge again. Damn.

The door of the building opens once more and I leap back to hide. It is not Vance, but two shorter men walking arm in arm in the opposite direction down the street, not seeing me. I notice then a pounding beneath my feet, like the rumbling of a subway train only more rhythmic and distinct. Music, I realize. Straining my ears, I can just hear

270

the techno song coming through the closing door to the building. I walk to the door and open it. The music comes louder now, pulsing up a dilapidated stairwell.

I start down the stairs. At the bottom is a large, muscled man in a tank top, wearing more jewelry on his right ear alone than I possess. He looks down at me. 'This is a private club.'

I should have worn a skirt. 'I'm sure you could make an exception. For me.' I smile as flirtatiously as I can, but he looks unimpressed.

'Private club,' he repeats.

I reach into my bag, pulling out all of the money I can grab. I look down at the handful of notes. It cannot be more than eighty pounds. I hand the money to him and smile hopefully.

'You're not someone's wife, are ya?' I shake my head vigorously. He shrugs. 'All right. But I don't think this is your type of place.' He takes the money and steps aside, opening the door behind him. Inside, I blink my eyes to adjust to the purple haze. The club is cavernous, running at least half a city block, I estimate, though I cannot see the far end. Despite its size, the low ceilings give the place a claustrophobic feel. Most of the room is occupied by a dance floor, bodies writhing to the now-earsplitting techno. I understand then what the bouncer meant about my type of place, why wearing a skirt would not have mattered. The club is almost entirely men, dancing in various states of undress. A quick scan of the room reveals only two women, or what appear to be women, making out in the corner.

I cross to the bar on the left side of the room,

feeling the stares as I pass. 'Cosmopolitan,' I say, then survey the room once more. At the far end of the bar, I see Vance, talking to a burly, shirtless man. Striking in his orange coat, he stands out, even here.

I pay the bartender and take my drink, then head toward Vance, trying not to spill as I weave through the crowds. 'Excuse me,' I say as I come up behind him. He does not hear me but continues speaking to the other man, back turned. I touch his shoulder lightly. 'Vance Ellis?'

He jumps, then turns toward me. 'Yes...' he replies politely, as if girding himself for another round of praise from a theatergoer, a faint undercurrent of annoyance at being bothered by the public at his favorite haunt. Then recognizing me, his eyes widen. 'Jordan. What are you doing here?'

'I just need a minute of your time. Please.'

Vance hesitates. 'It's okay, Martin,' he says to the other man.

As Martin scrutinizes me, I try not to stare at his nipple rings, connected by a gold chain. 'If you're sure. I'll be right over there.' He pats Vance's arm and walks a few feet away to a group of dancing men, still eyeing me suspiciously over his shoulder.

'Mind if I sit down?'

'Suit yourself.' Vance pulls out a pack of cigarettes, seemingly oblivious to the NO SMOKING sign behind the bar.

I climb onto the bar stool, then gesture to the three empty shot glasses in front of him. 'What are you drinking?'

'Bourbon.' He waves over the bartender, who

272

places two shots on the counter. Vance slides one of them toward me, then picks up the other. 'Bottoms up,' he says, draining his glass. Closer now, I can see the dark circles under his eyes, a tiny smudge of greasepaint at his left temple.

I tilt my head back and down the shot, trying not to gag as the brown liquid scorches the back of my throat. 'I thought those were supposed to be bad for your singing voice,' I remark as Vance lights a cigarette.

'They are,' he replies, taking a long drag. 'And I hadn't smoked for eight years.' He exhales. 'Until yesterday.' His voice is heavy with recrimination.

I fight the urge to swat away the smoke that drifts in front of me. 'You mean since Duncan left.' He does not respond. 'Why did he go?'

'As if you didn't know.'

'I really don't. That's why I've come to you. I'm sorry to bother you like this. But I have to find him. It's very important.'

'I can't help you.'

I reach out and touch his arm. 'Vance, I'm not the enemy. I don't want to hurt Duncan or to interfere with your lives in any way. But I'm working on a very important investigation, one that could save lives. And Duncan has information I desperately need.'

He pulls his arm away. 'So you're asking me to trade his life for theirs? Forget it.'

'Trade his life? I don't understand.'

Vance grinds out his cigarette and motions to the bartender once more, not speaking until two more shots of bourbon are placed before us.

'Look, after you met with Duncan, he came home as scared as I've ever seen him. I haven't seen him look that afraid well ... not in a very long time.' He raises the shot glass, downing the bourbon with ease. 'He said he needed to go and I helped him get the hell out. He didn't say why and I didn't ask. He won't be back.'

I can tell that he will not risk his lover's safety by telling me where he went. 'Why do you think he was so afraid?' I ask instead. He shrugs. 'Vance, if you know something, anything...'

He bites his lip. 'It has to do with that business at college with Jared.'

'Jared.' My breath catches. Vance thinks I'm here about Jared, as Duncan did originally. I start to tell him that's not what I wanted to talk to Duncan about, then stop again. Let him keep going, a voice inside me says. 'What business?'

'You really don't know, do you?' he asks and there is a hint of smugness in his voice. His college lover shared a confidence that mine did not. 'The last year at college, Jared came to Duncan to ask for help with something in his research that troubled him.'

'But I don't understand.' This time I cannot keep myself from interrupting. 'Jared was a historian and Duncan read finance and economics.'

He nods. 'It seemed a little odd to me at the time, too. I really didn't understand much about it. But it seems that in researching war criminals, Jared found something about Nazi money.'

'Gold?' I blurt out. Legends of a lost cache of Nazi treasure have circulated around the department for years.

But Vance shakes his head. 'I don't think so. At least not that Duncan mentioned. It was more like a large bank account of some sort. Anyhow, Jared discovered information that suggested the bank account was still active, in use somewhere. So he came to Duncan, who was a finance major, to track it down.' He pauses, taking a long drag on his cigarette.

'What did they find?'

He shrugs. 'I don't know. They wrote some sort of paper on their findings and they were supposed to give it at a conference but they never did. Anyway, something happened there, and Duncan came back terrified. He said he told Jared that he was done with the research. But Jared insisted, said he would publish it alone, that Duncan couldn't stop him.'

'What happened after that?'

'Well after, you know...' He trails off and a guilty expression flickers across his face. His lover is still alive and mine is not. 'After graduation, Duncan seemed to relax. It never really came up again.' His face darkens. 'Until now.'

'Any idea why he would get scared again now?'

He shrugs. 'I assume it has to do with your questions.'

I didn't ask Duncan about Jared, I want to say. But I can't tell Vance that without going into the Infodyne investigation. 'Anyway, that's all I know,' he adds.

I hesitate. He is telling the truth. 'Thank you, Vance.' I can see his eyes working, wondering if he has said too much, if his words could somehow hurt his partner. 'If you speak with Duncan, tell

275

him that I'm thinking of him and that I hope he's all right. That I'm sorry.' I pull out a pen and scrawl my cell phone number on a napkin. 'I already gave Duncan my mobile but here it is just in case. He can reach me at this number if he wants to, anytime, day or night.' I can tell from the way he shoves the paper in his shirt pocket that Duncan will never see it. I stand to leave and Vance turns from me, reaching for another cigarette. 'Oh, one other question. The conference Jared and Duncan went to. Do you remember where it was?'

His eyes drift upward, remembering. 'Spain, I think. I remember being mad that I had rehearsals and couldn't get away to go with him. Barcelona maybe, or Madrid.'

Madrid. My heartbeat quickens. I reach for the second bourbon shot, which sits untouched on the bar, and down it in one gulp. 'Tell Duncan to call me,' I repeat.

I start for the door, my mind racing. I'd assumed that Duncan's disappearance had to do with Infodyne. But Vance thinks it's related to Jared and whatever they were planning to present at Madrid. Could Duncan possibly know something about the reason Jared was killed as well? The room, suddenly too warm, seems to wobble around me. Everything is turning out to be different than I thought. I asked Duncan about Infodyne and he immediately thought of Jared. We asked Lord Colbert about Jared, and the backlash came over Infodyne. Something exceedingly strange is going on.

'Leaving so soon?' the bouncer asks, his tone mocking. I do not answer. As I climb the stairs

276

my dizziness grows. What is wrong with me? I shouldn't feel this drunk from two shots.

I struggle to remain upright as I reach the street. It has begun to rain, thick drops smacking against the ground, freeing earthy smells from the pavement. I tilt my face upward, hoping that the cool wetness will revive me, but it does not help – I am dizzier than ever. I've got to find a taxi and get home. I make my way between two parked cars, holding on to the hood of one for support and looking out into the street. A horn blares loudly. I leap back as a truck barrels down the road, just inches from where I stand.

The buildings are spinning more quickly now, my vision growing blurry at the edges. I've got to get help. Blindly, I reach for my cell phone. Who should I call? Sarah cannot help me now and I don't want Mo to find out where I've been. I start to hit the button to call Chris. Then thinking better of it, I hang up and redial. The phone on the other end of the line rings once, then again. 'Pick up, dammit,' I whisper. Sebastian's voice mail answers. 'It's Jordan,' I say. The ground seems to tilt beneath me. 'I found something, uh...' It is becoming hard to speak. I have to tell him where I am. 'I–I'm on Brick Lane,' I manage, looking up desperately for a sign to give him a crossroad. 'South of Liverpool Street.' I feel very hot, then freezing cold. I'm going to be sick, I think, racing toward a nearby alleyway as vomit rises in my throat. The drink. There must have been something in the drink. 'I need...' Then the ground rises swiftly up to meet me and everything goes black.

the MAY TERM

chapter SIXTEEN

Through the darkness comes a low, persistent ringing. My alarm clock, I think groggily. As I roll over to turn it off, my outstretched arm smacks something cold and wet. I am abruptly aware of the hard pavement beneath me, the drizzle of rain against my skin. My head pounds. I remember going to the nightclub, my conversation with Vance. What happened next?

The ringing noise comes again. I grope the ground beside me, closing my hand around my cell phone and bringing it to my head. 'Hello?' I manage, inhaling the smell of fresh vomit on the ground beside me.

'Jordan, can you hear me?' Through the haze, I recognize Sebastian's voice. 'Are you all right?'

'I–I don't...' I falter.

'Stay on the line,' he orders. 'Do not hang up.'

'Okay.' I press the phone weakly to my ear. A few minutes later I hear footsteps. I try to turn my head toward the sound but cannot. Out of the corner of my eye, I see a figure approaching from the shadows. Panicking, I reach for my gun, but my movements are slow, as if I am swimming through mud.

Then the figure is above me. I struggle to sit up. 'Don't move!' a familiar voice hisses.

'Sebastian!' I cry weakly.

'Shhh!' He crouches low, looking in either

281

direction. I can see that his gun is drawn.

'How did you...?'

'Don't try to talk.' He places his hand underneath my neck and lifts me gently, as though I am a child.

A sharp pain shoots up from the base of my skull. 'Ouch!' I yelp.

Sebastian lowers me once more and I notice how the rain sticks his hair to his forehead, making him look almost boyish. 'Is it your back?'

'My head. It feels like someone used it as a football.'

He runs his hand over the back of my head. 'There's a bump. You must have hit it when you fell. Did you trip on something?'

'Hardly,' I reply, weak but indignant. 'I got dizzy out of nowhere. I'm pretty sure I was drugged.'

'What?' he exclaims, forgetting his own admonition to be quiet. 'By whom? And what are you doing in this neighborhood anyway?'

'One question at a time.' I swallow. Where to begin? My head throbs. 'I was here talking to Lauder's partner, trying to get a lead on where he went.'

'I thought you were going to talk to him at the theater.'

I swallow over the dryness in my throat. 'I tried, but I couldn't get him alone so I had to follow him and he went to some sort of gay club. When I went to leave, I felt sick. I must have managed to vomit before I passed out.' I reach for my waist, relieved to find that my gun is still there.

'Jesus, Jordan, you could have been killed! We've got to get you to a hospital.' He crouches

282

lower, examining the back of my head more closely. Despite the pain, I am aware of his closeness, the warmth of his hand against my neck. 'There's no blood, but you could have a concussion.'

I shake my head. 'No hospital. I'm fine.' Grabbing Sebastian's arm, I struggle to sit up. 'If I'm hospitalized, it's going to get Mo all stirred up.' I see his face working as he considers my point. 'She'll want to know what I was doing and why. It could set us back weeks, if not get us shut down for good.'

'Okay,' he concedes, helping me to my feet. 'But we should get out of here in case whoever did this comes looking for you. Can you walk?' He puts his arm around me and I lean on him for support as we walk. I look like a mess, I am sure, not to mention the smell of sick and dirt from the pavement.

At the corner he hails a taxi and helps me into the back. I slump against the seat as he leans forward and speaks to the driver. 'How long was I out?' I ask again, as we speed through the rain-slicked streets of East London.

'About twenty-five minutes, give or take. I found you as quickly as I could.' I start to ask where we are going. Then I lean back and close my eyes, too tired to care.

'Hey.' Sebastian leans over, pressing his hand against my brow. 'Stay with me, all right?'

I nod. 'Just resting.'

A few minutes later I feel the cab slow, turning one corner, then another, feeling its way through unfamiliar streets. I open my eyes as we stop in front of a warehouse building and look at Sebastian quizzically. 'Where are we?'

'Docklands. This is my flat,' he explains as he pays the driver. 'It's not that far from where you went down, so I thought it made sense to come here. We can go to yours if you'd rather.'

My shoulders sag with weariness. 'This is fine.' We do not speak as a creaky grated elevator carries us to the fifth floor. Inside, Sebastian's flat is an open loft, but with none of the polish that Chris's had. The wood floors are old and splintered and there is no furniture except for a mattress in the corner. 'I haven't lived here long,' he explains. 'I bought the place unfinished, hoping to do it up. But with all of the traveling...'

'I understand,' I reply, thinking of my own bare apartment in Washington. I walk to the broad windows that cover the far wall. The buildings across the street are lower set, allowing for a panorama of the river, the city illuminated on the far bank. 'The view is nice.' The rubbery sensation returns to my legs and I sink to the edge of the mattress. There is a blue cardigan at the foot of the bed I am certain belongs to Sophie.

Sebastian disappears around the corner and I can hear him moving around in what I imagine to be the kitchen, opening cupboards. A few minutes later he returns with two mismatched cups of tea, a glass of water, and a kitchen towel. 'Here,' he says, holding out the towel. I tilt my head, not understanding. He reaches out, pressing the damp towel to the corners of my mouth, then pulls away, revealing dried bits of vomit. Lovely. He hands me the water and two aspirin.

'Did Vance tell you anything?'

I put the aspirin on my tongue and swallow them down with a gulp of water, then shake my head. 'Not about Duncan's whereabouts.' Slowly, I remember the rest of my conversation with Vance. 'There's something else, though. Vance doesn't think that Duncan's disappearance has to do with my questions about Infodyne. He thinks it's about something that Duncan and Jared worked on together at college.'

He cocks his head. 'Jared?'

I hesitate. It feels awkward talking about this with Sebastian after he accused me of still being in love with Jared. 'I know, it sounds really strange.' Quickly, I tell him about Jared's research and the conference at Madrid. 'So Duncan and Jared were working together and Vance thinks that my questions about Jared dredged up something that made him scared enough to leave. It's wild, isn't it?'

'Maybe, maybe not.'

'Huh?'

He reaches around the side of the bed and pulls out a file, then hands it to me. 'I was going to give you these tomorrow at the office.' Opening the file, I recognize the documents in Arabic that I gave him. Behind are several sheets of neatly written English cursive. An image of Sophie, sitting here on the mattress translating, flashes through my mind. Pushing it aside, I try to read the paper, but the lines blur and my right temple starts to throb.

I hand the file back to him and lean against the wall behind the mattress. 'I can't manage this right now. Can you tell me what it says?'

'Have you ever heard of Mohammad Amin al-Husseini?' I shake my head. Diplomats who work on the Middle East are a very exclusive group, composed of officers who spend their entire careers studying the region. 'He was the Grand Mufti of Jerusalem before the war.'

'Oh right.' The name, vaguely familiar to me, calls back to some history course I'd taken as an undergrad. 'He led the Muslims in Palestine in the twenties and thirties.'

'That's him. When he was exiled in the late thirties by the British he went to Berlin, stayed there throughout the war. He created an alliance with the Nazis, raised regiments of Muslim SS for the Nazis in the Balkans. Worse yet, he stopped transports of Jews from going to Palestine. Children, who would have escaped but for him, wound up dying at Auschwitz.'

An alliance between the Nazis and the Palestinians, I think, trying to process the information. 'It makes sense. Those hating Jews bonding with those hating Jews.'

'It was more than common cause. The Nazis promised al-Husseini that after the war they would help to exterminate the Jews in Palestine, ensuring that the land would be kept for the Muslims.'

'Obviously that never happened.'

'Right. After Germany fell, the Mufti fled Europe and lost most of his political influence. He died in Lebanon in the early seventies.'

'Interesting.' I press my hands against my temples, willing the aspirin to work faster. 'But

286

how does it tie in with Jared's work? I mean, he was researching war criminals who disappeared. We know where this guy went.'

'That was just background from me,' Sebastian replies. He slides along the mattress to sit beside me, and leans closer, pointing. 'The documents you gave me are two versions of an agreement between al-Husseini and the Reich.' He indicates a place on the one of the original Arabic documents that has been underlined in pencil, then jumps to the same place on the translated page. 'This paragraph describes a fund, established by the Nazis as insurance to the Mufti of their promise to help after the war.' He turns to another page. 'But it was omitted from the final agreement.'

'So maybe they decided not to set up the fund.'

'Or maybe they decided that no one should know about it. Either way, the fund never made it into the agreement.' He looks from the paper to me. 'It's pretty remarkable, you know, a college kid finding these papers.'

I want to tell him that Jared wasn't just some college kid; he was a doctoral student, gifted and intense. 'He mainly did his research at the Public Records Office at Kew Gardens.' I had been there a few times for my own research and was surprised by the endless boxes of original documents, neither cataloged nor preserved, to which researchers were given access. 'I remember Jared saying that after the end of the Cold War, there were thousands of documents shared by the former Eastern Bloc nations with the West, information to which no one had access for nearly half a century. It was one of the things he was

287

most excited about in his research.'

'He well could have been one of the first scholars to go through some of the documents, especially if these papers were buried in a box that no one realized was important,' Sebastian agrees. He taps the papers. 'And these well could have been the reason Jared approached Duncan for help.'

'Duncan read finance at Cambridge. Jared could have been asking him for more information about types of funds, or how to find out if this one ever existed.'

'Right. But the question is, what did they find out about the fund?'

'It's hard to know without having the rest of Jared's research.' There are still papers in the trunk at Chris's apartment, I think. I am going to have to go back there. 'Or being able to speak to Duncan. When I approached him the other day, he thought I wanted to talk about Jared. But I didn't think to press him on it.'

'You couldn't have known.'

'Whatever they worked on together, Vance seems sure that's why Duncan has disappeared now, why he was so terrified years ago.'

'And Jared, was *he* terrified?' he asks gently.

'I don't know,' I admit. 'Scared enough to buy one-way plane tickets out of the country.'

'To where?'

'South America. Does it really matter?' I hear the sharpness in my own voice. 'Sorry,' I say, rubbing my eyes. 'I think I'm just tired. This isn't your problem. It has nothing to do with our investigation.'

'It's fine,' he replies. 'I think the whole matter is very interesting and I'm happy to help.'

'But do you really think that this' – I pause, gesturing to the file. 'That this research could be somehow connected to Jared's death? I mean, he was just writing a dissertation.' But as I say it, I know that Jared's work was never just that. Even at college, I knew from his intensity that whatever he was working on was real. I pick up the teacup from the floor beside me, closing my hands around the warmth. 'I need to find Duncan now more than ever. He's the only one who can tell me about Jared's work. But Vance was my last lead on finding him. I think I've reached a dead end.'

'Maybe with regard to Duncan. There might be another way, though. What about the paper they were going to give at Madrid? I mean it might contain the information that they were going to present, whatever it is that someone wanted buried.'

'Good point. But how am I going to get it? It's not like Duncan is just going to hand me a copy, even if I can find him.'

'Did Jared have a computer?'

'Yes!' Personal computers were just coming into wider use at colleges in the nineties. I see Jared's clunky, early-model laptop. 'Chris might know whether Jared's mother kept his computer. I should call him, tell him what I've found out about Jared's research.'

'Have you considered the possibility that he might already know?'

I snap my still-aching head back toward

Sebastian. 'What?'

Sebastian places his hand on my shoulder. 'Jordan, I don't mean to upset you, but haven't you wondered, even for a minute, why Chris contacted you? I mean, why now?'

'Someone sent him a newspaper article about Jared's death,' I reply quickly. 'It made him suspicious.'

'And he couldn't possibly have fabricated that because...?' he challenges.

'Chris wouldn't do that. I mean, I've known him–'

'Knew him,' Sebastian corrects. 'The two of you were out of contact for years.' He hesitates briefly. 'I ran a background check on Chris Bannister. After I saw you with him in the pub.'

'You did what?'

'Something about him made me uneasy.'

'Uneasy? Or jealous?'

Sebastian shakes his head. 'No. Or at least that wasn't why I did it. We have no personal lives in this business, Jordan. You know that. I wanted to know who you were associating with. I make no apologies for that.'

'And?'

'The bloke's a walking vulnerability. In the past ten years, he's had a divorce–'

'From Caren. I know.'

'Did you know he had a drinking problem for several years after college?' It was Cambridge, I think. We all had drinking problems. He continues. 'Financial troubles.'

'Money problems?' I interrupt. He nods. 'No way. Chris is from one of the wealthiest families

290

in Britain.'

'*Was* from one of the wealthiest families,' he corrects. 'I'm sure you don't get the British society pages in the States, but the Bannister family has fallen on hard times in recent years.'

'He's got his job at *The Times*.'

He shakes his head. 'He was let go six months ago. Seems he got too close to one of his sources and let that cloud his reporting. I guess he forgot to mention that.' I do not answer. I realize then how very little I know about Chris. Sebastian continues. 'Look, I know the guy is a friend of yours and I'm not saying he's done anything wrong–'

'So what *are* you saying?' I snap.

'Just that he's just got some ... baggage.' Haven't we all, I want to ask? 'That Chris Bannister may not be the man you once knew.'

'And that maybe Chris has his own reasons for wanting to find out what happened to Jared?' I finish for him. He does not respond. 'When were you going to tell me all of this?'

'Maybe never,' Sebastian replies, his voice sincere. 'You seemed to enjoy spending time with him and I didn't think it was any of my business. But now, given what Vance told you and your being drugged... I'm just asking you to be careful.'

'It makes no sense whatsoever.' I drop my head into my hands, overwhelmed. Chris found me, asked me to help him learn the truth because he was Jared's best friend. That's all. 'So what do I do now?'

'I think you should focus on finding the paper

291

Jared and Duncan were going to deliver at the conference.'

'Maybe if I head back up to Cambridge...'

'Well there's no question of that for a few days. Not until you get your head checked out, make sure you aren't concussed.'

'But what about the Infodyne investigation? I mean, now that I've hit a dead end on Lauder.' I shiver.

Sebastian walks to a pile of clothes in the corner and returns with a hooded sweatshirt. 'Put this on,' he instructs. 'And no worrying about the investigation, either. Let Sophie and me work some other angles for a day or two. You need to rest.'

I take the shirt from him, smelling his familiar cologne. 'Thanks, but I just need a good night's sleep and then I'll be fine. I should go.' I stand up, then grab the wall, dizzy again.

He comes to my side. 'There's no way you can be alone tonight. I can take you home if you want, or to your friend's house, or we can stay here, but I'm not leaving you.'

Exhausted, I sink back down to the futon, then take my gun from my waist and put it into my bag. 'Here's fine.' Sebastian sits down beside me, then takes the sweatshirt from me and starts to help me put it on. I pull back, suddenly aware of how filthy I am from lying in the street. 'Would you mind if I took a shower? I'm feeling fairly gross.'

'Not at all.' He stands and walks to the pile of clothes once more, produces a t-shirt and a towel and hands them to me. 'Loo is just through the kitchen,' he says, gesturing to a doorway.

The bathroom is small, with a standing shower, toilet, and sink pressed close together. I turn on the tap, and as I wait for the water to warm, open the medicine cabinet. A spare toothbrush, I suppose, would be too much too hope for. Finding none, I squeeze some toothpaste onto my index finger, running it over my teeth as well as I can. As I 'brush,' I think about what Sebastian said about Chris. The notion that he could be lying to me, that he might have ulterior motives for wanting to find out what happened to Jared, seems impossible.

I rinse, then pull out a bottle of mouthwash and take a swig. As I swish, I study my reflection in the mirror. I look as if I've been hit by a freight train, face smeared with dirt, hair pressed flat to my head.

'Better?' Sebastian asks when I emerge ten minutes later, still drying my hair with the towel. I drop to the mattress beside him and he holds out the sweatshirt once more, helping me put it on, half zipping the front. I lean back and he props up two pillows behind my head, then puts his arm around me protectively.

I look around the flat warily. I should offer to sleep on the sofa but there is none. Sophie's sweater stares up from the foot of the bed, recriminating. I want to ask about her. 'It's all right,' Sebastian says, following my gaze. 'No funny business, I promise. Just a colleague keeping an eye on you to make sure you aren't hurt too badly.'

Too tired to argue, I roll onto my side, leaning

my head against his chest and closing my eyes. Any port in a storm. He tightens his arm around me. My breaths grow longer and more even, matching his. This feels good, I think, then stiffen. The thought is as surprising as any I have had. I realize then that I *do* care that Sebastian has been sleeping with Sophie. The protestations rise up like floodwaters, threatening to drown me. I cannot like Sebastian. He is my teammate. Getting involved now, on top of the Infodyne investigation and worrying about Sarah and finding out about Jared's death, is simply too much. It is a moot point, I remind myself. You already told him no. He is with Sophie now. Pushing the feelings down, I close my eyes.

Sometime later, I wake with a start. The room is still dark, but outside the clearing sky has turned a lighter shade of gray. From the street below comes the sound of a truck engine, the banging of supplies being loaded onto a cart.

Above me, Sebastian shifts. I look up, expecting to find him still asleep. But his eyes are wide and alert. 'Hey,' he says.

'Hey,' I manage, pulling away as the feelings from last night surge back up within me.

He reaches out to touch the spot where I hit the back of my head. 'How are you feeling?'

The ache is nearly gone, dulled to a mere pinch. 'Much better. How long was I out?' I rub the nape of my neck, which has grown stiff from sleeping at an angle. Beneath my hair, my fingers brush against Sebastian's. He does not pull away.

'Just a few hours. I've been keeping an eye on you to make sure you're all right.' His face is expressionless, but there is a deeper tone, a protectiveness to his voice that I do not recognize.

'I think...' My voice catches. Staring into his eyes, I am unable to speak. Suddenly I do not care about Sophie or Chris or the fact that Sebastian and I work together. I lean over, brushing my mouth against his. For a second, he hesitates. Then he kisses me back softly at first, the intensity growing. He pulls me gently across the futon to him until I am half lying across, half straddling his chest. There is no hesitation, no more questions left to be asked. He reaches beneath my shirt, drawing me close.

Between us there is a vibrating sensation. 'You should...' I begin to mumble, my mouth still pressed against his. But he pulls the phone from his pocket and throws it so that it skids across the floor unanswered. A second later, my phone begins to ring beside the mattress. Reluctantly, I pull away. A number I do not recognize flashes across the screen. 'It could be Duncan,' I whisper as I open the phone, shushing his groan with my hand. He slips one of my fingers into his mouth and begins to suck. 'Jordan Weiss,' I manage, feeling my insides melt.

'Ms. Weiss, this is the Accident and Emergency Department at the University College Hospital. Your friend Sarah Sunderson asked us to call. She has been admitted to the Acute Admissions Unit.'

I pull my hand away, alarm rising in me. 'Is it serious?' Sebastian shoots me a quizzical look.

'It is, I'm afraid. Please come here immediately.'

295

chapter SEVENTEEN

Sebastian follows me as I take the front stairs to the building two at a time. On the still-damp sidewalk, I stop, looking desperately in both directions. 'You'll never get a cab around here at this hour,' he says, taking my elbow and guiding me gently to a black Vespa parked beneath an overhang by the side of the building. As he wipes off the seat, I start to tell him that it isn't necessary for him to come with me. Then looking both ways down the deserted street, I realize that he is right. He hands me a helmet I didn't see him pick up, then straddles the scooter. I put on the helmet and climb on behind him, forced close by the tiny seat. The bike lurches from the curb and I wrap my arms around his midsection quickly so as not to fall off. Inhaling his scent, I remember our kiss. 'What have I done? Chris, then Sebastian, in less than a day. And now something has happened to Sarah ... it is as if some rapid-fire karma is rising up, punishing me for my misdeeds.

What happened to Sarah? She seemed fine the last time I saw her. But I remember finding her on the floor when I arrived. Did she fall again, manage to injure herself? 'She's going to be fine,' Sebastian calls over his shoulder, seeming to read my thoughts. We weave in and out of traffic, barely stopping for lights. I look over my shoulder, praying we are not stopped by the police.

What seems like an eternity later, we screech to a halt in front of a no-parking sign by the hospital emergency bay. I leap from the bike and then stop as a wave of dizziness overtakes me. 'You should get checked out, too, while you're here,' Sebastian says, coming to my side.

'I'm fine,' I reply quickly. Sarah needs me and I have to leave whatever is going on between me and Sebastian behind. 'You don't have to go in with me.'

'I'll wait here,' he persists.

'Thanks but it isn't necessary. You go back to the investigation. We need you there and Sophie shouldn't be left on her own.' Her name comes out awkwardly. She is not just our teammate anymore; she is the other woman.

For a minute I worry that he will be hurt that I do not want him coming with me, but Sebastian is not Chris. He shrugs, willing to take what is offered. His lack of neediness, I decide instantly, makes him even more attractive. 'I'm sorry we got interrupted...' I say, faltering.

His face brightens. 'Me too. Rain check, okay?'

I turn away, fighting the urge to kiss him. 'I'll call you later,' I call over my shoulder as I race for the hospital door. 'Thanks for the ride.'

I burst though the doors of the emergency room. 'Sarah Sunderson?' I demand of the clerk behind the desk.

The woman looks up at me, then back at her computer screen. 'One moment, I'll just...'

'Jordan,' a voice behind me says. I spin around. Mo, in a pink cardigan and jeans, walks toward me.

'Mo! I don't understand. How did you...?'

'The hospital called the embassy looking for you,' Maureen replies. She seems to have aged overnight. It is, I realize, the first time I have seen her without makeup. 'Are you okay?' she asks.

'I'm fine,' I answer quickly, my own injury forgotten. The last thing I need is Mo knowing about Sebastian and me, or that I'd been careless enough to allow myself to be drugged. 'Where's Sarah?'

'She's in a private room. Follow me.' She leads me down a corridor, then stops before a closed door, blocking my way and putting a hand on my shoulder. 'Wait a second. Jordan, Sarah was badly hurt.'

'Was?' Bile rises in my throat. 'She's not...?'

'No, no, she's fine,' Maureen replies quickly. I inhale deeply as the hallway seems to right itself once more. 'I'll take you to her in a minute. But first we need to talk.' She looks in both directions down the corridor, then pulls me into the doorway of an empty room.

'This is serious: Sarah was attacked.'

'Attacked?' I grab the doorway as the ground starts to wobble beneath me once more. 'But I thought, with her illness, that maybe she fell again...'

Maureen shakes her head. 'The police said that two men broke into her flat. They were looking for something in her desk or her computer; they didn't mean for her to find them. But she woke up.' I nod. Sarah was always a light sleeper. 'When she confronted them, they attacked her and tied her up, turned on the gas. She wasn't

298

supposed to make it out alive. Fortunately the nurse arrived early and found her in time.'

'How bad is it?'

Mo squeezes my shoulder. 'It's not good. Her lungs were already compromised by the disease and the gas was really hard on them.'

'No...' I whisper, leaning against the door frame, tears springing to my eyes.

'But she's awake, Jordan. Alive. She's a fighter.'

I am not comforted. 'I've got to go see her.' I start around Mo, but she tightens her grip on my shoulder, holding me in place.

'One more minute. First a question: Why would someone attack Sarah?'

I shift uneasily. 'I don't know.'

'Did you tell her anything about the investigation?'

'Of course not,' I reply, unable to keep the indignation from my voice. 'It's classified.' My mind races. Sarah knows about Jared's death, my quest to find out what happened to him. I remember what Vance said about Duncan being terrified. Could whoever scared him have attacked Sarah? It seems impossible. But I cannot tell Mo about my conversation with Vance without divulging that I was looking for Duncan, that we still have not given up on Infodyne. And I do not have time for the thousand questions my revelation would surely bring.

Instead I gesture toward Sarah's hospital room. 'Has she said anything?'

'Not much.' Mo is staring at me now, lips pressed together.

'I don't like it,' she declares, exhaling sharply.

299

'This is getting serious.'

'It's okay, Maureen.'

'The hell it is!' Mo slams her hand into the door frame. 'Nobody makes a personal attack on one of our agents' families. And what kind of sicko attacks...' Before she can finish the thought, her cell phone rings. She whips it out, heedless of the fact that we are in a hospital. 'Martindale,' she says. A voice comes over the line, male and terse, but I cannot make out what it is saying. Her eyes dart back and forth, the creases in her brown deepening. 'Yes, I understand. Of course. Right away.'

Who calls Mo, I wonder, and barks orders like that? 'Was that about our investigation?' I ask as she closes the phone.

'No,' she says quickly.

I study her face. I am not sure if I believe her, but there's no time to press the issue now. 'I need to go see Sarah.' I start around her.

'We're not finished,' she says, blocking my way. She lowers her voice. 'Jordan, I want you off this case. And I want you to leave your other investigation – the personal one – alone, too.'

'Maureen, please. I'm so close.' That, I realize, is a lie. I have no idea who is behind Infodyne, or Jared's death. 'You can't ask me to give up now,' I press. 'You said yourself that you wouldn't, either, if you were in my shoes.'

She closes her eyes. I study her face, wondering if what I said got through. 'We'll talk about it tomorrow. You've got twenty-four hours.'

'Then what?'

'We'll see. A lower-profile assignment. Or a

300

desk job, if you're not good.' She watches as my face falls. 'Do we have a deal?'

'Yes.' I cross my fingers behind my back. I will continue the investigation, twenty-four hours or twenty-four years. Whoever attacked Sarah crossed a line. Now it is personal. 'Except for the desk job,' I add.

'Good.' Apparently satisfied, Mo gestures to the two guards posted outside Sarah's room. 'I also want round-the-clock security on you. One of these gentlemen will be escorting you home when you are done here. Got it?'

I start to protest that there is no way I can operate discreetly with a security detail following me around. But I stop. This is not a battle I can win. 'Security for Sarah, too, right?'

'Of course. We've coordinated with the police on this. They're sweeping her apartment as we speak, and watching there and here at the hospital.'

'Thanks, Maureen.'

'I'm going to go home and get some rest. I've been here since three.' I notice then the dark circles underneath her eyes. 'You never did say where you were last night, by the way, or why we couldn't reach you. I tried your cell phone for an hour.' I open my mouth to tell her it did not ring, but before I can speak, she continues. 'I even sent Sophie to your flat to check on you.' I raise an eyebrow. 'Yes, Sophie. She was the only one I could think to call without raising a fuss to the entire embassy. I couldn't reach Sebastian, either,' she adds pointedly.

'Fieldwork,' I reply, avoiding her gaze. 'I don't know what was up with the phone.'

I turn and walk toward Sarah's hospital room, still feeling Mo's eyes on my back. My stomach twists. Sarah is lying flat in bed, eyes closed, a system of tubes and wires coming out of her arms, beneath her gown. A heart monitor beeps above her head. As I step closer to the bed, I wince. Sarah has a large bruise on her cheek and her upper lip is cut.

She opens her eyes at the sound. 'Hey,' she whispers, managing a faint smile.

'Oh, Sarah, I'm so sorry.' I bend down and touch my forehead to hers.

'Don't be. It's not your fault.' She breathes heavily, as though she has been running.

'Yes it is.' I look around, desperately wanting to do something to help her. Then I spot a pitcher beside the bed. 'Water?' She nods. I pour a small cup. I press the button on the side of the bed to raise her head, then quickly stop as she winces in pain. 'Here.' I put my hand under her neck and bring the cup gently to her lips. Sarah takes a small sip, then stops, staring up at me. I pull the cup away. 'What is it?'

'What happened to your forehead?' she whispers. I touch my brow, feeling the scrape for the first time. Did Maureen notice? 'They got you, too, didn't they?' Her eyes grow moist and I can tell that my attack bothers Sarah more than her own.

'Someone slipped something in my drink is all. I hit my head when I passed out.'

'Any idea who?'

I shake my head. 'I went to see Vance Ellis at a bar, but I don't think he—'

'Vance Ellis?' Sarah interrupts, stronger now.

'Yes, Duncan's partner.'

Her eyes widen. 'Jordie, look.' She gestures with her head at a television mounted in the far corner of the room.

I look at the writing that scrolls across the muted screen. ACTOR KILLS SELF. My stomach drops. Vance's headshot, the same one that hung on the theater marquee, stares back at me. 'Oh no,' I whisper, as Sarah turns on the sound. Found in the restroom of an East End gay nightclub called the Pit. An apparent overdose, the announcer says. He was rumored to have been despondent over the decline of his relationship.

'They said it was likely a suicide,' Sarah offers, turning the volume low once more.

I picture Vance at the club last night, so fiercely protective of his partner. His relationship was not in demise and he wouldn't have done anything to compromise his ability to protect Duncan. No, Vance was murdered, just hours after speaking with me. And with his death, my only connection to Duncan had disappeared.

'You don't think he killed himself, do you?' Sarah presses.

I shake my head, remembering the shots of bourbon that Vance was downing. 'He wasn't suicidal. Despondent and drinking, but not enough to kill him.' The shots, I realize. I only had two and I was knocked unconscious. The second shot, the one I grabbed after the shock of hearing Vance mention Madrid, was intended for him. 'I think someone drugged his drinks, including the

303

one that made me pass out.'

'But why?' she asks. Because he knew more than he told me, I think. He knew more than he was letting on about what Jared and Duncan worked on, and someone wanted that to disappear forever. The realization slams into my stomach: the person or persons who murdered Vance well could have killed Jared because of his research. And if I am right, Duncan is in grave danger.

Sarah reaches out and touches my arm gently, pulling me from my thoughts. 'Does it have something to do with Jared?'

'What do you mean?'

'Last night after you explained what you and Chris learned about Jared's death, I started doing some digging online. I mean, I have a lot of time on my hands and I wanted to help. Jordie, did you know that Jared and Duncan worked together on some research related to Nazi money?'

I stare at her, amazed that she had been able to learn so much from the Internet. I might have, too, if I'd had time to sit down and do some real research since coming to England.

'I know. They were supposed to give a paper at a conference in Madrid about a month before Jared died. But they never did for some reason.' Even as I say this I know that her inquiries about Jared got her attacked. Guilt rises up in me. 'Did you get a look at who did this to you?'

She shakes her head. 'Not exactly. There were two men. Like I told the police, they were wearing masks, but I'd guess they're in their late twenties or early thirties, judging by their voices. Foreign, though I couldn't make out the lan-

304

guage. They dressed as though they were playing street thugs.'

'Dressed as though? I don't understand.'

'They were wearing torn trousers and dirty shirts and they had taken the trouble of growing stubble. But their hands,' she winces, touching her face, 'which I got a good look at, were manicured and smooth. And they were wearing Cartier watches.'

I tuck this information away to process later. 'What did they want?'

'I don't know. They didn't speak to me. I heard noise in the living room and I thought maybe it was the nurse. When I rolled into the room, they seemed startled. They were rifling around my desk and they had my laptop on, trying to get around the password. But after I interrupted them, they tied me up, turned on the gas, and left.'

'You must have been terrified.'

'Nah,' she replies. 'Death threats don't mean that much when you're terminally ill.'

'Oh!' Dropping my head onto the mattress beside her, I begin to sob.

'Hey now.' She puts her hand on my shoulder. 'It's okay, I'm fine. But Jordie, Jared's paper ... do you think that's why...?' She does not finish the question.

I lift my head from the crisp white sheets and wipe my eyes with my sleeve. I am, I realize for the first time, still wearing Sebastian's sweatshirt. 'Why someone killed him? I don't know. It seems impossible that someone could want to murder a student over his research, even one as brilliant as Jared.'

'I guess it depends on what he found,' she observes.

'True. I just don't know what to do.'

'You've got to find out what Jared and Duncan wanted to present at Madrid,' she replies logically. 'Once you know that, you'll have a better sense who would have wanted to stop them.'

'But Maureen said I need to give up investigating this. I told her no, of course, but now that I've seen you ... it's too dangerous. What if they come back?'

'That's all the more reason you've got to continue. I saw those men, saw the look in their eyes. They came after me because we got too close to something.' *We*, I think, my guilt rising once more. I never meant to drag her into this. She continues. 'They aren't going to give up just because we do. Do you understand what I'm saying?'

She's right, of course. We already know too much for these people to leave us alone. I have to find them before they come back and try again, and maybe Sarah or I wind up like Vance. I've got no choice but to keep going. 'I understand.'

She smiles, satisfied. 'Good. I want you to get those bastards for me. What's your next move?'

I remember my conversation with Sebastian last night. 'With Duncan gone, I need to find another way to get the paper that he and Jared were going to give at Madrid.'

'That makes sense. I scoured the Internet but it was nowhere to be found. Sorry.'

I squeeze her arm. 'You did great. We'll have to think of another way. There are some papers that

Chris got from Jared's mom that I can check. I'm supposed to go over there tonight.' I bite my lip, faltering.

'Jordie, what's going on?' Sarah demands, her cheeks brightening, then fading quickly to gray once more.

I look away. Normally I would dump all of my problems on Sarah. But now, while she is lying in this hospital bed, I cannot. 'Chris and I got a little too close. It's no big deal, I'm just being silly. That's the short version and I'll tell you the rest some other time. Right now I need to focus on getting that paper.'

'Maybe there was someone else from Cambridge at the conference,' she suggests. 'Someone who might have kept a copy of the paper.'

'Good point. But who?' I remember the hotel stationery I took from Jared's trunk. There were some initials scribbled on it, ending in an *A*, I think, followed by Trinity Hall, the name of one of the colleges. Another student or a professor maybe, who had been there, too? 'I have an idea.' I open my cell and dial Sebastian.

'Hallo,' he answers a moment later.

'It's Jordan,' I say, trying to still the fluttering in my chest.

'Oh, hi.' His voice lifts a note. 'How's your friend?'

'Okay,' I reply. 'I was wondering if you can do me a quick favor. Are you near a computer?'

'Sure,' he replies. 'Just give me a second to boot up.'

'Go to the Cambridge site, then to the page for Trinity Hall. Tell me what faculty members they have listed who have surnames beginning with an *A*.'

There is a pause and I can hear him typing. Sarah watches me, eyebrows raised. 'There are two,' Sebastian says finally. 'Marcelius Ang and Rosemary Alberts.'

'What are their subjects?'

'Alberts teaches literature. Ang is a history professor.'

'Marcelius J. Ang?' I ask, seeing the initials on the stationery clearly now.

'That's the one.'

'Perfect, thanks. Talk to you later.' A pang of longing pulls at my stomach as I close the phone.

'What happened?' Sarah asks. I explain quickly about the hotel stationery. 'I think Ang could have been at the conference also. I need to talk to him.'

'We could see if there's a phone number,' Sarah offers, but I shake my head.

'I don't want to call and risk having him disappear like Duncan. No, I think I need to speak with him in person. He's less likely to shut down on me that way.' I hesitate, looking around the hospital room. 'I hate to leave you alone, but if we're going to get these guys, I've got to keep going. Mo's only given me another twenty-four hours and after that she's going to pull the plug on the investigation.'

Sarah nods. 'I'll be fine. Those guys won't be back. Maureen's got her watchdogs on me.'

'I know, she's got them on me, too, and I've got to shake them. So I'm going to slip out and if anybody asks, I hope you don't mind telling them...'

308

'...that you went home to take a shower and get some sleep.'

I smile. 'Thanks, you're the best.' I stand and silently blow her a kiss.

'Be careful,' she mouths.

Outside the room, the guards stand as I exit the room and one starts to follow me.

'That's not necessary,' I say.

'But Ms. Martindale gave instructions–'

'Ms. Martindale would laugh,' I reply curtly. 'I'm going twenty feet down the hall to the toilet, where I'd prefer you not follow me, and then to the cafeteria. You can call her yourself if you want,' I add, pulling out my cell phone and holding it to them. 'But I'll be back before you reach her. She was here all night and I don't think she'll appreciate the interruption.' The guards sit back down uncertainly.

I walk as casually as possible around the corner, then turn into a room with three empty hospital beds. There is only one entrance, a row of high windows across the far wall. I take a deep breath, studying the windows, wondering if I can reach them to climb out. I have a minute at best before one of the guards comes to check on me. This may be my only option. Then I notice a pile of neatly folded scrubs on one of the beds. I grab a pair, duck into the toilet. Twenty seconds later I emerge wearing the blue cotton garb over my own clothes, my hair tucked away in a cap. I look both ways out the door then start down the hall in the opposite direction from Sarah's room, fighting the urge to run.

Outside, I race to the corner and hop into a

cab. 'King's Cross,' I say, looking out the rear window of the car to make sure I have not been followed. I rip off the surgical cap, then sink back in the seat, my mind racing. Vance is dead. Someone attacked Sarah. And as near as I can tell, both events have something to do with the paper that Jared and Duncan wanted to give at Madrid. I've got to get to Cambridge and talk to Professor Ang before something else happens.

My phone rings and I pull it out of my bag. 'Jordan?' Sophie's baby-powder voice comes over the line. 'Are you okay? Because the DCM was looking for you and–'

I cut her off. 'She found me, and everything is fine.' That might, I realize, be the lie of the year.

'Oh, okay,' she says, sounding confused. 'When you didn't call me back, I thought–'

'Back? Did you leave me a message?'

'Two of them. Last night.' I look down at my phone but the message light is not blinking. Strange, since Mo said she tried to reach me too. 'Jordan, I need to talk to you.' Alarm bells ring in my mind. Did she somehow find out about Sebastian and me? 'I think I've found something for the investigation. Can you meet me somewhere?'

'Sophie, I'd love to but I'm racing to catch a train out of town right now. I'm sure if you call Sebastian–'

'I can't,' she says more firmly than I have heard her speak, cutting me off. 'Not with this.'

'Does it have to do with the records he asked you to translate?'

'Records? I don't understand...'

310

Impatience rises in me. I need to get on the train to Cambridge, and I don't have time for a heart-to-heart with Sophie. Still, she is part of the team, and she might have found something important. I have an idea. 'Sophie, where are you now?'

'I'm on the Piccadilly Line near Ravenscourt Park, just on my way back from the Public Records Office. I was following up on a lead and...'

Not far at all from Hammersmith. Perfect. 'Mo gave you my key last night, right? I need you to do me a huge favor. Go to my flat and pick up the folder that is on the coffee table.' I picture the Madrid stationery as I left it the previous day. There might be something else that could help me in Cambridge. 'Bring it to King's Cross as quickly as you can. I'll be waiting by the W.H. Smith store. We'll talk then. But I need to make a train within the hour. So please hurry, and don't tell anyone that you're meeting me.'

'I won't,' she replies. Her voice is solemn, almost fearful.

Fifteen minutes later, the cab pulls up in front of King's Cross and I pay the driver. Inside, I make my way across the main concourse of the station, ducking downstairs into the toilet and removing the scrubs. As I wash my hands, I catch a glimpse of my reflection in the mirror. Cringing, I splash water on my face, trying without success to fluff some life into my matted curls. Upstairs I scan the concourse anxiously. It is too soon, of course, for Sophie to be here. I look up at the schedule board. There is a train to Cambridge in ten minutes, another in twenty-five. I've got to be on one of those before Mo realizes that I gave security the jump.

I walk to the row of shops that lines the right side of the concourse, get some cash from an ATM machine, then stop in front of the W.H. Smith newsstand and glance at the headlines on the tabloids. Five minutes pass, then ten. A voice comes over the loudspeaker, announcing the train to Cambridge. Staring at the door to the street, I fight the urge to pace. I walk to the coffee stand and order a cappuccino, keeping my eye on the door. Where's Sophie? Damn her, I swear inwardly, returning to the newsstand. I pull out my cell phone and dial the last number called but it rings several times and goes to voice mail. What is taking her so long?

'Train to Cambridge...' a voice announces over the public address system, calling the second train. I can wait no longer. I take a final, long look in both directions, then run for the platform.

May 1998
The voices and laughter fade as the door to the bar slowly closes behind me. Outside, the honeysuckle-laced night air is cool and still, the silence broken only by a chorus of crickets chirping from the bushes beside the stairs. Lights burn behind windows in the brick buildings that line two sides of the courtyard, illuminating students hunched industriously over dorm room desks.

It is the third week in May and an air of solemnity

has fallen across the college as exam time nears for the undergraduates. The college grounds are kept quiet, front gate closed even during the day, tourists shooed off by the porters. The bar was half as full as on a normal night – even Mark begged off from his usual pint and game of table footie to return to his books.

As I walk through the archway to First Court, I stop, looking up at the library, which runs along the third floor above the Porter's Lodge. Jared is seated at his usual carrel, head hunched over, bathed in yellow lamplight. I watch as he chews on the edge of his pencil, then scribbles something furiously. Usually I would stop up for a few minutes of whispered conversation, a quick kiss. But the past few nights he has seemed more distressed than pleased by the interruption, annoyance thinly veiled under a strained smile. So instead I turn away and start across the field toward home.

The change seemed to come abruptly a few days ago, like the swift storm that caught us on our ride to Grantchester. Or maybe there were signs, tiny fissures of changes I hadn't wanted to see. Jared had become distant again, stony. He's not unkind as he was when we first met, but troubled and withdrawn, spending less time with me and the others, speaking little when he is there.

I unlock the back door to the house and creep up the stairs so as not to wake Sarah, but when I reach the landing, light still burns beneath her door. I raise my hand to knock. It would be good to talk to her about Jared. Then I hesitate. How can I explain the problem, the subtle changes that are so difficult to articulate, even to myself? I turn and walk into my own room.

Jared's tension is understandable, I remind myself

as I undress and climb into bed. There's his disser-tation, which he is trying to finish writing and then submit; the May Bumps are less than a month away. The Eight is training as hard as ever, working to fine-tune our timing, to look for the tricks that will give us that extra bit of speed and power.

And then there is my departure. I close my eyes, listening to the crickets beneath the window. It is only five weeks until the semester ends and I leave England for good. Jared and I have not talked about what is happening other than in the most peripheral and perfunctory way, my casual mention that I had to book United because British Airways was completely full with summer holiday travelers, his suggestion that I give my belongings I don't want to ship home to Oxfam or one of the other charity shops. We have not discussed what is really happening, the fact that our fledging relationship will end.

'Maybe we could meet at the winter holidays,' he once said. 'A Weiss-Short summit in the States.'

I hesitated. Was he suggesting that we continue our relationship long-distance? I loved the idea that we could transcend the miles, keep things going until somehow magically reuniting. But even as I consid-ered it, I knew that it would never work. I had seen it all too often as an undergrad, the boyfriend in Wash-ington trying to keep a high school flame alive with a girlfriend in Texas or Colorado. The story was always the same: hours spent on the telephone, the nervously anticipated visit at Christmas, the realization that someone cheated or changed, that the circumstances and commonalities that once held them together were no longer there. I didn't want the resentment and repercussions that invariably came with trying to hang on to something for too long. Better to put the memories under glass and have them always than to try to take this where it could not survive, like a magical object unable to cross into the real world without disintegrating into angry dust.

But as he watched me expectantly, I could not bring myself to extinguish his hope. 'I would love to see you,' I replied instead slowly, choosing my words with care, wanting to keep the possibility alive.

A strange expression crossed his face and I knew that he was not fooled. Deep down, he understood that this was the bargain we had made with time in exchange for this happiness, written in indelible ink. 'You can show me Washington. It will be nice,' he added, clinging stubbornly to this thread as though it could stop the days that were slipping rapidly from beneath us.

I open my eyes in the darkness. I had drifted off, for how long I do not know. I run my hand along the empty space beside me. The sheets are cool, not rumpled as they are when Jared has been here. What time is it? I listen for the sounds of students calling to one another as they spill from the pubs on their way home. But the street is silent except for a garbage truck collecting cans at the top of Lower Park Street.

I roll over. Three-thirty, the clock on the nightstand reads. The library closes at one. Jared has been coming to me later and later, but he is always here by now. I stand up and dress swiftly, pulling on my leggings and splash top, which I had laid across the chair in preparation for the next day's row. Then I step into my still-tied sneakers and start down the stairs.

Easy, I think as I walk swiftly up Park Street to Jesus Lane, then turn onto Malcolm Street, studying the dilapidated row homes on both sides. Maybe Jared decided to stay at home tonight. But he always comes to me. I walk to his house and take the porch steps two at a time. I ring the door buzzer twice, pressing the button down for several seconds, but there is no response. Where is he?

The river, I think. There is a spot by the Fort Saint George pub where Jared likes to sit and think. A few times we have taken a blanket and a bottle of wine there at night when the weather was warm. We laid on our backs, staring up at the endless sky, the field of stars revealed by the perfect darkness. But would he have gone there alone at this hour?

I cut through college, race out the back college gate. Let him be there, I pray as I make my way across the deserted darkness of Jesus Green as if on my way to some strange middle-of-the-night outing. I am half-way across Midsummer Common when I spot him, a figure huddled along the riverbank, shrouded by the willow trees that dip low to the water. Drawing closer, I pause. He sits, hands wrapped around his knees, staring at the water. 'Jared?'

He does not answer. I drop down beside him, my panic at searching for him replaced by a new sort of alarm. I touch his shoulder, then rear back as he jumps, fearing that he might lash out, not recognizing me. But he only blinks, his eyes clearing. 'Jo?' He looks around disoriented, as if waking from a dream and trying to remember where he is.

'Are you all right?'

'Yes, of course,' he says, sounding as though he is trying to convince himself.

'When I woke up and you weren't there...' I hesitate, not wanting to nag.

316

'I'm sorry if I worried you.'

'It's okay. It's just that you've seemed different somehow these past few days.' I pause, struggling to find the right words. 'Withdrawn. Preoccupied.' I take a deep breath, hating the insecurity of my own words even before they are spoken. 'Is it me?'

His eyes widen. 'God, no!' He straightens, drawing me into his arms and kissing my forehead, cheeks. 'Not you. Never you.' His voice is forceful, sincere. But then he recedes again, looking out at the water once more, not speaking, still holding me tight. He bites his lip as though wanting to say something, trying to decide if he should. 'Come away with me, Jo.'

'For a holiday?' I blink. How can he possibly want to go away now, with the race just weeks away? 'I suppose, we could manage a weekend, see if there are any short breaks on special.'

He shakes his head. 'For good. Let's get on a plane, go to Bali, or Johannesburg maybe, and never look back.'

My mind races. 'After graduation?'

'I'm not talking about after graduation. I mean now.'

'But the race—'

'Is just a race!' he explodes. 'Just a fucking college game! Whether we win or lose, our lives will be the same the next day and then it will just be something to brag about or lament at a reunion dinner once every ten years when we come back and see who is fat and thin, rich and poor, divorced and miserable and dead. Is that what you want your life to be? This place is so damn trite, all the parties and drinking...'

'But...' I say, then falter, stung by his words. In truth I know that he is right. To me, Cambridge has been

317

Camelot, the happiest place I have known. But I see it now as he does, a rich kids' playground, a party in a castle.

He grasps me by the shoulders. 'Let's get out of here,' he says again, his eyes burning. 'Let's go do something that actually matters for once.'

He's been drinking, I realize, catching a whiff of acrid breath. I notice then his bloodshot eyes, the saucerlike pupils. This surprises me more than anything else. He doesn't usually drink the night before an outing, or touch alcohol at all this close to a race. 'I think,' I begin carefully, 'that we should get some sleep and talk about this in the morning.'

He opens his mouth and for a minute I fear that he will refuse to come with me, that he will launch into another tirade. 'All right,' he says, his voice calm and rational now. I stand and he reaches up, putting his hand in mine like a child and climbing to his feet. Wordlessly he allows me to lead him back to my house.

In my room, I undress once more and climb in bed to my usual place beside the wall. He climbs in, curving himself around my back, and I am surprised to feel his hardness against me, his arousal in spite of the alcohol. His hand brushes my breast and I wonder if he will try to make love to me, but he buries his head in my neck and a moment later begins to breathe long and even. But I am awake now, my mind active from our conversation. Why would Jared talk about going away now, with the race just weeks away? He is panicking, I decide. It is about more than just winning. The moment we've worked for all these months will soon be here and then, win or lose, it will be over. And I will be gone.

I burrow deeper into his arms, close my eyes, begin to dream, as I so often do, that I am in the boat. We are just beginning an outing, warming up in pairs, then fours as we make our way past the other boathouses. The sky is low with clouds, the air warm and close. As we turn onto the Long Reach, all eight begin to row. I open my mouth, wanting to rebuke the crew for not waiting for my command, but no sound comes out. The boat is gaining speed, moving faster than we ever have, but the strokes are jerky and unsettled, sending water splashing up at me. I look at Chris, mutely signaling him for help, but he stares straight ahead, not seeing my distress.

Jared, I think, craning to see over Chris's broad shoulders. But at Jared's normal place at five sits a substitute, a strange, dark-haired boy I do not recognize. Where is Jared? Perhaps he traded places with someone. I lean forward, struggling to look farther down in the boat. But he is not there. Terror rising in me, I stand up. The boat begins to wobble, then tilts sharply to the left, capsizing, and as I am swallowed by the cold abyss of the water, everything goes black.

I open my eyes to the darkness of my bedroom, trying to raise myself from the clutches of the dream, gasping for breath. But the air does not come. There is something around my neck, I realize, reaching up: Jared's hands clamped tightly around my throat.

'Jared,' I try to croak, but as in the dream the sound will not come, the effort instead pressing the last bit of air that remains from my lungs. In the moonlight, I can see his eyes shut tightly, pupils moving beneath lids, as he struggles in his own dream, oblivious to what he is doing. His grip tightens around my throat, pressing against my windpipe. I am going to die, I

319

panic, as my head grows light.

Desperately I raise my knee to his groin. He cries out, his hands loosening as his eyes fly open. I inhale sharply. 'What happened?' he asks, clutching himself. 'Why did you kick me?' I continue sucking in great gulps of the air, unable to answer. 'Are you all right?' He looks down at my neck. There are marks, I can tell. Red finger marks, accusatory across the paleness of my skin in the moonlight. 'Oh God,' he leaps up, oblivious to his own pain. 'I'm so sorry. What was I doing?'

'It's okay,' I say, still shaken. 'It was just a dream. Come back to bed.' The fact that he did not mean to strangle me is of little comfort to either of us, though. He walks from the room. He's going to leave, I think, gripped by cold panic. But a few minutes later he returns, his hair damp around the edges of his face where he splashed water. He sits on the floor beside the bed, holding my hand until I drift off to sleep.

In the morning, bright sunlight filters through my eyelids, waking me. I lie still for a moment, smelling freshly cut grass through the open window, wondering if the previous night was a dream. Then I open my eyes. Jared is lying on the floor, his hand raised up to hold mine, just as he had done at rowing camp before anyone knew we were together. I start to rouse him, to convince him to return to bed. Then I stop, knowing it is pointless that no matter how hard I try to persuade him, he will not get back into bed with me again. Part of me is relieved. I cannot be sure he will not hurt me, lost in his nightmares, beyond conscious reach. What if I had been facing away from him, unable to kick and wake him to save my own life? My stomach twists, both hating and guiltily grateful for the distance he has put between us, doing the only thing he can to keep me safe.

chapter EIGHTEEN

It is cool and cloudy as I step out of the train station at Cambridge, a sharp breeze blowing stray newspapers and other debris across the pavement. I do not bother walking this time but climb into one of the taxis that waits at the front of the station. 'Trinity Hall,' I say to the driver.

As I sink back in the seat, I catch a glimpse of my reflection in the rearview mirror. My hair, which I slept on while damp at Sebastian's, flares wildly from my head in all directions. If only I could shower again, or at least throw on a base-ball cap. Of course I never would have done that as a student; it would have been too American, and I was always trying to fit in. I remember once as I stood by the side of the rugby pitch, watching a game, Ollie Smith, an arrogant kid from Leeds, had sidled up beside me. 'Nice trainers,' he sneered pointing at my white Reeboks in a tone that implied no British student would be caught dead wearing those at a social occasion, even a sporting match. I walked away, eyes burning. I had forgotten I was not like the other students. But in that moment the differences came rushing back and I knew I would always be a foreigner.

But the next day after we rowed, the crew all came to dinner wearing white athletic shoes. 'I don't understand...' I said.

'I overheard what that ass Ollie said to you,'

Chris replied. I could hear the anger in his voice. 'That which you do to the least of my brethren...'

'...you do to me,' I finished for him, touched by the show of solidarity. 'Thanks guys.'

Chris, I think now, as the cab draws close to the city center. He has always been such a loyal friend. Sebastian has to be wrong about him. But why didn't he tell me about losing his job? I lean my head against the back of the seat, rubbing my eyes and puzzling over all that has happened. If someone had told me twenty-four hours ago that I would be suspicious of Chris and have feelings for Sebastian, I would never have believed it. Everything is muddled now. Not to mention the fact that Vance is dead and Duncan is still missing. The answers, it seems, are more elusive than ever.

I pay the driver and make my way on foot through the market square to the end of Trinity Lane, where Trinity Hall sits. Despite its central location, it is easy to miss, a simple arched doorway in a stone building sandwiched by two of the larger colleges. Inside, its ivy-covered, brick-walled courtyards are textbook Cambridge. I hesitate by the entranceway to the first courtyard, trying to visualize the address Jared scrawled, to remember where the professors' offices are located. For a second I consider asking in the Porter's Lodge but I do not want to risk drawing attention to myself.

Instead I start around the courtyard, studying the nameplate beside the first doorway. But there are no names that sound close to Ang. I move to the next door, scanning the list. Anxiety rises in me. I could have sworn Jared's notes gave a college courtyard address, but what if I am wrong? His office could be at the remote Sedgwick site, where the history department is located. I start toward the next doorway. The third name listed is M. Ang. I open the door and start up the stairway that leads to the fellows' rooms on the second and third floors. He might not be here, I remind myself. And even if he is, he might not remember anything from the conference or have kept his papers. At the second-floor landing, I walk toward the doorway to room three. But the space beside the door is an empty square, the drywall rough where something was taken down and not repaired.

I knock on the door, which is ajar. 'Hello?'

'Come in,' a female voice says. I push the door open. Inside, a plain, fiftyish woman stands behind a large wood desk, sorting stacks of books. Sunlight streams through the stained-glass window behind her, illuminating the dust mites that dance through the air. Overflowing bookshelves climb to the ceiling. 'Can I help you?'

'I'm looking for Professor Ang. Is this the right office?' She cocks her head, staring at me in a way that seems to warrant an explanation. 'I'm a former student of his,' I lie. 'Back in town and hoping to talk to him about a project we worked on together.'

'Oh dear,' she says, setting down the books and leaning against the desk chair for support. 'You haven't heard, have you? Then again, I suppose you wouldn't have, being from America and all. Professor Ang passed away.'

'He's dead?' Her eyes widen at the abruptness of my question. 'I'm sorry, I mean, I'm just so surprised.' I force sadness into my voice. 'What happened? I mean when did he...?' I choose my words carefully in case there is a long-term illness I should have known about.

'About five weeks ago. It was a car accident while on holiday in France.'

'I'm so sorry.' Easy, I tell myself. He died in a car accident. There's nothing suspicious about that. But my mind races, riddled with paranoia after all that has happened. Is it coincidence that Ang died now?

'If only he hadn't gone.' The woman's voice grows heavy with sadness. 'The professor didn't even want to go, you know,' she adds. 'He was never one for travel. But his wife insisted.' Her last words drip with disdain. Was this woman more than a secretary to Professor Ang, a lover maybe, or simply an assistant with an unrequited crush?

'How dreadful,' I murmur. I weigh the information, considering whether it has value to me, and decide that it does not. 'I was actually coming to see the professor to find a paper I worked on with him any number of years ago. I don't suppose you'd still have his files. Maybe I could look for it...'

'I'm afraid I don't. I sent all of his personal effects to his family in Exeter last week. All that's left are the books. College insisted that I get the office ready for a fellow they've brought in to teach for him.' Her tone makes clear that the room should have been left as a shrine indefinitely. 'You could try the library, though. They kept a catalog of the faculty's published works.'

Only this one was never published. 'Thank you anyway.'

I make my way back down the steps, then out of the college. On the street, I stop again, my shoulders slumping. Ang is dead, and so are my chances of getting the paper, at least from him. What now? I could just get on the next train back to London. Cambridge, it seems, is a dead end again. I start toward King's College chapel, set against an ominous gray sky. It looked so imposing just a few days ago. Then I feared its wrath, the questions it seemed to ask. Now I am demanding answers. But its grandeur seems to conspire against me, standing sentinel to obscure the truth I came to learn. I think of Sarah, lying in her hospital bed, of Vance, who was almost certainly killed for knowing too much. Of Jared. Anger rises white hot in me, boils and bubbles over. There is more to be learned here.

I turn and head north toward Lords, uncertain exactly of where I am going or what I am going to do. Halfway down Jesus Lane, I stop, looking toward Malcolm Street. A hand seems to grip my throat. From the top of the block I see it: Jared's house. No different than the rest, a dilapidated row house, three stories high, subdivided into rooms for a half-dozen or so students with shared bathrooms and a kitchen. Slowly, as if against my own will, I walk toward it. Then, standing in front of the house, I take a step forward, peer down. My throat tightens. Through a low gate, a set of steps leads to Jared's ground-floor flat. I turn

325

away and instead climb the stairs to the porch and study the door buttons that ring to each of the flats, names scrawled beside each on scraps of paper, covered by the tape that holds them in place. I run my finger across the bottom piece of paper. How many layers would I have to peel back to find Jared's name?

My thoughts are interrupted by a loud creaking sound. I leap backward as the front door swings open unexpectedly. 'Hallo!' a cockney voice booms. A stout, round-faced woman in a flower print dress and apron appears in the doorway, holding a mop. 'Can I help?' I struggle to catch my breath. 'Didn't mean to startle you,' the woman adds. 'Thought it was one of the students forgotten their key.'

Nettie, I recall. Though she was considerably thinner then, and her hair more brown than its present gray, I still recognize the woman as the same one who had been the bedder for this end of Malcolm Street, cleaning the student houses. 'Hi, Nettie,' I manage at last. 'You probably don't remember me, but I'm–'

'I know who you are,' Nettie interrupts. 'One of the students, or used to be anyway. You used to go with the young fella in the basement.' She presses her lips together. 'One who died.'

A lump forms in my throat. 'Yes. My name is Jordan.'

'That's it, Jordan!' she exclaims, as though she remembered on her own. 'Nice to see you. Come on in.' I hesitate, staring through the doorway behind her. I had not imagined actually going into Jared's house. But Nettie has turned and waddled down the hallway. As I step into the dilapidated foyer, a familiar smells fills my nostrils. It is the scent of old heaters and burned toast, of damp carpet and too many people living in too close a space, unchanged by the years. Nettie sets down her mop against the wall, wiping her hands on her apron. 'I was just about to make myself a spot of tea. Would you like some?'

I start to say no. It is only a matter of time before Maureen finds me missing and figures out where I have gone. I have to keep moving. But it may be worth asking Nettie some questions. And the kitchen is downstairs, beside Jared's old room. 'That would be lovely.'

I follow Nettie down to the kitchen. 'What brings you back here?' she asks as she fills the electric kettle.

Good question. I pause uncertainly, as a dozen answers flood my mind. 'I'm writing a book about my time at Cambridge,' I say at last, choosing an outright lie.

Nettie smiles widely over her shoulder. 'Ooh, will it be one of them romance stories?'

I fight the urge to laugh. 'Maybe. But right now I'm just doing some research. Trying to remember things. And I was wondering if I could take a look around.'

Nettie purses her lips. 'I suppose so. You'll want to see your fella's room, I suspect?'

'Please.' I hold my breath as she processes my request, remembering how the Master might have told the staff not to cooperate with Chris and me.

Nettie waves her arm. 'Go ahead. Have a look

while the water's boiling. Room's unlocked and the boy who lives there now won't be home for hours.' I walk out of the kitchen to the door beside it. Through a new coat of white paint, I can still see the scratch where Jared dented the door, trying to move a chair. Taking a deep breath, I turn the handle and step inside. Tears spring to my eyes. It is someone else's room now, adorned with posters of heavy metal rock groups, photos of students drinking and making obscene gestures at the camera, things that Jared never would have hung. But the furniture is the same, the tiny single bed, the spartan desk and dresser by the window. Even the smell, a damp basement odor, is unchanged.

I spin around slowly, then drop to the floor. A thousand memories race through my mind, nights spent whispering and making love in the narrow bed, waking up in Jared's arms. An image pops into my head, different from all the rest. It was May 3, my twenty-second birthday, and Jared surprised me with breakfast in bed, fresh-cut melon and strawberries. Afterward, he drew me into his arms, kissing me even more urgently than usual. When he put himself inside, I was surprised to feel him not wearing a condom. We'd been so fastidious to that point, despite the fact that I was on the Pill. He only planned to stay that way for a minute, I know, just to feel what it was like. But the indescribable closeness, the warmth of his skin against my insides paralyzed us both. Then he gave a slight shake of his head, an apology for what he could no longer hold back, and as he began to move toward the inevitable finish, I

328

knew it was too late, that in that moment something between us changed forever.

Enough, I shudder, shaking the image from my
mind. I only have a minute or two before Nettie
calls me for tea. I stare up through the window to
the street above, trying to piece together those last
few weeks, sifting through the information I
gathered, trying to get inside Jared's head. He was
frustrated that no one would listen to him about
the Nazi money. (Nazi money – the concept still
seems far-fetched, too impossibly remote for the
real world.) Scared enough to buy one-way plane
tickets. I remember then the long walks he'd
taken at night, the haunted look in his eyes after
he returned, his heart racing as though it would
burst through his chest. Who was chasing you,
Jared?

My eyes drop to the desk beneath the window,
a simple wooden plank on four metal legs. It is
bare and neat now, not like when Jared covered it
with so many books and papers you could barely
find the bottom. Something on the underside
catches my eye. A dark spot, too symmetrical and
defined to be a knot in the wood. I crawl closer
to get a better look. Grasping the edge of the
desk, I feel along the bottom. It is not in the
wood, I realize, as my hand brushes against a
hard, raised object, but something attached to it:
a key held fast by tape. I pry away the tape and
pull out a small key. What could it possibly open?
It is probably just a bike key.

Hearing footsteps outside the door, I stand up
quickly and shove the key in my pocket. A
moment later, Nettie pushes open the door,

holding two steaming mugs in her hand. 'Tea's on,' she announces. 'If you've had enough time here.'

'Yes,' I reply quickly. 'Thank you for letting me have a look. For old times' sake.' I follow her back to the kitchen. It is a classic shared student kitchen with cheap white appliances and counter-tops, and notes reminding the others to wash their own dishes and not borrow milk without asking stuck to the front of the half-sized refrigerator. I pull out a plastic chair from the table and sit. 'Nettie, can I ask you something?'

She carries milk and sugar to the table and sits down. 'Certainly, lovey. What is it?'

'Were you here the day Jared was found?'

Nettie tilts her head, stirring sugar into her cup. 'You askin' for your book?'

'No.' I swallow a mouthful of tea. 'I'm asking for me.'

'The morning he was found, I was. I come in and the police are everywhere. Don't touch noth-ing, they told me. I figured after a few days they would want me to pack up his stuff and send it to his folks. But the next day, I came in and it was all gone.'

'Did you clean the room then?'

Nettie shakes her head. 'It was already done. Looked as if no one had lived there.'

Nettie was, I knew, the only bedder for the house. 'Do you know who cleaned it?'

'Me, I didn't ask. I was glad for the help, what with looking after six houses and all. But it wasn't any of the other girls neither, I can tell you that.'

A fist seems to tighten around my stomach.

'How about before he died – do you remember anything unusual?'

'No, he was always right quiet. Never any girls here at all except for you.' I smile inwardly. 'So sad that he passed away.'

I can tell she has nothing more to offer. I finish my tea and carry my cup to the sink. 'Thanks, Nettie.'

'It was just tea.'

'For the conversation, I mean.' I reach over and pat her hand. 'For remembering Jared.'

'It's good to see you.' I start up the stairs. 'Wait,' she calls. I turn around to face Nettie below. 'There's one other thing.'

'Yes?'

'Well, it's just that I didn't see Jared that often. He wasn't one of those lazy student types, y'know. Not like some, always laying about and sleeping late, making it hard to clean. He was always out before I got here, what with his studies and rowing and all.' Nettie twists the front of her apron uneasily. 'I just think that maybe you might want to talk to someone who saw him more than me, like Tony.' Nettie blushes.

I nod. I had almost forgotten about the rumors that the boatman and Nettie were an item. 'That's a good idea.'

'Tony was running errands this morning but you should be able to catch him at the boathouse just before one. Jared spent a lot of time there, y'know. Tony always spoke so fondly of him. He might have some information.' She pauses, looking at me evenly. 'For your book, that is.'

I know then that she is not fooled by my story.

331

'Thanks, Nettie.' The older woman does not answer, but turns and disappears back into the kitchen.

I hurry onto the street, considering what Nettie said. I hadn't thought to talk to Tony. Jared would not have confided in him, and I doubt that the prickly boatman would have noticed anything – he was always sequestered in his shop, preoccupied with fixing broken riggers and smashed bows, replacing oars. But it is worth a try.

I look at my watch. Nettie said Tony would be back before one but it's not yet noon. My stomach grumbles, reminding me that I haven't eaten since yesterday. I walk to the far end of the road where it dead-ends into King Street. The road is best known for its large number of pubs, eight when I was a student, and for the King Street Run, a popular challenge where students attempt to drink a pint at each pub without breaking to go to the loo. I make my way to Saint Radegund's Free Press, 'the Rad' as it was simply known, the smallest of the King Street pubs, located at the end of the road on the left. It was a student favorite, most notably known for its lock-ins: as closing time neared, Perry the barman would ring the bell and shout 'half-time' instead of calling for last orders, resulting in loud cheers from the students who could stay and continue to drink well into the night.

The pub is deserted now, a young woman I do not recognize behind the bar where Perry should be, putting away pint glasses. 'Can I order a sandwich?'

'I'm afraid the kitchen isn't open for lunch yet,'

she replies, gesturing to the clock above the bar. 'I can ask if there might be some breakfast left, though.'

'That would be great.'

I walk to one of the tables and sink down into a chair. Above the bar, a soap opera plays on the television. Remembering the key I found beneath the desk, I pull it out. It's probably not even Jared's. Some kid is going to go looking for it and not be able to unlock his bike.

But the key is old, peeling at the bits of yellowed tape still stuck to it as though it hasn't been removed from its hiding place in years. And not a bike key, either, I realize, reading the fine engraving on the back: Hudson's PLC. Hudson's was a bank on Saint Andrews Street that catered to the businesses and shops. I'd never been inside, preferring like most students the Barclays branch with its simple, no-fee checking accounts that suited our low balances. The key must be to a safe deposit box there. That doesn't mean it was Jared's, I remind myself sternly. Any one of a dozen students who had lived in that room could have taped it to the desk.

But an image pops into my mind. I was walking back from the University Library one afternoon in May and as I came down Sidney Street past Sainsbury's supermarket, I'd seen Jared coming out of Hudson's Bank. It struck me as a little unusual, as I knew he had a Barclays student account like the rest of us. 'Clearing up a wiring issue with my stipend,' he'd offered vaguely by way of explanation. At the time, I didn't think to question it. But now, holding the key in my hand,

I wonder if it was something more.

I'll go to the bank after I see Tony, I decide, tucking it back in my pocket as the barmaid returns with a lukewarm cup of coffee and a plate of reheated scrambled eggs, beans, and tomato. I inhale deeply, savoring the familiar scent. It is hard to believe I haven't had English breakfast since I've been back. I take one big mouthful, then another.

Ten minutes later, my breakfast finished, I carry my dishes back to the bar. 'That was delicious, thanks,' I say, as the woman rings up the meal on the till.

'Four pounds, twenty pence.' I pass her a twenty-pound note, looking up at the television screen once more. The soap opera has broken for a newsflash of some sort, reporters clustered around a tall, red-haired woman. Maureen, I realize, freezing. I cannot hear what she is saying but she is still wearing the same clothes as when I saw her at the hospital early this morning. Had the media somehow learned about Sarah's attack?

But that is not it, I realize quickly. Something is different about Mo from when I last saw her. Her eyes are red, her hair wild. No longer just tired, she is distraught. Lights from emergency vehicles flash in the background behind her. 'Can you turn that up please?' I ask the barmaid.

She picks up a remote control. '...investigating all possible causes,' Maureen is saying, her voice raspy.

The camera cuts away to a male reporter standing a few feet from the throng. 'The gas explosion at the Hammersmith flat occurred just before five...'

That's my house, I realize with a start, recognizing the row of flats behind the reporter. Or was. A smoking pile of rubble is all that remains where my flat had been, a gaping hole of splintered wood ripped from the adjacent unit. Behind it sits the river, now fully visible from the street.

The barmaid clucks her tongue and says something about the dangers of gas cooking. But I do not answer. The screen cuts again, this time to earlier footage of something long and dark being loaded into an ambulance from the street. A body bag. My heart stops. Someone died in the explosion. The reporter's voice weaves through the buzzing in my ears, '...diplomat killed.' The screen cuts to a photograph of a young woman in a navy suit, black hair pulled back low and tight. An official diplomatic photo of ... me.

They think I am dead, I realize. Then I understand Mo's red eyes. I have to call her, tell her that it is a mistake. But that means someone else died in the explosion.

'Your change,' the barmaid says, but I do not respond. Sophie, I think. I sent her to my apartment for the papers. Now I know why she never made it to the train station. She was killed at my flat, in an 'accident' that was intended for me.

chapter NINETEEN

Sophie's dead.

The words reverberate in my brain. I see her walking up to my apartment, turning the door-knob. How far inside did she make it before the explosion? Had she sensed something was wrong and tried to leave? I lean against the bar and bury my head in my hands. This is my fault. I never should have asked her to go to my house for my own selfish purposes.

'Ma'am, are you all right?' the barmaid asks.

I look up at the woman's half-concerned, half-fearful expression. 'Just got dizzy for a moment.' I straighten. 'Keep the change.' The woman's eyes widen as her hand closes around the fifteen pounds. Breathe, I command myself as I walk from the pub. Think.

Sophie's dead. I remember my diplomatic photograph flashing across the television. Everyone thinks that it is me. I see Mo's grief-stricken face, her red eyes. I should call and tell her that I am okay. I reach for my phone, then hesitate. The safest thing for me right now is for my attackers to keep thinking that I am dead. Mo can be trusted, of course, but I cannot call her now, when she is surrounded by all those reporters.

My attackers. Someone blew up my flat, thinking I would be in it. And it was gas again – undoubtedly the same people who tried to kill

336

Sarah. I imagine her lying in her hospital bed, hearing the news report of my death on television. I have to tell her that I am alive.

I open my cell phone and scroll down the calls received, redialing the number for the nurses' station and asking for Sarah's room. As the call transfers, I hold my breath. What if someone is with her or listening in on the line? My thumb feels for the end-call button but before I can press it, there is a click and Sarah picks up the phone. 'Hello,' she says, and I can tell from her hoarse, cracked voice that she has been watching the news.

'Don't say anything,' I instruct tersely.

'B-but you're...' I hear her struggling for breath, trying to process the fact that I am not dead.

'I'm fine,' I say, realizing as the words come out of my mouth that it might be the overstatement of the year.

'Thank goodness.' Relief floods the phone line. 'When I saw–'

I cut her off. 'I can't stay on the phone but I wanted you to know. You can't tell anyone, though.'

'Not even M–'

'Not even her. I'll tell her as soon as the crowd clears.'

'Did you get to see the professor?'

'No, he died just over a month ago.'

'Oh, no! Do you think...?'

'That it was related?' I pause, considering the idea. 'I don't know. It was a car accident in France, so it could just be a coincidence. But in any case, we can't get the paper from him.'

'We'll just have to find it another way.'

We, I think, my guilt at involving Sarah rising once more. 'You just rest and concentrate on getting better. I have to keep moving.' Picturing Sarah alone in the hospital room, my uneasiness grows. Whoever succeeded in killing Vance and Sophie might come after Sarah again. 'Are you okay?'

'Fine,' she replies quickly, understanding. 'I'm feeling much better and the guards are here all the time. Don't worry about me. Just be careful.'

'I will. I'll see you soon.'

I close the phone. I could call Sebastian to see if he is all right, if he knows any more about what happened than what they said on the news. Then I decide against it. Before all this, I could have counted on him not to tell Maureen where I am, but now, if he's upset about Sophie ... is he upset about Sophie? I pause, considering the question. She was our teammate and he was dating her, at least for a bit. In fact, she might have been safe with him this morning, if it wasn't for me.

Pushing down my guilt, I continue along King Street until its end at a roundabout and cross to the edge of Midsummer Common, then stop again. Beyond the park sits the river, the boat-houses splayed across its far bank. My stomach knots and for a minute I contemplate turning around, running for the station and catching the first train to London. But Nettie said that Tony might know something. No, I have taken it this far and I owe it to everyone – not just Jared, but Vance and Sophie and Sarah – to see this through, run down every lead no matter how thin. I force myself to continue forward across the expanse of parkland, past the joggers and dog walkers, toward the footbridge at the Fort Saint George.

On the far side of the bridge, the boathouses lay in midday quiet, waiting for the students who have abandoned them to lectures and supervisions to come again. As the Lords boathouse comes into view, I stop. A lump forms in my throat and I look to the upstairs balcony, willing Jared to appear as he had the day we met.

I cannot do this. Suddenly I want to flee. I have done all that anyone expected me to do. But even as I finish the thought, I know that I cannot turn back now. No one made me come here today. This was my choice, the subconscious bargain I made with myself the day I walked into the Director's office and asked for London, sealed the moment I set foot on the plane. All roads led me here, and there is no going back, or around – only through. Steeling myself, I make my way to the boathouse.

Outside the door to the boathouse, I stop again. In the corner sits a small gold plaque. It is set low to the ground, easily missed if one is not looking for it. I kneel, running my fingers over the engraving. 'In memory of Jared Short,' it reads. That's all. No mention of who he was or how he died, even when he was here.

Straightening, I open the wood door and am assaulted by the familiar smell of dampness and sweat. Inside, I struggle to adjust my eyes to the dim light. To the left sit the darkened bays where long boats sleep on racks like giant birds nesting. The whirring sound of an ergometer, a lone rower training, filters down the stairs from the locker rooms above. Straight ahead I can hear the sound of big band music playing on a tinny radio. I knock on the half-open door. 'Come in!' a gruff voice bellows.

I push the door open and step through. Tony's workshop is exactly as I remembered it: floors and tables piled high with open jars and wood scraps, unidentifiable metal pieces and tools, the air a heady mix of cigarette smoke and turpentine (perhaps not the best combination). At the far end of the room sits a small man with white hair, hunched over a metal rigger, a stub of a cigarette dangling from his mouth. 'What do you want?' he asks, not looking up.

'Hello, Tony,' I begin hesitantly. He has seen almost thirty years of rowers come and go. 'I don't know if you remember me. I'm–'

'I know who you are,' he interrupts. 'You're the American who coxed the first May boat in ninety-eight. The Aylings shell.' Inwardly I smile. Tony might not remember names, but he knows every crew and piece of equipment that has passed through his boathouse. 'Busted up a boat the year before.' I cringe at this. I was hoping he would have forgotten the Great Crash of '97, as it came to be known. At the start of the May Bumps in my first year, the rudder fell off the bottom of the boat, unbeknownst to me. As we raced around Ditton corner, I wasn't able to navigate the sharp turn and we ran, at full speed, into the bank. Four of the rowers wound up on land, the boy at bow rowing against a tree. 'What do you want?' he repeats, still working the rigger.

I pause. The years, it seems, have not softened his demeanor. 'I'm Jordan Weiss. I'm back for a visit and Nettie suggested that I speak to you,' I add quickly.

He looks up. ''Bout what?' he asks, his voice relaxing at the mention of the bedder.

'Jared Short. Do you remember him?' He does not answer, but takes a long drag from his cigarette, then grinds it out in an overflowing ashtray on the workbench beside him. 'He sat in the five seat in my first May boat,' I persist.

Tony nods. 'He moved back from the seven seat to five after you two started going out.' I am surprised; I didn't think Tony would have noticed that Jared and I were dating. 'Drowned,' he adds. His face sags and I can tell that he regards the loss of one of 'his' boys to the river as a personal failure.

'Right. I was wondering if you remember anything that last semester. The last few weeks before Jared died.' I do not bother to make excuses as I did with Nettie. Tony either knows something or he doesn't.

'Nothing I can recall. It was a busy time, you know, during the Bumps. Lots of races, lots of wrecks. Jared was a good boy, not bothering me every day like some.' Tony's forehead wrinkles. 'I do remember ... one night that June, I heard him yelling at someone up on the balcony.'

Inwardly I shrugged. Jared yelled at everyone. 'That could have been me.'

'Nah. He never got angry at you, not like this. It was he and another fella arguing something fierce.'

'About what?'

'Can't rightly say. But it was nighttime and I remember thinking it was strange they were here, because it was too dark to row and too close to a race for them to be on the erg machines. And they wasn't fighting about rowing, I'm sure, or I woulda stuck my nose in and given them what-for. No, it was about something else, something I couldn't understand. The other boy wanted something from your boyfriend, or wanted him to do something, and he wouldn't. They got pretty heated. I told 'em to pipe down and they went away real quick after that.'

'Do you remember who he was talking to?'

He shakes his head. 'It was so long ago. Have you been to the site? Where he's buried, I mean?'

Caught off guard, I hesitate. 'Never. I mean not since–'

'It's a beautiful spot. I stop by every so often, to clear the brush and such. Haven't been there for a month, since I twisted my knee. But you should go, pay respects. Might help you put it all to rest.'

I look at him uncertainly. Tony does not know, of course, why I am here, that a simple visit to Jared's grave will not bring me peace. 'I would, but it will take at least an hour to walk there and another to come back. I need to get back to London before then.'

'And you never were much for bikes,' he recalls. 'You want to borrow my scull?'

I hesitate. Part of me wants to run from the boathouse. I have come far enough. But Tony is right: I should go. I need to go. 'Please.'

'All right,' he says. 'But don't break my bloody boat!'

I cannot help but smile. It is an old joke, his admonishment to each of the coxes as they set off down the river. 'I won't, I promise.'

Ten minutes later I am seated in the narrow, single shell, two oars resting neatly in my lap. 'You remember how to do it?' he asks, wincing as he crouches down on the bank beside me. I nod. It was Tony who taught me to scull over a few quiet Sunday afternoons in the Michaelmas Term of my first year. You couldn't be a good coxswain, he said, without knowing how to row yourself.

'I'll have it back in an hour.'

'Door will be unlocked if I'm not here.'

'Thanks, Tony.' I start to push off.

'Wait a minute!' He slaps his forehead, then grabs the edge of the shell so roughly it threatens to tip. Water splashes over the side, soaking the front of my pants, as he pulls me back into the bank. 'I just remembered who Jared was arguing with that night. It was the blond boy. Loud one.'

My stomach jumps. 'Chris Bannister?'

'That's 'im. He was captain that year, I think. Don't know how I could have forgotten. The two of them were always together. But it was the only time I ever saw them fight.' He shakes his head. 'I'm such a daft old man.'

'Not at all. But you don't happen to remember what they were arguing about now, do you?'

'I wish I could.' He releases the boat, staring off into the distance.

'Thanks,' I say again, pushing off gently from the bank once more. I look over my shoulder to make sure nothing is coming, then lean forward in my seat, arms extended toward my ankles. I bend my knees, sliding my bottom toward my feet, moving slowly so as not to upset the boat. I can feel Tony watching me from the bank, appraising my technique, how much I remember. As the oars enter the water, I push back, straightening my legs and drawing my arms into my lap, sending the boat backward with a short wobbly motion. As I begin the cycle again, my movements grow more confident, fluid. When I turn back, Tony has disappeared.

Looking over my shoulder once more, I guide the scull past the boathouses. This is not the river I knew; as a cox, I faced forward, steering us through the obstacles ahead. But now I see the scene behind unfold as the boys had, the town fading into the horizon, the houseboats that line this stretch of the river appearing then disappearing again in the mist.

As I paddle beneath Chesterton Footbridge, I can feel the river unfolding ahead. Grassy reeds line the bank, fens stretching endlessly into the gray horizon. Settling into the rhythm of my stroke, I let my thoughts return to what Tony said: Jared and Chris were fighting shortly before Jared's death. It wasn't unusual for them to disagree about running the boat club, but Tony said it wasn't about rowing. And it was strange for Chris to be the one yelling – he idolized Jared. Usually Jared's temper got the better of him, even after we started dating and I had, as the boys said 'mellowed him out.'

As I pass under the railway bridge into the Long Reach, I gaze over my shoulder once more.

The river is quiet at midday, broken only by the occasional fisherman along the bank. A vision pops into my mind of a spring evening. Jared and I had gotten Chinese takeout and carried it down the towpath, dropping to the ground by the water's edge and watching the sunset behind grazing cows as we ate, neither speaking. Things were so simple, peaceful. How did it turn into all of this?

I steer the shell around the gentle curve at Ditton Corner. The river grows narrower here, the banks thick with trees on either side. A few seconds later, I turn onto Plough Reach. Ahead, on the left bank, a lone willow leans heavily toward the water, marking Jared's grave. I take a final stroke, then brush the oars gently against the water's surface, letting the boat run until it slows, guiding myself into the bank. I climb out carefully, pulling my weight forward with my arms as I'd been taught and crossing the oars against the bank so the boat will not drift away.

Straightening, my breath catches. About ten feet from the bank stands the simple marble grave, lone and ill-fitting among the trees. Trembling, I walk to it, then kneel. The headstone was not here the last time I was; then the grave was marked by only a raised mound of dirt, a cross someone crudely fashioned with sticks. Now I run my fingers across the lettering: JARED SHORT, FEBRUARY 1, 1976–JUNE 12, 1998.

'I'm sorry,' I whisper. Sorry I didn't push harder to find out what was troubling you, that I let you down that final night. That I haven't been able to find out who did this to you, that I have been gone for so long. I fight against the tears Jared would not have wanted. But the regrets rush forth, and I sink to the ground, sobbing. I know now that finding Jared's killer is no longer just about finding the truth. It is about redemption.

Why did I come here? It is not, I realize, just because Tony suggested it. No, I came looking for answers. I put both hands on the tombstone, as though Jared might kinetically transfer his secrets to me. I am overcome by a wave of frustration. 'What!?' I shout through my tears, looking up at the unbroken grayness of the sky. 'What is it that you want me to know?' My voice disappears, swallowed into the thickness of the trees, and then the air is silent again, except for the sound of a bird chirping in the distance.

Wiping my eyes, I study the lone grave once more. I cannot help but contrast it to the American cemetery at Madingley, to which Jared and I biked that spring day, to the rows and rows of identical tombstones. Is Jared lonely here? No, I decide instantly. He would have wanted this, a quiet place by the water, only the trees and birds as company.

The silence is broken by the rumble of a train crossing the railway bridge in the distance behind me. There is nothing more for me to do here. It is time to go. Reluctantly, I stand up, wiping the dirt from my knees. I take a step backward, studying the trees, which grow thicker as they recede from the river bank. Suddenly I notice something moving a few feet beyond the grave. It

346

is a small rabbit, not much more than a baby, hopping among the trees, dwarfed by the thick trunks, nearly hidden by the brush. I watch as it moves closer to the gravestone, then disappears behind it.

Intrigued, I lean forward, peering around the stone to get a better view. Then I stop. The ground on the far side looks different. The grass seems fresher, not as long and unkempt as on the front. I might have thought that Tony cut the grass, but he said he has not been here in a month. Curious, I crawl around the stone and kneel, running my hand along the earth. Closer now, I can see that the ground is covered with grass clippings, as though someone has taken then from a mower bag and sprinkled them here. I brush the grass aside. Underneath, the dirt is fresh and damp, recently pressed into place. My heart quickens. Someone has been here.

Looking back toward the towpath, I wonder for a moment if it might have been vandals. But then I study the ground once more, running my hand along the line where it has been disturbed. The edges are neat, the lines meticulous, running several feet back behind the tombstone in a long, rectangular shape. The shape of a coffin.

No, whoever was here was professional, deliberate.

And they were digging at Jared's grave.

chapter TWENTY

I stare at the ground. Someone dug down to Jared's coffin, but why? I thrust my hands into the cool, moist dirt; I am seized with the urge to start tearing at the earth, to see what lies beneath. But it is too heavy and I cannot dig that far. I need to get help, to tell someone what I've found.

I race to the bank and climb into the scull, rowing back as quickly as I can, my strokes short and uneven. But when I reach the boathouse and pull into the bank, Tony's car is gone. 'Back in an hour,' reads a note on the door.

Damn. I need to ask him about the grave site. I retrieve my bag from inside the workshop, then hesitate uncertainly. What now? I still need to go to the bank, I remind myself. I can go there, check back with Tony later.

On the far side of the river, I make my way across Jesus Green. At Lower Park Street, I stop, eyeing the row of simple gray brick houses that line the left side of the road. Mine was the fourth on the left. I look up at the second-floor window, remembering long afternoons curled up in a chair, sipping tea as I worked on my thesis, breaking often to gaze out at an impromptu football game, children playing in the grass. Life here *was* the ultimate playground with high walls. Was it ever that simple for Jared, I wonder now?

Maybe once. But then he'd seen what lay on the other side of those walls and it changed him. He tried to protect me, to keep the truth of whatever he'd seen from me. And now that truth is the one thing I need, the only thing that would give me closure and make me whole again.

I press on and a few minutes later reach Saint Andrews Street and the main thoroughfare of shops. Hudson's Bank was just past Sainsbury's market, I recall. But when I reach the spot, the bank is gone, a discount travel agency in its place. I walk inside. A young male clerk sits behind a desk, typing on a keyboard.

Customer service here, I remember, is not what it is in the United States. 'Excuse me, but wasn't there a Hudson's Bank at this location?'

He does not look up. 'Closed about five years ago.'

My heart sinks. 'My family had a safe-deposit box there. Where would that have gone?'

The clerk, visibly annoyed that I haven't come to inquire about the cheap weekend getaway to Majorca advertised in the front window, stands up and walks to the back of the shop. I start to leave. 'Miss,' a voice calls after me. I turn back, surprised. 'My manager says that the boxes all went to the Barclays down the street.'

'Thank you.' I race out onto the street. Barclays Bank is a half block north on the same side. Inside, the cheap blue furniture and pressboard walls seem unchanged by the years. Bypassing the line of students waiting at the window, I walk to one of the new-accounts clerks seated at a desk. 'I had a safe-deposit box at Hudson's. I understand that they were moved here.' The clerk stares at me evenly and for a minute I wonder if she will ask for identification, proof that the box is mine. But she stands and leads me to the rear of the bank, punches in a code, and opens a door to reveal a wall of boxes.

The clerk leaves the room and closes the door behind her. I stare up at the rows of boxes. I do not even know if Jared had a box here. Even if the key does belong to him, the box could have been at a bank home in Wales, or anywhere. And if it is here, what would the number be? Perhaps I should just start trying each box. But there are hundreds; the clerk will surely come back before then. And I do not know if there is a hidden surveillance camera somewhere in the room. Think.

Would he have used his birthday? I go to the box with the digits that match the month, date, and year of his birth, 2176, but the key gets halfway in and sticks. I twist in both directions, struggling to pull it out. People here sometimes express the birth date before the month, I recall, but the key does not fit in 1276 either.

The hotel stationery, I remember then. The piece of paper that cost Sophie her life. There were numbers on it. Could those be related to the safe-deposit box? I close my eyes, pressing my hands to my temples and trying to remember. I can see the first three digits, 328. They struck me because March 28 was the very date that Jared and I first kissed. But the fourth digit is a blank. I walk to the place where the boxes begin numbered 3280. That box is high on the wall, so even standing on my tiptoes I can barely reach. They key will not go in the lock. I move to the next box and this time the key goes in but will not turn. My shoulders sag with disappointment. Perhaps the numbers Jared scribbled have nothing to do with a safe-deposit box at all. But I have to keep trying. Hurriedly I move onto 3282, then 3283, my heart sinking with each failed attempt. The clerk will be back any minute now. I insert the key into 3284 and it slides in easily. Holding my breath, I turn the key. The box opens with an easy click.

I pull the box from the wall and set it on the table, my heart pounding. A safe-deposit box. Jared's box. Why did he keep it? And why didn't his mother, or someone else, come to claim it after all these years? I pull the box from the wall and set it on the table. The room is silent except for the low whirring of a fan in the ceiling. I hold my breath as I open the lid, expecting to find the cash he asked his mother to wire, or perhaps some papers explaining his research. But inside it is empty, except for a small gray box. A jewelry box, I realize, lifting it.

I open it, then gasp. A diamond ring stares back at me.

The box falls from my hand and bounces on the floor. Hurriedly I pick it up. The ring is white gold, a modest diamond solitaire. Exactly the kind of ring I would have picked. I take the ring from the box and slip it on my fourth finger. The fit is almost perfect, a little too snug, but ideal for my thinner fingers of college days.

An engagement ring. Jared was going to ask me to marry him.

This explains so much – Jared's secretiveness, the money he asked his mother to send. Perhaps the plane tickets to Rio were intended for us to elope or take a honeymoon (though the tickets were one-way). But it does not help me figure out why he was killed.

I take off the ring and hold it again, considering. So Jared wanted to marry me. It seems unlike him to be so impulsive. When did he plan to give it to me? Had he changed his mind or simply never had the chance before he died? I was never one of those girls who dreamed of getting married. But now I picture him picking out the ring, nervously planning how to propose. What would my reaction have been? I imagine saying yes, the news spreading joyously throughout the college. We would have been married in the chapel, I am sure, a small ceremony. And then I would have canceled my plane ticket home and found a way to make a life here with Jared.

It would all have been so perfect. Knowing now what he wanted for us, the possibility of what might have been, makes his death hurt more than ever.

I shake my head, clearing the vision from my mind, and reluctantly place the ring back in the jewelry box. Then I hesitate. What should I do with it? Wearing it does not feel right, not when Jared did not give it to me. But I cannot leave it here. I put the jewelry box into my bag, then close the box and walk from the vault.

Outside, I look at my watch. One-fifty, nearly an hour since I left the boathouse. I start to retrace my steps toward the river.

As I near the edge of Jesus Green, I reach into my pocket for my cell phone. I need to call Mo, to tell her that I am alive. Much as I like to keep running with the impunity of the dead, it isn't fair to make her grieve much longer. And I need to get to her before she calls my parents and ages them a decade with misinformation. There is a certain comfort, I decide, in telling her from here, risking her wrath from a safe distance.

'Jordan!' A familiar voice calls behind me. Caught off guard, I jump. Chris, I realize, turning. What on earth is he doing here?

He kisses my cheek, then steps back quickly. I straighten my shirt, the awkwardness of seeing him for the first time since our having slept together rushing back. 'You startled me. I didn't expect to see you here.'

'Likewise.' He looks at me levelly. 'What are you doing?'

I can tell from his expression that he has not heard about the explosion at my flat, the misperception that I am dead. 'I'm just heading back to London actually. There's been a gas explosion at my flat.'

His jaw drops. 'An explosion? Thank goodness you're all right!'

'I am, but a colleague of mine was killed. Some of the news reports said it was me.'

'I'm sorry to hear that. But you didn't say what you were doing up here in the first place.'

I hesitate. I could tell him about the translation of Jared's research notes, about the ring. Ask him if he found a copy of the Madrid paper in Jared's things. But Sebastian's suspicions are fresh in my

353

mind. Chris has kept so much from me that I hardly know him anymore. For a second I want to turn the questions on him, ask him why he lied to me about his job. But I do not have time for a lengthy confrontation. Instead I search for an explanation that will get me out of there quickly. 'I thought I would check some records at the University Library, see if there is anything on Jared's research.' A look of disbelief crosses his face and I instantly realize my mistake. Chris knew I did not come from the library. How long had he been following me? Did he see me talking to Tony at the boathouse, coming out of the bank? My fingers close around the jewelry box in my pocket.

'And?' he presses.

I shake my head. 'Nothing. You?'

'Just asking a few more questions around college. But the Master seems to have clamped down on everyone speaking to us.' He is lying, too. Did things change the other night in his flat? Or was he this way all along? My initial instinct not to tell him what I've found was right.

'Jordan, I've been trying to reach you.' He reaches out and touches my arm. 'About the other night…'

'It's okay.' But he does not look appeased. He wants, needs to talk about it. Still, I tell him, 'I have to get back to the office, the explosion and all that. Let's have dinner tonight and talk then.'

His face brightens. 'Sounds great.'

'I'll call you later to set details.' I reach up and brush my lips past his cheek. Then I hurry past him, continuing on the path through Jesus

354

Green. A minute later, I look back at the spot where Chris stood. He is gone, or seems to be anyway. But my suspicion bubbles: What is he really doing here?

I jump as my cell phone vibrates in my hand. Sebastian's number appears on the screen. The news report said I died in the explosion, so why is he calling me? For a second I consider not answering. But I desperately want to hear his voice. And I cannot keep the fact that I am alive a secret any longer. 'Sebastian?'

'It's me.' His voice is raspy and hollow.

How did he know that I wasn't dead? But before I can ask, there is a shuffling sound of the phone being passed. 'Jordan, what's going on?' Maureen booms. Apparently, the fact I'm alive is no surprise to her either. What the hell are you doing out of town?'

Damn. In my haste I'd forgotten about the tracking device on the phone. 'I'm in Cambridge.'

'I told you not to leave town. Sophie's been killed.'

'I know. I'm sorry.'

'Forget sorry. What was she doing at your place?'

Quickly I tell her about my phone conversation with Sophie, our plan to meet at the train station. 'She never showed up.'

There is a pause. 'After the explosion, I thought...'

I can hear the pain in Mo's voice. 'I should have called you. I'm sorry.' I swallow. 'How did you know it wasn't me?'

'Sebastian figured it out, actually. We couldn't identify the body, but Sebastian recognized the

355

sweater Sophie was wearing.' My stomach twists, a strange ball of jealousy and guilt. 'Are you all right?'

'Fine, but Mo, there's something I have to tell you–'

'Not another word,' she interrupts. 'I want you to do exactly as I say: get on the first train back to Kings Cross. I'd send someone to get you but it's quicker this way. My car will be waiting for you at the station.'

'But–'

'No buts, Jordan. Get to the train, now. We'll talk about it when you get here.'

Ninety minutes later, I step off the train at King's Cross. 'Ms. Weiss?' A gray-suited man I've never seen before appears at my side. 'Diplomatic Security.' He opens his jacket, revealing a silver badge so that only I can see, as if someone might try to impersonate him or I might question his identity. 'Come with me, please.' As we walk from the platform through the station, he keeps close to me. Is he afraid I might try to slip away? He escorts me to Mo's car, closing the back door behind me before climbing in the front passenger seat. We pull from the curb, weaving as swiftly through the streets as traffic will allow.

Twenty minutes later the car speeds around Grosvenor Square, screeching to a halt in front of the embassy. The flag out front flies at half-mast. Sophie, I think, the rock of guilt in my stomach growing.

'Wait,' the agent orders firmly now from the front passenger seat as I start to open the car door. It is the first time he has spoken since the station. He gets out of the car and comes to my side, opening the door and taking me expertly by the arm. I notice then that he has his pistol out, drawn low at the waist. His head swivels in both directions. 'Come on.' It is not my fleeing, I realize then, that he is worried about. Does he really think someone is going to take a shot at me in front of the embassy, in broad daylight? Suddenly I am back in Liberia, racing for the helicopter. I lower my head, quickening my pace to match his as we make our way up the steps to the door.

Inside, the man releases me but follows closely as I head toward the elevator. 'She's in the Bubble,' the agent says, pushing the button for the subbasement. Downstairs, he waits by the door to the Bubble as I punch in the code and open it. Then, his work done, he turns and disappears.

Maureen paces the front of the room. Sebastian is seated at the table, head in his hands. He does not look up as I enter. The memory of our kiss rushes back to me and I fight the urge to go to him, make sure he is all right. I half expect to see Sophie seated at the front of the room, overeager to please, willing to do whatever is asked.

Mo strides across the Bubble, her expression twisting between wanting to hug me and hit me. 'Thank God you're okay,' she says at last, gripping me by both shoulders.

'I'm sorry I didn't call. I was...' Hearing a rustling sound behind me, I stop and look over my shoulder. A short older man with gray hair stands in the corner of the room. He is, I realize, the man I saw Mo speaking with in the lobby the other day. I look at Mo, puzzled.

'Jordan, I'd like you to meet Roger Newsome of the Serious Organized Crime Agency,' Maureen says.

I turn to Sebastian, searching for an explanation. But he looks away, not meeting my eyes. I face Mo once more. 'I don't understand. What's going on?'

The man in the corner clears his throat. 'Why don't we all sit down?'

I lower my voice. 'Mo, I need to talk to you. Alone.'

'Jordan, Mr. Newsome is fully cleared,' she replies, loudly enough for everyone to hear. 'You can speak about the investigation in front of him.'

I look at her, amazed. The confidences we've shared in the past have never been about security levels. Something has changed with Mo. Is it because I lied to her about being dead? But there is no time to wonder. 'It's not that, exactly. It's about—'

'Jared Short,' the man in the corner finishes for me.

I turn to stare at him. 'How do you—?'

'Sit down,' Mo repeats. I drop into the chair she's pulled out. 'Jordan, Mr. Newsome is Sebastian's boss. He's in charge of the Albanian investigation for the British government.'

'I don't understand,' I say. 'What does that have to do with Jared?'

Mo blinks once. 'Sebastian?'

I look down the table at Sebastian, who shifts uncomfortably, still staring at his hands folded in front of him on the table. 'Jordan, you and I talked about the possibility that there was a joint fund between the Grand Mufti and the Reich.'

Yes, we discussed that in your bed, I think, though I can tell from his tone that he has not revealed what happened between us. He continues, 'After we spoke, I did some digging. It appears that Jared discovered that, at some point toward the end of the war, the money in the fund disappeared.'

'Who took it?' I ask, sitting down.

Sebastian opens the file that sits in front of him on the table. 'The Germans and al-Husseini didn't trust each other that much, so the account that contained the Jerusalem Fund, as it was loosely called, was set up with certain safeguards in place, a dual lock system. Neither could touch the fund without the other. But look at this.' He hands me a newspaper clipping, written in Cyrillic.

'My Russian is a little rusty.'

He shakes his head. 'Not Russian. Serbo-Croatian.'

'Sorry, my Serbo-Croatian is just as bad. What does it say?'

'This article talks about the death of SS-Brigadier Brunhuller. He was a senior officer, in charge of organizing military divisions in the Balkans during the war.' He looks up at me. 'Including the Albanian nationalists in Serbia, especially Kosovo. He appealed to the group by promising a greater Albania, including Kosovo, after the war.

'But what does that have to do with the fund?'

'As part of his alliance with the Reich, the Grand Mufti sent Akbar al-Hakim, one of his most trusted deputies, to the Balkans during the war to help form regiments. But al-Hakim and Brunhuller became close and they formed a secret alliance of their own.' I struggle to keep up as he delivers the history lesson in rapid fire bursts. 'As the Allies advanced, they realized that their bosses in Berlin would not be in power much longer. So they made a plan to steal the money, continue their anti-Jewish initiatives in exile. But al-Hakim, it seems, betrayed Brunhuller and killed him once they accessed the fund. Then he disappeared with the stolen money.'

'And that's what Jared discovered?'

'Yes, at least in part. He took his research to Duncan, who was reading finance. He wanted to figure out where the money went. They were able to trace the funds to a man called Igor Dusinski.'

'Dusinski is al-Hakim's illegitimate son,' Newsome interjects. 'Fathered during al-Hakim's stay in Kosovo during the war. Dusinski,' he adds, 'was one of the leaders of the KLA.'

'Jared and Duncan discovered that the Nazi fund was being used to fund the KLA during the war in Kosovo,' Mo recaps.

I look from Mo to Sebastian, then back again. Jared's research is linked to the KLA. Now I understand why he was always so passionate, so engrossed. It was never about the past. 'But how did you...?'

'When you mentioned the connection between Duncan and Jared, I had one of my colleagues at MI6 run a search of their archives,' Sebastian says.

I look down at the newspaper clipping. 'And all

of that is in here?'

He shakes his head and pulls out another sheet of paper. 'Unholy Alliance: The Utilization of Nazi War Funds by the Kosovo Liberation Army,' it reads. 'Duncan Lauder and Jared Short. May 9, 1998.'

'You found the conference paper,' I say. 'This is what I was looking for in Cambridge.'

He shakes his head. 'This is only the abstract that they submitted in advance of the conference. We haven't been able to locate a copy of the actual paper.'

'How did you get this?'

'Jared and Duncan tried to go to the British government, to share what they found,' Mo replies. 'But no one took them seriously.'

'It was the mid-nineties, and we were too preoccupied with trying to stop the killing to listen to the conspiracy theories of a couple of college students,' Newsome replies, a note of defensiveness in his voice.

'No one listened, so they decided to try to publish their findings,' Mo adds. 'They were set to share their work at a conference in Madrid but the presentation was canceled at the last minute. The official reason was a scheduling conflict, but a government investigation later revealed that there was a security threat. KLA operatives threatened to detonate a bomb if they were permitted to speak. So they returned to Britain having not shared their discovery.'

And a month later Jared was dead. 'You think the KLA killed him?' I ask.

A strange look, one I cannot decipher, crosses

Mo's face. 'Yes. It seems that after Madrid, Duncan was scared enough to give up. But Jared continued trying to publish his findings, talking to anyone who would listen. The KLA tried bribing him into silence, and when that didn't work they resorted to threats. They weren't just battling the Serbs; it was a public relations battle for the support of the West. They couldn't afford to have the world see that their struggle for freedom was funded in part by the Nazis.'

I swallow, trying to process it all. It is before me, the answer that I have been looking for: Jared was killed by the KLA for knowing too much, for not being willing to remain silent. I stand up. 'I need some air.'

But Mo presses her hand on my shoulder. 'Jordan, please. I know this is a lot to process but there's more.'

I sit back down again. 'I don't understand. I mean, I'm glad to know the truth about Jared's death.' I pause. 'But why do you care? I mean, why all of this?' I wave my hand in the direction of Newsome.

Sebastian clears his throat. 'As we discussed the other day, the modern Albanian mob has its roots closely linked to the KLA. We believe that the KLA funds Jared discovered are now in the hands of the mob.'

I look around the table, finally acknowledging the connection: Jared's research, the cause of his death, is somehow linked to our investigation. Then I turn to Mo. 'Is this true?' She nods. 'How long have you known?'

'Just today,' she replies quickly. 'I mean, I

thought it was a strange coincidence when you knew Duncan Lauder. But I had no idea that this connection existed.'

'Jordan, we need your help,' Sebastian says. 'Our mission objective is to find out who is laundering the money. But if we can get to the money itself...'

'You think Jared had information about the location of the money?' I drop my head to my hands, trying to process it all. 'But even if he had discovered the account, surely it would have been moved since then.'

'If we can find the account, even where it existed a decade ago, there will be markers our financial experts can use to track it down,' Newsome replies.

This is about so much more than the money, I think. My mind reels back to Anna B. Crippling the mob financially would hinder all of their operations, including the human trafficking that had caused Anna and the other girls so much pain. Sebastian's eyes meet mine and I know he is thinking the same thing.

'It's not a sure thing,' he says gently. 'But it seems that whatever Jared discovered is close enough to the mob's present-day operations to be valuable. They want to keep it from us very badly. Enough to kill Vance Ellis, to try to kill you...' His voice trails off and I know he is thinking of Sophie.

'When Jared died, his research, all of his information, disappeared with him,' Mo says gently. 'We need to find that now.'

'I've been searching for the same thing,' I reply.

'My friend Chris got a trunk of papers from Jared's mother. That's where I got the research notes about the Mufti's agreement with the Nazis. We started going through it the other night.' I look down, avoiding Sebastian's gaze. 'But we still had more to look through.'

'We need you to get to those papers, bring us anything of significance,' Newsome says. 'Can you do that?'

I nod. 'Chris wants me to come back to go through the trunk tonight.' The room seems to grow warm. 'I've got to get out of here. I'll let you know what I find.'

I stand. 'Jordan wait!' Mo calls as I reach the door.

Before she can say anything else, I storm out the Bubble and up the stairs, out the front door of the embassy. Mindless of any danger, I run down the stairs and start across the square. My mind whirls, trying to process everything I have learned. Jared's research is linked to my investigation. It is almost too much to believe. And if it is true, then the Albanians killed Jared, and Sophie and Vance, too. Which means that Duncan is in great danger. I've got to get a hold of him, but how? I pull out my cell phone, dial his number, tapping my foot impatiently as it rings a third, then fourth time. 'Duncan, it's Jordan Weiss,' I say after the voice mail recording and the beep. I debate whether to mention Vance, then decide against it. 'I need to speak with you. It's a matter of life and death. Please call me.' I hang up, then send him a shortened version of the same message by text.

As I close the phone, I hear footsteps behind me. 'Jordan, wait.' I turn to face Sebastian, who has run after me, jacketless. 'You really do like to make me chase you across parks.'

I smile weakly. 'What is it?'

'Nothing,' he says quickly, looking over my shoulder in the distance. 'I'm sorry. That I didn't come to you first with what I found. It's just that, well, after Sophie, I was afraid–'

'It's okay,' I say quickly, cutting him off. 'I understand.'

'You do?' Relief floods his face as I nod. 'I just feel so guilty,' he adds.

'Don't. I'm the one who sent her to my flat.'

'You couldn't have known.' He pauses. 'I still wish we hadn't gotten interrupted last night...'

'Me too.' Impulsively I step closer to him and lean my forehead against his chest. He buries his fingers in my hair, his other hand finding mine. Desire rises in me as I breathe his scent, remembering last night. 'I'd take you up on that rain check tonight, if I didn't have to go to Chris's.'

He steps back, his expression turning serious once more. 'I don't like it. Like I said last night, I think the guy's got ulterior motives.'

'It'll be fine.' I look up at his face, a mixture of protectiveness and jealousy. 'But Sebastian, there's something else I didn't say in there. When I was in Cambridge, I went to Jared's grave. Someone was digging.'

His jaw drops. 'Digging? The weather's been really unsettled lately. Maybe the earth just shifted.'

Inwardly I shake my head. I know that I am not

imagining things. 'It was real digging, with shovels and tools.'

'Who do you think would do that?'

'I don't know.' Across the square, the clock chimes six. I want to go see Sarah, and visiting hours will end soon. 'I have to go.' Fighting the urge to reach up and kiss him, I turn and walk quickly across the square.

June 1998

I hear the crowds before I can see them, a dull murmur of voices as we near Chesterton Footbridge that rises to a din as we turn onto the Long Reach. The crowds for May Bumps have grown with each day. Now, as we make our way to the lock for the start of the third day of races beneath an eggshell blue sky, they gather around picnic tables at the Pike and Eel, swelling the banks three or four deep the entire length of the towpath, basking in the sunshine. 'Eyes in the boat,' I remind quietly into the microphone. I give the rudder string a small tug to the right, adjusting our course, aiming for the railway bridge.

A minute later, an orange-vested race official in a small launch directs all of the ascending crews to pull aside in order to let the second division race by. We pull into the far bank and a cheer rises from crowds as the crews come into view at Ditton Corner, barreling down the Long Reach from the opposite direction.

Watching the boats race past us, my skin tingles. Bumps are serious business. The notion of trying to hit the next boat in front makes it especially dangerous for the cox who sits at the rear of the boat being chased, closest to the point of impact. There have been accidents, injuries, even rumors of a cox being killed.

I look at my watch anxiously now. Four-forty, twenty minutes until our division goes off. Our arrival at the start has to be timed just right. Too late and we will be rushed and harried turning and getting on station; too early and we will sit around, the boys' now-warm muscles growing tight. I look down the boat at the crew. For once they match in black Lycra shorts and white zephyrs, short-sleeved shirts with a fine band of red and black around the neck and sleeves. Their faces are pale, their expressions grave. The fact that we have done exactly the same thing each of the past two days does not calm my nerves or theirs. If anything, we are more tense now. We rowed over the first two days of the races, completing the entire course, escaping being bumped by the Downing crew behind us but not managing to bump Trinity Hall ahead. We only have today and tomorrow left, and there is an unspoken sense that time is running out, the goal of the Headship slipping through our fingers.

For a minute I consider making a joke, lightening the mood. Then I decide against it. I want them this nervous. 'All right boys,' I say at last, when the race has passed and the official has given us the all-clear. 'Let's take it on.'

We continue forward in small fits, moving slowly in the queue of boats making their way to the start. There is no stretch of clear water, as I had hoped, to do another warm-up exercise. As we round the corner, a cheer goes up from Ditton Paddock, where a contingent from Lords is assembled, groups of students in red and black, well-dressed parents and alumni picnicking and drinking Pimm's with lemonade.

Finally we near the lock, and as we turn around I scan the bank, looking for our station. Then, spotting Tony, I guide us into the bank at the second of the seventeen starting posts lined up along the course. Behind Tony on the towpath, Lord Colbert appears on his bike. 'Good row, Lords,' he calls, Churchill addressing the troops.

'Five minutes,' Tony announces, not looking up from his stopwatch. A chill runs up my spine as the boys begin checking their shoelaces, tightening the gates that hold their oars in place. Tony hands me the chain that I am required to hold until the start to keep us on position, and whispers instructions about the current and wind that I cannot hear over the buzzing in my ears.

There is a loud explosion, cannon fire signaling the one-minute mark. My stomach drops and I fight the urge to jump out of the boat, desperate to be anywhere but here. But it is too late. Tony has picked up a long wooden pole and is pushing the boat out into the middle of the river, positioning us parallel to the bank for the start. 'Thirty, twenty-nine,' he counts, pulling back the pole. I cannot bear to look at the boys in front of me, to see the terror and hope in their eyes. 'Bow pair, take a small stroke,' I instruct instead, concentrating on getting the boat as far forward as possible. My arm stretches behind me and I struggle to hold onto the now-taut chain that keeps us in place. 'Now just bow.' The front of the boat straightens. 'All eight, come forward.' The boys slide to the ready position, knees compressed, oars poised.

There is another boom. 'Wind it up!' I cry as I drop the chain, but there is no need. They are already off the start, using the twenty short hard strokes we

368

agreed upon to get momentum going. *Fifteen, sixteen,* I count inwardly, leaning forward in my seat, trying to control the adrenaline that surges through me. *'Lengthen in three, in two, stride now!'* The boat settles into a rhythm as the boys begin the longer strokes that will set the pace for the rest of the course.

Behind us I hear the chopping of oars against water, the terse voice of Downing's cox, commanding her crew to catch us. My nervousness rises. *Are we about to be bumped?* I fight the urge to look behind me, forcing myself to concentrate instead on the race ahead, on steering smooth and tight around Grassy Corner so as not to disturb the crew, on getting closer to Trinity Hall. *We've gained on them,* I realize, as we enter the Long Reach. I consider calling a bumping ten. But I cannot do that unless I am sure we will get them – crying wolf will damage the boys' spirits. *'Legs for ten,'* I call instead.

Suddenly everything comes together. All eight oars catch in perfect unison, buried to exactly even heights. Legs lock and drive back against the water and the boat sails, seeming to soar really, and fly forward. I hold my breath as the boys recover, willing them to do it again. The boat leaps once more, even stronger and more smoothly, perfectly synchronized strokes falling into a rhythm now. My heart lifts as the distance between our bow and Trinity Hall's stern closes. *We are doing it.* But we came close the previous two days also, only to fall away. *Can we actually do it this time?*

My eyes meet Chris's then and he nods, ever so slightly. *'This is it, boys,'* I say, lowering my voice to convey my seriousness. *'Bumping ten. In three, two, one, now!'* There is a palpable surge on the next stroke,

369

an acceleration through the water as legs push, arms pull harder than they ever have.

We lurch forward and there comes a scraping sound from the bow. A hand shoots up in the air from beyond the front of our boat. It is the Trinity Hall cox, signaling that they have been bumped, acknowledging defeat. 'We did it!' I cry into the microphone, my voice cracking. 'I mean, take it down to light pressure.' It is my job to stay calm, to get us out of the way of the fourteen boats still barreling toward the finish line. Disbelief, then joy floods the boys' faces and a giant whoop erupts from somewhere in the bows as I guide us into the bank. We have done it. We have claimed the Headship.

Ten minutes later we pull into the boathouse. Students, gathered at the bank, swarm the boat so rapidly that I fear we might tip. As I step onto land, several hands lift me in the air, holding me high over heads. Normally I hate being picked up, but throwing the cox in the water after a bump is part of the tradition. I close my eyes, bracing.

Then I feel myself changing hands. Strong arms wrap around me, then sweep me low to the water so my foot touches the surface in a symbolic gesture before lifting me up once more. I open my eyes, expecting to see Jared, but it is Chris who has rescued me. 'We did it,' he whispers, smiling widely, and I notice then the wetness in the corners of his eyes.

'We did it.' I repeat, looking over his shoulders, scanning the crowd for Jared. He is standing back by the boathouse alone, watching the scene. His gaze catches mine and he smiles but his eyes are troubled, faraway, and I know in that moment that the thing that was chasing him these past several weeks was not the race at all.

Later in the evening, we make our way down the Chimney into college for the May Ball. Nick, Andy, and Mark, who have come stag, race ahead, while the other boys linger behind with their dates. As we cross into Chapel Court, my eyes widen. The college has been transformed, the courtyards festooned with enormous marquee tents illuminated brightly from inside, housing musical acts, dance floors, and cafés. From the biggest tent, a washed-up one-hit-wonder band desperately belts out the song that made it famous. Students, clad in tuxedos and evening gowns, mill among kiosks offering food of every possible kind – pad thai, kebabs, ice-cream sundaes. In the stair-cases there are smaller diversions: a fortuneteller, a massage booth. A crane on the outer edge of the rugby pitch offers bungee jumping. It is carnival and prom all rolled into one; I have never seen anything like it.

'Let's go!' Mark cries, gesturing toward the far corner of Chapel Court. A play area has been assembled there, with a Velcro wall and moon bounce, two students trying to knock each other off platforms with foam gladiator clubs.

'Don't get injured!' Chris calls as Mark runs off, Nick and Andy following. 'We still have to race tomorrow.' The other boys and their dates disperse among the attractions, leaving just Chris and Caren, Jared and me. We pause for a large group photograph that is being taken from above, then make our way into one of the large tents and find a table. A dance floor occupies the middle of the tent, overflowing with students writhing to a seventies disco song I do not recognize. Jared disappears and returns a few minutes later with drinks, a pink champagne concoc-

tion in sugar-rimmed glasses for Caren and me, a beer for Chris. He got himself a beer, too, I note with surprise. I had not expected him to drink with another day of racing yet to go.

The decision to hold the May Ball the night before Bumps ended was a huge source of controversy, the result of a scheduling mistake on the part of some college office. By the time the conflict was discovered, vendors and acts were already booked and there was no way to change the date without losing thousands of pounds. The crew debated whether to attend, especially since we bumped to first place. Trinity Hall, now in second place, would be gunning for us tomorrow and we had everything to lose. But the expensive tickets had been purchased and dates, with new dresses hanging in closets, were not apt to be forgiving. So the boys agreed to go to the ball, and we resigned ourselves to enjoying it a great deal less than we otherwise would have, drinking lightly if at all, and not making it to the survivors' photo that would be taken in First Court at dawn.

Jared is staring across the tent, brow drawn low, lips pursed. 'You okay?' I ask, slipping my hand in his. He does not answer. I kiss his cheek, trying to cajole him from his thoughts. 'We did it.'

He shakes his head faintly. 'It's not over. It'll never be over,' he says, his voice barely a whisper.

'What?'

He looks down at me as though just realizing I am there. 'Nothing. I was just saying that the race isn't over yet.'

'Tomorrow it will be,' I say, forcing my voice to sound upbeat.

'Of course,' he replies slowly. His eyes meet mine,

then look away. We both know he is not talking about the race. He stands up, pulling his hand from mine. 'I need to get some air.' Then he is gone, crossing the tent before I can ask if he wants me to join him.

I slump back in my seat. Annoyance mixes with my concern. It's the May Ball. We're the Head of the River. Can't he be happy, even for a night? I start to turn back toward Chris and Caren, wanting to shake off the heaviness, but they are engaged in a disagreement of their own, their voices low and terse. I stand up, making my way to the bar, shaking off the sense that Jared would disapprove as I order a vodka tonic.

'Hey.' Chris comes up behind me. 'I'll take one of those, too,' he tells the bartender, gesturing to my drink.

I start to protest that he has to row tomorrow, then stop. 'Where's Caren?'

'She, uh, left. Doesn't understand why I can't stay up all night shagging tonight.'

I start to laugh, then taking in his somber expression, think better of it. It must be so lonely for the other girls who date the rowers and aren't part of the Eight, always second to the needs of the crew. 'Well it will all be over tomorrow.'

'Yeah,' he says, but his voice is miserable. The Eight is everything to Chris. Even if we win, he will still be unhappy that it is ending. We carry our drinks back to the empty table. An uncomfortable silence passes between us. It is the first time we have been alone since I started dating Jared.

When did things change, I wonder? My mind eases back to the night of the Tideway. We all seemed so happy and carefree then. We bumped today, went to the Head; we accomplished what we had been working all year to achieve. This should be the happiest night of the year. Instead Chris and I are awkward, and Jared despondent.

I cannot take it. 'I'm going outside,' I say before walking quickly from the tent. The air, cooler now, is rich with the smell of damp earth and grass. Through the fabric I can hear 'Dancing Queen' and see silhouettes of students moving. I used to be like that, fun-loving and carefree. Tears begin to flow down my cheeks.

'Hey!' Chris catches up to me. He is balancing our drinks in his left hand, reaching out to me with his right. His expression turns serious. 'What's wrong?' I shake my head. 'Come here for a second,' he says, leading me to the low wall behind the enormous tent that separates Chapel Court from the playing fields. I remember as if in a dream how he used to protect me, seemed to be able to make everything all right.

He sets one drink down on the wall, then hands the other to me. 'Here.' I take a sip, watching as he finishes his in a single swallow. 'So what do you think?'

I know he means of our chances of hanging on to the Headship tomorrow. 'It could happen,' I reply carefully. So much in a bumps race is left up to fate – who gets a good start, breaks a rigger or an oar.

'I think we can do it,' Chris says but I can hear the doubt beneath his voice. 'You okay?' he asks abruptly. I hesitate, startled by the change of topic. Chris is not one to ask, does not dwell on trouble. 'I don't mean to pry but you seemed really upset.'

'I'm fine. Jared...' I hesitate. It is too awkward to discuss with him. 'We didn't fight or anything like that. Sometimes it just gets so...'

'Heavy?' he finishes for me.

I nod. I was going to say complicated but heavy is more accurate. The music changes to Madonna's

374

'Crazy for You.' I don't want to talk about heavy things. 'Let's dance.'

If Chris is surprised he gives no indication. I stand up, starting for the tent, but he blocks my way, arms extended. He thinks I meant for us to dance here. Too weary to argue, I step forward, letting myself be enveloped in his strong arms. We sway gently to the music in the narrow space between the wall and the tent. I lean my head against his chest, grateful for the respite from heaviness and worry. Then I look up. Chris lowers his head abruptly, his lips looking for mine.

I freeze. Then, as he draws me closer, my lips seem to respond on their own, kissing him back. Panic floods my brain. This cannot happen. Good sense taking over, I put my hand on his chest and push away. 'Chris, stop.' He comes at me again, a dazed expression on his face. I step back quickly and he stumbles. Looking into his eyes, I understand then why he has been so upset about Jared and me being together. He is not jealous about losing his best friend – he has feelings for me. 'Chris, I'm sorry but–'

I realize then that he is not looking at me but over my shoulder.

Turning, my stomach drops. There, standing behind me, is Jared.

Jared stares at us, eyes hollow. I take a step toward him. 'It's not what–' But he turns and disappears through the archway. 'Jared, wait!'

I start after him but Chris grabs my arm stopping me. 'Jordie, we need to–'

I pull away. 'No Chris, I'm sorry if I gave you the wrong impression.' I run through the arch. 'Jared!' I cry. But he is gone, and the only sound is my own voice, echoing in the darkness.

chapter TWENTY-ONE

I walk quickly down the hospital corridor, glancing at my watch. It's almost seven, just an hour left to visit. At the door of Sarah's room, I stop. There is a man in a dark suit standing over her bed. Alarmed, I duck around the door frame, reaching for my gun. Then I step into the room. 'Who the hell are—' I begin.

But Sarah, seeing me over the man's shoulder, smiles. 'Jordie!' The man turns and I recognize him as one of the security detail Mo assigned to protect her. I tuck my gun away, feeling foolish. 'This is Officer Ryan Giles.' Her cheeks flush slightly. Has she been flirting, I wonder?

I take in the guard, who is fortyish, graying at the temples with a gentle smile. 'Nice to meet you,' I manage.

'And you.' He nods. 'I'll leave you two to talk. Be just outside if you need anything.' He directs this last comment at Sarah, a note of protectiveness in his voice.

I move closer, studying Sarah's face. Most of the tubes have been removed and the bruise around her eye has faded to yellow. Still, she looks paler and more vulnerable than before. 'Well he's very handsome,' I manage, trying to keep my voice light.

'What are you doing here?' she asks, ignoring my comment, her voice low and concerned. 'I mean, I thought no one was supposed to see you.'

'It's okay,' I say, kissing her cheek. 'Mo knows I'm alive. I've already been to the embassy. How are you feeling, anyway?'

She waves her hand. 'I'm perfectly fine.' I study her face, unconvinced. 'What did you find out?' she presses.

I hesitate, wondering if I should be talking about Jared's death now that it is somehow linked to the classified investigation. But Sarah put her life on the line. She's part of this now. Quickly I tell her about Jared's research, the possible link to the mob. 'That's absolutely unbelievable,' she says when I have finished.

'I know. And it gets worse. They want me to get Jared's papers from Chris to see if they contain the information about the bank account that he and Duncan found. And Sebastian thinks that Chris has been keeping his real motives from me, that he could be on the wrong side of all this.'

'What do you think?'

I shrug. 'I just can't believe it. I mean he's acted a little strange since, well, you know...'

'No, I don't know,' she replies pointedly. 'All you said was that you guys got too close, that you'd tell me the rest later. What happened?' I look away. 'Oh no, Jordie! You didn't sleep with him, did you?'

'I was upset, emotional. It just kind of happened.' I clear my throat.

'How was it?' she asks, eyes twinkling.

'Bad. Good. I don't know. I mean, physically it was fine, but it was a mistake and I knew that the minute it happened. Setting that aside for a second, Chris was Jared's best friend. One of us. It doesn't seem possible that he could betray Jared. Or me.'

Sarah's brow furrows. She never liked Chris, but it's still hard for her to believe he could do such a thing. 'So what are you going to do?'

'Get the papers, I guess. We need to find that information. Sebastian...' My voice catches as I say his name. 'Sebastian thinks...'

But my hesitation is not lost on Sarah. 'Sebastian.' She cuts me off, raising an eyebrow. 'I know that tone, Jordie.' Because she heard it once before, I think, remembering a conversation ten years ago at one of our Sunday pizza lunches. It was shortly after the Tideway, the day I told her about my getting together with Jared. I tried to play it off as just a hookup, brought on by too much alcohol and adrenaline after a race. But then, as now, she called me on it, made me acknowledge that there was something more. She continues. 'What gives? Did you sleep with him too?' Her tone is chiding, nonjudgmental.

'No,' I say quickly. 'I mean we kissed, but...' I cannot bring myself to tell her that we were interrupted by the call that she was hospitalized. 'And yes, it was good,' I add, before she can ask. 'Very good. But I don't know. I mean, he's very attractive and I think he likes me. It's probably just physical.'

'Or you could really have feelings for him.'

'It's complicated right now. There's the investigation, all of this business with Chris. Not to mention the fact that he was dating Sophie.

We'll see. Maybe when all of this is over...'

'But when will that be?' She's right, I realize. Even if we learn what happened to Jared, and find the Albanian fund, there will be more steps, developments. It could take months. 'You've changed, Jordie. In a good way, I mean. A few months ago, you would have cut and run from anything real. You're more open now, like you were at college. It's the first time I've seen you like anyone since Jared. But there's always going to be an excuse to shut a man out. I think you should let it happen.'

'Maybe.'

'Anyway, you should go to my place, grab a shower and some sleep. You look like hell.'

I do not, I remember, have a place of my own. 'Thanks. I have to get to Chris's tonight, but I could do with a shower first.'

'So you're going to get the papers from him.'

'I think so.' My stomach twists. 'I hate lying to him, but what other choice do I have? If Sebastian is wrong about Chris having other motives, then there won't be anything to find. And if he's right, well then, Chris is no friend at all. I don't think we'll find what we're looking for, though.'

'Then what?'

Before I can answer, my cell phone vibrates in my bag. 'Excuse me,' I say, pulling out the phone and opening it. A text message flashes across the screen: 'Meet me ton. at river beneath Embnkmnt Tube stat. at 8.30 D.L.' Duncan. My breath catches. So he got my message after all and he's here in London. Had he never left or did Vance's death cause him to come back?

379

I text back 'yes' then close the phone. 'Just work,' I say uneasily to Sarah. It is not exactly a lie. 'But I need to go. I'll see you tomorrow, okay?'

As I walk down the street to the Tube station, my mind races: Duncan is back. But why did he return and contact me now? It could be a result of Vance's death, an angry decision that he has nothing more to lose. Is he really going to tell me what I need to know? Originally I wanted to learn what he and Jared were working on at college. But now, with that answer in hand, my questions run so much deeper. 'Where is the information Jared possessed and what did he do with it before he died? Hopefully with that knowledge we can find the answer to who killed Jared and help stop the Albanians at the same time. It is almost too good to believe.

Twenty minutes later I step out of the Tube station and make my way down the sloping street past the darkened shops to the path that runs along the river's edge. Close to the water now, the air is dank and clouded by faint mist. I pace back and forth, trying without success to stay calm. 'What if Duncan doesn't show? Impulsively I pull the ring box from my bag and slip the ring on my finger, as if it will bring Jared and his long-buried secrets closer to me. Duncan will be here, a voice seems to say. He has to.

And if I do get the answers I've been seeking, what then? An image passes through my mind of a future self I do not recognize, happy and relaxed, all of the ghosts put to rest. England will never be just another assignment, of course. But with the questions behind me, I can focus on helping Sarah, maybe find a life of my own. Sebastian, I think, feeling a surge of warmth as his face appears in my mind. When the mission is over, maybe he and I can be together, despite my guilt about Sophie and everything that has happened.

A train rumbles across the bridge above, startling me from my thoughts. I jump, looking behind me. By the pillar of the bridge, there is a figure, hiding in the shadows.

I inhale sharply. 'Duncan?' I call. How long as he been standing there?

'Jordie,' a familiar voice says. But it is not Duncan.

'Chris?' As he steps into view, alarm rises in me. 'What are you doing here?'

'I got a message...' he begins, then falters.

He's lying, I decide instantly. I hadn't contacted him and Duncan surely meant to meet with me alone. He must have followed me again. Then the pieces of the puzzle start to fit together: Sebastian's suspicions about Chris's motives, Chris turning up wherever I am. Could he really be working for the other side?

'You said Duncan,' he presses. 'Are you meeting him here? What's going on?'

I hesitate, calculating the least I can say that will satisfy him. 'Yes, but it's not connected to Jared. It's something else, Chris. Something to do with work.'

'But I thought...' His expression changes, a deep crease forming across his brow. 'Is that it?' he asks eagerly, stepping forward. There is an intensity to his voice that I have never heard before.

I step back, puzzled. 'What?'

I notice then that he is pointing to my left hand. 'The ring,' he asks, moving closer. 'Can I see it?' he asks, reaching out his hand.

A chill passes through me. How does Chris know about the ring? He must have seen me coming out of the bank and somehow figured out what I found in the safe-deposit box. But why does he care?

I look nervously over my shoulder. Duncan won't show if Chris is here; I need to get rid of him quickly. 'Here.' I turn away slightly and start to slip off the ring. As it passes over my finger pad, I notice for the first time the ridged, uneven texture of the underside. I hold it up to the light. There are dark lines on the inside of the band. The ring is engraved. Did Jared inscribe our names on the inside, or perhaps a message of endearment to me?

Drawing it closer to see the engraving, I gasp.

I know then why Jared never gave me the ring. It is more than a declaration of love – it is a message to me, a voice from beyond the grave, left behind in case anything should happen to him. Inscribed on the ring is a series of numbers. The numbers I am sure are somehow connected to the bank account that Jared found, the one linking the KLA to the Nazi fund.

I turn back toward Chris, flooded with disappointment. Now I understand his turning up here, his interest in the ring. Chris never cared about finding Jared's killers. The whole thing was a set-up – he tricked me into finding the information Jared had hidden so he could confiscate it for the mob, or whoever he is working for, before I could turn it over to the government. My anger grows. Everything Sebastian said is true. But for how long had Chris been a traitor? I remember then what Tony said about Jared and Chris fighting at the boathouse. Was Chris somehow involved with Jared's death as well?

But Chris is still watching me expectantly, unaware that I am onto him. I slip the ring tightly back on my finger, then hold out my hand like a newly engaged fiancée, hoping the glance will be enough. 'It's beautiful, isn't it?' I manage. 'I guess Jared was planning to surprise me but he never got the chance.'

He reaches for my hand, trying to slide the ring from my finger. 'What does it say?' he asks. 'Can I see?'

I pull back, covering my hand. 'I–I don't know what you're talking about.'

'But you said...' Chris steps toward me, hand outstretched for the ring. I cannot let him have it. I move backward, trying to put as much space between us as possible. My back brushes against the pillar of the bridge, blocking my retreat.

'Chris, stop.'

He is nearly on top of me now, his thick arms blocking me on either side. 'It's okay Jordie. Just give it to me and everything will be all right.' Putting one hand on my shoulder to hold me in place, he reaches for his back pocket. He has a gun, I think, panic seizing me. Desperately, I reach around and pull out my own pistol, closing my finger around the trigger. 'What are you doing?' Chris catches my arm, trying to keep me from raising the gun, and as I struggle to pull away, my finger presses down harder. A shot rings out. He jerks back with a grunt, a stunned look on his face. Red seeps across the front of his shirt. 'Jordie...?'

Oh, Chris,' I cry as he slumps against the wall. I am seized with relief and remorse at the same time. Dropping my gun, I help him to the ground. 'I'm so sorry. I didn't want to...'

'Then why?' he asks weakly, grimacing.

'You came after me. You were trying to take the ring, to give the information to the Albanians. I couldn't let you.'

'Albanians?' he gasps, a mixture of confusion and pain twisting his face. 'No. I came because you asked me to...'

Cold terror shoots through me. 'What?'

He pulls his hand from beneath his body and I see then that he was not reaching for a gun but for his mobile phone. 'Your text,' he pants, his face a deathly gray. 'You asked me to come here, to take the ring for safekeeping.'

I take the phone from him and open it. There on the screen is a text message, asking Chris to meet me here, telling him I have found information inside the ring. My initials are at the bottom. But the sender's number is not mine – it is the same number from which I received Duncan's text message. And I had not known about the information inside the ring until just now.

Someone had summoned Chris here, too, and tipped him off about the ring, pretending to be me. But who could have possibly known? Was it Duncan? I turn to Chris, but his eyes are closed, head rolled back. 'Chris!' Dropping to my knees, I shake him but he does not move. I've got to get help. I open the phone, but the signal is too weak, blocked by the overpass. I do not want to leave him, but I have no choice. 'Hang on. I'll be back in a second.' I look in both directions down the deserted path, then start for the road. But a dark figure appears in front of me, blocking my way. Duncan, I think, but as he steps into the glow of the streetlight, my jaw drops.

There, standing in front of me, is Sebastian.

'Sebastian?' I stop, staring at him in disbelief. 'What is he doing here? This time I had not called him for help. 'Thank God you're here. I received a text from Duncan and came here to meet him, but Chris showed up instead some- how. And Chris's been shot, that is, I accidentally shot him.'

'I know.' He smiles. 'Thank you for that. Saved me the trouble.' I notice then the pistol, drawn low at his waist.

'I don't understand.' A chill shoots up my spine. 'You...'

'Sent you the text? Yes. Did you really think that coward Lauder would come back to London?'

My stomach twists. 'And you texted Chris too.'

He grins, his face a twisted mask I do not recognize. 'Poor fool really was just a guy who cared about his friend. Wrong place, wrong time.' I can tell from the casual way he glances over his shoulder that he thinks Chris is dead. 'But I'm afraid the time for explanations is running short.' He holds out his hand. 'Ring, please.'

Sebastian knows about the ring – but how? I

385

hesitate, not wanting to acknowledge the realization that crashes down on me like an icy wave. Sebastian set Chris up, tried to make me think that he was the traitor, when in fact it was Sebastian all along who was working for the mob, trying to get Jared's information before I could turn it over to the government.

'I don't understand.' I pause uncertainly, eyeing my gun, which lies on the ground by Chris where I dropped it, too far away for me to reach. I need to stall him, figure out how to keep him from getting the ring. But Chris needs help now, before it is too late – and if he moans or does anything to give away that he is alive, Sebastian may finish him. I lick my lips, stalling for time. 'I thought we–'

'Liked each other? You're an attractive woman, Jordan. I'll give you that. Under different circumstances, we might have had something. But here you were just in the way.'

'Sophie, too?' He does not answer. 'But why?'

He hesitates and I can tell he is wondering how much to say. Then he shrugs. 'I suppose it doesn't matter now.' And in those six icy words, I know that he means to kill me as well. 'We had to stop the information from getting to the government.'

'How long have you been working for the Albanians?' I demand. Had he developed some sort of allegiance to the mob during his years in the Balkans or did it go back even further?

A harsh laugh rips from his throat. 'The Albanians?' Without warning, he lunges for me, pinning me against the bridge pillar, slamming the back of my head against the stone, the very same spot on my head I'd hurt just a day earlier. I bite my lip, fighting the urge to cry out against the fireworks of pain, not wanting to rouse Chris. Sebastian presses his body hard against mine, pinning my arms to my sides as he reaches into my pocket, then my bag, searching for the ring. I can feel every inch of him against me, the desire that this power brings out in him.

He takes the box from my bag and opens it, his eyes widening slightly as he realizes it is empty. 'Where's the ring?' he demands and before I can answer, he draws his hand back, slamming me across the face with his gun. Blood spurts from my lip and splashes across his cheek. I close my eyes, bracing for another blow. The ring is the only thing that is keeping him from killing me. Then a look of realization crosses his face and he reaches down and grabs my hand. I struggle to pull away, but it is too late: he pulls the ring from my finger and holds it up to the light. 'You sentimental fool. That's the key to forty-six million dollars and you're wearing it like a lovesick schoolgirl.'

He shoves the ring into his pocket. Then he looks over his shoulder in both directions and I can feel him calculating the risk of another gunshot, the attention it might bring. Still holding me firmly in place, he brings his hands to my throat, feeling around my neck for my carotid artery. He's trying to find the pressure point, I realize, panicking. With the right choke hold, he can cut off the blood supply to my brain. I will be unconscious in seconds, then dead in less than a minute.

I try to kick but it is useless. His fingers are pressing down harder on the base of my neck. My vision begins to blur, dark spots appearing in front of me. 'Just let go,' he says softly, as though rocking a baby to sleep. For a second I see Jared hovering beside me.

In the distance, tires screech faintly. It's a dream, I think. But there are footsteps, growing louder and more real. Sebastian loosens his grip slightly as he turns in the direction of the noise, and as he does I inhale sharply, then slam my forehead into his nose. He cries out as he falls away from me. I look toward the direction of the footsteps. A man I faintly recognize as one of the security detail from Sarah's hospital room scrambles down the hill, his weapon trained on Sebastian, who has recovered and is climbing to his feet.

'Glad you've arrived, mate,' Sebastian says brightly to the guard. 'Sebastian Hodges, Serious Organised Crime Agency. I've just caught this American diplomat passing classified material to this bloke.' He gestures toward Chris with his head. 'He came at me and I had no choice but to shoot him.'

'He's lying.' I cry out. The officer looks from Sebastian to me, then back again and for a minute I think he is going to believe Sebastian. 'You've got to stop him. Please.'

'All right, folks,' he says. 'Let me call an ambulance and then we'll all go back to the station and sort this out.' But Sebastian is moving now, raising his gun. I lunge after him, but it is too late: he points the gun at me, backing away.

From the road above come sirens, growing

louder. 'It's over, Hodges,' the officer says, his gun trained on Sebastian. 'Give yourself up.'

But Sebastian stares at me evenly, a man undefeated. 'Sorry Jordan,' he says, raising his gun to his mouth. Then, his eyes not leaving mine, he puts it inside and pulls the trigger.

chapter TWENTY-TWO

I sit up and stretch, blinking my eyes against the sunlight that streams in through the window, trying to figure out where I am. From behind the sofa on which I lay comes the sound of glasses clinking, wheels rolling on linoleum floor. Sarah's flat, I remember.

I stand and walk to the kitchen, where Sarah is pulling silverware from a drawer. 'Good morning.'

'Morning?' She laughs lightly, gesturing to the window. 'It's nearly dinnertime. I ordered us some Chinese takeaway. It should be here soon.'

I look at her, confused. 'I slept all day? I'm so sorry. I had no idea.'

'You needed it,' she replies. She's right. Last night was the first time I've gotten any real sleep in weeks. She points to a cabinet above the counter that is out of her reach. 'When did you get back, three, four?'

'Sometime before dawn.' I pull down two plates from the stack she indicates. 'I hope I didn't wake you.'

'I didn't even hear you come in. How's Chris?'

'Better. He's conscious now.' I swallow over the lump in my throat. 'The doctors say that he'll be fine.'

It has been more than a week since the confrontation at Embankment. Chris had emergency surgery to repair a tear in his colon where the bullet passed through. But he developed an infection as a complication from the operation and drifted in and out of consciousness as the doctors struggled to bring down his fever. I spent almost every minute at the hospital, leaving only to check in once at the embassy for debriefing and to attend the memorial service held for Sophie at a nearby church. As I kept vigil by Chris's bedside, listening to him babble deliriously, my heart broke. I did this to him. He had to be all right.

Finally, last night, as I lay half doubled over against the edge of his mattress, my head buried in my arms, I felt movement, his fingers brushing against my hair. 'Jordie.'

'Hey,' I sat up, rubbing my eyes. 'You're awake.' I ran my hand over his brow, which was palpably cooler.

He paused, considering. 'My stomach hurts.'

'You're in the hospital. You had surgery, but you're all right now. Do you remember what happened?' He nodded. My eyes filled with tears. 'I'm so sorry. I never should have doubted you.'

'It's okay,' he replied, stroking my hand. 'I can see how you might have thought it was me. I mean, I was kind of obsessive, you know?' He breathed hard, determined to speak. 'When we

390

were at college, I was on top of the world. But after Jared died, things just seemed to fall apart. My career, my relationship with Caren – I couldn't make anything work. I kept thinking if I could go back to that night, change what happened...'

'I know.' It's a place I've been a thousand times in my own mind. But Chris let it take over his. 'It was Sebastian all along it seems, working for the Albanian mob. They killed Jared, for knowing too much about the Nazi money they had, for trying to tell the truth. But we were able to turn the information about the bank account that Jared found over to the government. They'll be able to use it to freeze the mob's assets, prosecute those who have been laundering money for them. Jared's mission will be accomplished at last.'

'So it's over now?'

'It's over.' I watched as first relief, then uncertainty, washed over his face. The quest that consumed him for so long has been fulfilled.

'You should go get some rest,' he said. 'You're welcome to use my place.'

I stood to leave. 'Thanks, but I need to check on Sarah. She was discharged a few days ago.'

'That's great news.' He hesitated, then released my hand. 'Good-bye, Jordan.'

'I'll check on you later,' I promised. And though I knew I would, I also knew that things would be different now.

Afterward, I came back to Sarah's, collapsing onto the couch and falling into a deep sleep. 'It will still be a while until the food gets here,' Sarah says now. 'I left out a fresh towel and some clothes, if you want to have a shower.'

Noticing then my wrinkled clothes, I walk to the bathroom and undress. Then I turn on the hot water tap in the shower full blast, welcoming the scalding pressure against my skin. Sebastian appears in my mind. I see his face, twisted in the moonlight, ready to kill me to get the information he wanted. I still cannot believe it was him. I always prided myself on my instincts about people. But I liked Sebastian; I thought we could be close. How could I have been so wrong? I have only spoken to Mo a few times briefly since the night of the shooting, but she seemed as surprised as I was by Sebastian's betrayal. I am eager to get to work tomorrow, to find out more about why he did it, what they've learned about the person he really was.

A few minutes later, I step out of the bathroom in the too-long cotton shirt and jeans Sarah left for me, still towel-drying my hair. I carry the plates of Chinese food she prepared from the kitchen to the living room and set them down on the coffee table, then refold the blanket Sarah placed over me when I was sleeping.

'So how are you doing?' she asks between bites of fried rice.

I hesitate, considering the question. 'I don't know. I mean, for the past week, all I could think about was Chris. But now that he's all right, there's everything else. Like Sebastian. How could I have been so wrong about him?'

'Jordie, there was no way you could have known.'

'Maybe, but that doesn't change the fact that I

392

blamed the wrong man. I almost killed Chris. And I would be dead myself.' I pause. 'If not for your boyfriend.'

'Oh, Jordie!' Sarah's cheeks color. At least one of my suspicions had proved correct: Officer Ryan Giles has a crush on Sarah. The night I left her hospital room so abruptly to meet Duncan, she'd been concerned and asked him to send a colleague after me to check. The guard arrived just in time to stop Sebastian from killing me. 'He's not my boyfriend,' she adds.

'Well he'd certainly like to be.' Even through my concern for Chris, I'd noticed how attentive Officer Giles was to Sarah in the hospital, how he insisted on escorting her home when she was discharged. A bouquet of tulips from him sits in a vase by the window.

She shakes her head. 'We enjoy each other's company, that's all. Besides, what kind of future can he expect with me?'

'A wonderful one,' I reply quickly. 'Full of love and family.' She does not reply. 'Anyway, he said he'd take leave to accompany you to Geneva. Have you given any more thought to that program?' Another good thing besides Officer Giles came out of Sarah's hospital stay: a visiting doctor told her about a promising new Swiss clinical trial for ALS patients. He thought she'd be perfect, offered to refer her.

She shrugs. 'I completed the paperwork, but there's a waiting list so it's a long shot. We'll see what happens. Anyhow, you were saying about Sebastian.'

I slump back in my chair. 'I never expected it,

you know? I mean any of it, this crazy assignment, the link to Jared. People getting killed. I
mean, when I got your letter, I thought I'd take
the transfer to London and spend a couple of
years pushing–'

'Letter?' Sarah interrupts. 'What letter?'

'Your letter, silly.'

'I don't know what you're talking about.'

'The one you sent to me about a week before I
came over. You said that it would be really great
to see me and–' I stop midsentence. Sarah's face
is blank and for a minute I wonder if her medicines are interfering with her memory. But her
eyes are clear. 'You mean you didn't send me a
letter?'

She holds up her right arm limply. 'Me write a
letter, with this hand?'

'It was typed.'

'Impossible. My printer has been broken for
months.'

'But I still have–' I stop. Sarah's letter is gone,
of course, in the explosion at the flat with everything else I owned.

'Jordie, you know I love you. But I never would
have asked.'

She is right, of course. My stomach drops.
Sarah did not write to ask me to come. The letter
was a hoax. 'Oh, no.'

'You're saying that someone impersonated me
to get you here?' she asks. I nod. 'Who?'

'I don't know. But I'm going to find out.'

My mind races. Someone set me up, got me to
come to England, but who? Not long ago, I might
have said Chris. Was Sebastian somehow in-

volved? I need to talk to Mo, I realize. If I leave now, I can still catch her at work. I look over at Sarah, who sits with her half-eaten dinner in front of her. 'I need to run out for a little while,' I say. 'Will you be all right here?'

She waves her left land. 'I'll be fine. Just be careful. Don't go getting in any more scrapes.'

'I promise.' I carry my plate to the sink, then grab my jacket and head out the door. On the street, I pull my cell phone from my bag and start to dial Mo. Then I close it again. This is a conversation that needs to be had in person.

Half an hour later, I walk through the lobby of the embassy, take the elevator to the fifth floor. The outer door of Maureen's office is unlocked and the reception area deserted. Amelia is gone for the day, chair pushed in behind a perfectly organized desktop. I walk to Maureen's door, knocking once before turning the handle. 'Mo?'

There is no answer. I step inside, looking up at the clock on the wall. Six-thirty. Mo usually works this late. I walk to her desk. To anyone else it looks like chaos, but I have no doubt that she knows where every piece of paper is located. The documents are routine, cables to and from Washington, invitations to social occasions. 'Reception at seven,' reads the paper calendar she still insists on keeping, notes in her bold scrawl. She must have left already. I slump against the edge of her desk. I'll have to ask her tomorrow.

I scan the office. Who faked Sarah's letter to get me here? Had Mo known?

My eyes stop on a file cabinet that sits in the far right corner of the room. Do I dare open it?

Housekeeping, or someone else, could come in at any second. I walk to the cabinet, studying the dial lock. What would the combination be? I know from needing access to Mo's files during various assignments over the years that it is always something related to the twins. I turn to the twins' birthday numbers: 3-17-87. But the lock doesn't open. Hurriedly, I invert the numbers, still without success. What else could it be? The date she officially adopted them in Vietnam: July 4, 1987. I remember her telling the story of an Independence Day spent in a squalid Hanoi hotel room with two sick infants, wondering what on earth she had just done. Impulsively, I invert the date, twist to the numbers. There is a split-second pause, followed by a sharp click that seems to echo across the office, breaking the silence.

I pause, guilt rising within me. I am about to cross a line. I've done almost everything in my ten years in the Foreign Service – been shot at, killed a man. But I have never broken the trust of a fellow officer or superior, much less one who is also a friend. I started down this path the day I agreed with Sebastian and Sophie to continue investigating Infodyne behind Maureen's back, I realize. A thread, once picked, that could not be stopped from unraveling. Then I see Maureen's face in the Bubble earlier this afternoon, the conflict in her eyes when I questioned why I was brought here. I do not want to believe she had anything to do with this. But I have to know.

Taking a deep breath I open the drawer slowly. Inside, there are personnel files, arranged alphabetically. The top drawer goes only through the N's. I close it and open the next drawer, thumbing to the W's. I find my file and I pull it out, then hesitate. 'What is the penalty for accessing one's personnel file without permission? But I have gone too far now to turn back.

I open the folder. Inside is a copy of my dossier, similar to the one I'd seen in the Director's office the day I requested the transfer. This file has more documents, though, which seems odd since I've only been here a week. I turn the page. There is a photograph of a group of college students, standing in front of the Rijksmuseum. My own face, third from the right stares back at me. The charity hitch to Amsterdam, I remember. There are other pictures of me at Cambridge, too. One in the boat during a race, another standing beside Jared at a party. I am not entirely surprised; the Department investigated me thoroughly before granting my security clearance, including – perhaps especially – my time overseas. But these photos should be in my official file back in Washington. How did Maureen get them?

I turn to the left side of the file, which contains my personnel actions, the pink carbon copies still used by the Department to note transfers, salary increases, promotions. They are held in place by a two-hole punch clip, the most recent action filed on top. I scan the first sheet, the order transferring me from Washington to London. It is routine: cost codes for my travel, the Director's signature scrawled at the bottom, authorizing for my hastily booked plane ticket.

I flip the page. The next sheet should be my orders assigning me to Washington for a year after

Liberia. But instead, it is another transfer order for London. It must be an extra carbon copy, I decide, scanning the page. But this order is printed in a smaller font. I flip back to the first page, comparing. The preprinted requisition numbers are different, one ending in a 3, the other in a 7. No, they are not the same orders. I turn back to the second page that is missing the Director's signature, scanning it quickly. The order is dated April 14 – a full week before I walked into the Director's office to ask for London.

I stare at the paper in disbelief. I was assigned to London before I even requested it. Someone knew I would ask even before I did. Because they sent me the one thing they knew would prompt me to request the transfer – a forged letter from Sarah, asking me to come to her.

My eyes drop to the bottom of the paper and at the sight of the familiar scribble on the approval line, my heart stops: M. Martindale.

'Ahem,' a voice behind me says suddenly. I jump, dropping the file. There, standing in the doorway to the office, is Maureen.

'M-mo,' I manage. 'I came to see you, but your calendar said you were going to a reception.'

'I was. I forgot something. It's a little late for a social call, don't you think?'

'I was just...' I falter, searching for an explanation and finding none.

'Snooping through my files?'

'Looking for answers.' Anger replaces my nervousness as I pick up the file. 'You did it, didn't you? Forged the letter from Sarah to get me to come to England?'

Mo shifts, then looks away. 'Not personally. But I was aware of it.'

So there were others involved. 'I don't understand.'

'We knew you would never come back to this place, not without a very good reason. And we desperately needed your help.' She walks to her desk. 'Look, Jordan. What I told you in the Bubble was true: Jared and Duncan tried to come to the government years ago and no one listened. Much later, we realized we needed the information they had found. Your background, your connections to both of them, made you a natural fit.'

'But why didn't you just ask me? I mean, this is my job, for Christ's sake!'

'Would you have done it? We ignored Jared, and look what happened. Part of you has to blame us for that. So we thought we would bring you here and assign you to the investigation, have you get the materials from Duncan and be done with it. We never counted on Sebastian turning on us, or your friend Chris digging around.'

I sink down into one of the chairs in front of Mo's desk, the realization sinking in: she set me up. 'Let it go, Jordan,' she says. 'It's over. You found the information and even as we speak, agents are en route to confiscate the funds. The mob's operations will be seriously crippled because of what you did. You can leave London now. I'll see that you get assigned anywhere in the world you want to go, and send Sarah to get the very best care available.'

I look down at the file again, considering what she has said. Just leave London again. If only it were that easy. Didn't she know that even if I got on a plane right now and never came back, I would never really be able to leave?

I begin to page further down in the file, not caring if Mo will object, wanting to see if there is anything else. Toward the bottom, a corner of a manila envelope juts out from beneath the other papers. I pull it out. Addenbrooke's Hospital, the return address reads. The envelope, neatly slit open, addressed to me. Dr. Peng's report, I realize. 'When did this arrive?'

'Yesterday morning.'

I swear inwardly as I slide out the contents. Inside is a folder containing the same report we saw at Dr. Peng's office. There are two additional sheets, though, each containing a single grainy black-and-white copy of a photograph, blown up to full-page size. I lift the first sheet closer to get a better look. It is an image of the front of a torso, up close, bloated and thick from the water. My stomach turns. The image cuts off at the neck, I note, relieved. I do not want to see Jared's face, not like this.

I start to close the file. Then slowly I reopen it, turning to the final sheet. The photograph this time is of Jared's torso from behind. But the image was taken slightly higher than the last and I can see the wisps of his dark hair, matted against the back of his neck. I trace my finger along the hairline, letting my mind go places I never had. My vision blurs. 'What was his last thought? Did he see the waters rise up around him or was he already gone? Was there pain, enough time to be afraid?

I blink studying the photograph once more. My eyes reach Jared's shoulder, lock in. Something about the picture is wrong. My pulse pounds hard against my temples. I turn to the final page, nearly tearing it in my haste, staring at the image of Jared's back. The skin is smooth, unbroken. It cannot be.

Suddenly I am in the tattoo parlor the night of the Tideway, holding Jared's hand as the needle dug into his back and the blood ran. His shoulder was not unmarked when he died; it bore the swan tattoo of the Eight. I know then that the man in the picture is not Jared. Whoever was buried that day was someone else.

I look up at Mo, struggling to speak. 'This isn't Jared.'

'I don't know what you're talking about,' she replies evenly. But something on her face, beneath all of her makeup, betrays her.

'You're lying,' I say.

She takes a step backward, flinching as though she has been hit. 'Jordan Weiss, you and I are friends. I would never—'

'Never what, lie to me? That's funny. Tell me everything, Mo. Otherwise I'm going to pick up that phone and call the Director. He'd love to have your head and you know it. Unless he's in on it, too.'

'No, he's not.' She exhales sharply, defeated. 'What do you want to know?' But her face is still guarded, and I know I will have to ask the right questions to get anything out of her.

'Is Jared alive?' I demand.

She does not answer for several seconds. 'I

don't know. Maybe. At least we think he was at some point. We believe that after he tried to tell the government about the Nazi funds and was threatened, he faked his own death somehow, and disappeared.'

No, a voice inside me screams. Jared never would have deceived me like that, left without saying good-bye. He had plane tickets for both of us. Then I remember his protectiveness, his distance at the end. Something must have happened to convince him that it wasn't safe to take me with him. So he simply left.

'Faked his own death? But how? There was a body and...' I turn to her. 'How long have you known?'

'For years it was assumed that the Albanians found him and killed him. But then several weeks ago when your friend Chris started nosing around, we realized that he might still be alive. The British government had his body, that is, the body that was placed in his grave, exhumed, which confirmed our suspicions: it isn't Jared.'

My mind whirls. 'He would have had to have help.'

She nods. 'Someone who could get to the accident site before anyone else. Identify the body. Arrange for a burial, pay off a coroner to substitute an unclaimed corpse for Jared's.'

Lord Colbert. I remember then his defensiveness at the dinner, his insistence that we leave the past alone. He wasn't trying to protect the college, or Infodyne or even himself. He was protecting Jared.

So the grave had been dug up after all. But

something about her explanation still does not make sense. If the government was only interested in the information Jared had discovered, why go to the trouble of exhuming the body to confirm he was dead? If it was really only the KLA-Nazi fund that the government was after, they could have used any operative to get close to Duncan. They would not have needed me. No, I realize suddenly. This was never just about more than Jared's information; this was about Jared himself. Someone knew, or suspected, that he was alive, even before the body was checked. And whoever it was wanted to find him, draw him out of hiding to silence him once and for all. I remember then Sebastian's words beneath Embankment before he killed himself, his scorn at the notion that the Albanians had done this.

'Who was Sebastian really working for?' I ask quietly. She shakes her head. I reach for the phone on her desk. 'Mo, it's the middle of the afternoon in Washington. The Director is surely at his desk and he'd love to hear about all this. I don't want to call, but I will if you don't tell me everything, now.'

She blinks, surprised. I have never spoken to her like this before. But she can tell from my tone and expression that I am serious. Her shoulders slump.

'Raines.'

'Raines?' I picture the paunchy ambassador. 'What does he have to do with this?'

'Sebastian was working for him. Or was, before he went rogue and tried to steal the forty-six million dollars for himself.'

'I don't understand.'

'Raines used to be CEO of Dynan Industries. It's a defense firm.' And a sister company of Infodyne, I think, remembering the corporate records Sebastian showed me. 'In the nineties, Dynan had a number of large contracts in the Kosovo region, providing services to the U.N. forces there. But they had to kiss some rings in order to get in.'

'So you're saying the company was in bed with the Albanians?' She nods. 'What was it – arms, money?'

She shrugs. 'Maybe both and then some. I've never been privy to the details. Anyway, when Jared came forward with the information about the Nazi-KLA fund in the mid-nineties, Raines panicked because the account Jared had found contained transactions that conclusively linked Dynan to the KLA. And the KLA didn't want to be publicly affiliated with the Third Reich just when it was waging a public relations battle for the goodwill of the West. Together they pressured Jared and Duncan to be quiet and turn over what they had found. Duncan acquiesced – he even took a position with Infodyne in exchange for his silence. And Jared was killed, or so most people thought.'

'And then everything was quiet, right?'

'Until now. A few months ago, the British government opens this investigation into money laundering for the Albanian mob, surfaces Infodyne as one of the suspect companies. And Raines is Ambassador now.'

'Not to mention the presumptive nominee as

404

the next secretary of defense.'

'Right. Given the close connection between the KLA and the mob, Raines was terrified about his company's activities in Kosovo coming out if the account information Jared found ever surfaced. And then your friend Chris starts digging around and we find that the body isn't Jared's and–'

Raines wanted Jared dead, to shut him up for good, I finish silently. Mo walks to me. 'Jordan, you have to believe I didn't know. Raines lied to me, said it was just about putting you on the team to get the information Jared and Duncan found. I didn't know how far he planned to take this, that he planted Sebastian on the team to do his dirty work. I started getting suspicious after we were pulled off Infodyne, but by then it was too late. Sophie was dead.'

And Vance and nearly Sarah, too. 'But why?'

'You were getting too close, it seems, to the information linking Raines to the KLA. Sebastian, in his eagerness to get to the money, fed you clues that brought things too close to the Ambassador. We think that Sophie may have made the connection, and that she was trying to tell you the day she was killed.' I swallow over my guilt.

Mo continues: 'Anyway, I confronted Raines, but my name was on the orders transferring you. He said that if we were exposed, both of our careers would be over. But if I kept quiet...' She stops mid-sentence and in that moment I understand. Raines must have promised Mo something in exchange for her cooperation, and knowing Mo, it wasn't money.

'He said would help you become an ambassador, isn't that right?'

She looks away. 'I thought that if we could stop the Albanians at the same time ... the good I could do would justify it in the end.'

'Jesus.' Suddenly the pieces in my mind all fit.

'I know. It spiraled out of control.' She slumps against her desk. 'So what now?'

I lean against the desk, uncertain. I could call the Director, turn Raines and Mo in. There would be a huge investigation, months of endless bureaucracy. I turn back to Mo. 'You said Jared is alive. Where?'

'He may have been in London as recently as a few days ago. We think he might have been following you, checking if you were all right.' I remember the sense on the running path that I was being followed. Was that Jared? My heart aches at the thought of him being so close, of not having been able to touch him. Mo continues, 'But after Duncan fled and things started heating up, we think he left again. He's been everywhere these past ten years, Jordan: Morocco, Rio, Cape Town.'

I hold out my hand. 'What information do you have?'

She hesitates, then reaches into her desk, pulling out another envelope. 'That's everything, Jordan. There's an address in Monaco where he stayed briefly a few months ago. That's his last known location.'

I start to open the envelope, then close it again. I need to get out of here. 'I'm leaving, Mo.'

'That's a good idea. Go see Sarah, get some

406

rest. Tomorrow, when you feel better, we'll talk again.'

I shake my head. 'You don't understand. I mean, really leaving.' I scoop up the envelope, the photos, my personnel file.

'What are you going to do?' she asks uneasily.

'You mean, am I going to turn you in? I should, but right now I don't have the time. I have more important things to do. But I'm taking this as an insurance policy. Raines will never be secretary and I wouldn't buy anything with the ambassadorial seal on it just yet.'

'You're going after Jared, aren't you?'

I hesitate. Although I'd known it deep down, I did not realize until Mo said it aloud that it was exactly what I was going to do. 'Yes.'

'You'll never find him, Jordan. He's spent years on the run. If our best operatives couldn't locate him, what makes you think you can?'

It is a good question, but one that I do not have time to answer. 'That's my problem. But if anyone comes after me or tries to hurt Jared, I'm going to the newspapers with everything I've learned.'

Mo nods and I can tell from her grave expression that she believes me. 'There's one more thing,' I add. 'Sarah mentioned a clinic in Switzerland with a new trial protocol for ALS. I want you to pull whatever strings you have to in order to get her admitted. And I want her sent there by medevac right away, if she'll go, and the costs to be covered.'

'When will you be back?'

'I won't. I quit.'

Mo's jaw drops. 'Quit?' I cannot work for her,

or for any of them again after what they did. 'But what will I tell the Director?'

'That's your problem. Good-bye, Mo.' I tuck the folder in my bag and walk out the door.

chapter TWENTY-THREE

Heathrow's Terminal One is nearly deserted except for a few backpackers sleeping across benches in the corner, a janitor mopping the floor by the entranceway. I walk to the British Airways desk, where a clerk is organizing papers, seeming to wind down for the night. 'I'd like to purchase a plane ticket to Nice.'

'Tonight?' The clerk blinks at my request. 'Let me see.' Her fingers click against the keyboard. 'Last direct flight has already gone for the evening. You'll have to transfer in Paris, or Milan, unless you want to wait until morning.'

'Milan,' I say quickly, knowing that I will not use the second half of the ticket but will take the train from Milan to Monaco to keep a lower profile. I don't think Mo will have me followed or detained. She has too much to lose now. But I'm not taking any chances. And I'm eager to get going, get close to Jared's last known sighting in hopes that it is not too late. 'One way, please.'

'One hundred eighty-three pounds.' The clerk's eyes widen as I pass her four fifty-pound notes. 'Any bags?'

I shake my head. 'None.' I smile inwardly,

thinking of the two suitcases that lay among the charred rubble of my flat. Suddenly I am twenty-two again, backpacking through Europe on holiday, climbing aboard the train in Prague as the sun sets through the open end of the station, headed for points unknown. Free.

The clerk wrinkles her nose and I know that but for the diplomatic passport there would be questions – a last-minute one-way ticket, my lack of luggage, would all scream security threat. I hold my breath, exhaling only after she hands me back my passport and a boarding pass. 'Gate twenty-six at ten-fifteen.'

I clear security. As I cross the concourse, I reach instinctively into my pocket for the cell phone, then remember I left it at the front desk of the embassy before departing. Instead, I walk to a bank of pay phones, dialing Sarah's number. 'Hello,' she answers.

'It's me,' I say quickly.

'Jordie, are you all right?'

'Fine, I– ' I stop, hearing a male voice in the background. 'Do you have company?'

'Ryan, I mean, Officer Giles stopped by,' she replies, and I can hear the blush in her voice. She is not alone, I realize, flooded with relief. 'So what happened?'

Quickly I tell her about my confrontation with Mo, the information I learned. 'Jared didn't die that night, Sarah.'

'What?' There is a moment of stunned silence. 'How is that possible?'

'It's a long story. But he might be alive,' I repeat.

'*Might*. Jordie.' I can hear the concern in her voice. 'You're going after him.' It is not a question.

'I am. I have to see this through to the end, you know?'

'I know. Reminds me of someone else.' And I know she is talking about Jared, his dogged quest for the truth.

For a moment, I consider telling her about the arrangements I've made with Mo for her to go to Switzerland. Then I decide against it, knowing she will argue. 'I'm sorry I didn't have time to say good-bye.'

'It's fine, Jordie,' she says quickly, and I know that with her, as always, it really is. 'I love you. We'll meet up in an airport, say, in three weeks.' Her tone is light but there is a weakness there that I have not heard before. I wonder then if the clinic will be able to help her or if I have seen her for the last time. But part of her will always be with me, traveling where I go, waiting to talk about it all over tea at the end of the day.

'I love you, too. I'll call you soon.'

I hang up and start to walk away. Then I pick up the receiver once more and dial another number. The porter answers and when I make my request, he hesitates. I hold my breath, waiting for him to refuse because of the late hour, but there is a pause and then the phone rings again. 'Hallo.' Lord Colbert's voice comes on the line.

'Sir, it's Jordan Weiss. I'm sorry to disturb you at home. I know it's late.'

'Ms. Weiss.' If he is surprised by my call, he gives no indication.

'I just wanted to say I know what you did for Jared. That is, I wanted to thank you.'

'I don't know what you're talking about,' he replies quickly, and I realize that he is still protecting Jared. I imagine then Jared going to him, scared and alone, the Master doing whatever he could do help. 'He was one of my students,' he adds. For a minute I consider asking him where Jared went but even if he knew, even if Jared had not moved around dozens of times, he would not tell me. 'Goodbye, Ms. Weiss,' he says. 'And good luck.'

As I set the receiver back on the hook, Jared's face appears in my mind. I cannot believe that he might be out there somewhere, alive. Has he changed? I wonder where he is, if he is alone, scared, what he looks like now. A kind of hope, more terrifying than any of the pain or fear or returning to England, rises in me. He might be dead, I remind myself, or impossible to find. But the flame of possibility that began to burn when I saw the coroner's photo in Mo's office refuses to be dampened. There is only one way to find out.

Adjusting the shoulder strap to my bag, I start down the concourse toward my gate, past the duty-free shops closing for the night. All around me are groups of people, flight crews in matching uniforms, couples and families going on holiday, small groups of business travelers. People together. And me, setting out on another journey, once again on my own. An unfamiliar pang of loneliness shoots through me. Then I remember Jared's words on the chapel roof, hear his voice,

411

as clearly as though he is walking next to me. Sooner or later, we all go home alone.

Sarah was right, though. Jared gave me something that I carry with me, a driven need to follow this through to the end, to find the answers, wherever they may lead me. I am running again, but for the first time in a decade, not running away. This time I am running toward something.

Running toward the truth.

Acknowledgments

The Officer's Lover is the magical fusion of new and old for me. It represents the first of a new kind of novel and the beginning of a partnership with a wonderful publishing team. To that end, I would like to thank my gifted editor, Emily Bestler; her assistant, Laura Stern; and the entire team at Atria for their remarkable work in bringing this book to life.

At the same time, *The Officer's Lover* is the culmination of a vision that I have been seeking to bring to life for more than a decade. So I must recognize those who have been supporting and encouraging this work for so many years: my friends Stephanie, Joanne, and Pugsley; my writing instructor Janet; the many writers who have reviewed pieces of the book in its various forms; and the other friends and coworkers who have encouraged me along the way. Special thanks to Alison, for her perspective on British life and culture.

And, of course, my eternal gratitude to my friend and best-agent-in-the-world Scott Hoffman at Folio Literary Management, who believed in my work before anyone else in publishing and stayed with me longer than anyone in his right mind should have until that faith was validated.

Your keen insight and tireless efforts made my career.

My deepest appreciation must be reserved for my family: my husband, Phillip; brother Jay and parents; Marsha and Gene. Without you, none of this would be possible, or worthwhile.

There are some people who will look at the parallels between Jordan's life and my own (Cambridge and State Department) and wonder, 'How much of the story is real?' To those readers, I say first and foremost – it's all fiction, the characters, the story, everything. Let me say also that I believe that while real life makes for a terrible plot, it makes for a wonderful setting.

So with that, I'd like to pay tribute to two groups of people who inspired the setting of this book: first, the many Foreign Service Officers and other government workers I've been privileged to know, whose heroism, skill, and sacrifice have continued to awe me long after our professional affiliation has ended.

Second, I'd like to recognize my friends, with whom I experienced that brief illumination of Camelot known as Cambridge, a time and place that left its mark on all of us and created a common bond that lives on. Beyond all else, *The Officer's Lover is* a tribute to that real-life fairy tale, and a love song to those who lived it.

The publishers hope that this book has given you enjoyable reading. Large Print Books are especially designed to be as easy to see and hold as possible. If you wish a complete list of our books please ask at your local library or write directly to:

Magna Large Print Books
Magna House, Long Preston,
Skipton, North Yorkshire.
BD23 4ND

This Large Print Book for the partially sighted, who cannot read normal print, is published under the auspices of

THE ULVERSCROFT FOUNDATION